INTO THE FURY

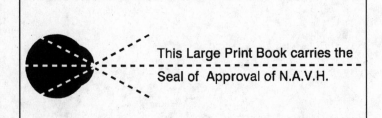

This Large Print Book carries the
Seal of Approval of N.A.V.H.

A BOSS, INC. NOVEL

INTO THE FURY

KAT MARTIN

THORNDIKE PRESS
A part of Gale, Cengage Learning

Farmington Hills, Mich • San Francisco • New York • Waterville, Maine
Meriden, Conn • Mason, Ohio • Chicago

GALE
CENGAGE Learning®

Copyright © 2016 by Kat Martin.
A BOSS, Inc. Novel #1.
Thorndike Press, a part of Gale, Cengage Learning.

LIBRARY OF CONGRESS CATALOGING-IN-PUBLICATION DATA

Names: Martin, Kat, author.
Title: Into the fury / by Kat Martin.
Description: Large print edition. | Waterville, Maine : Thorndike Press, 2016. |
    ©2016 | Series: A Boss, Inc. novel ; #1 | Series: Thorndike Press large print core
Identifiers: LCCN 2016000509| ISBN 9781410489401 (hardcover) | ISBN 141048940X
    (hardcover)
Subjects: LCSH: Large type books. | GSAFD: Romantic suspense fiction.
Classification: LCC PS3563.A7246 I58 2016 | DDC 813/.54—dc23
LC record available at http://lccn.loc.gov/2016000509

Published in 2016 by arrangement with Zebra Books, an imprint of
Kensington Publishing Corp.

Printed in Mexico
1 2 3 4 5 6 7 20 19 18 17 16

INTO THE FURY

CHAPTER ONE

Seattle, Washington
SINNERS, SLUTS, and WHORES-- BEWARE. Your TIME is at HAND.

Standing next to the long mahogany table in the conference room, Ethan Brodie reread the note he'd just been handed. Printed on a plain sheet of white paper, the ominous words were typed in different fonts and sizes, all of them in big bold letters.

Fairly old-school for the twenty-first century, Ethan thought. But then, e-mail was a helluva lot easier to trace.

The client, Matthew Carlyle, was head of operations for La Belle Lingerie, a retail fashion chain, kind of a knockoff of Victoria's Secret with slightly less expensive garments. In his midforties, five ten, lean and fit, Carlyle had silver-threaded dark brown hair, hazel eyes, and a thin scar that ran close to his ear along his jaw.

7

The other man in the room was Ethan's boss, his cousin Ian, owner of Brodie Operations Security Services, Inc.

"I imagine in the lingerie business you get threatening notes all the time," Ethan said to Carlyle.

"We get kooks all right. Plenty of them." Carlyle accepted the note Ethan returned. "But a letter like this was mailed to each of our ten top models, sent to them at our flagship store here in Seattle, and the company isn't happy about it."

"You talk to the police?"

"Not yet. We'd prefer to handle the problem discreetly, avoid any bad press. That's why I came to BOSS, Inc. Ian and I have worked together before. I trust him to handle the problem."

Ethan turned to his cousin, conservatively dressed in tan slacks and a yellow button-down shirt. While Ian was blond, Ethan was dark-haired, like most of the Brodie men. Both were tall, Ethan taller, at six foot three. "You have the notes checked for prints?" he asked.

"I did," Ian said. "Papers were all clean. The letters were mailed out of different post office locations in the area so that led nowhere. Since the models are about to go on tour, Matt's decided to temporarily beef-up La Belle security, just to be on the safe side."

"Probably a good idea." Though Ethan wished someone else was taking the job. The thought of traveling for weeks with a group of airheaded fashion divas was the last thing he wanted. Still, he worked for a living, and this was exactly the kind of job he was good at.

Silently communicating his dislike of the assignment, he flicked a hard glance at his cousin, whose blue eyes lit with amusement.

"Ethan's the best man for the job," Ian said, not the least repentant. "He's an ex-cop, worked personal security for some of the top execs in the dot-com business. You can be sure he knows what he's doing."

Carlyle nodded. "I read his résumé. Looks like he can handle the job." He returned his attention to Ethan. "Aside from working protection, you're a private investigator, correct?"

"That's right. Before I went to work in Seattle, I was a homicide detective on the Dallas police force."

"Good. I'd really like to find the guy who sent those notes. I've got a feeling about this, and I'm not liking it. I'm hoping with your background, you'll be able to sniff around, talk to the models and the hands backstage. If the guy's part of the crew, we want him out."

"I can do that."

"You'll need to be discreet. I don't want people shook up before we go on tour. But it'd be best for everyone if you could come up with something that will help us track this bastard down."

"Understood." And he'd rather be busy than standing around waiting for trouble that probably wouldn't come. With any luck, the most he'd have to worry about was crowd control and a few overzealous fans.

"How many more men do you think you'll need?" Ian asked Carlyle. Though they'd gone into the conference room for privacy, they hadn't bothered to sit down. The meeting wasn't going to take that long.

"We've hired a couple of guys already, but we could use at least one more man with a background in personal protection."

"That would be Dirk Reynolds," Ian said. "I'll talk to him, see if he can take the job."

Dirk worked freelance for the company, same as Ethan and his brother, Luke, as well as his cousin, Nick. Nick was married. With his little wife pregnant, he preferred to stay close to home.

Luke was on a case. Even if he weren't, his specialty was bail enforcement, not personal protection. Dirk Reynolds was one of Ethan's best friends, a former Ranger and a damned good man.

"I'll leave you two to discuss this further," Ian said. "Matt, I'll get back to you after I talk to Dirk."

But Ethan figured his friend would take the job. The money was extremely good, and having just wound up an assignment, Dirk was currently looking for something to do. The tour might provide an interesting escape from Seattle.

Ethan thought of the weeks ahead and inwardly groaned. For him, babysitting a bunch of hot-bodied women in scanty underwear would be a twenty-four-hour-a-day headache. He'd had more than his share of trouble with the female sex — still did — and he didn't want more.

"One thing I need to make clear," Carlyle said as Ian walked out of the room and closed the door. "These are some of the most beautiful, sexiest women in the world. They're every man's fantasy. That's the reason La Belle has a strict no-fraternization policy. There's no way you can do your job if you're thinking about getting laid. We expect you to be pleasant, but steer clear of anything more than that. You with me so far?"

11

"Oh, I'm with you."

"I realize you're only human, but I need to know you understand and accept our policy. Any breach is grounds for automatic dismissal."

"All right. One thing you need to know. I wouldn't accept the job if I thought my dick would get in the way. I admire a beautiful woman, same as any other man. But I'm being paid to do a job and that's exactly what I'll do."

Carlyle seemed relieved. "I hope you're speaking for your friend Reynolds as well."

"Dirk's a professional. Beyond that, he'll have to speak for himself."

"Okay. Sounds like we understand each other. We'll be doing dress rehearsals for the rest of the week. Then our first show is here in Seattle on Saturday night. You can report to the Paramount Theatre at eight tomorrow morning. At that time, I'll introduce you and Reynolds to the rest of your team and our ten top models. Just keep in mind what I said."

Ethan made no reply. If Carlyle knew how much he wasn't looking forward to meeting a gaggle of vain, self-absorbed females, he would probably do handstands. But actions spoke louder than words. It shouldn't take the man long to figure out Ethan was off women indefinitely.

His ex-girlfriend, Allison Winfield, had done everything in her power to make sure of that.

"Oh my God. Would you look at the eye candy that just walked backstage?"

There was awe in her friend Megan O'Brien's voice. As Val bent over to fasten the buckle on her strappy high heel, she tried for a glimpse but couldn't actually see who'd just arrived.

Megan kept staring and just kept talking. "You see the one on the left? The guy with the sexy mustache? He looks like he walked out of a biker fantasy. He can knock on my door any time, day or night." She rolled her eyes. "Especially at night. And the big one on the right turns the words tall, dark, and handsome into an understatement. I think I'm in love."

Val finally looked up. Two men stood next to Matt Carlyle. One was about six two, good-looking, with medium brown hair, and a horseshoe mustache that framed his mouth, curved down to his jawline, and made him look like a real badass. A real sexy badass.

It was the bigger man who snared her attention, at least six three, with dark brown hair, dark eyes, and a face any red-blooded female would be hard-pressed not to admire. His hair was trimmed cop short and fit his hard-jawed, handsome face perfectly. The way he filled out his black T-shirt said he was two hundred pounds of solid male muscle.

When those dark eyes moved in her direction and skimmed lightly over her frame, an unexpected zing of electricity shot through her body.

"Who are they?" The little shot of awareness was new to her. Val was too busy for men. Being a La Belle model was difficult and demanding. At the same time, she was taking online college courses, getting ready to start a part-time job at the end of the tour and go back to school in the fall to finish her degree.

"They're extra security," Megan said. "After we got those threatening notes, Matt hired a few more men. The big guy's heading up an additional team." Megan sighed. "Those two look yummy enough to eat."

"You know the rules. No fraternizing with the staff."

"I know. I don't usually care, but in this case . . ."

Val grinned. "Down, girl. Best not get your thong in a twist. Far as we're concerned, they're untouchable."

"Yeah, more's the pity."

Val laughed. She glanced back at the men, saw the bigger man looking the other way, and enjoyed a long, unabashedly thorough appraisal. Sometimes pure masculine beauty deserved to be appreciated.

Hearing the voice of Daniel Clemens, the show's choreographer, along with the light rustle of feminine laughter, reminded her where she was. Shoving the men into a far corner of her mind, Val went back to work on her shoe so she could take her place in the lineup with the rest of the models.

CHAPTER TWO

Carlyle gave Ethan and Dirk a brief tour of the theater where the girls were rehearsing and would later be performing the first show of the summer tour. The Paramount in downtown Seattle was a landmark, a performing arts theater that could seat up to twenty-eight-hundred people. Built in the twenties, it was a wildly ornate structure with gold leaf on the walls and Baroque plaster moldings overhead.

Carlyle looked up at the huge crystal-beaded chandeliers hanging from the ceiling, scanned the ornate designs painted on the walls. "I hope the setting doesn't overpower the costumes," he grumbled.

Ethan figured mostly naked women in sequins and feathers wouldn't have much trouble holding the audience's attention.

Carlyle led them toward a big muscle jock with a shaved head and earrings in his ears. "You need to meet our chief of security.

He's got his own crew, so hopefully you won't be bumping into each other too much, but you need to know who's who."

Carlyle stopped in front of the beefy man, about Ethan's height but bulked up more in the chest, arms, and shoulders. An overzealous Arnold Schwarzenegger. Ethan wondered how many hours a day he spent at the gym.

"Beau Desmond, meet Ethan Brodie," Carlyle said. "The guy with the 'stache is Dirk Reynolds."

Desmond reached out a hand and Ethan and Dirk both shook.

"Ethan's heading up the additional security team we've hired. He's also a PI, so he'll be doing some digging, trying to find out who sent those notes."

"Long as he keeps his nose out of my business he can do whatever he wants," Desmond said.

One of Ethan's eyebrows went up. So it was going to be a pissing contest. Who's the toughest, who's the best at his job. He'd been afraid of that when he'd spotted the earrings.

"I'll do my best to stay out of your way," Ethan said diplomatically. He was there to do a job. He'd do it with or without Beau Desmond.

"Make sure you do," Beau said, determined to get the last word.

Carlyle made no comment, but clearly he had picked up on Desmond's belligerent attitude. As they walked away, Dirk was grinning in anticipation. He loved nothing better than making a dickhead look like a fool.

"Beau's good at his job," Carlyle said. "Be helpful if you kept that in mind."

"Oh, I will," Ethan said.

Dirk wisely made no comment.

Leaving Beau Desmond behind, Carlyle led them into a room where four men stood drinking coffee. They each wore jeans and a black T-shirt with a white La Belle logo on the front left corner, the symbol for male and female, a round circle with a cross at the bottom and an arrow off the circle at the top.

The shirts made them easily identifiable as La Belle security. He and Dirk had been given a stack when they'd walked in that morning and each was wearing one now.

Carlyle made the introductions. "Listen up, you men. The guy on my right is Ethan Brodie. He's heading up additional security for the show. That means the four of you. The guy next to him is Dirk Reynolds. They're both professionals. They know what they're doing, so listen and do what they say."

The men introduced themselves one at a time. They all had some security experience, not much. A sandy-haired, thirtysomething parking lot guard named Sandowski, a tall beanpole of a guy named Walt Wizzy who had worked for Walmart. A Hispanic named Pete Hernandez who was built like a brick house but stood only about five foot six and, by the jut of his chin, probably had a little-man's complex. Ethan figured if there was trouble in the group, Hernandez would be it.

A black guy named Joe Posey was an ex-cop, but he was older and out of shape. The men were hardly first-string, but Ethan figured unless something really bad went down, they would do just fine.

He gave the guys a brief rundown of what he expected them to do. "Your job is to keep people out of the theater who aren't sup-posed to be here. With this many women around, there's bound to be a handful of smart-asses who think they're God's gift. Handle them pleasantly but firmly. Whatever bullshit story they come up with, don't let them anywhere near the models. You get in over your head with one or more of them, use your radio to call for backup. Questions?"

No one spoke.

"The second part of your job is to keep an eye out for anyone or anything that looks suspicious. Someone who has ill intent, no matter what it might be. Report anything out of the ordinary directly to me or Dirk, and don't be afraid to say something, even if it seems insignificant. It's always better to be safe than sorry."

Joe Posey raised a dark hand. "I heard a rumor someone sent threatening notes to some of the models. That true?"

It was, but Carlyle didn't want the media getting their hands on the information, turning the show into some kind of circus.

"These women model lingerie," Ethan said. "They get all kinds of mail, some good, some not so good. Carlyle has his own men escorting the ladies to and from the theater, so you don't have to worry about that."

He ended by filling them in on what Carlyle had told him. "Rehearsals the rest of the week. They start at eight in the morning, go till they're finished. We're here before they get here until after they leave. The show is on Saturday night, then we travel. You all understand we'll be spending some time on the road, right?"

20

The men rumbled an affirmative.

"One last thing: Keep your hands off the girls. No fraternizing, no hassling the women. Stick to that rule and we'll get along just fine. Break that rule — you're fired."

They had all been warned, but it didn't hurt to repeat the warning. "Now, I'd like you to spend some time getting familiar with the theater. You need to find all the nooks and crannies, places some joker could hide. Take your time and make it thorough."

It was a task he and Dirk would be performing, too, as soon as Carlyle was finished with them. The group of men broke up and headed out the door.

Ethan turned to Carlyle, who had been standing quietly to one side. "What's next?"

"Now I introduce you to our ten top models. There are thirty in all, but these are the stars of the show, the ones who got notes like the one I showed you. These are the women I'd like you to focus on."

Carlyle led them out of the room, back to the rear of the stage, where all thirty models were lined up, ready to start rehearsing.

"There are five segments to the show," Carlyle explained. "Countries of the World, Nashville, Devil-Angel, Winter Wonderland, and Diamond Jubilee. There's a wrap with the entire cast, then we're finished. Each of the women makes at least two costume changes. They're working on the World segment now. Follow me."

Ethan and Dirk followed Carlyle toward the group of women standing in a semicircle, taking direction from the choreographer of the show, who stood in front of them.

"That's Daniel Clemens. He can be a little pissy, but he's damn good at his job. We couldn't do the show without him."

For rehearsal, most of the women were wearing black leggings under a collection of very short skirts, cutoff jeans, long T-shirts, and cutoff sweatshirts.

"For the next few days they'll be working on their routines. There's a full dress rehearsal the day before the show. That'll include final costume fittings, live orchestra, everything."

Ethan's gaze ran over the women. At least for the moment, they were decently covered. Their casual dress didn't change the fact that each woman was incredibly beautiful, their faces right out of a magazine.

Carlyle roll-called ten names and the women came forward. A couple of redheads, five blondes, two brunettes, and an ebony-skinned beauty with amazing cheekbones and long jet-black hair.

Ethan flicked a glance at Dirk, who carefully kept his eyes straight ahead.

"Ladies, these men will be working as additional security while we're on tour. Ethan Brodie is the big guy on the right. Dirk Reynolds is the guy with the 'stache."

Carlyle smiled. "Do me a favor and cut them some slack. They have a job to do, same as you. It's easier if they don't have to contend with naughty smiles and flirty remarks."

The women chuckled good-naturedly.

"Introduce yourselves. First names are enough. Start at the far end and work this way."

A redhead stepped forward. "I'm Caralee," she said with a soft Southern drawl.

"I am Katerina." A beautiful, smiling blonde with a hint of Russia in her voice.

As the women each spoke their names, Ethan mentally attached the name to a face, knew Dirk would be doing the same. The redheads were Caralee and Megan. The blondes were Heather; Katerina, the Russian; Delilah, with very high cheekbones; Ursula — either German or Austrian; and Valentine.

The brunettes were Isabel, a young Sophia Loren look-alike; and Carmen, a pretty, dark-eyed Latina. The exotic ebony-skinned woman was Amarika. From Africa, maybe. He couldn't be sure.

He let his gaze travel over the women a final time, paused for a moment on the one who called herself Valentine. He liked blondes, always had. All five of them had gleaming long blond hair, some straight, some wavy. Valentine's was the color of honey. It curled softly down her back and swung around her shoulders.

She was maybe five nine, about an inch shorter than the redhead named Megan, who stood beside her. Most of the girls were around five ten; a couple, including Amarika, appeared to be at least six feet. All of them wore strappy high heels that pushed them up another five or six inches.

In a room full of gorgeous women, it took a helluva lot to stand out. He heard throaty laughter, realized it came from redheaded Megan. Next to her, the blonde flashed a grin, and a stunning pair of dimples popped out. He'd remember that one now, *Valentine.* Sounded more like a stripper than a classy underwear model, but hey, what did he know?

And even in their nondescript rehearsal clothes, all of them were perfect. Chosen for their flawless faces and exquisite bodies.

Too perfect, as far as he was concerned.

Even if the women weren't off-limits, he wouldn't be interested in a female whose entire focus was on herself. Hell, if it weren't for sex, he'd give up women completely.

Unfortunately, he had needs, just like any other red-blooded male. As he looked over the tantalizing buffet of femininity and felt his body stir, he figured it was past time he made a date with one of his lady friends.

Women he had known for years, the sort who understood where he was coming from, made no demands, were fun to be with, and in it to satisfy their own needs, same as he was.

Not tonight. Tonight he was having supper with his cousin Nick and his wife, Samantha. Tomorrow night, maybe, if he could find the time. His gaze swung back to Valentine, and he felt a little kick. The sooner, he thought, the better.

"Ethan! Come on in." Samantha Brodie stepped back so Ethan could walk into the single-story, wood-sided house on a heavily treed, oversized lot in the Newcastle area. The home wasn't far from Brodie Operations' main office in Bellevue and was also close to the Perfect Pup pet-grooming parlor where Samantha worked.

25

Ethan looked down at her and couldn't help smiling. "Hi, sweetheart, how you feeling?" He was off women, had very little use for the female sex, at least for the moment, and yet Nick's petite wife had won him over completely.

"I feel great." She grinned, went up on her toes to give him a hug. "We both do." Samantha was almost four months pregnant, with the little baby bump to prove it. With her freckled nose and bouncy nutmeg curls, she was the image of the girl next door. Nick was crazy in love with her and over the moon about having a kid.

"I heard you got the job with La Belle," she said, still smiling.

"I got the job. Not really looking forward to the travel, but the money's damn good."

"It's only for a few weeks, isn't it? The show starts here in Seattle, goes to five other cities, then comes back home."

"That's right." He didn't ask how she knew what was going on with La Belle. He didn't want to think of his cousin's pretty wife in a pair of lacy bikini panties. He didn't think Nick would appreciate that, either.

"Nick's out in the backyard. Supper's almost ready. Come on back."

He followed her into a kitchen made cozy

by warm wood cabinets, cream-colored ceramic tile counters, yellow walls, and yellow-and-brown curtains. When she turned sideways, Ethan couldn't help noticing how much the bump had grown since he had last seen her.

He smiled at the thought. It had only been a few months since his cousin had quit his job as a homicide detective in Anchorage, moved to Seattle, and started working for Brodie Operations. BOSS, Inc., they called it.

Ethan's smile turned into a grin. Nick hadn't wasted any time getting his little wife pregnant.

Thinking of the baby Samantha carried reminded him of his own child, three-year-old Hannah, and the smile slid from his face. He hadn't seen his little girl in weeks — not that he hadn't been trying.

Ethan stepped into the kitchen. The aroma of garlic and tomatoes penetrated his dismal mood and his mouth watered. "Damn, that smells good."

Samantha's pretty lips curved up. She was wearing jeans and a snug little short-sleeved top that curved over her belly. It had never occurred to him that a pregnant woman could look cute, even kind of sexy.

"I'm making spaghetti. It's almost ready."

Nick walked into the kitchen just then, nearly as tall as Ethan, with wavy black hair and intense blue eyes. "How about a drink?" Nick asked. "You look like you could use one. Wine, beer, or something stronger?"

"A straight shot of whiskey might help, but I'll just have a beer." Ethan pulled out a chair and took a seat at the kitchen table.

Nick walked to the fridge, grabbed a bottle of Budweiser, and tossed it to him, then grabbed one for himself. "So, which is it? Your new job or something to do with your little girl? Allison still giving you ten kinds of grief?"

Ethan twisted off the bottle cap and took a long swallow of the ice-cold brew. "Both. I called Ally on my way over. As usual, she gave me some bullshit reason I couldn't talk to Hannah." His ex-girlfriend still blamed him for their failed relationship, though she was the one who had ended the affair.

"You're lucky she refused to marry you," Samantha said. "I know you wanted your daughter to have your name, but you told me yourself the two of you were a bad combination. You deserve someone who loves you."

Ethan just grunted. After what he'd been through, going the love route was the last thing he wanted.

Nick grabbed his wife, turned her into his arms, and gave her a smacking kiss. "What else do you need me to do?"

Samantha laughed and pushed him away. "Salad's made. You already set the table. Why don't you sit down with your cousin and relax?"

Samantha was a fabulous cook, a wonderful homemaker, and one sexy little gal. She was also smart and a hardworking businesswoman, part owner of the Perfect Pup, a chain of dog-grooming salons. Lately, she'd been bugging Nick to let her bring home a puppy. Nick wanted to wait till she had the baby. Ethan figured the pup would be part of the household by the end of the week.

"I hear you started working with La Belle today," Nick said, taking a seat across from him at the table. "That's one job I'm glad you got and not me." Like Dirk, Nick was a former Ranger. Like Ethan, he was also a former police detective. Nick was capable and tough as boot leather. But he was a married man, and he took that role seriously. "Should be an interesting assignment."

"Yeah, well, if there was any way I could have gotten out of it, I would have. But the pay's really great and the hours aren't bad. As long as the women behave themselves, it'll be fine."

Nick snorted a laugh. "Not many men would want the most beautiful women in the world to leave them alone."

Ethan took a swallow of beer. "Yeah, well, most men are a lot more naïve than I am. As far as I'm concerned, the only place in a man's life for a woman is in bed." He glanced over at Samantha, who held up a wooden spoon as if she were about to slam it against his skull.

Ethan grinned. "Present company excepted."

Samantha grinned back and returned to her cooking.

"What about the women in the show? Anyone look interesting?"

"They're all beautiful. Sexy. Knockout bodies. Everything a man could want — in bed. Out of it, I wouldn't know." He looked up to see Samantha walking toward him. The spoon was gone, so he figured he was safe.

"Speaking of the show," she said. "There's a . . . umm . . . favor I'd like to ask."

Ethan smiled. "Name it, sweetheart; anything."

"A friend of mine is one of the models. She goes by Valentine Hart. Maybe you know which one she is."

"Valentine. Yeah, with a name like that, who could forget? Dimples, right?"

"That's right."

"What about her?"

"Val got this terrible note. I guess some of the other models got them, too. She said it was kind of scary, called the women sluts and whores."

"I know about the notes. That's one of the reasons they decided to beef up security."

"Well, I was wondering if . . . maybe you could kind of keep an eye on Val. She's a really great girl, you know? You're a bodyguard. You could make sure she's safe."

"That's not a favor, Samantha. Keeping the girls safe is why they hired me. That's my job."

"Yes, but Val isn't —"

"You don't have to worry, I'll take care of her." He didn't want to hear about the woman. He didn't want to know any of the models on a personal level. "If she's your friend, I'll keep her on my radar, okay?"

Just what he didn't need. Any sort of up-close-and-personal with one of the women. But Samantha was family. If Valentine Hart was her friend, he'd keep an eye on her.

"Thank you," she said softly.

Ethan nodded, though he figured a lingerie model had more than enough experience with men to know how to handle herself.

"That smells delicious," he said, hoping to change the subject. "I'm starving."

Samantha smiled. "It's just about ready. Nick, how about helping me serve?"

Nick stood up. "You got it, baby." Moving behind her, he slid an arm around her waist, dragged her nutmeg curls out of the way, and kissed the side of her neck.

Samantha laughed.

The sweet sound made Ethan think how lucky his cousin was, and just how rotten his own luck was when it came to women.

CHAPTER THREE

The only lights on in Val's Montlake duplex apartment were the lamp beside her bed and the screen on her computer. She was up late studying, trying to catch up on the Internet courses she was taking.

Snoozie, her big gray cat, slept on his pillow on the back of the desk. Even asleep, he was great company.

Val sighed. With rehearsals, she wouldn't be doing much studying this week. She'd be getting home late and she needed her beauty rest, needed to look her absolute best for the dress rehearsal, then the fashion show on Saturday night. She owed it to the people who were counting on her.

The Internet contest she'd won six months ago had secured her a place as a La Belle Lingerie fashion model. Out of thousands of women, she was the lucky winner.

The work was grueling. She'd never understood how hard a fashion model worked.

Though La Belle models weren't half-starved, anorexic women like high-fashion, couture design models, they had to be in top physical condition. The women were expected to ooze sexuality. They'd been chosen for their full breasts, small waists, and perfectly curving hips. La Belle models wore lingerie designed to appeal to men — which was the reason women bought it.

A strict diet regimen was required, along with the two to three hours a day she spent with a trainer to ensure her body stayed perfectly toned and fit.

The job had required her to drop out of school to train for the fashion show and do PR work for the company, but La Belle was paying her a boatload of money, enough that she'd be able to finish at the U of Washington next year with a degree in veterinary medicine.

Val loved animals and always had. Becoming a vet was a longtime dream, but her scholarship had run out after she'd earned her bachelor's degree. With her parents' help and working two part-time jobs, she'd managed to get through her first year of vet school, but the tuition was nearly twelve thousand, with fees on top of that, living expenses, food, and travel to and from campus.

On a whim, she'd entered the modeling contest, and to her amazement, she'd won.

God and the genes she'd inherited had blessed her with excellent bone structure, as well as a really good body. Though a lot of women would think the high-paying, seemingly glamorous life of a model was the job of a lifetime, running around half-naked in sequins and feathers just wasn't the life for her.

Instead, she was using her physical assets to pursue the goals she had set for herself when she was in high school.

Val glanced at the clock, saw it was after midnight, reached over and turned off her laptop. Tomorrow was another rehearsal day. At the end of the summer, her contract with La Belle would be up and she could finish her final term at school. Her job as a fashion model would be over and she could return to a normal life again.

Val smiled. After the whirlwind tour and her fifteen minutes of fame, it might take a while to figure out exactly what normal was.

Sitting in front of his laptop on the desk in his bedroom, the man moved the mouse and changed the font. He chose another font and typed the next word, then changed the font again, continuing, one by one, until he finished the note. The printer hummed as he printed the words on a plain white sheet of paper.

Sinners, SLUTS, and WHORES-- BEWARE. REPENT *or you* WILL be NEXT.

He was proud of his handiwork. This note matched the first, its message more than clear. When the note was found, there'd be no doubt who was responsible. And he'd be careful to leave no clues that could be traced back to him. He just had to work out the timing, then make sure everything went the way he planned.

As he mentally went over his preparations, he began to look forward to the encounter, always an adrenaline rush. He'd been missing that lately. He settled back in his chair and studied the note.

Soon, he'd deliver it.

He smiled, anticipating the challenge, then the satisfaction of a job well done.

Ethan's second day at the theater was hectic. The women were busy rehearsing, and for the first time, he began to see what a difficult job they had. Not just walking out on the stage tossing their hair and smiling but placing each step exactly right, moving in ways that best displayed the garments they were selling. They had to learn dozens of different poses and cues from the choreographer, who was constantly making changes and asking them to relearn something they had only just learned a few minutes before.

Add to that, the way they took care of their bodies required tremendous work. Ethan regularly pumped weights and worked out in the gym in his apartment complex. It was just part of his job. These women worked with trainers, dieted furiously, limited their alcohol intake to practically zilch, and went to bed early. When in the hell did they have any fun?

After watching them a while, when a woman he'd dubbed Heather-with-the-silver hair strutted down the runway in her sky-high heels, stepped wrong and went down hard, he was only a little surprised.

Being close to the stage, he jumped up on the runway and walked over to help. Her nails dug into his arm as she took hold and tried to stand, released a grimace of pain.

"Take it easy." Crouching beside her, he urged her to lie back down.

"Don't move her!" Daniel Clemens and his young assistant rushed forward. "Someone call Dr. Harrison!"

"I'm okay," the blonde said, but he could hear the anxiety in her voice. "Please — just give me a minute, Daniel. I'll be fine."

Clemens was tall and slender, with light brown hair moussed into some kind of bed-head style. Ethan had a hunch he was gay, but he wasn't flamboyant. And as Matt Carlyle had said, he was clearly good at his job.

The choreographer knelt next to Ethan. "We can't stop rehearsal. We need to get her off the stage, but she can't walk on that ankle. Do you think you could carry her back to one of the dressing rooms?"

"Not a problem." Bending, Ethan scooped the girl up in his arms and started striding toward the back of the stage.

Heather slid her arms around his neck. "Wow. If my ankle wasn't hurting so damn much, I'd be impressed."

His mouth edged up. "You aren't that heavy."

"Oh, you are a sweet talker." Heather flashed him a pain-filled smile, then returned her attention to Clemens, who hurried along beside them. "I'll be okay, Daniel, really. It only hurts a little. I'll be fine by tomorrow."

"Sorry, dear girl. You know show policy. We'll have to see what the doctor says. I'll go make sure he's on his way."

Daniel hurried off as Ethan carried Heather into one of the dressing rooms. He tried not to notice the array of hot-pink panties, skimpy lace bras, feather boas, sequined thongs, and God-only-knew what else. Gently, he settled Heather on the sofa against the wall and stood up just as another woman pushed her way into the already cramped quarters.

Though her dimples weren't showing, he recognized the blonde. *Valentine.*

She reached down and gently caught hold of the injured woman's hand. "How are you doing, Heather?"

At the contact, the girl fought not to cry. "Oh, God, Val, I can't believe this."

"You're going to be okay. Just lie back and let me take a look, all right?" Valentine knelt next to the platinum blonde. "Somebody get an ice pack. We need to keep the swelling down."

She glanced over, spotted him standing in the doorway, and seemed to remember who he was. "Ethan, can you find someone to get an ice pack for us?"

He nodded. "I'll take care of it." His last glimpse as he walked out of the dressing room was Valentine moving the ankle. He heard Heather's hiss of pain, and then she started to cry.

"I've got the ice coming," Daniel told him when he reached the open area behind the stage. "We keep a couple of physicians on our payroll, on call for emergencies like these. It shouldn't take Dr. Harrison long to get here."

"Will she be able to do the show?" Ethan asked.

Daniel shook his head. "From the looks of that sprain, it isn't likely. La Belle has liability concerns when it comes to job-related injuries. Besides, I don't think she'd be able to walk the runway in a pair of spike heels."

Ethan didn't think so either. But then, he couldn't figure out how the models managed to do it when there was nothing wrong with them.

Daniel glanced back toward the dressing room and released a long sigh. "Heather is going to be crushed. These women prepare for the show all year."

He was beginning to figure that out, coming to respect the models in ways he hadn't expected. He liked the way Valentine had shown up to help her friend. There had to be a lot of competition between them. They were, after all, still women.

He looked up, spotted Dirk walking toward him in that lanky, restless stride of his.

"We got a problem?" Dirk asked.

"Yeah, but not the kind we're here for. One of the women took a fall, sprained her ankle. She's probably out of the show. They'll have to run the production one model short."

"Which one was it?"

"Heather."

"Platinum blonde. I remember her. Told me she's from LA. Guess she'll be making the trip back home."

Ethan cocked an eyebrow, leaving the words *hands off* unsaid.

"I know, I know. It wasn't like that. She was just killing time between set changes." He grinned, moving the short-cropped mustache that framed his mouth and trailed down to his jaw. "Besides, I prefer redheads. That one, Megan, with the big blue eyes, is just my style."

Ethan chuckled. "Too bad about the no-touch rule. You could pretty much find anything here you wanted."

Dirk grinned. "I'm looking forward to the dress rehearsal."

"Or undress, as the case may be."

"Yeah. Even better."

"Just remember to keep it in your pants."

Dirk grunted. "With you around, the

Grinch Who Hates Women, how could I forget?"

Ethan couldn't stop a smile. "I don't hate women. Hell, I've got a daughter, remember? I just don't need another pain in my ass right now."

Dirk just chuckled, turned, and sauntered away. A glimpse of his tattoo flashed, just at the neck of his T-shirt. Ethan noticed two of the models staring after him, whispering and smiling. It seemed the ladies liked Dirk as much as he liked them.

It was a couple of hours later that Ethan spotted Heather again. She was resting quietly on a sofa backstage, her ankle propped up and wrapped with an Ace bandage, an ice pack situated on top.

He'd been quietly asking around, talking to the girls who'd received threatening notes, hoping one of them might have an idea who could have sent them. He'd talked to a few of the stagehands, just to get an overall impression of how things worked, see if any of them seemed overly interested in the women. So far, nothing had clicked.

He walked up to Heather. "I thought you'd be home by now, taking care of that ankle."

She shrugged. "My home's in LA. Those of us from out of town are staying at the

42

Fairmont."

"I heard that."

"Daniel asked me to stay, help him get Carmen and the other girls ready to take over my segments in the show." Her big brown eyes filled and she glanced away.

"I'm sorry about what happened, Heather. You got a really tough break."

She sniffed, wiped away a tear. "Yeah, but stuff like this happens. I'll get well and I'll be back. Thanks, by the way, for helping me out there."

"No problem. Maybe you could return the favor by answering a couple of questions about that note you got."

"Sure. I'm happy to answer, but I really don't know anything."

"From what I was told, the notes were mailed to the company's flagship store here in Seattle."

"That's right. Generally, fan mail is opened, read, then forwarded to our home address. In this case, all ten of us were already here in Seattle getting ready for the show when the notes arrived."

"The company reads them for inappropriate content, I imagine."

"Yes. It's for our protection, really. If they're too explicit or say something raunchy, they get tossed. Because these seemed threatening, Mr. Carlyle took us aside after our first group meeting and showed them to each of us individually, asked if any of us knew who might be responsible."

"But you didn't."

"No. No one did. I just figured it was some crackpot. Some of the other girls were worried, but I'm from LA, land of ten thousand nut jobs."

Ethan chuckled. "The postmarks came from six different locations in the Seattle area. How long have you been in town?"

"I stayed with friends for a couple of days before I moved to the hotel."

"You didn't notice anyone following you, either before or after you got to the Fairmont? Anyone who stood out in some way?"

She frowned, trying to remember. "I don't think so. I wish I could be more helpful."

He nodded. "Thanks for trying."

"You aren't really concerned about this wing nut?"

Ethan smiled. "When you put it that way, no. But keeping everyone safe is my job. That includes finding wing nuts like this one."

She gave him a flirty smile. "You know, I'm not part of the show anymore. So the no-fraternization rule no longer applies."

His mouth edged up. "Unfortunately, as

long as I work for La Belle, the rule applies to me. Take care of yourself, Heather. And thanks again."

He didn't miss the smirk on Dirk's face as he walked away.

Val spotted Ethan Brodie outside the door of the break room. Arms crossed over his chest, biceps bulging, he watched her approach, his dark eyes alert but at the same time reserved.

She knew he was related by marriage to her good friend, Samantha Brodie. Sam's husband, Nick, and Ethan were cousins. Nick was amazingly handsome and so was Ethan, which made the family resemblance clear. Nick was hot. So was Ethan.

Besides his good looks, there was something about him: an aura of physical strength, maybe, or confidence, or a mixture of both. Whatever it was, a little kick of awareness went through her whenever she felt his eyes on her.

He unfolded his arms and stepped away from the door. "Valentine, you got a minute?"

Her heart did a little jerk and started beating faster. She didn't like the feeling, but it didn't go away. "Sure. What can I do for you?"

"I was hoping you could answer a couple of questions about that note you and some of the other girls received."

"All right."

He tipped his head toward a quiet area a few feet away from the break room, and Val walked in that direction. She was tall, but he was way taller. When he spoke, she had to tip her head back to look at him.

"You live here in Seattle, right?"

"That's right. In the Montlake area."

"Have you noticed anyone around your house, someone who might seem out of place, someone you aren't used to seeing? Or maybe there's someone who seems to keep popping up wherever you go."

She thought that over. "I can't think of anyone. I spend time with a trainer at the gym not far from my place. Once in a while one of the guys can be a little overfriendly, but if they get too pushy, Mark — that's my trainer — usually puts a stop to it."

"Which gym is it?"

"Ajax Fitness. It's on Twenty-Fourth Avenue East."

"What's Mark's last name?"

"Dargan, but I really don't think —"

"When can I find him there?"

"He works mornings and evenings. I don't know his hours this week since I won't be working out with him."

"People like the guy who wrote those notes? It can be anyone. Sometimes it's a neighbor, someone who develops a fixation just watching you walk in and out of the house."

"I live in a duplex. My neighbor, Mrs. Oakley, is seventy-five years old. She feeds my cat when I'm out of town."

"You a churchgoer?"

She saw immediately where he was headed. "You think there might be some kind of religious connection because he calls us sinners?" She grinned. "If that's the case, it could be one of my long-lost cousins." When a dark eyebrow lifted in interest, she added, "I'm kidding. I haven't seen any of them since I was twelve years old."

A reluctant smile touched his lips. "So you don't go to church."

"Actually, I do go once in a while. Not that often. Mostly weddings and funerals. Back a ways, I occasionally went with my family." She didn't say it wasn't her real family. Mom and Pops were her adoptive parents, but she loved them as if they were tied by blood.

She glanced toward the break room, desperate for a cup of coffee. "Unless there's something else, I've got to get going." She started to turn away, but he caught her arm and a little zing of electricity shot through her. The surprise on his face said he felt it, too.

His features went from pleasant to dark. "One more thing. Samantha Brodie's my cousin's wife. I gather the two of you are friends."

"That's right. Sam's really terrific."

"She is, and she's worried about your safety. That means if you get into some kind of trouble, you come to me. I'll be there if you need me. You understand?"

She didn't really. Why would she get into trouble? And if she did, the last person she would call would be some macho, overprotective male like Ethan Brodie. "Okay."

He nodded. "Thanks for the help."

"Probably won't turn out to be much, but you're welcome." Walking away from him, she headed for the break room, checked her watch, and realized they were ready to start rehearsing her segment of the show.

Val sighed. Thanks to Ethan Brodie, it looked like she wasn't going to get that badly needed cup of coffee.

CHAPTER FOUR

The rehearsal ran late. Instead of going home after, Ethan headed for the gym in Montlake on 24th East. It wouldn't be dark for a while. The July days were long, and according to Valentine, Dargan worked evenings.

It was overcast, a leaden sky hanging above the city, but the temperature wasn't cold and the forecast was for clear skies tomorrow.

After he'd talked to Heather and a couple of the other girls about the notes they'd received, he'd decided to concentrate on the four women who lived in the Seattle area, since the note had likely come from someone in the vicinity.

That meant Valentine, Megan, Delilah, and Isabel. He'd spoken to all but Isabel and come up with zilch.

He figured Mark Dargan, Valentine's trainer, was worth talking to. As Ethan shoved through the glass front door, the familiar sounds of clanking metal and the thud of weights dropping onto rubber mats reached him. The air conditioner hummed, keeping the rooms just shy of chilly, exactly the way he liked to work out.

At the front desk he asked for Dargan, found him easily. Six feet tall, blond, and athletic, the guy seemed popular with everyone in the gym. He was working with a client, midforties, balding, and probably fighting to keep the weight off. Fortunately, the workout was coming to an end.

Finished with the last set, Dargan's client set down the barbells, said good-bye, grabbed his workout towel, and headed off to the showers.

"You're Mark?"

"That's right."

"Ethan Brodie. I'm working security for La Belle. You know the name, right?"

"Yeah. One of my clients models for La Belle."

"Valentine Hart."

"That's right. What can I do for you?"

"With the show coming up, we're trying to nail down any potential problems before they arise. Valentine mentioned she'd had trouble a couple of times with guys working out at the gym. Said you'd handled them."

Dargan shrugged a set of lean-muscled shoulders. The guy was in great shape. But he got paid to be, same as Ethan.

"Wasn't any big deal," Dargan said. "One or two got flirty, tried to get a date. One got a little pushy." Mark grinned. "I told him I was Val's boyfriend and he'd better leave her alone."

"Are you?"

Mark shook his head. "Don't I wish. She's too busy for men. Or at least that's what she says. We've never really been more than friends anyway, and besides, I've started seeing someone."

"Good for you."

"Val's the best," Mark said. "She's got a beautiful figure, not overly muscled, you know? Just smooth and toned and fit. That's what La Belle wants in a model. It's my job to keep her that way."

Ethan thought of how she'd looked in black tights under a pair of cutoff jeans, midriff bare, her top cut just low enough to hint at full breasts. His mind conjured an image of what she'd look like in nothing but skimpy lingerie, and an unwanted tightening started in his groin.

"Any chance the guy who gave her trouble would pursue the matter, send some kind of threatening note to Val and some of the other models?"

"I don't think so. The man never bothered her again, only came around here a few times after that. Most guys start working out but stop after a couple of months." Mark's gaze ran over Ethan. "Not you, though. You stay in shape."

"Part of my job, same as you."

"You're a bodyguard, right? How about keeping a special eye out for Val? Like I said, she's the best."

"Seems you aren't the only one who thinks so."

Mark glanced over, caught a wave from his next customer. "Anything else?"

Ethan handed him a card. "Not unless you think of something."

Mark took the card and walked away, and Ethan headed for the door. As he reached the parking lot, he looked down at his big stainless-steel wristwatch. It wasn't that late. Clouds still hovered above the city, but a weak sun pushed through in places.

It wasn't Hannah's bedtime yet. His daughter would still be awake, and he wanted to see her. Since he would soon be leaving the city, he was determined to make that happen, and this time Ally wasn't going to stop him.

The porch light was on when he rolled up

in front of the big two-story house, parked his black four-door Wrangler hardtop at the curb. Through the curtains, he could see the yellow glow of the lamp next to the sofa in the living room.

He had almost reached the front door when he heard Allison's laughter out in the backyard. Ethan stepped off the cement path and headed in that direction. Stopping at the side gate, he lifted the latch, shoved the gate open, and kept walking.

Allison Winfield sat in a blue canvas swing on the big covered patio. A man in a short-sleeved yellow Izod shirt, sandy brown hair neatly combed, sat in the swing beside her.

In the fading light, Ethan could see Hannah sitting cross-legged on the patio a few feet away, playing with the doll he had given her. Her silky blond hair, pulled up in a ponytail, swung from the top of her head, and her blue eyes danced as she spoke to the doll she'd named Martha, God only knew why.

His heart squeezed. Surely his little girl couldn't have changed so much in the few weeks since he'd seen her. Surely she didn't look older, more grown up. Yet, as he watched her, it seemed that she did.

He started striding toward her, heard her squeal of delight when she spotted him, felt a tightening in his chest.

"Daddy!" She was on her feet and racing toward him, the ponytail on top of her head bobbing madly. "Daddy!"

Ethan bent and scooped her up in his arms. She smelled like cinnamon graham crackers mixed with a child's natural sweetness. Just holding her made his heart hurt.

"Hi, sweet cakes. How's Daddy's best little girl?"

She giggled, slid her arms around his neck. "I'm Daddy's only little girl."

Ally's shrill voice had him turning. "What are you doing here, Ethan? You know you aren't welcome." Allison Winfield was auburn-haired, of average height, and very pretty. She had a great figure and came from a family with way too much money.

She was also spoiled and conniving. When he'd met her, he'd been so in lust he hadn't been able to see her faults. By the time she was pregnant with Hannah, it had been too late.

"I've got a job that'll take me out of town for a while," he said. "I wanted to see Hannah before I left the city." He kissed his daughter's soft cheek and she giggled. Hannah made up for all the trouble Ally gave him.

"The least you could do was call before

you showed up uninvited."

"Every time I call, you say you're just leaving. There's never a time that's convenient. She's my daughter, too, Ally. If you don't start making it easier for me to see her, I'm going to take you back to court."

He'd had to hire an attorney and get a DNA test to prove he was Hannah's father. He'd spent a small fortune on legal fees to establish his rights, and if Allison continued to block his visitation, he was going to have to go to court again.

"Do whatever you like," Allison said smugly. Because she was still on Daddy's purse strings, legal fees and court costs weren't a problem for her. "You should have thought of Hannah before you left me."

"You're the one who ended it, Ally. I would have married you and you know it."

"And divorced me. You made no bones about it. You said from the start you didn't think it would work."

"I couldn't make you happy. Both of us knew that." He tipped his head to the man who stood watching from a few feet away, back straight, shoulders rigid. Slender, athletic, and handsome, he looked like a guy who played tennis or golf; not a tough guy, but ready to defend his damsel in distress.

"Who's your friend?" Ethan asked.

Allison glanced behind her, tossed her shoulder-length auburn curls, gave the poor fool a come-on smile. "That's Arthur. If it's any of your business, which it isn't."

Ethan ignored the guy, tried not to feel sorry for him. "I just want to see Hannah, Ally. I'd think you'd be happy about it. Seems like you could use a little time to yourself once in a while."

Arthur walked up beside her, set a hand possessively at her waist. "If you want me to make him leave, Allison, I will."

"Take it easy," Ethan said. "I'm just here to see my kid." He turned to Ally. "Give me five minutes and I'm gone."

Her mouth curved into a catty smile. "Why should I?"

"Because if you don't, there's going to be trouble and your friend will feel obliged to interfere. That won't go well for him. Five minutes. That's all I want."

She cast Arthur a glance. He was puffed up and ready to fight. Ally must have known what the outcome would be if she goaded him any further.

"Fine. Five minutes. Then you leave."

"We'll be out on the front porch." Hannah clung to his neck as he strode back in the direction he'd come from and walked out through the side gate.

"I missed you, Daddy."

He hugged her tighter. "I've missed you, too, cupcake. I've got to go away for a while, but when I get back, we'll work it out so Daddy can see you more often, okay?"

She grinned, her ponytail bobbing up and down. "Will you be back in time for my birthday?"

The tour would be over by then and he'd already made plans for the occasion. "Absolutely. We'll do something really special, I promise."

"Will you take me on a pony ride?"

"I will, if that's what you want to do and your mom says it's okay." Though there was every chance Ally would pitch a fit just to cause trouble.

They sat on the porch together, Hannah in his lap. Five minutes turned into six or seven before the door jerked open.

"Okay, that's it. Tell your father good night, Hannah."

"Can't he stay a little longer, Mommy?"

"No. He has to leave. Besides, it's your bedtime."

Ethan gave her a last quick hug and kiss and set her on her feet.

She waved. " 'Night, Daddy."

" 'Night, cupcake."

Allison grabbed the little girl's hand and

hauled her inside, gave him a last hard glare, and slammed the door.

Ethan took a deep breath and let it out slowly, started walking back to his Jeep.

Friday night, the man decided. He'd waited too long already. Soon the models would be leaving on their tour.

Using a Kleenex to pick up the note so he wouldn't leave fingerprints, he lifted it out of the desk drawer and set it on the desk, giving it a final check to be sure it was exactly right.

The message looked the way he intended: the stark white paper, the eerie, uneven words. He smiled, wishing he could be a fly on the wall when they found it. *And her.* He wondered how much trouble she would give him before she died. Not much, he was fairly sure. Women liked him. Always had. In the end it wouldn't matter. The result would be the same.

He put the note back in the drawer. Planning was everything, and he was ready. Once the task was completed, he could relax, enjoy the fruits of his labor. He thought of the night ahead and cold anticipation pumped through his blood.

The day of the dress rehearsal arrived and

the Friday event had the theater packed with people, all of them scurrying around doing their myriad jobs. Set designs were being touched up, added to, and changed. Lighting people tested the huge overhead spotlights. Sound gear was readied, the volume and balance checked, the mics and speakers.

The orchestra was setting up, testing their instruments. The security guys were moving around, quietly doing their jobs. A TV camera crew wandered around out front and also backstage, getting ready to film the chaos and excitement of the dress rehearsal, which would be posted on the Internet after the first show of the tour was over.

Val was already nervous and the show was still a day away. But she had never done any sort of modeling, no TV work, hadn't done high school or college theater. Unlike most of the girls, who'd had a good deal of experience in the field. She was out of her element and working hard to handle the pressure.

A good shot of vodka might help, but it wasn't going to happen. Too much was at stake. Val had promised to give the job her very best effort and she intended to do just that.

"Valentine!" A stout woman named Rosa

bustled toward her. "There you are. We're ready for your fitting." Each model had been assigned to a seamstress for the final fitting of her costumes.

Val nodded, followed the broad-hipped woman toward one of the dressing rooms. She caught a glimpse of the big bodyguard, Ethan, who had helped Heather after her fall. She did her best not to stare, but damn, he was an amazing-looking man.

She wondered if he might be gay, since he never seemed to notice any of the women. But she hadn't gotten gay vibes when he'd talked to her — just the opposite — so maybe he was simply doing his job the way he was supposed to.

She remembered the little zing they had shared, remembered the way his eyes had darkened. Definitely not gay, more likely a macho type who thought all women existed merely for his own personal pleasure.

She followed Rosa into the dressing room, found two other models inside, Isabel and Delilah. Delilah wasn't one of her favorites. She was way too full of herself, plus she loved gossip and had a knack for spinning it in whatever direction would make her look good. Still, she was mostly okay.

Dark-haired and sultry, Isabel Rafaeli was a lot of fun. She came from a big Italian

60

family who were all really proud of her. Izzy had told her the Rafaelis had flown in from Brooklyn: mother, father, two brothers and their girlfriends, even her older sister, Maria, for Izzy's first La Belle fashion show.

Val felt a pang in her chest. She would love to have a family with lots of brothers and sisters. But her mom and dad had died in a car accident when she was ten years old. The only family she had, a distant cousin and her no-good husband who lived in Seattle, had stepped in to raise her.

But living with them was hell, nothing at all like the loving family home she'd had before. When she was twelve years old she ran away, then eventually wound up in the foster care system. By the time she turned sixteen, she had a chip on her shoulder the size of a boulder and was always in some kind of trouble. If it hadn't been for the Hartmans, an older couple living on a small farm in Bellingham . . .

She jumped at a light slap on her rump.

"Pay attention, young lady. I've got a lot of other girls to take care of besides just you."

"Sorry, Rosa." From the beginning, she had been self-conscious about stripping buck naked in front of a bunch of women she hardly knew. She had learned to steel

61

herself and just get it done, which she did now.

For the first segment, Nashville Country, she was wearing a pair of red lace hip-hugger panties that dipped low in front, rode high in back, and showed the lower portion of the cheeks of her behind. The push-up bra was red, too. Beautiful garments for a woman's boudoir.

Unfortunately, tomorrow night she'd be wearing them on national TV.

Once she had on the panties and bra, Rosa tied a red bandanna around her neck.

"Sit down and put on your boots," the woman commanded.

At Rosa's no-nonsense tone, Val obeyed, pulling on an amazing pair of red high-heeled cowboy boots with a ruby-studded eagle on the front. Red stones flashed around the brim of the white felt cowboy hat she settled over her long blond curls.

"Walk across the room, turn, and walk back."

She did as she was told, glittery red earrings dangling from her ears, sparkling with every step.

Rosa frowned. "Stand still, now. I don't like that little pucker on your right hip." The fit of each garment had to be exact. There wasn't a fabric bulge, a loose button, or a flyaway thread, not an uneven hem. Nothing but perfection was allowed.

Rosa took scissors, then a needle and thread to the offending pucker, and it quickly disappeared.

"All right, that's it. You can go. They're waiting out there for you now."

"Thanks, Rosa."

The woman made a shooing motion and Val hurried out as Caralee Peterson walked into the dressing room.

Val grinned. "She's a tyrant. Good luck."

Caralee grinned back. "Rosa's gonna make that little ol' bustier I'm wearin' fit like a glove. Gonna make all the men go Southern crazy."

Val laughed, liking Caralee. She took a deep breath and headed for her place in the Nashville Country lineup, spotted Ethan and a pair of biceps that threatened the seams of his black T-shirt. At the little lift she felt in her stomach, she carefully kept her eyes straight ahead, determined to ignore him. But she couldn't help wondering if he would approve of the way she looked in her sexy red lingerie.

CHAPTER FIVE

"I don't know about you," Dirk grumbled, "but I don't know how much more of this I can take. I've been walking around with a hard-on for the past two hours."

Ethan chuckled. When he'd seen Valentine Hart walk out in her tiny red lace panties and a bra that shoved up her breasts like a feast for a king, he'd had to fight damned hard to maintain his highly prized control. *Damned hard.* He almost smiled.

"You like that one, don't you?" Dirk said. "*Valentine.* Gotta love the name."

"Sounds like a stripper, and I don't like her — I don't even know her. She's Samantha's friend. Sam asked me to keep a special eye on her."

Dirk laughed. "Well, you shouldn't have much trouble doing that."

Ethan flashed him a look. "Somewhere in your testosterone-fogged brain you do recall there's no mixing with the staff?"

Before Dirk could reply, one of the girls walked past wearing nothing but a silver thong and a strapless silver bra. She slid a sexy smile toward Dirk, and he groaned.

"Oh, yeah, I recall. I'm reminded every few minutes."

The corner of Ethan's mouth edged up. He could hardly blame his friend. He had never seen such an astonishing array of beautiful faces and drop-dead gorgeous bodies.

He looked up just then, caught a glimpse of Valentine in her cowboy costume, felt a jolt of lust so strong his body went rock solid and his nostrils flared. Long, honey-blond hair, full breasts temptingly displayed, nice high ass, and legs that went on forever.

Ethan clenched his jaw. *Dammit.* He was off women. And because she was a friend of Samantha's, especially off that one. He wondered how the two women could possibly have anything in common, a home-maker like Sam and a lingerie model who flaunted herself half naked in front of a million men.

"We need to make a sweep," he said, his voice a little gruff. "I'll take the left wing, you take the right."

Dirk nodded, and they moved off in opposite directions. An orchestra provided the music, country for this segment of the show. As a Shania Twain song began to play and the rehearsal continued, Ethan made a point of seeking out each of his men.

"Everything okay?" he asked Joe Posey, who was posted not far from the dressing rooms.

The black ex-cop just smiled, his eyes riveted on the beautiful ebony-skinned Amarika, standing to his left, talking to another girl. "My wife's gonna get lucky when I get home tonight."

Ethan bit back a groan. "At least you have a wife."

Posey grinned. "She's real pretty, too. And sexy. I won't need to fantasize about one of these gals here."

"That's just cruel," Ethan said.

Posey laughed. "What? Big strappin' fella like you? I imagine you got someone you could call."

"I imagine." But the more he thought about sleeping with some old flame, the less interested he was.

He thought of Valentine Hart and began to get hard. *Damn.* He hated when this happened, when his interest fixed on a particular female. It was exactly what had happened with Allison, and look how badly that had turned out.

Joe's smile faded as he glanced around. "No sign of trouble. I'll head downstairs, check the basement again."

Ethan nodded. La Belle had its own men posted at each entrance, both inside and out. Ethan had spotted Beau Desmond a couple of times, along with his buddy, a blond guy named Bick Gallagher, who looked more like a surfer than a private cop. Fortunately, there was plenty to do so they rarely crossed paths.

Ethan's men were mobile, moving quietly, keeping watch in and around the theater. All carried radios in case there was any sign of trouble, along with expandable batons. None carried firearms — though Ethan and Dirk would both be armed during the show tomorrow night.

Near the front entrance, Ethan spoke to Pete Hernandez, the short, muscular Latino, got the same answer he'd gotten from Posey.

"Not much going on. A couple of guys got past the outside guard. I saw them walk in. When the inside man tried to stop them, they got in his face. I was close enough to help. We talked to them, calmed them down, suggested they come back tomorrow night if they wanted to see the show. They got the message loud and clear and left without any more hassle."

"Nice work. The idea is to stop trouble before it can escalate into a serious problem. Better to use your head than your fists or that baton you're carrying."

Pete nodded.

Ethan figured Pete had passed his first test, hadn't flown off the handle, had kept his cool and done his job.

"Keep your eyes open," Ethan said as he walked away.

The rehearsal went smoothly, the fittings, the music, the staging and routines in all five segments. He'd been surprised to learn the Diamond Jubilee portion featured the girls in actual diamond necklaces worth hundreds of thousands, even millions of dollars.

The jewelry, provided by David Klein Jewelers, an upscale national chain, would arrive in a Seattle Armored Transport vehicle, protected by four armed security guards.

"I don't like surprises," Ethan said when Carlyle told him. "I especially don't like surprises that involve that kind of money."

"Sorry. I guess I should have mentioned it sooner. As far as we're concerned, the jewelry's just part of the costuming. It's the Klein company's problem to get the stuff in and out safely."

"Something worth that much is an attractive nuisance. It poses a risk to everyone."

"You're right. Again, I apologize. We've been using the stuff in the show for the last couple of years without a hitch. I guess I got a little apathetic. The good news is, the jewelry won't be worn today. It doesn't arrive until just before the show tomorrow night."

But diamonds worth millions added another layer of potential trouble for Ethan to worry about.

"I'll make my men aware," he said and took off to accomplish the task.

The day turned out to be shorter than he'd figured. By six o'clock on Friday afternoon the dress rehearsal was over. Carlyle wanted everyone to go home, take it easy, and get a good night's sleep. He wanted the crew alert and the models rested and looking good for the big show tomorrow evening.

Ethan couldn't imagine how twenty-nine gorgeous women could possibly look any better.

"We'll celebrate when the show is over," Carlyle promised the group of models clustered backstage at the end of the day. "You've all done a great job so far. Tomorrow night the world will see how beautiful you all are. And how sexy La Belle lingerie can make a woman look and feel."

The group applauded and started breaking up. La Belle security was escorting the local models back to their homes, the others over to the Fairmont Olympic. Ethan waited until everyone on the stage crew had left the theater; then he and his men made a sweep to ensure no one was still inside after the doors were locked. They needed to make certain no one could hide and get to the women tomorrow night during the show.

Satisfied everything was in order, and leaving Beau Desmond and some of his men to do the final lockup, Ethan climbed into his Jeep and headed for his Belltown apartment.

He'd only driven a couple of blocks when his phone started ringing. He didn't recognize the number as he hit the hands-free button.

"Brodie."

"Ethan, hi, it's Debbie Bryant."

A woman he had dated a few times last year. "Hey, Deb. What's up?" Debbie was the regional head of marketing for a big retail home decor company. She was based in Los Angeles but flew into Seattle every four months. Deb was smart, sexy, and interesting, and she had no expectations of

70

anything more than a night out and a good time in bed.

"I'm only in town just today," she said. "I thought maybe . . . if you weren't busy . . . we might get together for a drink after work."

He knew where a drink would lead, told himself to say yes. Maybe a night with Debbie would ease some of the sexual frustration he was feeling. "I appreciate the call, Deb. It's great to hear from you. Unfortunately . . . I'm . . . on a job. Maybe we can get together next time."

"Sure. Same goes if you're in LA. You've got my number. Take care, Ethan."

"You, too, Deb." Ethan hit the disconnect button. He couldn't believe he'd turned down Deb's offer. Maybe watching all those half-naked women had addled his brain.

Whatever it was, it looked like he was going home alone again tonight. Ethan reminded himself he was off women. He told himself staying celibate for a while was exactly what he needed.

Ethan clenched his jaw and called himself a fool.

CHAPTER SIX

It was a sunny July Saturday morning, the skies clear after three days of sullen gray. According to the weatherman, no rain was expected until the first of the week.

Sitting at the pretty little round oak table in the kitchen of her duplex apartment, Val sipped a cup of strong French roast coffee and read the *Seattle Times* on her iPad. Snoozie curled up in her lap, purring as she scratched behind his ears.

When her cell phone started playing a string of soft jazz notes, the cat leaped down and sauntered haughtily off to the living room, irritated at being disturbed.

Val grabbed the phone off the breakfast table and smiled as she recognized the number. "Hey, good morning, Samantha."

"Hey, Val, I'm sorry to bother you. I know you must be busy getting ready for the show and all, but —"

"What's going on?"

"I've got a problem with one of the dogs and I'm hoping you can help."

"Sure. I don't have to be at the theater till this afternoon, and I hate sitting here trying to make the hands move faster on the clock. This week, I've had a manicure, a pedicure, a facial, a massage, and two appointments at the hair salon. I am sooo ready to do something besides look at myself in the mirror."

"Great, because Mrs. Murphy's poodle has something wrong with its paw, and I was wondering if you could take a look. Mrs. Murphy's almost eighty. She barely gets by on her Social Security. She can't afford to pay a vet bill."

"Hey, it's not a problem. Just hang on, I'm on my way." Hair up in a ponytail, dressed in jeans, sneakers, and a bright-blue Seattle Seahawks T-shirt, Val hung up the phone and grabbed her car keys and purse.

She saved most of the money she was earning as a model for college, but she had indulged herself in a slightly used snazzy little red Nissan 370Z sports car. Decent mileage, fun to drive, and not too expensive, at least in the pre-owned model she had purchased.

A few minutes later, she was driving the 520, crossing Lake Washington, making the ten-mile drive to Samantha's pet-grooming parlor in Bellevue.

With her nerves already on edge because of the show tonight, she couldn't think of a better way to calm down than spending time with one of her best friends.

Ethan got the phone call at ten thirty A.M. Since he didn't have to be at the theater until noon, he sat at the computer in his apartment, Googling the ten women in the show who'd received the threatening note. He had already read their personnel files but decided to see what might turn up on an Internet search. So far, he'd finished the first five without anything jumping out at him.

He sat back in his chair and looked out the window. His furnished twelfth-floor apartment had a balcony off the living room and great views over the city. It wasn't fancy, but with two bedrooms and two-and-a-half baths, he had plenty of room, and he liked living in Belltown, being where the action was in Seattle. A remnant, he supposed, of his cop days in Dallas.

His cell had signaled twice before he pulled it out of the pocket of his jeans and pressed it against his ear. "Brodie."

"We've got a problem, Ethan." Matthew

Carlyle's voice vibrated with tension.

"What's going on?"

"An hour ago, Delilah Larsen was found dead in her condo. She was strangled."

"Jesus."

"Yeah."

"What're the circumstances?"

"Could be a break-in. The cops think maybe a burglary gone wrong."

He thought of the note Delilah and nine other women had received. "Or not."

"Yeah, that's the problem."

"Have you given the police the info on the notes?" Ethan asked.

"Met with the lead detective on the case this morning, guy named Bruce Hoover. He wasn't happy we hadn't reported the letters."

"I'll bet. What about the rest of the girls? Are they all accounted for?"

"We're in the process. We're putting a man on every woman in Seattle who got a note and placing guards on every floor of the Fairmont."

Ethan thought of Valentine Hart and the promise he'd made to Samantha. Worry slid through him. "What about Valentine? She's a family friend. You got someone with her?"

"Haven't been able to reach her so far. I'll stay on it, though."

"I'll find her. I'll let you know as soon as she's covered."

"All right."

"I want to take a look at the crime scene." Getting as much information as possible was his second priority — after he had Valentine secured. "What's the address?"

"It's 342 Lakeside Avenue. It's a luxury condo right on the water."

Ethan figured Delilah Larsen could afford it. One of the models had told him her fee was five thousand dollars an hour.

"I'm not sure the cops will let you in," Carlyle said.

"They'll let me in." He was a former police detective, and though Hoover was hard-nosed and set in his ways, Ethan had worked closely with the Seattle PD on a number of occasions since he'd started at Brodie Operations. There was a good degree of mutual respect. "I'll take a look and get back to you."

Retrieving the shoulder holster he'd planned to wear to the theater, he pulled out his Glock nine mil, dropped the clip, and checked the load. In Dallas, he'd carried a Sig P226, but he liked the Glock better. He shoved the pistol back in and slid the harness across his shoulders. Grabbing a lightweight black leather jacket, he pulled it on, covering the weapon, and headed for the door.

As he rode the elevator down to the underground garage, Ethan swore softly. They had tried to cover their bases. Clearly they hadn't done enough. He wished he'd programmed Valentine's cell number into his phone, wished he'd given his number to her, but at the time it hadn't seemed appropriate. Now his stomach tightened at the thought that something might have happened to her.

Sliding behind the wheel of his Jeep, he fired up the engine. Since he didn't have Valentine's cell, he brought up Samantha's number on his hands-free, heard the smile in her voice when she answered.

"Hey, Ethan. What's up?"

"I need Valentine's number. You got it?"

"Valentine? I've got her number, but if you want to talk to her, she's right here."

Relief trickled through him. "She's at your house?"

"No, the shop. She's —"

"By herself?"

"Yes, but —"

"Keep her there. Don't let her leave." Ethan ended the call. He wasn't about to relay news of a murder over the phone. He called Carlyle, told him he had found

Valentine with a family member and was on his way to provide protection. Then he pulled out on the street.

He needed to look at the crime scene, but Valentine's safety came first. Receiving threatening notes was no longer some nebulous problem. No matter what the police believed, Delilah's death wasn't the result of a failed robbery — there was a killer out there.

And Valentine Hart was on the killer's hit list. She was a friend of Sam's, and Ethan had promised to protect her. Pressing harder on the gas, he drove onto the freeway and headed for the strip mall on Bellevue Way where the Perfect Pup was located.

Val had been to the Perfect Pup any number of times in the last couple of years. She and Samantha had met through their volunteer work with the Humane Society, and though Samantha was petite and half a head shorter, a married woman and pregnant, they had a lot in common.

Mostly, their love of animals. Val was studying to be a vet. At one time, Samantha had wanted to be a veterinarian herself. Though it hadn't worked out, the pet-grooming business was a natural fit for her.

Val looked down at the little white poodle

shivering on the stainless-steel worktable in the grooming room. Using a fresh swab, she finished cleaning the dog's injured hind paw, wrapped its tiny foot in gauze, and gently taped the gauze in place.

"Missy doesn't seem to mind the bandage," Samantha said, stroking the dog's soft white curls to help keep it calm.

The dog looked up at Val, then nudged her fingers, as if to say thank you. "Mrs. Murphy can probably take the wrapping off tomorrow," Val said, giving the dog a friendly rub.

"I can't believe someone would do a thing like that to a helpless animal."

Someone had slipped a thin rubber band around the dog's hind paw. The soft curls had kept it hidden. The constriction had started to dig in, hiding it even further, cutting into the flesh until it had started to bleed. Eventually, it could have cost the poodle its foot.

"People can be cruel, that's for sure," Val said.

A loud *woof* reminded them another dog, brought in just as Val had arrived, waited in grooming room number two.

Samantha grinned. "Harry's calling. I guess he's ready for his bath." Harry was the exact opposite of the little poodle except he had the same white coat, a gigantic, shaggy, Old English sheepdog right out of a Disney movie.

"I've got to take care of him." Sam tipped her head toward the waiting area. "Ethan ought to be here any minute. Why don't you wait for him out front? I really appreciate your coming in, Val."

"I'm glad I could help, but I'm not going to stand around and do nothing while you battle with that monster dog." As if he heard, Harry started woofing. "Come on, I'll help you."

"You've got a big production tonight. You should be getting your beauty rest, not washing some oversized mutt."

"I can't leave till Ethan gets here, and it'll go a lot faster with both of us working." She thought of the man who was on his way to the shop, a professional bodyguard whose appearance left no doubt he could handle the job. She had no idea what he wanted, but a little ripple of anticipation went through her at the thought of seeing him again.

It was ridiculous. So he was hot. So what? Between the gym and her modeling, she saw hot guys all the time. She had no idea why she felt such a ridiculous attraction to this one.

With a grateful smile, Samantha led Val into the other shampoo parlor, which smelled like perfume and wet dog. "Okay, Harry, you know the drill. Come on, boy."

Sam unhooked the leash attached to the wall, and the big dog rose to all fours. Samantha led him over to the big stainless tub filled with hot soapy water, and he jumped up in, sending water and soap bubbles flying.

Sam grinned at Val, and she grinned back, then both of them dipped into the water up to their elbows and started giving Harry a scrub.

CHAPTER SEVEN

Worry rode Ethan's shoulders all the way across town. What if the murdered woman had been Valentine? What if she was the killer's next target? Thinking of Samantha's beautiful friend lying dead made his stomach burn. He'd promised to protect her. If something happened, what would he say to Sam?

He was in a dark frame of mind when he climbed out of the Jeep and pushed through the door of the Perfect Pup. What the hell was a pampered woman like Valentine doing at a dog-grooming parlor on the day of her show?

He scoffed. Probably having ribbons tied on the topknot of some little rat dog. Maybe one of those prissy little lassa-assholes, or whatever the hell they were called.

No one was behind the counter in the waiting area, but he could hear feminine laughter coming from the back of the shop.

Ethan headed in that direction, his mind on the steps he needed to take once he had Valentine secure.

At the door to one of the shampoo rooms, he spotted Samantha's mop of nutmeg curls as she shampooed a gigantic white dog. A blond woman stood next to her, both of them up to their elbows in soapy water.

Ethan jolted to a halt as the great beast leaped out of the tub, soap bubbles flying, knocking down the taller woman, who went sprawling on her behind, the wet dog landing on top of her.

She let out a squeal of laughter matched by Samantha's burst of hilarity. Ethan just stared. Good Christ, it was Valentine Hart.

"Get off me, you big ox!" Valentine gave a fierce shove that didn't budge the animal at all. Ethan finally managed to collect his wits enough to start forward. Sensing he wasn't in the mood to be disobeyed, the dog lumbered to his feet and ambled a few steps away.

"Hi, Ethan." Samantha grinned. "That's Harry." Just then the dog gave a mighty shake, sending a barrage of water droplets flying.

Sam and Valentine broke into fresh gales of laughter. Valentine's dimples popped out, and Ethan couldn't stop staring. Her soggy

T-shirt clung to a pair of perfect breasts, but it was the joy in her pretty blue eyes that made his chest feel tight. He reached a hand down to help her up, and she grabbed hold. Ethan felt a jolt all the way to the soles of his low-topped boots as he pulled her to her feet.

"Thanks," she said, smiling.

Ethan couldn't stop a smile in return. "You're just full of surprises, Ms. Hart." His gaze traveled from the messy ponytail on top of her head, all the way down her long, jeans-clad legs, to a pair of worn sneakers.

Behind him, Samantha snapped a leash onto Harry, and the big dog politely sat down.

"I think it's time I introduced you two," Sam said. "Ethan, this is Valerie Hartman. Valentine Hart is her stage name. She's not really a model. I mean, she is, but it's only temporary. Val's actually a student at the university. She came over to help me take care of an injured poodle. She's studying to be a veterinarian."

"A veterinarian," he repeated dumbly, still trying to get his head wrapped around this latest bit of news.

"I tried to tell you," Samantha said, "but . . ." She shrugged her small shoulders and let the words trail off, and Ethan felt like a fool.

He turned to the pretty blonde. "I think maybe we should start over . . . if that's all right with you."

Her pink lips curved. "Okay."

"I'm Ethan Brodie." He stuck out a hand. "It's nice to meet you, Valerie."

She shook his hand. "Valerie Hartman. A pleasure, Ethan." Her smile brightened and he felt the kick. "Val works just fine for both my names."

She must have noticed his gaze drifting down to the wet shirt clinging to her breasts because soft color washed into her cheeks. When she modestly crossed her arms to cover herself, he remembered how he'd thought her name sounded like a stripper's and felt stupid all over again.

"You . . . umm . . . came here to see me," she reminded him. "What's going on?"

The moment of levity was over. He was there to keep her safe. "I guess you haven't gotten a call from Matthew Carlyle or anyone from La Belle."

"My cell's in my purse. Half the time I don't hear it ring."

"I'm afraid I've got some bad news, Val. Earlier this morning, Delilah Larsen was found dead in her apartment. She was murdered."

"What?"

"She was killed sometime last night."

Val swayed, and Ethan gently caught her against him. "Easy. Maybe you'd better sit down."

"There's a sofa in the office," Samantha said, leading them in that direction.

Val didn't argue when he guided her inside and settled her on the couch. Her face looked so pale, he urged her head down between her knees. "Give yourself a minute. You'll be fine."

"I'm okay. I don't faint. I'm studying to be a doctor." But she waited a few seconds before she lifted her head.

"I'll get you some water." Samantha hurried away and returned a few moments later with a cup.

Ethan handed the cup to Val just as the buzzer above the front door sounded, announcing a customer's arrival.

"Hold on a minute," he said. Turning away, he moved quietly off toward the waiting room, pausing out of sight beside the door. A gray-haired woman, clearly no threat, walked in with a tall, long-haired Afghan dog.

Ethan returned to the office. "Go ahead,

86

Sam. Take care of your client."

Samantha nodded, took off for the waiting room. Val leaned back against the sofa, her face still pale, but some of the color had returned to her cheeks.

She looked up at him. "Delilah and I weren't really friends, but we worked together. She didn't deserve to be murdered. How did it happen?"

"She was strangled."

She swallowed. Her eyes widened as the possibility sank in. "Oh my God, it wasn't the guy who wrote those notes?"

"We don't know yet. I'm on my way to her place now. I'll know more once I take a look at the crime scene."

"What about the other girls? Are they okay? Oh, God, what about Megan? Meg O'Brien? She got one of those notes."

"Carlyle's making sure all the models are covered. He knew I was coming to get you. You need to call him, tell him you're okay."

"Let me get my phone." She hurriedly retrieved it and came back. "Looks like Matt's been calling."

"Call him back. Tell him you're with me. Tell him I'll be bringing you to the theater for the show."

"Okay." She was still shaken up, he could see, trying to process the information. She phoned Carlyle, told him she was safe.

"Ethan Brodie is with me now."

Carlyle said something on the other end of the phone.

"Yes, of course. I didn't think you'd cancel. I'll be there on time." Val hung up and released a shaky breath.

Ethan pulled out his iPhone. "What's your cell number?"

She gave him her number and he programmed his phone. "Now input mine."

She flicked him a glance but punched in his number.

"Are you okay to drive?"

"I'm okay. It was just such a shock."

"Where do you live?"

"Montlake, over by the university."

He mentally calculated the best route to take. "I'll follow you home, then drive you down to the theater later. I gather they aren't canceling the show."

"I didn't think they would. Too much money's been spent. They'll put another model in Delilah's place." She glanced down, swallowed.

Ethan didn't reply. He hadn't thought they'd cancel either. "You ready? I need to get moving."

Pulling herself together, Val got up from the sofa, stopped on the way out to say good-bye to Sam. Ethan followed her out of the building and walked her to her vehicle, a frisky little red Nissan sports car.

"Nice ride," he said. When she clicked the locks, he leaned down and pulled open her door.

"Thanks. It was kind of a splurge, but it was worth it." She slid in behind the wheel. "You don't have to follow me. I'm okay. Really. I'll see you down at the theater later."

"I don't think you get this, Val. You're with me until we figure out what's going on. What's your address in case we get separated on the road?"

"I really don't think —"

"I need your address."

She frowned as she gave him the number of her duplex on East Calhoun. "I have to get ready. I need to —"

"I'll be right behind you." Ignoring the unhappy look she cast his way, he walked back to the Jeep and climbed in, reached down, and programmed her address into his GPS.

He'd done everything in his power to avoid the attraction he felt for Valentine Hart — Valerie, he corrected. Now a murder had thrown them together.

As he fell in behind her little red sports car and Val wove her way through the Bellevue traffic, he thought about the woman he had misread so badly. A memory arose of her and Samantha, wet and soapy as they shampooed the big hairy dog. He thought of the dimpled grin on Val's face.

For the past three years, he'd been nursing his anger, harboring a grudge against women; not just his ex, but women in general.

Watching Samantha — the best thing that had ever happened to Nick, seeing Valerie on her all-important day helping a friend with an injured dog — it was hard to hang on to that anger.

It was past time to let it go and he knew it.

Ethan scrubbed a hand over his face. Since now wasn't the best time to be examining his life, trying to figure out what it was he really wanted, he needed to focus on his job. He had a theater full of women to protect and a murder to solve.

Which meant he'd have to be even more careful to keep his distance from Valentine Hart.

Val pulled up in front of her garage and opened the door as Ethan parked in front of the duplex, got out of his big black Jeep, and walked toward her.

Why was it he seemed to get better look-ing every time she saw him? When he smiled, which he didn't do that often, he was a devastatingly handsome man.

"Wait here," he said, joining her in the garage. He opened the door into her kitchen and disappeared inside to check things out, returned a few minutes later, and led her into the apartment.

"I've got to get over to the crime scene," he said. "That means you have to come with me. Pull on a dry T-shirt and let's get go-ing. I'll bring you back as soon as I'm finished."

Her hackles went up. "I can't go running off with you, Ethan. I have to get ready for the show."

"I thought they were doing hair and makeup at the theater."

"They are, but I have to shower, throw a few personal items into a bag. I was plan-ning on doing a little meditation, try to get myself relaxed before tonight."

"You'll still have time for that. Dry T-shirt, or I take you the way you are."

She couldn't believe it. He might be hand-some, but he was still an overbearing, macho jerk. "You're kidding, right? Now you're threatening to manhandle me?"

Amusement touched his lips and his hard

look softened. "Sorry. I'm a little out of practice dealing with women. I need to keep you safe, Val. I have no idea where the crazy who killed Delilah might turn up next. Until we know more, I need you somewhere I can protect you."

He had a point. A woman was dead. Val had also received one of those letters. She sighed. "Okay, I see your point. But you'd better get me back here in time to get ready."

"No problem."

She hurried into the bedroom, dragged off her wet Seahawks tee, pulled on a yellow T-shirt with *I heart Seattle* on the front, then returned to the living room.

Ethan was occupying himself with a perusal of her apartment. "Nice place," he said, his gaze going over the antique bookshelves, the overstuffed nutmeg tweed sofa and chair that complemented the flecks of brown in the beige carpet. One of her mom's framed samplers hung on the wall next to some cute dog and cat prints.

"Homey," he said. She noticed Snoozie had wandered in and was winding his way between Ethan's long legs. He didn't seem to mind.

"Another surprise?"

"I would have guessed modern and expensive."

"Why is that?"

"Because you don't exactly look the homey type." He picked up the big gray tom and absently stroked his fur. Val felt the movement of his fingers as if they were touching her instead of the cat.

"I'm saving my money to finish vet school," she said, shaking off the thought. "Sam told you that. This place is as much as I can afford until I graduate. And if you want to know the truth, I like it — so there."

His lips twitched. God, the man had a beautiful mouth. Just looking at the way it curved did funny things to the pit of her stomach.

"You live alone?"

"Just me and Snoozie."

"We've met." Ethan scratched the cat beneath his chin one last time, then set him back on his feet. "No boyfriend, then. Sam didn't say, but I don't see any sign of one."

"What, you were prowling around while I was changing?"

"I'm a detective. Prowling is what I do."

She shook her head. "No boyfriend. I don't have time."

She didn't say more as Ethan opened the front door and she walked out of the apartment, crossed the old-fashioned covered front porch, and made her way along the walkway out to his Jeep — a big black Wrangler four-door hardtop that looked like a smaller version of a Hummer and shouted *too much testosterone.* She couldn't deny it seemed to fit him.

He opened the door on the passenger side and Val climbed up in the seat. Ethan walked around, slid in on the other side, and cranked the engine.

"How much college do you have left?" he asked as he pulled away from the curb.

"One more year. It's taken me longer than other students. I'm twenty-six, almost twenty-seven. I . . . umm . . . had a couple of setbacks in high school, didn't graduate on time. My . . . umm . . . parents got me a tutor and I started getting good grades. Even with a partial scholarship, I still had to work."

She smiled. "I've already had an offer for a job in one of the local animal clinics as soon as I get my degree."

A dark eyebrow arched in her direction. "You don't think you'll miss being a model? Most women would go blind with joy if they could work for La Belle."

Val laughed. "I'm not most women."

Ethan flashed her a look that made her

stomach lift. "Yeah, I'm beginning to get that."

He turned off I-90 onto Lakeside Avenue, then began to follow the shoreline, eventually pulling up near an expensive set of condos with views out over the lake.

"Modern and expensive," Val said, repeating Ethan's earlier words. "It would have suited Delilah perfectly."

"But not you." He cast her a sideways glance. "Now that I've been to your house, I stand corrected. Not you at all."

She didn't know if that was a compliment or an insult. The thought slid away as she noticed the police cars lining both sides of the street in front of the residence. Seeing them there made her stomach roll. It reminded her why Ethan had insisted she come with him instead of staying home by herself.

Delilah was dead. She'd been young and beautiful, her whole life ahead of her. As Ethan stepped out of the Jeep, Val closed her eyes and said a prayer for the woman who had died so needlessly and whatever family she had left behind. When she looked up, she caught Ethan's gaze through the window.

He opened the door on her side of the vehicle. "I won't be gone long. Lock the doors. I'll have an officer keep an eye on you until I get back."

"That isn't necess—"

"Just sit tight."

She blew out a breath as he walked away, his strides long and determined. He paused to speak to a uniformed policeman and the officer nodded, his gaze swinging her way as Ethan disappeared inside the building.

Val leaned back in her seat. For the moment at least, there was nothing she could do but follow orders.

She thought of the years she had bounced from one foster home to another, the bad attitude she had carried that had protected her and at the same time caused her nothing but grief. She was older now and wiser.

But she still wasn't much good at following orders.

CHAPTER EIGHT

Delilah Larsen's lakeside condo was a million-dollar chunk of real estate, more like two mil the way property values had inflated. The entire back wall of the living room was glass, the window providing a spectacular view of Lake Washington. White carpet covered the floor. The furniture, an L-shaped sofa and chairs, was upholstered in a nubby white raw silk fabric. Dark wood accents grounded the space.

The place was glamorous, something a movie star might live in. Being a world-class model had its advantages. But Delilah had paid a terrible price for fame and fortune.

A price Ethan was determined none of the other women would pay, especially not Valentine Hart.

He stopped at the door and grabbed a pair of crime-scene booties, stretched them over his low-topped boots. Pulling a pair of surgical gloves out of the box on the entry table, he snapped them on, then headed for the lead detective, Bruce Hoover. The lieutenant was not quite six feet, early fifties, with a bald head fringed by light brown hair. One thing you could count on with Hoover: He was always in a bad mood.

The detective looked up as Ethan walked toward him. "Brodie. I heard you were working this."

"Matt Carlyle brought me in to help with La Belle security a couple of days ago. He beefed up the manpower after some of his models received threatening notes. I presume you know about that."

"I got the info this morning. A little late for Ms. Larsen. But yeah, we know about the notes."

"Carlyle made the call. The women are lingerie models. They deal with crackpots every day. No one expected the guy to take it this far."

"Maybe he didn't." Hoover turned his gaze toward the door from the living room into the kitchen. "Looks more like a break-in. Disabled the alarm. Lock-picked the back door, came in through the laundry. Jewelry box is empty. Purse has been cleaned out. She probably walked in on the guy and he offed her."

Ethan walked over to where the woman's

body sprawled on the floor, covered by a clean white sheet. There was a lamp broken on the floor, but not much sign of a struggle. He knelt and drew back the sheet, saw dark bruises discoloring the woman's throat and her head tilted at an odd angle. Silky blond hair formed a halo around her face.

Ethan's jaw tightened. Yesterday Delilah had been a beautiful, vibrant woman. Today she was a corpse.

He drew the sheet back farther, took in the length of her perfectly formed body. "She's still wearing her nightgown." An expensive lavender silk with beige lace trim. "Hadn't gotten dressed for the day when it happened. What's the preliminary time of death?"

"Sometime between three and five A.M. Still dark, happened before the sun came up."

The slinky nightgown hugged her curves but hadn't been shoved up, hadn't been torn as she'd fought to breathe. "Doesn't look like she's been raped."

"Not at first glance. We'll know more after the autopsy."

He lowered the sheet back into place, hiding the woman from view, wished he could blot her image out of his head that easily. "Preliminary cause of death?"

"Strangulation. Her neck was also broken."

But the bruises said her heart was still beating while her killer was asphyxiating her.

"Big," Ethan said. "Strong enough to break her neck without much effort."

"If he was the guy who wrote the notes, he knew what he was doing. It didn't take him long to kill her. Personally, I'm leaning toward a burglary gone wrong. There's been a rash of break-ins in the area. So far no one's been home at the time."

"Why would he think she wasn't home?"

Hoover shrugged. "Maybe she spends her nights with a boyfriend. We'll give that angle a look."

"Good idea. I'd appreciate it if you'd keep me in the loop on this."

"Yeah, well, I'd appreciate it if you stayed out of police business. The only reason you're here now is Paul Boudreau is a friend of the mayor." Boudreau, the owner of La Belle, was extremely wealthy and a big philanthropist in Seattle. "Carlyle is Boudreau's top man and he wants you in. Just don't press your luck."

Ethan bit back a smile. Grumpy as the detective was, he was good at his job. They had worked together before and respected each other. Ethan was glad Hoover was on the case.

"I'll just take a quick look around and be out of here."

Hoover grunted.

Figuring his time was limited and needing to get Val back to her house to shower and change, he made a quick perusal of the condo, heading for the master bedroom, noting that the bed was turned back, as if Delilah had gotten up at some sound and gone to check on it.

Nothing out of the ordinary in the big marble bathroom. Clothes — and there were plenty of them — neatly hung in the oversize closet. Some still had price tags. He read the tags, dollars in the high hundreds, even thousands, designer fashions that cost a small fortune.

He tried to imagine Val wearing the expensive garments, yesterday could have, not today.

He walked into the kitchen. Alarm was the wireless kind, probably disabled remotely. He walked into the laundry room, took a look at the back door. Frowned. Carefully opening the door, he walked out on the back deck. Guy was good with a pick, only a tiny scratch where he'd jimmied the lock and opened the door.

The entry was neat and clean; just a

couple of twists and the door was open. The chain lock had been cut, probably with a pair of bolt cutters.

He walked back into the house and made his way to the living room. "What about fingerprints?" he asked Hoover.

"The place is wiped. Burglary makes the most sense. But we can't disregard the wacko and his notes, at least not yet. Our guys are canvassing the area. Maybe we'll get a hit."

Ethan stripped off his plastic booties and gloves and tossed them into the trash the CSIs had set beside the front door. "Keep me posted. I'll do the same."

"You're a pain in the ass, Brodie."

Under different circumstances, Ethan would have smiled.

Val looked up as Ethan approached the Jeep. Beneath his black T-shirt, heavy muscles bunched as he slid in behind the wheel.

"What did you find out?" she asked.

"Not enough." He started the engine. "Cops think it was a break-in. Burglary gone wrong."

"They think she walked in on someone?"

"They do."

"But you don't."

He shrugged those wide shoulders. "It

makes sense. The guy knew what he was doing. No prints. Easy in and out. Took jewelry and money, nothing else that we know of, at least not yet."

"Delilah had some really expensive jewelry. She was popular with the men."

He sliced her a look as the Jeep rolled along the road at the edge of the lake. "She have a boyfriend?"

"I've only heard gossip. I'd rather not repeat it."

"A woman's been murdered."

She sighed, nodded. "You're right. I'm sorry. Rumor was she had several very wealthy men friends over the last couple of years. Delilah loved jewelry. The men . . . umm . . . earned her favors by giving her expensive gifts."

"Did she keep the stuff in her apartment?"

"I don't know."

"You know the men's names?"

She shook her head. "We weren't close friends."

Ethan's phone signaled. He hit the hands-free. "Brodie."

"Hoover." The detective's voice rattled over the line. "The guy hit her safe. It was hidden in the back of her closet. We missed it the first time. Killer took whatever was inside."

"She had boyfriends who gave her jewelry," Ethan said.

"Must have been in the safe. I'll follow up. The thing is, Brodie, the box was empty, but the guy left a note inside. Pretty much the same as the last one. 'Sinners, sluts, and whores. Repent or you'll be next.' "

"Fuck."

"Yeah, that pretty well sums it up."

"How'd he crack the box?"

"Either he knew the combination or the guy was a real artist. I'm thinking he forced her to give him the numbers before he killed her."

"How'd he know about the safe?"

"Hell, I don't know. Maybe she offered him the jewelry as a bribe, tried to use it to get him to leave."

Ethan started nodding. "Instead, he got the combo and killed her anyway."

"Works for me. Considering the note he left, that would make sense."

Ethan ran a hand over his face. "That it?"

"For now."

"Appreciate the call, Lieutenant. If I run across anything, I'll be in touch."

Ethan ended the call and turned to Val. "That was Detective Hoover. He's the lead on the case."

"So it wasn't a burglary," Val said softly.

"No."

"You never thought it was, did you?"

"No," he said.

Val looked at Ethan, feeling a kernel of respect. The man knew what he was doing. She was glad he was the guy keeping her safe.

Ethan flicked a glance at the beautiful blonde sitting rigidly in the passenger seat. Her face had paled as the ramifications of the note in the safe sank in. "Now you understand why I needed you with me."

"Yes . . ." She glanced down. "I'm sorry."

Her hands were clenched in her lap. He reached over and covered them, gave them a squeeze. "We're going to get this guy, Val. Before he hurts anyone else. The police are working the case. Carlyle asked me to help. We'll find him, okay?"

She frowned. "So you're a detective. I thought you were a bodyguard."

"Personal protection's my specialty." He cast her a glance. "Before I moved to Seattle, I was a homicide detective in Dallas. Now I work as a private investigator whenever I catch a case. Hoover's good. I'm just as good or better. We'll find him, okay?"

Val looked at him and nodded, but she didn't seem convinced. "I need to call

Megan. She got a note and she's one of my best friends. I want to make sure she's okay."

"Go ahead. Be better if you don't give her too much information, though. This is a police investigation. They're cooperating so far. They'll stop if they can't trust us with what they know."

"I understand."

She called her friend. He knew which one she was: the redhead with the big blue eyes, the one Dirk had in his sights.

Hopefully, his friend would wait till the tour was over before he homed in on his target.

"Meg, it's Val. Do you know what happened? Are you okay?"

Ethan couldn't hear what the other woman said, but Val was nodding. "I'm okay," she told her friend. "I'm with Ethan Brodie. He's bringing me to the rehearsal. What about you?" She started nodding again. "So the other guy, the one named Dirk, is there? He's at your house now?" She looked over at Ethan but spoke to her friend. "He's bringing you to the theater. Okay, that's good. I'll see you there."

Ethan silently cursed. Looked like Dirk wasn't waiting. But then, Ethan hadn't waited to go after Val. He could make all the excuses he wanted, but the truth was, he wanted her safe.

"Megan is at her house with your friend Dirk," Val said. "You work together right?"

"That's right. We both work at Brodie Operations. My cousin Ian owns the company. Dirk's a good man. Your friend is in good hands."

She didn't reply, just leaned back in the seat. A few minutes later, he pulled up in front of her duplex, went inside to make sure she had no unwanted visitors, then brought her into the living room.

"You've still got some time before you have to be at the theater. Why don't you take a shower, maybe nap for a while? You're going to have a long night ahead of you."

When her pretty blue eyes filled, he reached over and lifted her chin. "You don't have to be afraid, Val. I'll be right out here. I won't let anyone hurt you."

She turned away from him, walked over and stared out the window. "That's not it. I just . . . I keep thinking about her. Did she struggle? How long did it take him to kill her? Did she suffer? I can't get it out of my head."

Ethan came up behind her, settled his hands on her shoulders. "He was big, powerful. It was over quickly. He didn't rape her. That's all I know. I hope it's some comfort."

She turned to look up at him, her eyes swimming with tears. "How could someone do that to a defenseless woman?"

"There are a lot of sick people out there, Val."

She swallowed, brushed away the wetness that escaped down her cheeks. "Thank you for coming to get me, making sure I was safe."

"It's my job."

"You could have sent someone. You did it because I'm Sam's friend, right?"

His eyes locked with hers, dark brown into worried blue. "Mostly," was all he said.

For the next few hours, while he waited until it was time to drive Val to the theater, Ethan worked by phone. He talked to Matt Carlyle, but they had both spoken to Hoover, so neither had anything new to report. He mentioned Delilah's men friends, and Carlyle agreed to see what he could find out.

Even after finding the note in the safe, they couldn't afford to make assumptions. There were lives at stake. They needed all the information they could gather in order to find Delilah's killer and protect the other women.

A phone call to Dirk had him grinding his teeth. "I take it you're with the redhead."

"Megan. That's right. They were going to send one of the guards, but I volunteered. She's a nice girl. I didn't want anything to happen to her."

"Yeah, well, she's also Valerie's best friend. Val's a friend of Samantha's. That makes her family, which makes Megan hands-off. You get what I'm saying?"

"I'm just doing my job — same as you. And who's Valerie?"

"That's Valentine's real name. She's studying to be a vet. Long story. Just remember why you're there, and it isn't to screw one of the models."

Dirk ignored him. "You get a look at the crime scene?"

"Yeah."

"Was it him — the nut job?"

"Looks like. Safe was robbed, looked like a burglary at first, but the guy left a note similar to the first. This one said 'repent or you'll be next.' "

"Fuck."

"Yeah."

"What's your take?"

"The guy's no amateur. He was in and out slick as grease, killed her quick and easy, broke into her safe, stole her money and jewelry — very expensive jewelry. That doesn't sound like a wack job to me, but still. . . ."

"But there's no reason a wack job couldn't have taught himself a few tricks along the way. Maybe even decided to make a little money while he was doing his dirty work."

"Could be. Could also be this isn't his first rodeo."

A pause. "You aren't thinking serial here?"

"Gut instinct? No. Cops will be checking that angle, though, looking for some kind of pattern."

Dirk sighed into the phone. "I hope to hell the cops can keep this quiet. We get a leak, we won't just have to worry about the killer. We'll have half a dozen copycats crawling out of the woodwork, sending notes to those girls on the tour."

"You got that right. Keep an eye on the redhead," Ethan said. "Just not too close an eye."

"Same goes for the blonde." Dirk hung up the phone.

CHAPTER NINE

Val showered, washed and dried her hair, perfumed and lotioned her body, fed Snoozie, then did her best to psyche herself up for the important night ahead.

She was ready to leave for the theater with plenty of time to spare. Ethan was pacing by then. She figured she would give him a break and go in a little early. Security would be tight at the Paramount. She would be safe there, and Ethan could do whatever he needed to help find the killer.

In a flirty little short black skirt that fluttered around her thighs when she walked, a peach silk, off-the-shoulder blouse, and a pair of open-toe, black high heels decorated with rhinestones, she was ready to face the photographers and TV media that would be waiting backstage before and after the show.

Val was fairly certain the after-party would be canceled. The murder of La Belle's top model wasn't something to celebrate.

A little shiver ran through her. She could have been the victim. Or she could be next. The murderer might go after Megan, or any of the girls who'd received a threatening note.

"You ready?" Ethan asked, breaking into her thoughts.

Val steeled herself; she had a job to do. Pasting on a smile, she grabbed her tote and her purse. "Ready as I'm going to get," she said.

Ethan parked the Jeep near the rear entrance of the Paramount, came around and helped her down, then started walking her toward the back door.

"Dirk's already here," he said. "That black Escalade's a BOSS, Inc., vehicle. Dirk usually drives his Viper or rides his Harley. The SUV is better for clients."

She smiled. "A Viper or a Harley. He certainly has good taste."

"I rode a 750 till I had a kid. I figured I couldn't risk getting myself killed and leaving her alone."

Her interest sharpened. "You have a child?"

He nodded. "Little girl named Hannah. She'll be four her next birthday. Sweetest little towhead you've ever seen."

Val's stomach tightened. "So . . . you're

married?"

"No. I offered, her mother refused. You might say we weren't exactly a match made in heaven."

She shouldn't have felt so relieved. But the heat in those dark eyes whenever he looked at her was hardly appropriate for a married man. Nor was the hot surge of desire she felt in return.

"Why didn't the two of you get along?" she asked.

"Since I'm not into name-calling, you'll have to ask her."

He reached the rear entrance and the outside security guard pulled open the door.

"Any problems?" Ethan asked.

"Not so far." The guard turned to Val. "Everyone's heard the news. I'm sorry about what happened to your friend."

Val swallowed. "Me too." She walked into the theater, past another guard just inside the door.

The place was already buzzing as Ethan led her into a big room backstage where rows of makeup tables had been set up, each with a lighted mirror. Some theaters had a row of dressing rooms. Here, every girl was assigned a table where a makeup artist would apply her makeup and a stylist would finish her hair. The room was already half full.

Val turned to the powerful man beside her. "I'll be okay now. Thanks again for coming to get me."

"I'll be waiting for you after the show."

"Oh . . . that's right. I don't have my car, so I guess I'll be needing a ride."

Something hot moved in those dark eyes; then it was gone. "I'll keep you safe, Val. For now that's all you need to worry about, yes?"

She nodded, smiled. "Thanks." Turning away, she took a deep breath and walked through the door into a completely different world from the one in which she actually lived. An exclusive world of beauty and glamour and fashion.

She thought of Delilah and the image changed to the dark reality of murder. Then she remembered that Ethan would be waiting to see her safely home.

She took a deep breath. She could do this, do the job she was being so highly paid for. Val headed for her makeup station.

Ethan spotted Dirk walking the redhead, Megan, toward the busy dressing area backstage. Like all the models, Megan O'Brien was a beautiful woman. At the same time, she seemed more approachable than some of the others, more of a high-school sweetheart than a sophisticated fashion model. Maybe that was part of what Dirk liked about her.

Dirk grinned down at her, whispered something. Meg smiled up at him, turned, and disappeared into the room.

Dirk walked toward him. "Everything okay?"

Ethan nodded. "You?"

"Meg was pretty shook up. I think she felt better after Valentine called. I gather they're close friends."

"Seems that way. You behave yourself?"

"Meg made it easy. She has about ten thousand guys trying to get in her pants. She's pretty cautious when it comes to men. What about you and Miss Dimples?"

Ethan let out a slow breath. "She's not what I thought. She's smart, saving her money to finish vet school. She was helping Sam wash a big hairy dog when I found her."

Dirk's mouth edged up. "Smart, hard-working, not prissy, and sexy as hell. So I guess you're no longer off women."

Ethan grunted. "I'm off them till this is over. I need to keep my head on straight and so do you. We need to find this guy before he kills someone else."

Dirk sobered. "So where do we go from here?"

"If you'll keep an eye on things, I've got a couple of errands to run. I'll be staying with Val until the tour leaves or they catch this guy, so I need my laptop and a few other things from my apartment. I need to head down to the office. I want to talk to Sadie, see if she can come up with something that might be useful."

Sadie Gunderson was a middle-aged woman who worked part-time at BOSS, Inc. With two grown kids and a couple of grandkids, she was the most unlikely computer whiz on the planet and dynamite good at her job.

"I'll keep an eye. You'll be back before the show?"

Ethan's lips curved faintly. "What? Miss all those beautiful half-naked women? I'm over thirty, but I'm not dead yet."

Dirk laughed. But the truth was, Ethan was more interested in seeing one particular half-naked woman, and because he didn't like sharing, he would rather she be all-the-way naked just for him. Beyond that, he would worry about her safety until he got back.

Ethan headed for the door.

■ ■ ■ ■

The sign etched into the plate-glass window read "Brodie Operations Security Services, Inc." The relatively small freestanding building took up two floors of a brick structure on NE 8th in downtown Bellevue. The reception area, conference room, employee lounge, and an open area with rows of desks, each with its own computer, were located on the first floor.

Upstairs was Ian's office, plus a room with a couple of beds where the guys could crash if they got in late, and the office Sadie sat in to work her computer magic.

Ethan shoved through the door into the reception area. Modern in design, with a butter-soft black leather sofa and chairs and a black granite coffee table, the waiting area as well as the rest of the decor was expensive, masculine, and comfortable.

Heading into the main part of the office, he spotted his brother, Luke, sitting at his desk.

"Hey, bro," Luke called out. At six two, he was an inch shorter than Ethan, with a hard, lean-muscled build. A year younger than Ethan's thirty-two, with his short-on-the sides, sun-streaked brown hair and brilliant blue eyes, Luke was an unrepentant ladies' man with no intention of changing anytime soon.

As Ethan walked up, he grinned. "Say, you wouldn't happen to have a backstage pass to the titty show, would you?"

Ethan felt a shot of irritation. "It isn't a titty show. These women are high-class models. They've been working twelve hours a day to put this show together."

One of Luke's dark eyebrows went up. "That so? Seems to me it was you who was grumbling about taking a job babysitting a bunch of airheaded women."

"Well, I was wrong. They aren't what I thought. At least most of them aren't. The bad news is, last night one of them was murdered."

The teasing light slid from Luke's handsome face. "Don't tell me it was the creep who sent those notes." His brother knew the reason La Belle had wanted to add more security. Luke's specialty was tracking down bail skips. He made a fat living as a bounty hunter, but he could handle just about anything.

"Guy left a second note," Ethan said. "Threatened to kill another model if the women didn't repent."

Luke hissed in a breath. "You need some help?"

"Appreciate the offer, but it isn't more men we need; it's a lead that'll give us a way to find this guy." His brother might be a little wild at times, but he'd been Delta till he'd taken a bullet next to his heart on some secret mission too classified to talk about. He was capable, reliable, and strong as steel. And beneath his lighthearted banter, Luke was the kind of man who believed in protecting a woman at any cost.

"I've got to check my messages," Ethan said. "Then I'm heading up to see Sadie. I'm hoping she can help."

"Good idea."

Ethan walked toward his desk.

"Listen . . . sorry about that crack about the girls. I was just trying to fire you up a little. With the trouble you've been having with Ally and Hannah, you've seemed a little down lately. I meant what I said — you need help, just call."

"Thanks. I will." Aside from being his brother, Luke was a man Ethan could count on. He wouldn't hesitate to ask for his help.

Crossing the office, Ethan sat down at his desk and picked up the phone. The days of an actual person taking messages were long gone, so he checked his voice mail, which he usually did from his cell. Unless it was necessary, he didn't give out his cell number. He liked to keep his private life private.

There were only a couple of messages, phone calls that pertained to his last assignment. Those he returned, then headed upstairs.

Ian's office door stood open, the room decorated in the same black-and-chrome motif as the rest of the building. Sitting behind his desk, blond hair a little rumpled, head bent over as he worked, Ian looked up as Ethan approached.

"How's the show going?" his cousin/boss asked. He was tall, like the rest of the Brodies, with an athletic build and a too-handsome face. There was a time Ian had had women falling at his feet, but since he'd met his wife Meri, those days were past.

"Everything was going just fine till one of the models got murdered last night."

Ian came out of his chair. "Sonofabitch. What the hell happened? Christ, don't tell me it was that crazy who sent those notes."

"Looks like. The vic was strangled. Her name's Delilah Larsen. The police don't have jack. I'm here to talk to Sadie, see if she can come up with something."

"Good idea. You get into the crime scene?"

"Yeah. Looked like a burglary gone bad

till they found another note in the victim's safe. Note made a second threat similar to the first. Be best if they canceled the show, but that's not going to happen. We really need to find this guy."

"Yes, and the tour leaves for Dallas on Tuesday. Security's going to be a bitch."

"Exactly. Sadie's usually in on Saturdays. She in her office?"

"She's there."

"I'll head on down. I need to be back at the theater before showtime."

"I'll do some digging," Ian said. "If I come up with anything, I'll let you know."

"Thanks." Heading out the door, Ethan strode down the hall into the office that was Sadie Gunderson's domain. She sat at her desk behind three computer screens, a big woman in her fifties, broad-hipped, with very curly shoulder-length silver hair.

There were photos on the desk: her son and his family, her daughter and her two kids. Ethan thought of Hannah and felt a pang in his chest. His daughter lived in Seattle, but he rarely got to see her. Nick, Luke, and Ian lived there, too, but the rest of his family was spread across the country.

He and Luke had been born and raised in Texas. Their mom had died five years ago. Two years later, their dad had remarried and moved to North Carolina. Jim Brodie was happy again, had adopted his younger wife's two kids. Ethan and Luke were both glad for him.

Ethan looked at Sadie and eased farther into the room, approaching quietly, like coming up on a Doberman chewing on a bone.

"Sadie?"

She glanced up, lines instantly forming across her forehead.

"I'm sorry to bother you, but I've got a problem and I'm hoping you can help."

Shrewd green eyes fixed on his face. "Everybody has a problem, hotshot. You'll have to get in line."

Ethan didn't back off. He was used to Sadie, whose bark was worse than her bite. Mostly. "My problem's murder, Sadie. And if I don't come up with something soon, it's going to happen again."

The woman's hard look softened. "Well, you better sit down, then, and tell me what's going on."

Ethan sat in the chair beside her desk and laid it all out: the notes the top-ten models had received, Delilah Larsen's murder, the second note left in the safe.

"So where do you want me to start?" she asked.

"I'm thinking we start with the women, each of the models who received a note. Get into each woman's past, go deep, see if we can find someone with a grudge, a guy who's willing to murder to get even."

"If he's mad at one of them, why would he send notes to ten of them?"

"I don't know. Maybe he doesn't care which one pays. Maybe Delilah was just the easiest to get to. Look at their backgrounds, their religion, since he keeps calling them sinners. Look at guys they've dated, anything that might give us a lead."

"Get me the names and I'll get moving."

Ethan smiled. "I e-mailed you a file with all the data. Names, addresses, ages, places of birth. You've got the basics, but I need a whole lot more. I need the personal info, stuff only a wizard like you can come up with."

Sadie scoffed. "You ought to know by now, dear boy, flattery isn't going to work."

"How about tickets to a Seahawks' game?"

"That'll work." She grinned. "I'll send the info to your e-mail as soon as I'm finished."

Ethan bent and kissed her forehead. "Thanks, Sadie. You're a peach."

"Yeah, well, just don't forget those tickets."

Ethan grinned. "Not a chance." Turning,

he left the room, hoping the information, once he got it, would actually be helpful. Giving up a pair of game tickets was a high price to pay.

His smile faded as he left the building, anxious to get back to the theater before something else went wrong.

CHAPTER TEN

The voluminous, high-ceilinged chamber backstage at the Paramount hummed with activity. Most of the original thirty, now twenty-nine, models were inside the giant dressing room in some stage of preparation for the show.

Besides the women, there were costume people, makeup artists, hairstylists, and general gofers. The room was thick with the odor of hair spray, powder, and perfume.

Face made up and hairstyle complete, Val was just getting out of her folding chair in front of the lighted mirror when Meg walked up, also show ready except for her costume. Her long red hair had been trimmed into a saucy, flyaway cut that enhanced the beauty of her heart-shaped face.

She was wearing black silk Capri pants with a silver belt, black high heels, and a black-and-turquoise halter top.

By unspoken agreement, they walked to a quiet corner out of the way. "Are you okay?" Meg asked. "Because I'm really not."

Val glanced at the activity around them. "I'm okay — sort of. I called my parents this morning. I knew they'd be worried when they heard about the murder. I told them everything was under control, that we each had our own personal bodyguard, and they seemed relieved."

Meg nodded. "I talked to my folks, too. And a detective named Hoover. He asked me a bunch of questions. I don't think my answers helped any. I didn't know Delilah that well."

"He talked to me, too, but I didn't know her much either." Val sighed. "I still can't believe it. The murder just doesn't seem real."

"The whole thing shook me up pretty good. I mean, ten of us got those notes, you know? Could have been you or me instead of her."

Val felt a chill, though the room was warm. Meg was right. It could have been any one of them. "That big bodyguard, Ethan? He's related to Samantha's husband, Nick. I guess that got me special treatment. He came to pick me up after the murder. He wanted to make sure I was okay."

"Lucky girl."

"Under different circumstances, maybe. He's definitely a hunk. But I've got to keep my mind on the show, and you know the rules about mixing with staff. I need this job, and even if Ethan was interested, which I'm not sure he is, he doesn't seem like the kind of guy who would break the rules."

"Too bad. Maybe after we get back home."

She shrugged. "Maybe." But she would be busy getting ready for school and he would be working another job.

Megan grinned. "I got the other hot one. And I'm not even related to one of his friends."

"Dirk. I've seen the way he looks at you. He wanted to make sure you were safe."

"I really like him, but a guy who looks like Dirk? He's probably a dog. I've had enough of those in my life already."

"Isn't that the truth?"

"Plus I've got a son to think of. If I ever fall for another man — God forbid — I'd want someone who'd make a good father. A guy like Dirk Reynolds . . ." She shook her head. "Getting involved with a woman who's got a child is the last thing he'd want."

"I suppose." Val thought of Ethan and his daughter, the way his eyes sparkled when he mentioned his little girl. "On the other

hand, Charlie's so cute he's almost irresist-
ible."

Megan laughed. "He's still in the terrible
twos. You wouldn't say that if you were with
him twenty-four seven."

Val grinned. "I love kids, but I think I'll
stick with animals for a while."

Meg grinned back. "Good call."

They eased a little farther into the corner.
Once they walked out of the room, they'd
be fair game. By now, the media had arrived full force backstage. A few cameras
were rolling in the makeup room. The rest
would be waiting like a horde of hungry
lions as the models left the prep room. The
murder of the show's top model only made
them more rabid.

"Dirk says they're trying to keep those
notes we got out of the press," Megan said.
"Officially, the murder is still under investigation. The cops are saying it was probably
a burglary gone wrong. They're afraid if
those notes get published, it might stir up a
bunch of psychos."

The thought made Val's stomach churn.
They'd been warned not to say anything
after the first notes arrived. Matt Carlyle
had reminded her again as soon as she'd arrived at the theater.

"I'm not saying anything," Val said. "The

police have enough to worry about just trying to keep us safe."

"Dirk says Carlyle stepped up security on all the models who live in Seattle. The out-of-towners are staying at the Fairmont. Dirk says they've got hotel security beefed up, too."

"What's going to happen when the tour goes on the road?" Val asked.

"Maybe they'll catch the killer before we leave."

Val glanced at the chaos around them. "Whatever happens, at least we'll all be together, all of us staying in the same place. That should make security a little easier."

"Yeah, and Dirk and Ethan are coming with us. Just knowing that makes me feel better."

Relief and something more trickled through her. She hadn't known the men were coming along. "They definitely seem capable."

"Yeah, hot and capable. Nothing like a man who looks like Dirk Reynolds, has a body that makes you drool, and knows how to protect you. Makes him a tough temptation to resist."

She was thinking the same thing about Ethan. "We need to let them do their jobs and we need to do our own."

"I know. Plus I don't want another broken heart."

"Right. And I don't need the hassle. I have too much on my plate as it is. Add to that, I have a hunch Ethan has more than enough trouble of his own."

"Then we don't have to worry, right?"

Val sighed. "Not about men. Just about not getting murdered."

By the time the pre-show started, the murder of Delilah Larsen, La Belle's most famous model, was all over the television and in every newspaper. Media trucks, camera crews, and reporters all jammed together outside the back entrance and lined the walkway up to the front door.

The press backstage had interviewed the nine remaining top models, and photos had been shot from every angle. They'd been fawned over and leered at. Ethan figured the pre-show was the red carpet of lingerie modeling.

As the start of the show drew near, he checked in with his crew, all of whom had been brought up to speed on the murder and cautioned to be alert so it wouldn't happen again.

"I saw the cops talking to some of the models before the pre-show," Ted Sandowski said. He was round-faced, a little soft, but not overweight, a nice guy the girls had dubbed Sandy, either for his name or the color of his hair. As long as they smiled at him, Sandowski didn't seem to care.

"Carlyle didn't like the models being interrogated," Sandy said. "He was ranting at one of the detectives, said he didn't want the girls upset so close to the start of the performance."

"The cops are just doing their job," Ethan said. "They've been at it since early this morning, trying to find out if one of the models or someone on the crew knows anything that could be relevant to the case. The longer it takes to find the killer, the higher the odds he'll get away with it."

"I wish it hadn't happened on my watch," Sandy said darkly.

Ethan just nodded. It wasn't Sandowski's fault. No one was to blame but the sick SOB who had murdered Delilah. But Ethan had been on enough cases to know it always felt like there should have been something he could have done to prevent it.

"Stay sharp," he said. "Don't get side-tracked by everything that's gone on."

Sandy nodded and Ethan continued his rounds, pausing to talk to some of La Belle's own security people, even sparing a moment to speak to Beau Desmond, who was his usual dickhead self.

"I thought you were a detective, Brodie. If you'd been doing your job, you'd have found the guy who wrote the notes before he murdered Delilah."

Ethan's jaw tightened. He disliked Beau a little more every day. "Unfortunately, it isn't always that easy. If it were, even you might be able to handle it."

Ethan knew he shouldn't bait the guy, but Desmond made it hard to resist.

Beau snarled a smart-ass remark to his blond, surfer-dude friend, Bick Gallagher, as Ethan walked away.

By eight thirty, the show was in full swing, the Paramount a glittering backdrop for the beautiful, sparkling jewels of femininity who were the La Belle fashion models.

Though the theater was filled to capacity and backstage was organized mayhem, Ethan was constantly aware of Valentine's movements.

At the moment, she was in the dressing room, just minutes away from doing her bit in the Nashville Country segment. He didn't have to see her walk down the runway to know exactly how she looked in her tiny red-lace hip-hugger panties and red high-heeled cowboy boots. The image was burned into his brain.

Still, he paused for a moment when she appeared, allowed himself to watch the way she strutted her stuff onstage, caught the wink she cast one of the photographers as she made the turn and started striding back down the runway, tried not to wish she'd been looking at him.

He told himself to remember how hot he'd been for Allison and what a disaster that had turned out to be, but it didn't keep him from getting hard as she passed him again on her second round and flashed a dimpled grin clearly meant for him as she headed back down the runway.

She was a different person up there, he thought, a beautiful sex kitten the men in the audience would be fantasizing about for weeks. A vision in sheer lingerie who made all the women want to buy the garments she wore in the hope their husbands would look at them the same way.

As the music swelled, along with the applause, he glanced around to see if he could spot anyone in her family in the audience. He caught sight of Samantha sitting next to Nick, who, at Sam's prodding, put his fingers in his mouth and gave a shrill whistle.

Ethan chuckled. As Val disappeared behind the curtain, he headed in that direction. It occurred to him that the confident, haughty female, Valentine, who caught and held the men's attention so easily, was nothing like the Valerie he had seen in Samantha's pet-grooming parlor.

A frown began to form between his eyes. Maybe he'd been wrong about her. Maybe this was the real Valerie, not the one he'd glimpsed earlier that day.

Then he spotted her just outside the door of the dressing room, head down, bent over, hands propped on her knees. As he approached, he saw she was trembling.

He glanced around, quickly scanning the area for any kind of trouble. "What happened? Are you okay?"

She looked up at him, seemed to relax a little when she realized who it was. "I'm fine. I just . . . getting up there and doing my routine . . . it's really hard for me. I have to psyche myself up, you know? Turn myself into Valentine. When I come off the runway, the adrenaline stops pumping and it hits me. I'll be okay in a minute."

The tension seeped from between his shoulder blades. She was Valerie Hartman, pet lover and friend of Samantha. Not Valentine Hart, hot-bodied sex kitten. It shouldn't matter, but it did.

Val ducked into the changing room and the show continued. Ethan worked behind the scenes until he saw Megan head for the stage. A glance around and he spotted Dirk, who'd moved into a spot where he could watch her. Megan was on the walkway in the Winter Wonderland segment. She looked like a fairy princess in nothing but a white sequined bra and white ruffled hipster panties. What looked like a tiara made of snow perched above her saucy red flyaway hair.

Even from a distance, he could see Dirk practically drooling.

Damn. He'd known this job was going to be a bear when he'd taken it. He didn't know it was going to be a grizzly.

Worse yet, tonight he'd be sleeping in the place where Valerie lived.

He hadn't told her yet and she hadn't figured it out. Until the tour left for Dallas, there were a dozen men assigned to the women at the Fairmont and one man assigned to each of the models who lived in Seattle.

He'd spoken to Carlyle, reminded him Val was a family friend, and said he'd be the one providing her protection. He didn't ask permission and Carlyle took his meaning. He was on the job. She was family. He'd quit and protect her on his own if he had to.

Carlyle needed him, so he didn't argue. "Someone's got to do it," Matt had said. "I guess it might as well be you. Just keep it professional and we won't have a problem."

"Goes without saying."

Carlyle signed off and Ethan hung up the phone. Until this was over, he was in charge of Val's security, though he would also be looking out for the rest of the women. Dirk would be doing the same, keeping a special eye on Megan. How his best friend had managed the assignment, Ethan didn't want to know.

The noisy cheers of the audience as Megan waved one last time and strode back toward the rear of the stage muffled Ethan's sigh.

One thing was certain. Neither he nor Dirk would be getting much sleep tonight.

CHAPTER ELEVEN

Val was exhausted. The show was over, a complete and total success, TV viewership heightened by the drama of the brutal murder of a famous fashion model.

So far no one knew about the notes. Both Matt Carlyle and the police were determined to keep the information out of the press. They were afraid it would put the women in even more danger.

After the show, Val had changed back into her floaty black skirt and peach silk blouse, spent a few minutes talking to Samantha and her husband Nick, the only friends who had come to see her in the show.

One of the reasons she was using a stage name was so she could go to school without the rest of the students knowing who she was. She wouldn't know if it worked until the tour was over and she started school again in the fall.

Val bent to hug Samantha, petite and half

a foot shorter, her light brown curls framing her pretty face. Nick kissed her cheek, and both of them congratulated her on a job well done. Val thanked them for coming and for worrying about her safety, told them what a capable job Ethan had been doing.

"You can trust him," Nick said. "Ethan won't let anyone hurt you, Val."

She flicked a glance toward where she'd last seen him, but he was off somewhere working. "I really appreciate the way he looked out for me. I felt better just knowing he was there. I heard he's going on tour with us."

"That's right," Nick said. "Ethan, Dirk, and the additional men Matt Carlyle brought in to help with security."

"After . . . what happened, I'm glad they'll be coming along."

They talked a few minutes more, then Nick and Sam said good night. Eventually, the theater emptied out, but instead of a celebration, Val joined the members of the cast and crew backstage for a few brief words in remembrance of Delilah Larsen.

At the beginning of the evening, Matt Carlyle had dedicated the fashion show to her memory, then asked for a moment of silence. Now the words Matt spoke, saying her life was like a bright star that had flashed and burned out far too quickly, made a lump rise in Val's throat.

Daniel Clemens said Delilah was one of the best models he had ever worked with and told them how much he would miss her, words that weighed heavily on all of them.

Now it was time to go home and get some badly needed sleep. Val returned to the dressing area to grab her tote and purse and was walking back out when she spotted Ethan standing just a few feet away.

Something eased inside her. She hadn't realized how anxious she was beneath the layers of fatigue until she saw him. Ethan would take her home and make sure she was okay.

He strode toward her in a pair of black jeans and a black blazer over his T-shirt. When the jacket swung open, she caught a glimpse of the shoulder holster he wore underneath.

She had noticed the weapon when he'd come to the Perfect Pup. It should have bothered her. When she'd been in foster care, she'd seen the terrible damage a gun could do, had seen kids shot by gang members, been with one of the teenage boys when he had been killed. The memory still haunted her dreams.

But Ethan was a professional. She didn't doubt he knew exactly what he was doing. Knowing he was armed just made her feel safe.

"You ready to go?" he asked.

"I've been ready for hours, but I still had work to do." She gave him a weary smile. "I'm finished now. I don't have to worry about the show for a couple of days. Not until we get to Dallas."

Ethan motioned toward the back door and she started walking in that direction. Before she reached the exit, he caught her arm, stopping her in the hall, his hold strong and reassuring. Val looked into his handsome face and a curl of heat slid into her stomach.

"What is it?" she asked, forcing her thoughts in a safer direction.

"Paparazzi. They're everywhere, front and back. No easy way out."

Worry slipped through her. "What should I do?"

His sexy mouth edged up. "Nothing." He left the purse hanging on her shoulder but took her tote and tossed it to one of the security people, who seemed to know where to take it. "Getting you out safely is my job. Just follow my lead."

It sounded easy. "Okay." But when one of the guards shoved the back door open, she saw it wasn't going to be easy at all. A sea of reporters rushed forward, cameras rolling, microphones thrust into her face.

Ethan stepped in front of her. "Let the lady through, gentlemen." A dark-haired female reporter thrust a microphone toward her. Ethan blocked her approach. "And ladies," he added.

All the while, he continued easing Val toward his Jeep, which was driving toward them, rolling through the crowd in their direction.

The brunette with the mic didn't budge. Val recognized her as an anchor with KIRO News. "How did you hear about Delilah's death, Valentine? Was she a close friend? Will you be going to the funeral?"

"Ms. Hart has no comment," Ethan said, nudging the reporter aside and moving Val forward through the determined throng pushing toward them.

A fan, a tall young man with a wide grin, broke through the line and rushed toward her. "Valentine, I love you! Will you marry me?"

Ethan had him in an armlock and was moving him out of the way before her admirer even got close. "Take it easy, buddy. The lady's not interested." Then he was back, moving a little in front of her, using his body to protect her, at the same time urging her forward.

"Valentine! Valentine! We love you, Valentine!" It was a group of young girls. They were high school age at the most. Val blew them a kiss, waved, and grinned so big her dimples popped out. All the while, she kept walking.

"Where's the damned Jeep?" Ethan grumbled, though the driver was moving the vehicle as fast as safely possible through the crowd. "We need the effing Jeep."

She could feel the heat of his big, hard body, his muscles flexing and bunching against her as he moved. Though she shouldn't be thinking about the way it felt to have him so close, a wash of heat spread through her.

Another reporter, a pretty woman with short black hair, rushed forward, microphone in hand. "Hey, Ethan! How about giving us a break? Just a few words from Valentine. What do you say?"

Ethan managed to smile, though Val thought it looked a little forced. "Valentine's had a rough day, Sheryl. Call La Belle's media people, see if they can set something up."

Like that was going to happen.

"Come on, Ethan." Moving along with

them, Sheryl held the mic toward Val. "How do you feel about the murder, Valentine? Was Delilah a friend?"

"Leave her alone, Sheryl. I'm sure La Belle will be holding a press conference sometime tomorrow."

The woman started to argue, but Ethan ignored her and closed the last few feet to where the Jeep was just pulling up. He jerked open the back door and settled her inside, followed her in, and slammed the door. She noticed her tote in the back of the vehicle as she snapped her seat belt in place. The man was efficient for sure.

In the front seat, a middle-aged man with shiny black skin pressed his foot down on the accelerator, and the vehicle rolled forward, the big Jeep bullying its way through the crowd.

"Val, meet Joe Posey," Ethan said, relaxing back against the rear seat. "He's going to get us out of here."

Val smiled. "Hi, Joe. Thanks for your help."

"My pleasure, Ms. Valentine." Joe checked the mirror as Ethan turned in his seat to look out the rear window.

"Christ, the bastards are following us," Ethan said.

Val turned, saw some of the reporters

scrambling for their cars, some already inside, pulling out behind the Jeep.

Joe just grunted. "The lady's a celebrity, chief. After what happened, they'll dog her and the rest of the models till they get some kind of story."

"Lose 'em. You buckled up?" he asked Val, saw she was, and snapped his own belt in place. "Joe's an ex-cop. He'll get us out of here safely."

The engine gunned and they were off. Ethan was right. Joe knew exactly what he was doing, when to slow, when to run a yellow without chancing a wreck, when to put the pedal to the metal and shoot through an opening in traffic.

A slow smile stretched across her face. She'd been wild as a kid. She'd loved motorcycles and fast cars, loved the feel of the wind in her face and the adrenaline rush. That hadn't changed.

Ethan's eyes came to hers. "So I guess you like speed," he said, amusement in his voice.

Val grinned. "Long as it doesn't kill me."

Ethan chuckled. Joe made a couple more fancy turns before they were completely in the clear.

"Nice job," Ethan said to him as the car slowed, began to roll quietly on down the street.

A mile or so later, Joe pulled over to the curb near one of the bigger hotels. "Good spot to catch a cab," he said. "My car's parked a few blocks down from the theater."

Ethan nodded. "You'll find cab fare and a little extra on your paycheck. Good work tonight. I'll see you Tuesday at the airport."

"Ten A.M. sharp. I'll be there." Joe got out of the Jeep, waved, and started walking. Ethan climbed out of the back and slid into the driver's seat. He looked surprised when Val slid into the front seat beside him.

She gave him a smile. "I don't need a chauffeur. Just a ride back to my house."

He smiled slightly, started the Jeep, and headed for Montlake. As the car rolled along, fatigue trickled through her. Resting her head against the seat, she closed her eyes, trusting Ethan to get her safely home.

Ethan pulled the Jeep up in front of Val's duplex apartment. She'd fallen asleep on the way. As he opened the door, she straightened in her seat, blinking owlishly up at him.

"We're home. Can you make it inside all right?"

She yawned, then smiled. "What, if I say no you'll carry me? I make it home by myself every night."

His lips twitched. As she started up the

sidewalk toward the front porch, he fell in beside her, then took the key from her hand and unlocked the door.

Ethan walked into the living room, heard her big gray cat meow, and flicked on the light switch, which turned on the lamp on the table next to the sofa.

"Stay here." Pulling his pistol, he cleared the house, checking every room to make sure the place was secure. He had no idea who was next on the killer's hit list, but if the guy was as crazy as the notes made him seem, the perp was going to do his best to murder a second victim.

Ethan walked back into the living room, saw Valerie kneeling to pet the big tom. He holstered his weapon. "And here I thought you were a dog person."

Val laughed at the reminder of her encounter with the big English sheepdog. "I love dogs. Cats. Horses. Birds. Fish. That's why I want to be a veterinarian. I like animals a lot more than most people."

"Yeah, I get that." He thought of the man who had coldly murdered Delilah Larsen. A crazy, or a cold-blooded killer? Either way the woman was just as dead. "Lots of good people around, though, if you look for them."

"I know. Like Nick and Samantha. They

146

were there tonight for my show. It was really sweet of them to come."

"They like you." And he was beginning to understand why. Besides the superficial turn-ons like a great body and a fabulous face, Val had substance. She was smart and hardworking, and she was kind to other people. He was beginning to like her, too. Which, under the circumstances, wasn't necessarily good.

"What about your family?" he asked. "I saw Isabel talking to her mom and dad and half a dozen brothers and sisters. I figured some of your family might show."

Val shrugged. "No siblings. Mom and Pops are older. They live up in Bellingham, and Pops wasn't feeling too well. Besides . . ." She let the words trail off and shook her head.

"Besides what?"

"They're pretty old-fashioned. They know what I'm doing and why, and they're okay with it, but seeing me up there almost naked . . . I'd just rather they didn't."

He cocked an eyebrow. "You know, Valerie, the show wasn't what I thought it was going to be. It wasn't sleazy. It was entertaining. You did a great job."

She shrugged. "Maybe. On the other hand, how would you feel if your girlfriend was up there strutting around in nothing but skimpy lingerie?"

There was no point in lying. He was who he was. "You want the truth? I wouldn't want my woman doing it. I'm a selfish bastard when it comes to a lady I'm involved with. I'd want her all to myself."

Her eyes searched his face. "So I guess you're a little old-fashioned yourself."

"Maybe . . . yeah, in some ways I guess I am."

Val glanced away. Walking to the front door, she pulled it open, letting in a rush of cold night air. "Thanks, Ethan. I really appreciate everything you've done. I'll see you at the airport on Tuesday."

He'd been putting off this moment. He had a feeling this wasn't going to go well. He walked over and closed the door. "Obviously, you still don't get it. I'm not going anywhere. Not until they find the bastard who killed Delilah Larsen."

Her dark blond eyebrows drew together. "What are you talking about? I'm exhausted. I need to get some sleep. You checked the house. There's no one in here. Now it's time for you to leave."

He just shook his head. "I'll take the sofa. If it makes you feel any better, there are five other women under personal protection tonight in Seattle, including your friend Megan."

"Megan?"

"That's right. I don't mind the couch, but I could really use a pillow."

She cocked her head, eyeing him with suspicion. "Who's with Megan?"

"Dirk Reynolds. She's in very good hands."

"*'Good hands?'*" She glanced down at the big hand he'd jammed into the pocket of his jeans and he couldn't help thinking how good he could make her feel if only he could touch her. When the corner of his mouth kicked up, her shoulders stiffened. "Are you telling me I don't have any say in this?"

"Not if you want to keep your job."

"I need this job and you know it."

"A lightweight blanket would be nice, too."

She made a huffing sound and flounced away, and Ethan couldn't stop a smile. She was going to be even less happy when he told her she'd have to leave the bedroom door open. He was a very light sleeper, so any little sound and he'd be wide awake.

On the other hand, considering the skillful way the killer had entered Delilah Larsen's condo, Ethan was giving her a break not insisting he sleep in her room.

Val returned with a pillow and a blanket, tossed them on the couch, which looked comfortable but about six inches too short. With a sideways glance, she turned and marched back down the hall. The sound of her bedroom door slamming shut made him grin with anticipation for the coming confrontation.

Ethan couldn't remember the last time a woman had made him grin.

CHAPTER TWELVE

Val overslept Sunday morning. Maybe it was staying up into the early hours last night. Maybe it was the pressure of her first-ever fashion show, one being televised across the country. Maybe it was being questioned by the police about a murder.

Whatever it was, she rolled out of bed at ten fifteen, feeling nearly as tired as she'd been when she'd finally closed her eyes. As she grabbed her robe and pulled it on, then walked out into the hall, it took a moment to remember that Ethan Brodie had spent the night on the sofa.

When she saw him standing in the kitchen with his phone against his ear, bare-chested, barefoot, and wearing only his jeans, the shock hit her like a hot flash twenty years too early.

Oh my God! She knew she shouldn't be staring at all those beautiful muscles, at a chest carved in granite and a set of bulging biceps that made her mouth water, but she couldn't force herself to look away.

"You're up earlier than I expected." He reached for the pot of coffee sitting on the counter and poured her a cup. When she didn't walk over to get it, he carried the cup into the living room and pressed it into her hand.

Fascinated, Val turned as he walked past her and watched the view from behind, the broad back and slim hips, the long, jeans-clad legs and big, manly feet. She didn't look away as he pulled a clean dark blue T-shirt out of an orange canvas duffel and dragged it on over his head, making all those gorgeous muscles flex and tighten as he moved.

Once he was covered, she seemed to regain her wits enough to take a drink from the steaming cup in her hand.

"Sleep okay?" Ethan asked mildly as he started back to the kitchen, unaware — thank God — of her former near-catatonic state.

"Yes, thank you." Knowing he was close by, feeling safe and protected, she had fallen deeply asleep and hadn't stirred till morning. But she didn't tell him that. He was in her space too much already.

He folded his blanket and set it on the

sofa, placed the pillow neatly on top of it. She watched as he zipped his orange duffel closed and set it on the floor next to the couch.

"I see you came prepared," she said with a trace of irritation. She didn't like being ordered around, no matter the reason.

"I keep a go-bag in my car — a couple of T-shirts, a razor, deodorant, enough under-wear to last a few days. I dropped by my apartment yesterday during the rehearsal and packed a suitcase to take with me to Dallas. It's in your hall closet."

"If you're planning to stay here that long, you must not think they're going to catch the killer any time soon."

"I hope they do. I was on the phone with Lieutenant Hoover when you walked in. I was hoping the cops would find fingerprints, footprints, DNA — something useful at the crime scene. But the place was clean. This guy knew what he was doing. That makes finding him a whole lot harder."

She glanced down at the laptop sitting on her mahogany dining table and wandered in that direction. She and Mom had hit local yard sales to furnish the duplex. They'd stumbled on the Duncan Phyfe drop-leaf table and four matching chairs, and Val had instantly fallen in love with the set.

"So you've been working," she said. The silver apple on top of his open computer dubbed him a Mac user. She was a PC girl herself.

"I'm collecting background information, trying to find out if any of the girls who got notes had contact with the killer at some point in their lives. A guy one of them might have pissed off, someone who might want revenge."

"Lieutenant Hoover questioned me about that when I talked to him. He asked if there was anyone I might have known, someone I had a run-in with who might want payback."

"Was there?"

She shrugged. "Not that I know of." She glanced down at the screen, saw Carmen Marquez's high school transcripts, and uneasiness crept through her. Carmen was one of the models who'd received a note.

She pointed to the screen. "How did you get that information?"

Ethan's dark eyes searched her face. "A lot of it's public record. You just have to know where to look."

"So that's it? You're just looking at what's in public records?"

His gaze seemed to sharpen and she wished she had left the subject alone.

"Does it matter where the info comes

from? We're trying to catch a killer before he kills someone else."

He was right. Finding the killer was more important than her personal privacy. *He won't find out,* she told herself. Her juvenile records were sealed. No way could he get into sealed police records.

"What is it, Val?" Ethan asked softly. "If there's something in your past, I'm going to find it. If it's important, be easier if you just told me now."

Her unease turned to worry and her chest clamped down. It was none of his business. Not anyone's business but her own. "It isn't important. I was just a kid back then."

He looked at her, and there was something in his face. It was compassion, she realized, and it made her eyes sting. "It was a long time ago," she said with a hint of panic. "The records are sealed. I told you, I was only a kid."

Ethan walked toward her, reached out and tipped up her chin. "We all make mistakes, Valerie. Whatever you did back then isn't important unless it somehow ties to the murder. I can find out. But I'd rather hear it from you."

"You can't find out."

"I can, honey. If you tell me, whatever you say won't go any farther than this room."

She turned away, walked over to the window, stared out at the lawn she had paid one of the neighbor kids to mow. What did it matter? It was all in the past. So what if Ethan Brodie thought less of her because of it?

She released a shaky breath, resigned to telling him what he was so determined to know. "My parents were killed when I was ten. Car accident in Michigan."

"I'm sorry, Val."

She ignored him, kept talking; she wanted this over and done. "I didn't have much family, just a few distant relatives. One of my older cousins was married. Alice and her husband, Ray, lived in Seattle. They took me in. From the start they made it clear they didn't want me. They treated me like a servant, kept me cleaning and doing their dirty work from dawn till dark. I didn't mind the work so much. It was the attitude, the feeling that they were doing me a favor just letting me stay in their house."

She didn't look at Ethan, just forced air into her lungs and kept going, desperate now to get it all out. "The abuse was mostly verbal, but I took a couple of slaps I didn't deserve and I started getting a bad feeling about Cousin Ray. He came into my room one night and just stood there in the dark watching me. The next day I ran away."

Ethan moved up behind her, turned her around to face him. "How old were you?"

"Fifteen."

"You live on the street?" There was something intense in those dark eyes.

"For a while . . . only a couple of weeks. The cops picked me up and I went into foster care." Sadness swept through her at the girl she had been. "I was pretty much a hellion. I didn't like my foster parents and they didn't like me. I went from one home to another, never seemed to fit in. When I was sixteen, I sneaked out one night with a couple of the older boys in the house. One of them had a friend with a car."

She glanced away, wishing she didn't have to remember the rest.

"Go on, Val. Finish it."

She forced her gaze back to his face. She was five nine, but Ethan was so tall she had to look up at him. "The guy with the car was in a gang. He got into a fight with another kid, and suddenly everyone was shooting. Bobby Rodriquez — he was the boy in the home where I lived — Bobby got shot in the chest. He . . . he died in my arms."

She didn't realize she was crying till Ethan handed her his handkerchief. His jaw was iron hard, his body rock solid. If she hadn't known better, she would have thought he was holding himself back, forcing himself not to touch her, comfort her. But maybe he was just disgusted.

"I don't like to talk about it," she said, wiping her eyes. "I'm not proud of what happened."

"You turned your life around, Val. You aren't that young girl anymore. You're a woman now. A beautiful woman who's made something of herself."

Some of the pain slipped away with his words. He wasn't condemning her. Why had she thought he would?

"It was Mom and Pops Hartman. They took me in. They put their arms around me and walked me out of that police station, and I swear I could feel their love right then. They lived on this little farm in Bellingham. They raised chickens, had a couple of milk cows. It felt like home from the moment I stepped out of the car. I changed because of them, because I wanted them to be proud of me. I still do."

She blew her nose, wiped a last tear from her cheek.

Ethan's smile was gentle. "I know they're proud of you, Val, and I'm glad you told me. I don't think it's important to the case, but you never know."

She just nodded. He'd listened and seemed to understand. She shouldn't have felt somehow lighter, but she did.

"I need to shower and get ready." She smiled, the pressure gone from her chest. "Thanks for the coffee."

He nodded. "Thanks for trusting me."

She didn't say more as she walked away and neither did Ethan, but she could feel his eyes on her all the way down the hall.

Ethan spent a couple more hours on the computer, but nothing in the files he had checked so far looked promising.

He was beginning to feel frustrated and restless when Val walked back into the living room.

"I'm going crazy sitting in the house all day," she said. "Any chance I could talk you into taking me to the gym? Weekends are usually slow, especially if the weather's good. What do you think?"

He smiled. "I'm feeling a little housebound myself. Let me give them a call, see if I can convince them to give us private access for a couple of hours."

"Seriously? You think they might?"

"Yeah. With the right inducement, I do."

Not surprisingly, the Twenty-Fourth Street

gym agreed. He'd send the bill to La Belle, but it wouldn't cost as much as he'd figured, and the benefits of a good, solid workout were worth it to both of them.

By the time they had finished and returned to the house, he and Val were both feeling better. The stiffness was gone from his muscles, along with some of the tension he'd been feeling.

All but the sexual variety. Thank Jesus, Val had worn loose-fitting yoga pants and a T-shirt, not the skintight gym clothes a lot of women wore. Still, watching her moving gracefully through her workout routine had him gritting his teeth to keep from getting hard. No way around it, the woman flat turned him on.

Once they got home, he kept his distance. Val worked on some of her Internet study courses and, that evening, called out for pizza, which they ate watching an old movie on TV. He didn't expect to feel so comfortable sitting next to her on the couch, wished to hell he didn't.

After Val went to bed, Ethan checked the house and grounds half a dozen times before curling his tall frame into the too-short sofa.

Early Monday morning, the day of the funeral, he was sitting at his laptop, going over the last of the background information Sadie had dug up on the top models. They all had interesting stories: a lot of them were world travelers, some married, some even had kids. Hard to believe with their perfect figures, but apparently true.

A fanatic might think a mother was an even bigger sinner than the rest. He made a note to speak to Caralee Peterson, the woman he remembered as the Southern belle from Atlanta. Caralee had a husband and a four-year-old daughter. He hadn't seen anything in the file that pointed to a problem with anyone from her past, but he wanted to speak to her, make sure she stayed alert.

He was surprised to see Megan O'Brien was a single mom with a two-year-old boy. Dirk hadn't mentioned it and neither had Megan. He needed to talk to her, too, make sure she didn't get singled out because she had a kid.

With the biblical tone of the notes, Ethan had asked Sadie to cross-check any religious affiliation, but Ian's middle-aged computer whiz had come up with zip. The women's religious preferences were as varied as their backgrounds: Agnostic, Protestant, Jewish, Catholic, Buddhist, nothing that specifically connected them to anyone who might be a threat.

He wanted to talk to the men Delilah had dated, hoped to get the names from Hoover, see if the cops had come up with anything in that regard. He also wanted to know if the police had found any old murders with a similar MO.

He glanced up to see Val walking out of the bedroom dressed for the funeral in a black knee-length suit, black high heels, a wide-brimmed black felt hat that dipped over one eye, and a veil that wasn't pulled down. She looked elegant and remote and completely untouchable. A shot of lust rippled through his blood like a heat wave.

Her blond hair was swept up severely and her face looked pale, but her unadorned appearance did nothing to deter the kick Ethan felt.

Damn, she was beautiful. He went hard just standing there watching her. And now that he knew the brutal past she had endured, how she had worked to lift herself out of it, he was even more attracted to her.

It didn't matter. He had a job to do and it didn't include hauling one of La Belle's top models down the hall into bed. It didn't involve ripping off those dark, forbidding clothes and taking her every way he could

162

imagine.

Exactly what he felt like doing.

"I'm ready," she said, and the tremor in her voice calmed his raging libido. This wasn't a day to be thinking of anything but a needless death and catching the bastard who had stolen a young woman's life.

He picked his shoulder holster up off the side table and slid into it, walked over to the entry hall closet to retrieve the black blazer he'd brought to wear over his T-shirt and black jeans for the service.

His cell chimed just as he shrugged on the coat. He dug the phone out of his jeans, saw Dirk's name, and pressed it against his ear. "What's up?"

"Turn on the TV. Local news. KIRO 7."

Ethan picked up the TV remote and pressed the power button, brought up the guide and tuned in the channel.

"What is it?" Val asked, but as their attention focused on the flat screen above the bookshelves, the reason for Dirk's call was clear.

". . . new information has surfaced on the brutal murder of supermodel Delilah Larsen. A reliable source has confirmed that within the last two weeks, Delilah, as well as nine other top La Belle models, received notes threatening their lives."

A cell phone image of the first note flashed up on the screen, the photo clear enough for each word to be read.

SINNERS, SLUTS, and WHORES-- BEWARE. Your TIME is at HAND.

Ethan swore softly. "Just what we didn't need."

"A second note similar to the first was found at the murder scene," the commentator went on, "which clearly establishes the killer as the same man who had previously threatened the women."

A photo of the second note appeared.

Sinners, **SLUTS,** *and* **WHORES-- BEWARE. REPENT** *or you* **WILL** be **NEXT.**

The reporter's voice came through the speaker. "The question now — will another La Belle model be the target of this deranged killer? And if so, what are the police doing to protect them?"

Ethan silently cursed.

"For more on this breaking news story and the killer the press is calling the Hellfire Preacher, we go to Sheryl Altman, standing outside the Evergreen Memorial Cemetery where Delilah Larsen's funeral is set to commence today at one P.M."

Angrier by the minute, Ethan listened to the rest of the segment, then clicked off the TV.

"The Hellfire Preacher?" Val repeated. "That's what they're calling him? How did they find out about the notes?"

"I don't know, but I'd like to get my hands on the bastard who leaked the information."

"A lot of people knew about them. It's hard to keep a secret like that for long. It's going to make everything more difficult, isn't it?"

Ethan worked a muscle in his jaw. "Yes." He didn't say more, and in the silence that followed, the sound of voices coming from outside filtered in through the window.

Crossing the living room, Ethan pulled back the curtains and stared through the panes at the crowd of reporters gathering on the front lawn. "Jesus, they didn't waste any time."

Val walked up beside him. "Oh my God."

Still connected on the phone to Dirk, Ethan lifted his cell back to his ear. "You still there?"

"I'm here. Meg's with me. I've got you on speaker."

"The vultures are already out front." Even the heavy mist hadn't deterred them. "No way we can get to my Jeep without a problem. We're in Montlake. How far away are you?"

Megan answered, her voice tinny over the open speaker. "My house isn't far from Val's. It won't take us long to get there."

"There's an alley behind the house," Ethan said. "Call me when you get close and we'll meet you out there."

"On my way," Dirk said.

"Get away from the window," Ethan said to Val. "We don't want to stir them up."

She cast him a glance. "You mean like a nest of angry hornets?"

His mouth edged up. "Exactly."

"My neighbor, Mrs. Oakley, is going to freak out."

"You can phone her as soon as we get on the road. Let's head for the back door, be ready to go when Dirk calls."

"Give me a sec." Val ran back to her bedroom, came out a few seconds later wearing her sneakers, her black high heels in her hand. "I'm a heckuva lot more sure-footed in these." She lifted a shoe to show him and he chuckled.

"Good thinking."

The call from Dirk came a few minutes later. So far the media hadn't wanted to risk trespassing into the backyard, and the alley

166

was kind of hidden by the foliage at the end of the block, not easy to spot if you didn't know where to look.

Val grabbed her umbrella. Ethan strode over and opened the back door, stepped out into the chill. "Let's go."

CHAPTER THIRTEEN

Val folded her umbrella and slid into the backseat of the big black Cadillac Escalade Dirk Reynolds was driving. Ethan followed her in. Megan sat in the front seat next to Dirk.

"Thanks for the ride," Ethan said as the vehicle shot on down the alley, and Val hurriedly buckled her seat belt. The windshield wipers slopped back and forth as the SUV pulled into the street. The weatherman had nailed it. Dark and overcast, perfect day for a funeral.

Meg turned around in her seat. She was also dressed in black: black leggings, black boots, a black wool skirt, and a black V-necked sweater. "You okay?" she asked Val.

"I can't believe someone leaked those notes. Now we have to contend with an even bigger batch of reporters."

"I know. I was really glad Dirk was there

when I saw the news. The Hellfire Preacher. Can you believe that? We were lucky to get out of there before they showed up at my place."

Val was thankful Ethan had been there, too. She sent him a glance, tried not to think how good he looked, how he seemed to fill up the entire backseat. Though she'd been glad for the exercise yesterday, the hours at the gym had been torture. No one looked better in a T-shirt and gym shorts than Ethan Brodie.

She had never been in lust before — had sex, yes, had boyfriends, but this was different. At least she was smart enough to recognize the feeling for what it was, nothing but a normal female reaction to a male who looked as good as Ethan. She just needed to keep that reaction under control.

"I've got to call my folks," she told Meg. "I didn't tell them about the notes. They'll be worried sick when they see this on the news. Good thing you sent Charlie off to his grandparents' house."

"Who's Charlie?" Dirk asked, his head swiveling toward Megan.

"He's . . . umm . . . my son."

Val shared a glance with Ethan, who apparently knew about the boy. But then, he'd been digging around, finding out everyone's secrets. Not that Meg was ashamed of her son; just the opposite. She only wanted to keep him out of the media blitz that went with the show.

"Why the hell didn't you tell me you had a kid?" Dirk asked, clearly annoyed.

"Because you don't strike me as a kid kind of guy," Megan replied.

A muscle tightened in Dirk's jaw. "You got a husband hidden out there somewhere you haven't mentioned either?"

The atmosphere in the car went heated. "No. I'm divorced. And Charlie's staying with my parents till I get back, so I didn't think it was any of your business."

"You're right," Dirk said darkly. "It isn't."

Silence fell inside the vehicle. When Dirk just kept driving, Ethan started talking. "I saw the boy in your file, Megan. Charlie O'Brien. Two years old."

Dirk glared at Ethan in the mirror. "What, you knew about him, too?"

"Ethan's been checking into our pasts," Val explained, trying not to feel a sense of betrayal. She didn't like him digging around, even if it was his job. She didn't like that she had let him see how vulnerable she was when it came to her past. "He's trying to find something that might connect one of us to the killer."

"A couple of the models have kids," Ethan said. "And while we're on the subject, if the killer's the fanatic he seems, he might not approve of a mother modeling sexy lingerie. Delilah might have just been a convenient target. Can you think of anyone who might be outraged at you or Caralee? Someone who strongly disapproves of what you do because you've got kids?"

Megan fell silent, taking time to consider. "There's no one I can think of."

"What about Charlie's dad?" Ethan pressed. "He the kind of guy who'd be pissed you're up onstage without your clothes?"

"She wears clothes," Dirk defended her. "Just not that many."

Val caught Ethan's look of amusement. Clearly the two men were close friends.

"I stand corrected," Ethan said with a wink at Val that made her grin.

"My ex-husband wouldn't have the least objection to anything I did," Meg said. "Jonathan started cheating on me a few days after we were married. I was just too stupid to realize the kind of man he was. He's long gone and good riddance. And he doesn't give a damn about Charlie or me — for which I'm immensely grateful."

Silence fell again and Ethan let the subject

drop. Val made a quick call to her parents, telling them she was safe and in good hands and that she'd call them when she had time to talk.

Then she phoned Mrs. Oakley and explained about the news cameras in front of the duplex. The older woman assured her it wasn't a problem. Typical Mrs. O.; she was enjoying the excitement.

At the end of the call, Val took off her sneakers and put on her high heels, then settled in for the ride to the Evergreen Memorial Cemetery, south of Seattle. With each passing mile, her mood grew more somber. By the time Dirk pulled up in front of the chapel, her chest felt tight, her heartbeat sluggish.

"Just stay close to me," Ethan said, and some of her anxiety slipped away.

A sea of reporters surrounded the funeral home, but the media was roped off, kept at a respectful distance, none of them close enough to ask questions or inject themselves into the mourners' grief.

As the SUV pulled up in front of the gray-carpeted walkway leading into the chapel, Dirk stepped out from behind the wheel and a valet slid in to take his place.

Ethan came around and opened Val's door. She pulled her black veil down over her face and stepped out on the carpeted walkway. Ethan moved in behind her, silently protecting her as she made her way inside the chapel.

Though it wasn't nearly large enough to accommodate the hundreds of mourners who had come to pay their respects, a block of seats had been reserved. All of the La Belle models, Paul Boudreau, Matthew Carlyle, a few other La Belle executives, and a number of Delilah's closest friends sat in that section.

Val recognized David Klein, the wealthy jewelry merchant who supplied the extravagant necklaces for the show, sitting next to Jason Stern, the president of the company. Undoubtedly Klein, who lived in San Francisco, had arrived in La Belle's private jet.

Val seated herself in one of the pews and Megan slid in beside her. At the front of the chapel, a cherrywood casket inlaid with mother of pearl rested on the dais, covered by a thick blanket of dark red roses. Behind a thin curtain off to one side, Delilah's family sat grieving.

From the corner of her eye, Val spotted Ethan standing near the wall at the end of the row, long legs splayed, hands crossed in front of him, in full bodyguard mode. His dark eyes moved restlessly over the crowd, scanning the room for any sort of threat. She felt better just knowing he was there.

The thought stirred a trickle of uneasiness inside her. She was beginning to depend on Ethan, and that was dangerous. She'd learned a long time ago, the only person she could truly depend on was herself. Even Mom and Pops wouldn't always be there for her. They were already in their late sixties, and Pops was frail.

She sat up a little straighter in the hard wooden pew. She'd always stood on her own two feet. No matter what happened, that wasn't going to change.

Still, until Delilah's killer was found, her life could be in danger. She wasn't stupid enough to deny she needed a man with Ethan's skills to ensure her safety.

She tried not to remember the lonely young girl who had depended on her boyfriend, Bobby. The sixteen-year-old who had foolishly believed Bobby Rodriquez would keep her safe.

Bobby had tried, but instead he'd wound up dead. She'd been left to face the cops, her terrible guilt, and her awful grief. There'd been no one to turn to, no one who gave a damn what happened to her. If it hadn't been for Thomas and Ellie Hartman, she might have ended up as dead as Bobby.

Or worse.

The organ music began to play, jolting her back to the present. It wouldn't be for long, she told herself, but for now she'd allow herself the luxury of depending on Ethan Brodie.

If she wanted to stay alive, she really had no other choice.

With the funeral under way and Val surrounded by the protection of a church full of people and a couple of dozen uniformed police, Ethan made his way outside. He'd seen Lieutenant Hoover head out the door for a smoke and figured it might be a chance for an update.

Hoover bent his head into the breeze and cupped a hand around a match to light a cigarette, then tossed the dead match into a trash bin a few feet away. He took a long drag, then let the smoke drift away in the breeze.

"You know those things'll kill you," Ethan said.

Hoover looked down at the cigarette between his fingers. "My wife makes sure I know that every damn day. Now I gotta hear it from you?"

Ethan fought not to smile. "Hey, we've all got to go sometime. I say pick your own poison."

Hoover just grunted.

"You come up with anything?" Ethan asked.

"Yeah. The vic had insurance on the jewelry. 'Bout a half million dollars' worth of diamonds."

"Plenty of motive for murder."

"Yeah, except for the note."

"True enough. Maybe the whole thing was a setup to steal the jewelry."

Hoover squinted up at him through the smoke. "You think so?"

"No. I don't think it was about the jewelry. Guy who sent the notes . . . it's personal for him."

"Be my guess, too."

"Any chance he's done it before?"

Hoover flicked an ash off his cigarette. "A serial? Nothing came up in the search. He may be planning to kill again, but if he's a serial, I'm betting Delilah was his first."

"Damn professional job if it was."

"Those guys are smart. They make plans months in advance. Years. I'm thinking Delilah was La Belle's number-one girl. He hit her to make his point."

"Who's number two?"

"Isabel Rafaeli. We've got her covered nice and tight."

Ethan nodded, wondering where Val fell on the top-ten lineup, made a mental note to ask her. "What about the messages? Anything on the paper or the ink?"

"Regular copy paper. So far we haven't found anything that would identify the printer."

"Since Delilah's being buried today, you've obviously done the autopsy. Find anything interesting?"

"We put a rush on it, being it's such a high-profile case, but nothing turned up. No drugs, no excess alcohol. She was healthy and extremely fit."

"That's how the models keep their jobs."

Hoover blew out a stream of smoke. "What about you? You got anything?"

"I've looked at a couple of different angles, tossed them around. Some of the women have kids. From the sound of those notes, I doubt our killer would approve of a mother modeling scanty underwear for a living."

"Good thought. I'll make sure that angle's covered. Anything else?"

"Still thinking about the boyfriends. Most murders are done by someone close. Delilah had men friends. That's where she got the diamonds. You talk to any of them?"

Hoover let the smoke curl out from between his lips. "Guy named Reese Dawes. He's in the shipping business here in Seattle. Lots of money; bought her a lot of expensive gifts, mostly clothes. He's been out of the picture for a while."

"Who's in?"

"You see, that's the thing. I tell you, you'll stick your nose in and it won't make me popular down at the station."

"Why not?"

"Because he's a good friend of Paul Boudreau's. Big money; gives a bundle to charity every year, just like Boudreau. Unfortunately, he's got a wife who wouldn't approve."

"So Delilah was his mistress."

"Looks that way."

"He give her the diamonds?"

Hoover nodded. "Yeah."

"Any chance he might have wanted them back?"

The detective snorted a laugh. "Be a pittance to a guy like him."

"Maybe she cheated. He killed her and took back the diamonds, didn't think she deserved to have the gifts he'd given her."

"Doesn't hold water when you think about the note in the safe. The creeper who wrote it doesn't fit anywhere in the jealous lover picture you're drawing."

That was true. Unless her rich boyfriend was a psycho, which apparently Hoover didn't believe. "So you aren't giving me a name."

"I would if I thought there was a reason. I can't come up with one, and since I like being a lieutenant and don't want to wind up walking a beat again, the answer is no."

"I can find out."

Hoover dropped his cigarette and crushed it out, leaned down to pick up the butt, then tossed it into the trash bin. He turned to Ethan. "Knock yourself out." Turning, he took off the way he'd come, disappearing into the crowd of people outside the door of the church who'd been unable to find seats inside.

Maybe he'd do that. Odds were, once they were on the tour, the gossip would be flowing and he'd find out the guy's name without much effort. He figured Hoover would know that. The lieutenant could stay out of the line of fire and Ethan could quietly keep digging if it seemed there was someplace to go.

Hoover hadn't given him a name, but he'd given Ethan enough information to find out.

Unfortunately, the lieutenant had also pointed out there was very little likelihood the wacko who'd strangled Delilah was some rich guy who wanted to punish his mistress.

He'd pursue it down the road if he thought it would lead somewhere. For now, the boyfriend angle looked like another dead end.

As the service ended and the group made its way out of the chapel, Meg felt a hand on her arm. She wasn't surprised to see Dirk walking beside her, part of a smaller, more intimate group that was heading across the wide stretch of rolling green lawn for the final graveside portion of the funeral service.

Meg wished she didn't have to go. She'd been holding it together fairly well, but Delilah was one of their own. She was young and vibrant and she hadn't deserved to die at the hands of a killer.

Meg glanced over at Dirk, caught the set of his jaw, the faint motion of his head, urging her to step away from the others. Letting him guide her, she made her way beneath the boughs of a pine tree where they wouldn't be overheard.

"What is it?" Meg asked.

"You could have told me about Charlie. You didn't have to lie about it. I like kids. I've never had any, but they're okay."

Her chin went up. "I didn't lie."

"A lie by omission is still a lie. I cleared your house. I've been staying there. I must have been in his room, right? I didn't see any toys or anything."

"I put them away after my mom came to get him. I'm kind of a neat freak, in case you haven't noticed."

His mouth kicked up, lifting his sexy mustache. "I noticed."

"Plus, we just moved to a bigger place with a yard. I haven't had time to fix his room up the way I wanted, so there isn't any little boy's wallpaper or anything."

"Any more secrets you're keeping?"

"Charlie wasn't a secret. I just . . . I didn't see any point in telling you, since there isn't a chance we'll be seeing each other after this is over."

His hazel eyes darkened. "You wouldn't say that if you knew how much I wanted to kiss you right now."

Her stomach contracted. "Don't. Don't even think it."

"Why not? It's the truth. I can't get you out of my head. I've tried, Meg, believe me, but there it is."

Her cheeks flushed as she glanced away. "We need to go. People are starting to look at us."

"I'm your bodyguard. I'm supposed to stay close so I can protect you."

She looked up at him, lifted a dark red eyebrow. "Oh, really? And who's supposed to protect me from you?"

She heard his soft chuckle as she slipped into the crowd standing around the grave. She felt him moving into position behind her, putting her where he could keep her safe. Meg closed her eyes and reminded herself that a guy like Dirk Reynolds was not the guy for her and Charlie.

If she was interested in settling down — which, after Jonathan, she definitely was not — she would need a nice, stable kind of guy, not a bodyguard/whatever else he did for a living.

She told herself that and tried to keep her gaze from wandering in his direction. Because every time she did, she saw that his eyes were firmly fixed on her.

Chapter Fourteen

The funeral was over. Val lifted the veil and pulled off her wide-brimmed black felt hat, sat back in the car seat next to Ethan, and clicked her belt in place. Dirk was driving, heading the big SUV into the rain that was falling steadily again, building puddles on the street. Meg sat up front beside him.

"You holding up okay?" Ethan asked.

She sighed. "It's just so sad. None of this feels real."

"Call your neighbor. See if the barbarian hordes are still parked in front of your house."

She took a deep breath, pulled her phone back out of her purse, and punched in the older woman's number. Mrs. Oakley answered on the second ring.

"It's me, Mrs. O."

"Valerie, dear, are you all right? I've been watching that poor girl's funeral on the television. Such a terrible tragedy."

"Yes, it is. Is the news media still out front?"

"They're gone. I think they went to the funeral, too."

"I thought they would, but I wanted to be sure."

Ethan spoke from beside her. "Tell her they'll be back. Tell her you'll be by to pick up the clothes you need for the trip, but you won't be staying there tonight. She needs to start taking care of Snoozie."

From behind the wheel, Dirk snorted a laugh. "*Snoozie.* I hope Val doesn't have a secret kid, too. At least not one named Snoozie. That'd be downright cruel."

"Snoozie's my cat," Val said, fighting a grin.

Meg leaned over and punched Dirk's arm. "He's very sweet. He just likes to sleep a lot."

"She needs a dog," Dirk said. "They're always up for a little action."

Val bit back a laugh. It felt good to smile again after all that had happened. She relayed Ethan's message to her neighbor. Said, "Thanks, Mrs. O. You're the best." She ended the call and turned to Ethan. "If we can't stay at my house, where are we going tonight?"

"You and Meg are spending the night at

the Fairmont. Carlyle will have the media under control and there's plenty of security."

She'd rather be home, but she didn't argue. She was leaving with the tour in the morning anyway. Another night on the road wouldn't matter.

Dirk was driving toward her house when Ethan's cell started chiming. He dragged it out of his pocket, didn't seem to recognize the caller ID. "Brodie."

Val couldn't hear the conversation, but she watched some of the color leach from his face. "Which hospital?" The caller said something. "Calm down, Chrissy. Just tell me which hospital she's in. I'll be there as fast as I can." He started nodding. "Seattle Children's. I'm on my way."

"What's going on?" Dirk asked, all business.

"Hannah's in the emergency room. I've got to get there as quick as I can. I need you to drive me back to Val's to pick up my car."

"You said Seattle Children's, right?"

"That's right."

"I'll drive you." He flicked a glance at Megan. "Right, Meg?"

"Yes, of course."

"Val?" Dirk asked.

"Absolutely. Ethan needs to get to his

daughter."

Ethan's shoulders relaxed as Dirk stepped on the gas. Still, he was clearly worried about his daughter, and Val didn't blame him. If she had a child, she would be freaking out right now.

"What happened?" she asked him softly.

"Hannah fell off her tricycle and hit her head. Her mother isn't answering her cell phone. She's off somewhere with her boyfriend. *Arthur.* That's his damned name."

Val wondered if Ethan was jealous, if he still had feelings for his ex.

Never one to miss anything, he drilled her with a glare. "What? What were you thinking just now?"

She shrugged, not about to tell him. "Is she a bad mother, your ex?"

"Not usually. Just vindictive as hell. After three years apart, Allison still carries a grudge because it didn't work out between us."

"You know what they say about a woman scorned."

"Yeah. I wouldn't care except that it affects our daughter. I want to spend more time with Hannah. Ally does her best to keep us apart."

So not jealous. Just concerned about his child. She wished she didn't feel so relieved.

They pulled up in front of Seattle Children's Hospital, and Val and Ethan jumped out while Dirk and Meg went to park the car. Inside the emergency room, Ethan walked up to the desk, and a no-nonsense nurse directed him toward one of the curtained enclosures.

Focused on his daughter, he started walking in that direction, remembered his job, turned, and set a hand at Val's waist, urging her along beside him. She stepped out of the way as he drew back the curtain and walked into the cubicle.

"Daddy!" With her blond hair in pigtails and a wide white bandage wrapped around her head, Ethan's little girl was adorable. As soon as she saw her father, tears welled in her big blue eyes, and she reached out her arms to him.

Ethan moved close to the bed and the child threw her arms around his neck. "I'm so glad you're here. My head hurts, Daddy."

"I know, sweetheart. But the doctors are going to fix you up and give you something to make the pain go away."

"Chrissy said you were coming. But I wasn't . . . I wasn't sure."

Ethan hugged her close. "I'll always come, sweetheart, whenever you need me."

He looked up as a woman in green scrubs

walked into the cubicle, black hair pulled into a twist at the nape of her neck, iPad in her hand. Her name tag read Dr. Villarosa.

"Hello, Doctor," Ethan said. "I'm Hannah's father, Ethan Brodie. What's going on?"

"Maria Villarosa. Hannah fell and cut her head. The gash required a couple of stitches. She also has a slight concussion. We don't think it's serious, but we're keeping her here for a couple of hours for observation. Once she's released, you'll need to keep an eye on her overnight. If there are no complications, she'll be fine in a couple of days."

He nodded, flicked Val a sideways glance. She could feel the wheels turning in his head. He had a job to do, but he was also a father, and his little girl needed him.

"It'll be okay," Val said to him softly, resting a hand on his arm. "I'll be staying at the Fairmont. You said yourself there's plenty of security."

His eyes remained on her face. He sighed. "I don't like it, but I guess it'll have to work. Dirk can take you down there with Meg."

She smiled. "Don't worry, I'll be fine." But she could see he didn't like handing over her protection to someone else, even his very close friend.

"Hannah, honey, this is Valentine," he

said. "She's a friend."

Val smiled at the little girl. "Hello, Hannah."

The little girl smiled at her shyly. "I fell off my trike and hit my head."

"Yes, I see your bandage. Your daddy was really worried."

Just then the curtain jerked back and a very pretty woman with curly, shoulder-length auburn hair walked into the cubicle.

"What happened to Hannah?"

"She fell off her tricycle and cut her head," Ethan said. "The babysitter called the ambulance. Hannah's got a slight concussion and a couple of stitches. When Chrissy couldn't reach you, she called me."

The woman's head went up. "The battery went dead on my cell. I saw the messages when I plugged in. I'm sorry if your daughter being in the hospital inconvenienced you."

Ethan's shoulders stiffened. "She didn't inconvenience me. She never has."

The woman turned to Val, her eyes burning with a light that didn't bode well. "Who's this? Your latest piece of ass? I can't believe you brought her here."

"Ms. Hart is my current assignment, Ally. She's under BOSS, Inc., protection. I brought her with me because your teenage babysitter wasn't able to find you."

The woman turned to Val as if she hadn't heard a word Ethan had said. "Don't let him fool you, honey. He only wants to get in your pants. He won't hang around long after that. We're all just conquests to Ethan."

Ethan's jaw went rock hard. He looked as if it was taking supreme force of will not to say something in front of his daughter that he would regret.

Dirk appeared just then, Megan close beside him. "Come on, Val. I think Ethan could use a little privacy."

She just nodded, grateful Dirk had been insightful enough to intervene when he'd seen Allison. They stepped into the waiting room and closed the door. Twenty minutes later, Ethan walked in, his features carved in stone.

"How's Hannah?" Val asked.

He relaxed a little. "She's doing great. The docs have decided to let her go home with her mother."

"That's good."

"Yeah, I guess." He shook his head. "I'm . . . ahh . . . sorry about what happened in there."

Val managed to smile. "Don't be. I think I get why things didn't work out between the two of you."

"Ally was right about one thing: She *was* a conquest. I went after her because she was beautiful and I wanted her badly. It didn't take me long to figure out what a mistake I'd made."

He seemed to be trying to tell her something, but she wasn't exactly sure what it was. "She gave you a darling little girl, so it was worth it."

Ethan finally smiled. "You're right. Hannah is a great kid, no matter who her mother is."

"You ready to go?" Dirk asked. "I imagine these ladies would like to get home and get out of their funeral clothes."

Ethan's gaze shot to Val. The hot look was back in his eyes. Clearly, there was nothing he'd like better than to *help her* get out of her clothes. A frisson of heat rolled through her, making her stomach muscles clench.

As they walked out of the hospital toward the big black SUV, she couldn't help recalling Allison's warning. *We're all just conquests to Ethan.* He'd admitted it was at least partly true.

Considering the way his hot look had melted her insides, it was definitely something to consider.

CHAPTER FIFTEEN

A chartered seventy-passenger Bombardier jet carried the remaining twenty-eight models, Matthew Carlyle, Daniel Clemens, costume people, makeup artists, Beau Desmond, Bick Gallagher, and some of the regular La Belle security team, as well as Ethan and Dirk. Another flight would be bringing the rest of the security people, along with the lighting and sound crews and various and sundry members of the tour.

The four-hour flight from the Sea-Tac Airport to Dallas/Fort Worth put them in Texas by midafternoon. Limousine buses shuttled the group to two different hotels: the models and higher-ups at the Ritz-Carlton, the rest of the group at the Warwick Melrose, not far away.

Though there was nothing planned for the balance of the day, the models at the Ritz were told not to leave the premises unless they were in a group and accompanied by security personnel. Dinner was catered for them in a banquet room at the luxurious hotel.

Early the following morning, while most of the La Belle security people stayed at the hotel to protect the models, Ethan and his crew, along with Beau Desmond and some of his men, were shuttled out to the theater where the production would be held, the Music Hall at Fair Park.

Though Ethan had been living among the dense foliage and tall evergreens of Seattle for the past few years, the flat, dry Texas landscape still felt like home. His Southern drawl had mostly disappeared, but he and Luke were Texas born and bred, along with a parcel of Brodie cousins scattered around the state. His connection to the land ran deep.

But he loved Seattle, had since he'd made the decision to leave the Dallas PD and join BOSS, Inc. The job Ian had offered him gave him the independence he had been craving. Now he couldn't imagine ever living anywhere else. Still, it felt good to be back in Texas for a visit.

Ethan glanced up as the shuttle arrived in front of a Spanish-style building constructed in the twenties. A Moorish influence showed in the architectural design of the structure's domes and arcades, and the theater was big — large enough to hold over three thousand people.

Which made it a very big headache for Ethan, his team, and the rest of the La Belle security crew.

Inside the theater, Ethan led Dirk, Sandy Sandowski, Walt Wizzy, Pete Hernandez, and Joe Posey into a small conference room.

"All right, you guys, listen up." Ethan waited for his men to form a circle around him. "As all of you know, after what happened in Seattle, the game has changed in a very big way. We aren't just keeping an eye out for guys who think they might get laid or just want to gawk at the women. We've got a murderer out there."

He paused a moment for effect, heard the men's muffled agreement, saw the grim expressions on their faces. "The guy who murdered Delilah Larsen is a single-minded killer with a bone-chilling agenda — he wants to take out another girl. The note he left at the murder scene makes that more than clear."

"Yeah, and some *chingadera* leaked the info to the papers," Pete Hernandez said darkly. "Which makes our job even harder."

"That's exactly right," Ethan said. "There's no way to know if our killer followed the tour to Texas. With any luck, he's back in Seattle, the police hot on his tail. But we can't know that for sure. Which means we have to be prepared. We have to be even more vigilant than we were at the last show."

Joe scratched his close-cropped, tight black curls. "That won't be easy. From the looks of it, this place is a real rabbit warren. Gonna be hell trying to keep things secure."

"The good news is we're in town two days early. During that time, we pick through every nook and cranny, find the places we'll need to be checking the night of the show." He motioned to a guard near the door, who walked over and handed him a set of floor plans.

Ethan unrolled the plans on top of the table and the men circled around it. "This gives us the basic layout." As several hands moved to hold the map in place, Ethan dragged a yellow marking pen out of his pocket and set it down on top.

"The floor plan's a copy I got from the manager. I want you guys to mark it up, highlight any spots that might be a hiding place, somewhere that isn't obvious. At the end of each day, we look at the map, make sure all of the yellow spots have been thoroughly checked out and secured."

"That makes sense." Walt Wizzy bent his tall, bone-thin frame over the table and began poring over the map. "We need to memorize the layout as much as possible."

"Walt's right," Ethan said. "This place has been remodeled a couple of different times. Walls have been moved or covered up with other walls. You guys take a good long look at the map, then I'll assign each of you a section you'll be responsible for."

"Sounds good," Sandy agreed.

"Dirk and I'll move around freelance. The girls will be arriving for rehearsal in . . ." He checked his watch. "About two hours. We'll meet back here in an hour and forty-five. We mark the map, then start providing security. After the rehearsal, we make another sweep. Same goes tomorrow. Any questions?"

No one made a comment.

"Good, let's get to work."

As the men headed out, Ethan walked up to Dirk. "Once the models are here, there's an errand I've got to run. I need you to be on top of things till I get back."

"No problem. What's up?"

"I've got a friend in the Dallas PD. I want to bring him up to speed on the murder in Seattle, ask him to keep me informed of any arrests, word on the street, anything that connects to the fashion show. I want to know if the guy who killed Delilah Larsen followed us to Dallas."

Dirk ran two fingers around his mustache down to his jaw. "I'll keep an eye on the girls."

Ethan nodded. They both knew which girls Dirk was talking about. "I know you will. Thanks."

Protecting Val was his job. That she was a family friend made it even more important. The attraction he felt for her complicated things, but he was doing his best to ignore it.

Ethan stayed at the theater until Val and the rest of the women arrived safely. Then he headed down to the Dallas PD on South Lamar Street.

He'd been gone a while from the homicide division. But a man you'd taken a bullet for didn't forget you. It was a debt that was never completely repaid.

Ethan thought of Heath Ford and smiled.

Val yawned as the afternoon rehearsal continued. Each of the models knew her routine, but the layout of the Music Hall was different from the Paramount, and so were the stage setup, the sound, the lighting. Heather's ankle had eliminated her from the show. After Delilah's brutal death, they were short two models.

Heather's segments had been reassigned to several different girls. Delilah was their number-one model, so her segments had gone to some of the top-ten girls. One segment had gone to Isabel Rafaeli, another to Megan. Val had been assigned to take Delilah's place in the Diamond Jubilee.

Costume changes had to be made and fittings done. Meg, Val, and Izzy, along with Carmen Marquez, had to stay late to work through their new routines.

As the hours wore on and the theater emptied out, Val found her gaze searching for Ethan. According to Dirk, he'd gone to see a friend who worked for the Dallas police.

He'd been a detective here, so he was bound to know people. Val wondered if he was visiting women friends as well and didn't like the spurt of jealousy she had no right to feel.

"I'm beat," Meg said as they took a break an hour later. "I'm way more than ready to get back to the hotel."

"Me too. Unfortunately, Daniel isn't quite satisfied with the changes yet. You know what a perfectionist he is."

Meg sighed. "I know."

"That's what makes him so good at his job."

"It's also what makes him such a prig."

Val grinned.

Meg grinned back, then they both glanced up as Dirk walked toward them. Val couldn't miss the warmth that came into her friend's blue eyes. Meg was fighting her attraction to Dirk the way Val was fighting hers to Ethan. She was very afraid both of them were going to lose their battles.

"You ladies have been at it a while," Dirk said. "You need anything? Bottle of water or something?" He spoke to both of them, but his eyes were on Meg.

"I'm okay," she said. "We should be finishing up pretty soon." He cast a questioning glance at Val.

"I'm fine," she said.

"Ethan just called. He's meeting us back at the hotel."

Val nodded, her exhaustion returning. Silly to feel disappointed.

"It's good to see you, Ethan." Heath Ford extended a hand. "How's Seattle working out for you?"

"Good. I like being my own boss." He smiled. "I've got a kid now, little girl named Hannah. No wife, though. I meant to stay in touch. Never seems to be enough time."

"Same with me. Still single, still looking. So what brings you to Dallas?"

"I'm working a security detail." Ethan explained about the fashion show tour, doing backup security and personal protection for the models.

"A lady friend mentioned the show was coming to town." Heath grinned. "I'm happy to say she's a customer." Six two, with a powerful build, dark blond hair, and brown eyes, Heath was a good-looking man and an even better detective. "Being paid for protecting a stage full of beautiful women — my kinda work."

Ethan grunted. "Might be, if it weren't for the no-fraternizing rule. Half the time the guys walk around with a set of blue balls."

Heath laughed. "So what can I do for you?"

"I guess you haven't heard — one of the models got murdered just before we left Seattle."

Heath sobered. "I've been working a case. I haven't heard anything about it."

"Some wack job strangled her. Claims he's going to do it again." For the next few minutes, Ethan brought his friend up to speed on Delilah Larsen's murder, the notes the ten top models had received, and the second note the killer had left in Delilah's apartment.

"I need to know if this guy's in Dallas, Heath. If he's following the tour. You guys pick up anything that points in that direction, I want to know. Even if it's a long shot, I want to know."

"I can do that."

"Not only do we have a dead model but the press managed to get wind of the notes, take photos, and broadcast them all over the country." Ethan dragged out his phone and brought up the image of the printed message.

Heath hissed out a breath. "Definitely not good."

"No, it isn't."

"A guy named Matt Carlyle is head of La Belle operations. He's good at what he does. I'm sure he's already been in touch with Captain Bridger or someone else in the department, but —"

"But you're a hands-on kind of guy and you want to be kept in the loop."

"That's right."

"Consider it done," Heath said. "By the way, how's that hole in your shoulder?"

Ethan's mouth edged up. "Healed just fine."

"I haven't forgotten what you did that

day." A back alley bar fight that had turned deadly. "If you hadn't showed up when you did, I wouldn't be here now."

"You would have done the same thing."

"I like to think so." Heath stuck out a hand, then leaned in to grip Ethan's shoulder. "I'll keep you posted."

"Thanks, my friend; I appreciate it."

Ethan left the office, climbed into the rental car he'd had delivered to the theater that morning, and headed back to the hotel. He had a job to do and part of it was finding a murderer, but he had been gone most of the day. He was beginning to get edgy about being away so long.

Dirk was with the women. Ethan told himself not to worry.

Didn't do a lick of good.

In the opulent Ritz hotel bar, the Rattlesnake, with its contemporary western theme, dark wood, and backlit golden onyx panels, Val sat at a table with Isabel and Meg. Sipping a glass of white wine, she tried to concentrate on the women's conversation. Across the room at the long polished bar, Dirk lounged on a stool drinking a Coke, watching the room, playing bodyguard.

He was armed, Val knew, a big menacing

pistol holstered at his waist beneath the black La Belle T-shirt he wore — though no one actually believed the killer would strike in a place as public as the luxurious Ritz-Carlton.

She tried not to look for Ethan. Their jobs aside, she didn't have time to get involved with a man. As soon as the tour was over, she was taking the part-time job she'd been offered at the animal clinic, waiting for school to start, then throwing herself into classes.

She'd be studying, preparing, taking on new responsibilities. She was getting her vet degree, then starting a career.

She glanced toward the door, saw Ethan walk into the room, and her whole body flushed with heat. In a pair of wraparound sunglasses, tall and broad-shouldered, built as if he'd just stepped out of the pages of a romance fantasy, he made the word *virile* look impotent.

Her stomach contracted. It was ridiculous. He was only a man. Maybe it was just that he made her feel safe, which no one had done in all the years since Bobby.

He pulled off the shades and tucked them into the top of his T-shirt, his dark gaze finding her as if he had some special radar. Instead of walking toward her, he headed for the bar and took a stool next to Dirk.

Val forced her attention back to the women, caught the tail end of a story about Meg's darling little boy, Charlie, smiled, and managed to say something that didn't sound completely inane.

When Matt Carlyle walked in and rounded them up to join the other models for dinner, she followed. Ethan and Dirk fell in behind the group, but instead of sitting at one of the tables, positioned themselves against the wall at opposite ends of the private dining room.

When the meal was over, the models headed up to their rooms, escorted by La Belle security guards. Dirk escorted Meg while Ethan accompanied Val, but they didn't talk along the way.

At the door to her suite, Ethan paused. "Get some sleep. You've got another long day tomorrow." His features were carefully blank, but his eyes were dark and hot, and she knew what he wanted, knew he was thinking about what it would be like if she invited him into her room, into her bed.

The knowledge made her pulse surge, and a feeling of power slid through her. Ethan might not admit it, but he was as attracted to her as she was to him.

When he took the key card out of her

hand and slid it through the lock, pushed open her door, and stepped inside, she felt a rush of yearning so strong it made her dizzy.

But Ethan just checked the living room, the bedroom, the closet, checked out the marble bathroom, then returned to the door.

"There's security on your floor around the clock. This high up, there's no way an intruder can get to you from outside. You're safe. You don't have to worry."

She swallowed, nodded. "Okay."

"Good night, Valentine."

He was using her stage name, reminding her of her job and his, and that they needed to keep their distance.

"Good night, Ethan."

He stood unmoving for another few seconds, his eyes on her face, waited until she moved back a little and closed the door. She heard his heavy footfalls as he turned and walked away.

CHAPTER SIXTEEN

Ethan couldn't sleep. Desire kept him hot and hard into the small hours of the night. Dammit, he had never felt such a clawing need for a woman, not with Ally or anyone else.

He finally fell asleep sometime after two, tossed and turned, and woke up a few hours later when his cell phone started to signal. He rolled over and checked the red digits on the clock on the bedside table. Six A.M.

Ethan looked at the caller ID, saw a Dallas area code, but didn't recognize the number. "Brodie."

"Heath Ford. I've got some bad news, Ethan."

The muscles across his shoulders went tense as he sat up in bed. "Tell me."

"A woman was murdered last night. Happened sometime between midnight and two A.M. Vic was strangled. Raped. She fought him and went down hard."

His grip tightened on the phone. "One of the models?" He'd thought they were all in and accounted for, prayed like hell they were.

"No. A stripper. Mandy Gee. At least that's the name she uses. Stella Davis is her real name. Works at the Tiger's Eye Lounge."

Ethan nodded, feeling both relief and regret. "I remember the place. Not exactly top-of-the-line entertainment."

"Maybe not, but it's always busy. Mandy left just before midnight. Her roommate found her body when she got back to the apartment around two thirty. The thing is, E, the first detective on the scene found a note. Same style as the one in the photo you showed me."

A hard knot balled in his stomach. "What's it say?"

" 'Sinners, sluts, and whores. You can run but you can't hide.' "

The knot tightened. "Printed note? Different fonts?"

"That's right. Could be him."

"First vic wasn't raped. Death was quick and easy. If it's him, he's escalated."

"I'm heading for the crime scene. I'll keep you posted."

"I'd like to take a look."

"All right, but we need to let the CSIs clear out. I'll call you later, try to make it happen."

"Thanks, Heath." Ethan ended the call. His thoughts went to Val, how badly she was going to take the news. He needed to see her, make sure she was okay. He wanted to be the one to tell her about the murder, not Carlyle or anyone else.

He phoned Dirk and filled him in, then took a quick shower, pulled on a clean pair of jeans and a black La Belle T-shirt, shoved his feet into low-topped boots, and headed out the door.

All nine top models had suites. Val's was on one of the upper floors. His smaller room sat on a lower one. He didn't like being so far away, but without causing trouble for both of them, there wasn't much he could do.

As of this morning, that was going to change.

He reached the sixteenth floor and strode out of the elevator, waved at the security guard, headed down the hall. He didn't know if she was awake. He didn't care.

She was going to take the news hard. He wanted to make it as easy on her as he could. He didn't bother telling himself it was because she was Samantha's friend.

That was a load of crap and he knew it. He cared about her. He shouldn't, but he did.

He knocked on the door and waited. Knocked again. Still no answer. His nerves kicked up. He had a pass key card, and if she didn't answer in the next five seconds, he was going to use it.

He was reaching for his wallet when the door swung open and Val stood in the opening. Her honey-blond curls were sleep tangled around her face and shoulders. She was wearing a sexy ankle-length peach satin robe that clung to her curves and shouted *La Belle lingerie,* and instantly he went hard.

Jesus, he wanted this woman.

Instead, he steeled himself. He had bad news to deliver. He needed to get it done.

Val raked back her long golden hair. She wasn't wearing makeup, which reminded him of the way she had looked the day he'd found her at the Perfect Pup. As far as he was concerned, she looked even better without it, fresh-faced and wholesome, which he was beginning to believe she was.

"Ethan. What is it?"

"I need to talk to you, Val. It's important."

"All right. Come in." She stepped back to let him walk past, then closed the door behind him. The suite was opulent, the living room done in soft golden tones accented with moss green, the traditional sofa and chairs upholstered in silk brocade with contrasting gold-striped pillows. There were mahogany tables and brass lamps, long moss green-and-gold draperies at the windows.

The models definitely lived the good life. Aside from the drawback that someone wanted them dead.

"What's going on?" Unconsciously, Val clutched the front of her robe, pulling it a little snugger across her breasts. He forced himself to look away.

"I think you need to sit down for this." He tipped his head toward the sofa, and her body went rigid.

"What is it? What's going on?"

"Val, you need to sit down."

"Tell me. I want to know what's happening."

He read the tension in her body, the way she held her back ramrod straight. No way was she moving from where she stood. "I got a call from a friend in the Dallas PD. There's been another murder, Val."

She swayed, made a little sound in her throat.

"Not one of the models," he hurried on. "A woman who lives here in Dallas. She worked in a strip club. She was killed in her apartment last night."

Val started trembling. Her face had gone paper white, not even a trace of color in her lips. He clamped down hard on the urge to go to her, to pull her into his arms and tell her everything would be okay. He was her bodyguard. He was there to protect her, nothing more.

"Was it . . . was it him?"

"The police don't know yet. Whoever did it left a note like the others, but the MO was different."

She started to shiver, looked even paler, still stood her ground.

Ethan clenched his fists. "You need to sit down, honey. Let me get you a glass of water or something."

She looked up at him, her eyes beseeching. "I'm . . . I'm scared, Ethan." Her voice trembled and her hands started shaking.

He couldn't do it. He couldn't stand there a second longer. It wasn't supposed to be personal, but it was.

"Fuck it." In two long strides he was there, hauling her close, wrapping her trembling body in his arms. Val turned into him, melted against his chest, pressed her face into the side of his neck. A soft sob escaped her throat.

"I've got you, baby," he said, tightening

his hold. "I'm not going to let anyone hurt you."

"Ethan . . ."

"It's all right, honey." He pressed his lips against her hair. She was tall. He hadn't realized how perfectly she would fit him. "You're safe, baby. Everything's going to be okay."

She made a faint little whimper, took a deep breath, and pulled away enough to look up at him. Her lips were plump but still pale, and they were just inches from his. If he moved just a fraction . . .

Val leaned up and kissed him. Her mouth, soft and damp, melded exactly with his. Ethan didn't hesitate, just dragged her fully against him and claimed the gift she offered. He was already aroused, his erection throbbing inside his jeans. When her soft lips parted, inviting him to taste her, his tongue swept in and the kiss went deeper. Vaguely, he heard himself groan.

The kiss went wilder, hotter. He tasted sweetness and the remnants of her fear, tasted hot desire. Val pressed herself against him, the vee of her sex pillowing the hard ridge of his. He wanted to be inside her more than he wanted to breathe.

Her robe had come partly open. He looked down at the luscious breasts he'd admired from too far away. Filling his hands with the smooth pale fullness, he tested the weight, ran a thumb over her nipple, and heard her swift intake of breath.

"Ethan . . ."

Her nipples were hard. When he bent his head to take the tip of one between his teeth, her head dropped back to allow him better access, and her fingers curled around the nape of his neck, holding him in place as he suckled and tasted.

Fisting a hand in her hair, he dragged her mouth back to his and kissed her again. Kissed her until neither of them could breathe.

"I need you," she said softly. "Oh, God, Ethan, I need you so much."

He wanted to tear the robe completely away, wanted to admire every inch of her beautiful body. He growled like a predator, felt like one as he lifted her into his arms and started striding toward the bedroom. Val didn't stop him, just clung to his neck, her head on his shoulder, her satin robe flowing around them.

Ethan kissed her long and deep as he crossed the threshold, his erection high and hard, straining for release. He'd almost reached the bed when an insistent knock sounded on the door.

Val whimpered. Ethan swore a dark oath and clenched his jaw against the pain of his aching arousal.

With a long, calming breath, he set Val on her feet, pulled her robe back in place over her breasts. "Stay here."

Striding out of the bedroom, he crossed the living room, looked through the peephole in the door, and saw Matthew Carlyle standing in the hallway. He'd been expecting Carlyle. Just not this soon.

Cursing himself for losing control, he looked back at Val, who had walked into the living room. "You okay? It's Carlyle."

Val pulled the sash on her robe a little tighter and raked back her heavy blond hair. "I'm all right. Let him in."

Even with his light brown hair unkempt, the shadow of a beard covering the scar along his jaw, Matthew Carlyle was an imposing man. And impeccably dressed as always, in beige slacks and a blue Oxford cloth shirt.

"I've been expecting you," Ethan said as Carlyle walked into the living room, though his arrival had been the last thing on Ethan's mind when he had been kissing Val. "I've got friends in the DPD. I know about the murder."

Carlyle looked past Ethan to Val. The

color was back in her face. The kiss had been good for something, at least.

"Ethan came to tell me what happened," she said, not venturing a glance his way. "I can't believe there's been another murder." She looked as if she'd just climbed out of bed, which she had. If Carlyle hadn't interrupted, Ethan would have had her back in bed again.

"It wasn't one of our girls, Val," Carlyle told her. "Everyone's okay."

"Not everyone," Val said. "A woman is dead."

Carlyle's mouth tightened. "That isn't what I meant."

Val's features softened. "I know that. I'm sorry, Matt. It's just —"

"Hey, I understand. This isn't easy for any of us." Matthew turned in Ethan's direction. "You said you had friends in the police department. What did they tell you about the murder?"

"Enough to make me wonder if it's the same guy as the one in Seattle. The woman who died wasn't a model. The man who killed Delilah sent threatening notes to ten women, killed one of them, said he was going to kill another. If it's our guy, he's changed his plans. He couldn't get to a model so he took out another woman."

"A stripper," Carlyle said. "That's what a police captain named Bridger told me. The killer must have considered her morally impure, same as he does the models."

"That'd be my guess. And she was raped, which Delilah wasn't."

"He raped her?" Val's voice quivered.

Ethan's gaze swung to her face. "That's right." There was no use holding back. It was going to be in all the papers. "And it wasn't quick like the first time. She fought him before he killed her."

Val sat down hard on the sofa.

"I'm going over to the crime scene as soon as it can be arranged," Ethan said. "I'll know more after that happens."

Carlyle walked over and sat down on the sofa next to Val. When he took hold of her hand, Ethan felt like growling again. The notion surprised him. He'd never been a jealous man. At least not until now.

Carlyle squeezed her hand. "Listen, Val, I know you're upset, but we've got all kinds of protection in place for you and the other girls."

"Maybe you should . . . consider canceling the show."

He shook his head. "I'm afraid that isn't possible. The company has millions of dollars invested in this tour. At this point we aren't even sure it's the same guy. As Ethan said, the note was similar, but the rest of what happened doesn't match." He patted her hand. "The tour's going forward, Val, but we aren't going to let anything happen to you."

She nodded but didn't look convinced.

Ethan spoke to Carlyle. "Valentine won't have to worry about anything happening to her because from now on I'll be sleeping on her couch."

Carlyle stood up, anger making the thin line along his jaw stand out. One of the guys said Matt got hit with a beer bottle in a fist-fight when he was a kid. It wasn't hard to believe.

"You can't stay in here," Carlyle said. "You know the rules."

Ethan crossed his arms over his chest. "I told you before, Val's a family friend. If I have to quit to protect her, then I will. You decide."

Carlyle's features hardened. His gaze swung to Val. "How do you feel about this? About Brodie staying in your suite?"

She opened her mouth, caught the dark warning glance Ethan cast her way. It said he'd be staying one way or the other.

Val closed her mouth and simply shrugged her shoulders. "It's a two-room suite. If

Ethan's close by, I won't be afraid."

Carlyle hesitated a moment, then stiffly nodded. "You've got connections with the Dallas police. I need you to stay on these murders — both of them. We've got to stop this guy."

"Like I said, I'll know more after I look at the crime scene."

"All right. For now, you can stay with Valentine. But the rules haven't changed. You step over the line, you're out. And you had better keep this quiet. We've got enough trouble without stirring up Beau Desmond and his security people."

Ethan didn't give a damn about Desmond. But he cared about Val, and he didn't want to make this any more difficult for her than it was already. "They won't hear anything from me."

Carlyle turned to Val. "Are you feeling up to making the rehearsal?"

"I'll be there."

Carlyle checked the time on his Rolex. "I need to go. I want to speak privately to each of the models who got a note. I've spoken to most of them already. I've called a general meeting to talk to the rest of the models and the crew."

His gaze went to Ethan. "You'll be with her on the bus?"

"Yes."

"Good. I'll see you both there."

The sound of the lock sliding into place as the suite door closed jarred Val out of the wide-awake nightmare she was living. Coming up off the sofa, she walked over to Ethan and stopped in front of him. She tried not to remember their fiery kiss, to think that if she just leaned in the way she had before . . .

She commanded herself not to move. "About . . . umm . . . what happened earlier . . ."

"Nothing happened, Val. Thanks to Matt Carlyle's very timely arrival."

She glanced away. *Nothing happened?* She would never forget that scorching kiss, or the hot yearning that had burned through her body as his mouth closed over her breast.

She looked into his handsome face, commanded her heart to slow. "Whatever did or didn't happen, I'm the one to blame. I just . . . this whole thing is so unreal. It's like it can't really be happening, but it is. I needed someone and I . . . I got carried away. I'm sorry."

One of his big hands unconsciously fisted, as if he were fighting the same battle she was not to move. "It wasn't your fault. I let

219

things get out of hand. I'm here to protect you, not take you to bed. It won't happen again."

But he would be staying in the suite with her. And the truth was, Val wanted it to happen again. Wanted to take up exactly where they had left off — with Ethan kissing her as if he would die if he didn't. With him carrying her off to bed.

She was fiercely attracted to him. Add to that, she hadn't slept with a man in years.

She wanted him. There was no denying the fact. But her instincts warned her to be wary. Ethan was an amazingly attractive man. Whenever he walked backstage, the eyes of every woman in the show cut in his direction.

We're all just conquests to Ethan.

The words rang in her head. Was that all she was to him? A conquest? She thought of the control that until this morning he had always maintained. Ethan had never pressed her for sex or any sort of relationship beyond that of client and protector.

She had been the one who'd lost control.

"You need to eat something," Ethan said mildly, as if that burning kiss had never happened. "I'll phone room service unless you want to go downstairs."

Room service. Staying in the suite would

mean spending more time alone with him. More time for her mind to remember the feel of his mouth moving hotly over hers, the way he had taken possession, the hard muscles bunching beneath his T-shirt.

More time for temptation.

"I'll get dressed and go downstairs. I'll call Meg. She must have heard the news by now. I'll see if she wants to meet me."

Ethan nodded. She could feel his reserve, firmly back in place. He was once more in control. He intended to stay that way.

If she wanted more from Ethan Brodie, it would be up to her.

Val told herself it had only been a moment of weakness.

But she had never been much good at lying to herself.

CHAPTER SEVENTEEN

Ethan drove his rented Buick out to the theater, following the limo bus. He would need transportation later, when he met Heath Ford at the crime scene.

All morning he worked with his team, going over possible problems inside the theater, security precautions they would need to take for the show on Friday night. He didn't get the call from Heath until two in the afternoon.

"CSIs are finished," Heath said. "I'll meet you out there."

With Dirk and a busload of security people at the rehearsal hall to cover the women, Ethan drove his rental car out the North Stemmons Freeway toward the Tiger's Eye Lounge, a fifteen-minute trip out of Dallas. The address Heath had given him for Mandy Gee's house was only five minutes from where she worked.

The July afternoon heat was stifling, at

least a hundred degrees. There'd been a time when he'd been used to the scorching weather, but not anymore. Ethan slid his wraparound sunglasses over his eyes, turned the air-conditioning up full blast, and tried not to think of the deep green forests of Seattle.

It didn't take long to reach his destination. Parking the Buick behind Heath's unmarked white sedan, he headed up the walk. Mandy Gee's small, gray-stucco, single-story, hip-roof house needed a paint job. The lawn was mostly dirt. What little grass grew in the yard badly needed mowing.

As he got closer, Heath walked out of the house and stood waiting for him on the porch. Yellow crime-scene tape stretched over the front door.

"They're finished and gone," Heath said. "Come on in."

Ethan removed his shades and hooked the earpieces into the top of his T-shirt. Walking in behind Heath, he paused in the living room to look around.

"Lots of blood, so be careful," Heath said. "The guy was a real crazy."

The place was a shambles. Broken lamp shades on the dingy brown carpet was soaked with the victim's blood. The worn sofa was bloodstained. Scarlet drops splattered one of the walls. Mandy and her roommate were lousy housekeepers, but the place was so torn up Ethan barely noticed.

"Body was sprawled on the floor in front of the couch," Heath said. "Way it looks, he threatened her with a knife, cut her pretty bad a couple of times as she fought him." He pointed to a blood smear on the edge of the coffee table. "Fell and hit her head. Fall knocked her unconscious. Killer raped her, then strangled her."

Ethan started shaking his head. "Not our guy," he said. "Not even close."

Heath's dark brown eyebrows went up. "One look and you're that sure?"

"Your perp got off on the violence, wanted to draw it out. He wasn't careful. Blood everywhere. Likely left fingerprints." He looked up. "I'm guessing you got DNA?"

Heath nodded. "Got semen. Hair follicles. Fingerprints. Blood beneath the victim's nails."

"And?"

Heath shook his head. "That's the bad news. Nothing in AFIS. Nothing anywhere that we've turned up so far. We're hoping for a DNA match, but —"

"But if he isn't in the system, he isn't in the system. You're probably not going to find a DNA match either."

"You could be right."

"Maybe that's the reason he didn't care what evidence he left behind. Maybe he isn't quite as crazy as he seems. Maybe he knew he didn't have to worry about you finding him. At least not through the system."

Ethan wandered slowly through the living room, careful not to step in any blood, then moved into the bedroom. The bed hadn't been made, but it didn't look recently slept in.

"What was she wearing?"

"G-string and pasties under a red silk robe."

"So she hadn't had time to change after she got home. Wonder why she didn't change at the club."

"House is just blocks away. I'll ask, but it's probably just her normal routine."

Ethan's gaze went to the bedroom window. It was open, the screen pulled off. "Guy went into the backyard, came in through the window."

He walked over to the closet. The sliding doors were open. He could see where the clothes had been pushed aside. "Hid in the closet till she was in the house, then went after her. The neighbors hear anything?"

"If they did, they aren't talking. Good chance he caught her by surprise. No time to scream, sound any kind of alarm."

That was Ethan's thinking. "Where was the note?"

"On the coffee table, next to the body."

He started nodding as the picture began to form in his head. "Killer saw the photo of the note on TV. Damned media showed it to the public and described it in detail. Started calling him the Hellfire Preacher. Killer liked the idea, got himself juiced up just thinking about what he was going to do."

They walked back into the living room for a final look around. Ethan briefly checked the kitchen, but it didn't look like Mandy had made it that far. He and Heath walked back out on the porch.

The detective paused at the top of the steps. "So it's not your guy. I guess that means you're done here."

"Not by a long shot. Whoever did this couldn't get to one of the models, so he killed Mandy Gee. He's scored a big victory. We don't have squat, so now he thinks he's smarter than the police. There's every chance he'll go after his original target. Thanks to the media, he's got the names of all the women who received one of the original notes."

"Or he might just figure any one of the models is fair game."

"Yeah."

"So . . . you gonna help me find him?"

Ethan smiled grimly. "You can bet on it."

Val and Meg sat side by side on one of the plush red-velvet wraparound seats on the limousine bus. The vehicle, designed to hold up to forty people, was equipped with color TVs, CDs and DVDs, a satellite tracking system, and a fully stocked bar.

Rehearsal was over. They were headed back to the Ritz. Dirk was aboard and so was Beau Desmond and his right-hand man, Bick Gallagher. Val wasn't crazy about either one of them. Beau was a control freak and Gallagher believed he was God's gift to women. At least they seemed capable of doing their jobs.

During the bus ride, she phoned her mom in Bellingham and asked how Pops was doing.

"Lord, you know you can't keep that man down. Doctor says it was probably the flu. He's outside feeding the chickens or I'd put him on."

"I'm sorry I missed him. Tell him to call me when he comes back in."

"I will, but you know how he hates talking on the phone. Maybe I can get him to text you."

Val grinned. Pops was determined to move into the twenty-first century. She liked that he wasn't giving in to old age without a fight.

"There's something else, Mom." She went on to tell her mother about the murder in Texas, making it clear the victim wasn't one of the models. She left out the part about the note since her parents didn't watch a lot of TV news and so far the information hadn't been released. "Love you," Val said and ended the call.

"You always smile when you're talking to your parents," Meg said as the bus rolled through the heavy Dallas traffic. "They must be really great."

"They're the best. I don't know what would have happened to me if they hadn't taken me in."

Meg knew about her childhood, her rebellion, her escape from her cousins, and the foster-care system she had barely survived.

"My folks are great, too. We're both really blessed."

"Yes, we are," Val agreed. But she knew from experience, the kind of unfeeling people she had lived with as a teen were more the rule.

"Have you talked to Ethan anymore about the murder?" Meg asked.

"I haven't seen him since breakfast. I know he was going out to look at the crime scene with a friend of his in the police department."

Meg shook her head. "That poor girl. What a terrible way for her life to end."

"I guess she tried to fight him. I like her for that."

Meg's chin firmed. "Me too. I'd fight. I wouldn't just let him kill me."

Val blew out a breath, rested her head against the back of the seat. "I acted like an idiot when Ethan told me. Two women murdered. It really scared me. I'm usually not such a wimp. The second murder freaked me out even more than the first, and that . . . umm . . . kind of freaked Ethan out."

"I was pretty freaked myself when I heard about it."

"I'm not supposed to say anything, but Ethan told Matt Carlyle that from now on he'd be staying in my suite."

"Yeah? I'm not really surprised. Dirk went ballistic after Ethan called him. He told me in no uncertain terms that he'll be staying in my room from now on."

"Matt agreed to that?"

"Dirk is a little different from Ethan. He didn't ask permission. He's just planning to show up."

"What about the security guard? Ethan says there's one on each floor."

"I get the impression getting past the guard won't be a problem for Dirk."

Val thought of Ethan. The look he'd cast her way had warned he would be staying with her, no matter what it took. "I guess you're right. So how do you feel about Dirk staying in the room with you?"

Meg toyed with a thread on the dark blue skinny jeans she was wearing with a sexy little tank and a pair of heeled sandals. "I'm really attracted to him. I've been thinking . . . maybe if I just, you know, slept with him, I could get him out of my system. Then we could both go back to normal."

After this morning, Val had been considering something along those same lines. "You think it would work?"

"I don't know. You've got a thing for Ethan. What do you think?"

"God, I don't know either. I can't figure out what it is about him that attracts me so strongly."

Meg laughed. "Besides the fact he's smart, gorgeous, has the ultimate male body, and

230

the superhero protective gene?"

Val managed to smile. "Yeah, besides that. Maybe they attract us just because we're so dependent on them. I mean, two women are dead. We could be next. Without Ethan and Dirk, we'd be a lot more vulnerable."

"Yeah, if it weren't for Ethan and Dirk, we'd have to pander to Beau Desmond's ego or screw Bick Gallagher." She grinned, tipped her head toward the back of the bus where Bick was sitting, and did a fake shiver, making Val smile.

"So . . . are you going to do it?" Meg asked.

"Do what?"

"Sleep with Ethan."

Val's skin went warm just thinking about it. "I kissed him this morning. Totally an accident and completely my fault. It was after he told me about the murder. I was pretty shook up and it just sort of happened."

Meg glanced around, then leaned closer. "Okay, dish. How was it?"

Val grinned. "Incredible. Scale of one to ten — it was a fifty."

Meg started fanning herself. "If I kiss Dirk, I'm going to combust. I just know it."

Val's grin faded. "Until someone catches this killer, we need to let them do their jobs. We don't want anyone else getting killed."

"You're right. Maybe when this is over we can think about having sex with them."

"Yeah, maybe."

Meg's cell started ringing. She pulled it out of her purse and pressed it against her ear, started smiling. "It's my mom." They talked for a while. Meg told her mother about the second murder but said it didn't have anything to do with the models, which was kind of a stretch, but Meg wouldn't want her mother to worry.

"She's putting Charlie on the phone," Meg said, her smile even brighter. She talked to her little boy for a while, told him Mommy loved him, and finally ended the call. When Meg looked away, her eyes were sad.

"I can't get involved with Dirk. I have a little boy to think of. If Dirk started coming around, Charlie would get attached to him. Dirk isn't a kid person. He rides a Harley, for God's sake. When things ended between us — which eventually they would — Charlie would be crushed. Just like when his daddy left. I can't let that happen to him again."

Val made no reply. She didn't have a child, but if she got involved with Ethan, she had a heart that could very well get broken.

We're all just conquests to Ethan.

After being around the tough teen boys she'd grown up with, then modeling in front of an audience full of hungry males, she knew most of them thought exactly that way. A woman was an object to be conquered, nothing more.

Besides, she didn't want to distract Ethan from doing his job, part of which was working to find a killer.

She didn't want to be the cause of another woman's death. Maybe even hers or Meg's.

She had to leave Ethan alone.

CHAPTER EIGHTEEN

Ethan spent the following morning with Heath Ford, meeting him for breakfast downtown at the Copper Kettle Café, not far from the police station.

"You were right," Heath said from across the red vinyl booth where the two of them sat waiting for their orders to arrive. "The guy's definitely not in the system. No DNA, no fingerprints, zip, zero, nada."

Ethan nodded. "I had a hunch. The crime scene was chaos. It was almost like he was leaving clues on purpose, daring us to find him."

"We're looking for similar cases — homicides or unsolved rapes — particularly anywhere in the Dallas area."

"He thinks he's too smart to get caught."

"Then he's in for a big surprise."

Ethan took a drink of his coffee, set the heavy china mug back down on the Formica-topped table. In the background, the clatter of silverware competed with friendly conversation. "You talk to the other girls at the club?"

"Talked to them all," Heath said, picking up his mug and blowing across the top to cool it down. "Got nothing we could use."

"No one hanging around, giving Mandy or the girls any trouble?"

"We got a few names. Guys who could get a little pushy. They're either in the system or have valid alibis. Got nothing that matches the evidence left at the crime scene."

"What about surveillance tapes? Someone lurking in the parking lot? Someone around Mandy's car?"

Heath just shook his head.

The waitress arrived, a saucy little blonde. "Bacon and eggs for you, cowboy," she said to Ethan, setting the hot plate in front of him. The delicious aroma made Ethan's stomach rumble.

"The usual for you, Detective." The glance the woman cast at Heath said she was at least half-smitten. "Corned beef hash and eggs over easy, just the way you like."

Heath winked at her as she set his breakfast in front of him. "Thanks, Sissy."

"My pleasure," she said in a sultry drawl that suggested she had already had the pleasure in a lot more personal ways.

Sissy took off to another table and Ethan and Heath both dug into their food.

Ethan shoveled in a bite of crispy hash browns, then took a drink of coffee. "You know, looking at the crime scene got me thinking. Who isn't in the system these days? DNA I can understand; it's still fairly new. But no prints, no hospital visits, nothing that came out of the school system? Even real estate salesmen are fingerprinted these days."

"Gotta be someone off the grid."

"Definitely someone who lives out in the country," Ethan said.

"Or did," Heath added.

"We need something, anything that will point us in the right direction."

"Maybe something will turn up."

"Tour leaves Dallas on Sunday. We've got a show in Atlanta Wednesday night."

"You think this new guy will follow the tour?"

Ethan's shoulders tightened. "He might. If he comes after one of the women, we'll be ready."

Heath took a drink of his coffee. "Like I said, maybe something will turn up before then and we'll be able to bring him in."

Ethan nodded. "At least we'd get one of

the crazy bastards off the street."

"I'm going insane," Meg said. "I can't stand being cooped up in this hotel a minute more."

"The show's tonight," Val reminded her. "We're supposed to relax and get mentally prepared. And you might recall, there's a murderer out there stalking us."

Meg, Val, Isabel, and Carmen Marquez all sat in Meg's suite. All of them were top models. Working together on the tour, the four of them were becoming good friends.

"I do not know about you," Carmen said in her soft Spanish accent, "but I am going out." She tossed the heavy, cascading black hair that fit perfectly with her big dark eyes and flawless olive complexion. "I do not care if I have to ask Bick Gallagher to take me. It would be worth sleeping with the devil himself for a little fresh air."

All of them broke into laughter. The guy might be well-built, with the blond good looks women usually liked, but he was also a conceited jerk. No way would any of them invite him into her bed.

Meg tossed a smile at Dirk, who stood next to the elegant moss-green draperies, his shoulder propped against the wall, a frown darkening his face. Meg figured he didn't like the thought of any of them sleeping with Bick.

"Maybe we could talk Dirk into taking us out," Meg said sweetly, pretending he couldn't actually hear.

Izzy and Carmen both jumped up from the sofa and hurried toward him, two lionesses on the hunt.

"You would do this for us, yes, Dirk?" Carmen leaned close. "Please say you will."

Dirk took a step back. "No. No way in hell am I taking four women out of this hotel. God knows how much trouble you could get into."

"We just want to get some lunch," Meg purred.

"Somewhere nice," Isabel added.

"Anywhere but here," Carmen finished.

Dirk cast Val a hard glance. "What about you? I don't hear you chiming in."

Meg bit back a laugh at Val's falsely innocent expression. "We wouldn't give you any trouble, Dirk. We promise. We'd do whatever you told us."

He rolled his eyes. "I'll just bet." He flicked a glance at Meg, who batted her eyelashes and tried to look seductive. One thing Dirk didn't try to hide: He wanted her. Unfortunately, Meg also wanted him.

"Just lunch, right?" Dirk said.

Sensing victory, Meg smiled. "That's all we have time for. We don't even have time to shop."

Dirk looked relieved at the news. "Where do you want to go?"

The girls glanced around. "Rosewood Mansion on Turtle Creek?" Izzy suggested. "I was there a few years ago with my sister."

"A mansion . . ." Carmen said thoughtfully. "*Sí*, that sounds like the perfect spot for lunch."

When Val and Meg grinned and nodded their agreement, Dirk blew out a breath. "Fine. I'll call down and arrange for a limo to pick us up. We can wait for the car in the lobby. Let's go."

Carmen's black brows shot up. "*Dios mío,* what are you talking about?" She planted her hands on her hips. "We cannot go dressed like this." She looked down at her khaki Capri pants and flat brown sandals. "We must all go and change."

"Jesus, I knew this was a bad idea."

"You said we could go." Isabel pouted, her full red lips curling down in a way that made her look even sexier than usual.

"Please, Dirk," Meg pleaded. "It won't take us long to get ready."

Dirk grunted. "I'll believe that when I see it." Izzy and Carmen both opened their mouths to argue, but he held up a hand. "Okay, fine. I'll have the limo pick us up in thirty minutes. Will that work?"

"I'll make a lunch reservation for twelve thirty," Val said, smiling, clearly eager to go along with the plan.

"Fine." Dirk walked to the door and pulled it open, walked out into the hall to talk to the guard. Izzy's suite was on Meg's floor, Val's two floors up. Carmen's suite was on the floor below.

Leaving Meg in her room under the protective eye of the security guard, Dirk walked the other three women to their rooms, alerted the guards on each floor, then came back up to Meg's.

Thirty minutes later, they were all together in the lobby, ready to go to lunch. Meg ended up sitting next to Dirk in the long black stretch limo that comfortably seated nine. She told herself to ignore the way her heart was racing, ignore the hard shoulder and sinewy thigh pressing into hers. But she couldn't ignore the look of burning intensity in Dirk's hazel eyes.

The girls were chatting, laughing, excited to be out of what felt more like a prison than a luxury hotel. All Meg could think of was the man on the seat beside her.

"I wish it was just you and me in here,"

Dirk said, low enough so no one else could hear. "I'd close the privacy panel, strip you naked, and tell the driver not to stop all night. I'd have you every way I could think of and start all over again."

Oh, dear God! Meg could hardly breathe and her insides had gone completely liquid. "You shouldn't talk like that, Dirk Reynolds. You're supposed to be thinking about keeping us safe."

"I think of that, Meg. No way would I let anyone hurt you."

"Except you."

"I wouldn't hurt you, honey. I'd never do that."

Her eyes stung. She couldn't remember a man affecting her so strongly. "Not on purpose, but in the end that's what would happen."

"You don't know that."

Across the way, Val laughed at something Izzy said, and Dirk bent to whisper in her ear. "No more sleeping on the sofa. Tonight when I come to your room, I want to sleep in your bed."

For too many reasons to count, that wasn't going to happen.

Meg flashed him a teasing smile. "We'll flip for it, macho man. Winner gets the bed. Loser sleeps on the sofa."

Dirk groaned.

"We're here!" Izzy clapped her hands excitedly as the car pulled up in front of the Mansion Restaurant, one of the most elegant dining rooms in Dallas. Outside the window, a white-coated valet hurried to open the limo door.

"I hope the food is still good," Izzy said. "My sister Gina had the tortilla soup and the chicken tagliatelle pasta with pesto and sun-dried tomatoes. I had the lobster macaroni and cheese. Everything was amazing."

"Pasta sounds fantastic," Val said. "I'm starving."

Dirk got out first, took a moment to check their surroundings; then Izzy scrambled to get out of the limo. As Carmen reached the door, a pair of long legs encased in black denim appeared in view.

"What the hell's going on?" Ethan's voice could have cut through nails.

Carmen tossed her thick black hair and smiled up at him. "Dirk — he is taking us to lunch," she said as she climbed out, making Ethan's scowl go even darker. "You are just in time to join us."

As Meg slid out, she didn't have to look to know where that scowl was directed. The knot that appeared in Ethan's jaw when Val stepped out of the limo erased any doubt.

Meg glanced at Dirk and both of them grinned.

"You should have called," Ethan said darkly. In concession to the heat, his shoulder holster was gone, his pistol clipped to the leather belt at his waist. Val could see the slight rise hidden beneath his T-shirt. She found it oddly comforting.

"When I got back to the hotel and you weren't there, I was afraid something had happened," he said. "I tried to call, but you didn't pick up."

She glanced down at the petite white leather handbag she carried. "I couldn't fit the phone in my bag. I didn't think I'd need it before we got back."

His jaw tightened. "From now on, you keep it with you. Understood?"

"You could have called Dirk," she argued. "Meg and I were with him when you left."

He tossed a hard look over his shoulder. "I tried. Call went straight to voice mail."

Dirk checked his cell as he moved the women toward the door. "Sorry. Looks like I let the battery go dead. Won't happen again."

Ethan's eyes cut back to Val. "Like I said, if you were going to leave, you should have called. It's my job to keep you safe."

"I wouldn't go off by myself. We just wanted to have lunch. Dirk agreed to take us."

Ethan scrubbed a hand over his face. "Dirk's a pushover. I would have said no."

Val just smiled and sailed past him into the opulent restaurant. "That's why I didn't call."

Ethan muttered a curse she couldn't quite hear, but his mouth edged up as he stepped in behind her. He'd been worried about her. Aside from Mom and Pops, no one had worried about her since she was ten years old.

Last night she'd been nervous about Ethan staying in her suite, but after the private supper La Belle had provided, he had simply escorted her upstairs, thoroughly checked the suite, and left. Ten minutes later, he'd returned. He was being discreet. He didn't want trouble with Beau and neither did she.

He'd arrived with laptop in hand. Once inside, he set up at the dining table and went to work answering his e-mail and checking in with his office. Val sat on the sofa in front of her own laptop, doing her best to concentrate on the Internet courses she had let lapse for the past few days.

When she glanced up, Ethan was on the

244

phone talking to Detective Hoover, the man in charge of the investigation in Seattle. From what she could hear, nothing new had turned up on the case.

All evening she worried. Would Ethan break the rules and kiss her again? Would she be the one to break the rules?

In the end, he suggested they end the evening early and go to bed. *Bed.* Just watching his lips move when he said the word had her nerves humming.

"You've got the show tomorrow night," he reminded her. "You need to get some sleep."

As if *that* was going to happen with him in the other room. But she didn't say that to Ethan.

In the morning, he left the suite before she woke up, leaving a note saying he had gone to his own room to shower and change, then returned. He was all business, as he usually was, worse since their ill-fated kiss. He escorted her to the theater for rehearsal, left her with Dirk and the rest of the La Belle security team, and went to meet his police detective friend.

Now he was here at the Mansion, standing next to a lovely arched window in the dining room, long legs splayed, hands crossed in front of him, watching over them with those intense dark eyes that missed nothing.

Seated at a round linen-draped table, Val's gaze went past the other three women to where he stood. She wondered if he would be as distant tonight, as calmly in control as he had been last night.

She wondered if he would continue to ignore her.

Val shot him another glance. She had never been very good at being ignored.

CHAPTER NINETEEN

The Music Hall was packed to overflowing. News of a second murder had sent the media into a frenzy and loaded spectators into the top row of the balcony seats. Matt Carlyle told Val the police had decided it might work in their favor to release the image of the latest note. Maybe someone out there would come forward with information.

From the dark look on Ethan's face, he didn't agree.

The pre-show began, the TV interviews rapidly descending into questions about the murders. Val stuck to the answers Matt had formulated for her and the rest of the models.

Yes, she was terribly upset that another woman had been killed, but the police weren't sure the murder of Mandy Gee was connected to the death of Delilah Larsen. Val had every confidence the Dallas Police

Department would handle the situation and make an arrest very soon. With so many capable security people watching out for the models, she wasn't afraid.

A third note like the first two, left at the murder scene, had revved media attention to even greater heights. According to the La Belle media staff, the publicity might sell even more tickets to the show.

Which was now under way, steaming along with perfect pacing, already down to the final few segments: Devil-Angel, followed by the Diamond Jubilee, then a wrap with all the models parading the length of the runway in various costumes from the show.

Trying not to think that she was taking Delilah's place in this segment, Val wore a sapphire-blue-and-silver bustier cut high on the sides, with a built-in, push-up bra that provided a sexy platform for the incredible million-dollar necklace the president of David Klein Jewelers, Jason Stern, personally draped around her neck.

She felt his long, slender fingers at her nape, lightly brushing her skin. "Hold still while I fasten the clasp."

With her hair swept up to display the stones better, the intricate, lacy pattern of diamonds fanned out in a glittering spiderweb around her throat, the platinum setting cool against her skin. As soon as the clasp clicked into place, she turned to check her image in the floor-length mirror set up backstage.

For a moment she forgot to breathe. Exhaling slowly, she stood there, completely enraptured by the sparkle of scarlet, amber, and brilliant blue glinting from each diamond prism.

"You look beautiful, Valentine." Jason Stern stood well over six feet tall. In his perfectly tailored navy suit, with his lean, athletic build, he looked every bit the high-powered executive. His thick black hair touched with silver near his temples and magnetic blue eyes only heightened the impression.

He rechecked the clasp and clicked the safety catch into place. "David Klein Jewelers couldn't have chosen a better spokesperson than you."

Her eyebrows went up as she turned to face him. "Spokesperson?"

"Of course. At least for the balance of your contract. Though the circumstances were painful, someone had to take Delilah's place. We think you make the perfect choice."

"I see." With everything that had happened, she'd forgotten that Delilah had also been the voice of David Klein. She did TV interviews and made special appearances. Val was surprised Matt Carlyle hadn't mentioned Klein's decision.

But then, he'd been up to his ears in the details of running the tour, to say nothing of handling the media after two women had been murdered.

"There'll be a bonus, of course," Stern continued. "And really, the job only requires a few extra duties. There'll be an interview wearing the jewels during the pre-show in Atlanta, along with a couple of morning TV shows, and a few online media events. Perhaps you'll join me for a late supper after the show tonight so we can discuss the details."

From the corner of her eye, she caught a glimpse of Ethan standing in the shadows not far away. He'd moved closer for this part of the show, keeping her and her million-dollar necklace in close proximity.

Even from a distance, she could read his body language. He didn't like Jason Stern standing so close. He didn't like the man's blue eyes skimming down her body with such blatant regard. He would come unglued if he thought she'd be leaving the theater with Stern after the show.

"I'll have a limousine waiting at the rear entrance," Stern went on, as if she'd already agreed. "Beau Desmond will escort you to the vehicle."

She told herself it was just part of her job. That all of this would be over by the first of September, when her contract ended and she went back to finish her last year of school.

She glanced at Ethan, saw that he had moved even closer, crossed his arms over his powerful chest in a gesture she was coming to recognize. She should have found his intrusion annoying. Instead, he made her feel safe.

She smiled into Stern's confident, attractive features. "I'm afraid I can't make it tonight, Mr. Stern."

"It's Jason, please. From now on we'll be working together."

"Jason . . . I'm sorry, but several of us already have plans, and Matthew has declared tomorrow a badly needed day of rest. Perhaps we can discuss the matter over lunch when the tour gets to Atlanta."

He smiled faintly. Half the women in the show were enamored of Jason. That he was married didn't seem to matter. From what she had heard, it certainly didn't matter to him.

He made a curt nod of his head. "I'll phone you as soon as you arrive, set up a time that's convenient."

"Three minutes, Ms. Hart!" one of the stagehands called out.

Stern made another curt bow of his head. "Until Atlanta," he said, turned, and walked away.

She wasn't completely sure why she felt such a wave of relief. Ethan uncrossed his arms and moved toward her.

His dark gaze followed Stern's movements until he disappeared, then returned to her, sliding over the necklace and down her body, a trail of fire that licked over her skin. The tension she'd been feeling returned, different now. Not nerves, just burning sexual heat.

"The diamonds suit you," Ethan said mildly, though there was something hidden in his words. "You look like you were born to wear them."

She studied his face. "I lived on the street, remember? One lesson I learned — there are a lot of things more important in life than diamonds."

A muscle tightened in his jaw. He flicked a glance to where Stern had disappeared. "You sure?"

He thought she was interested in Jason

Stern? Not hardly. She smiled. "Positive."

His broad shoulders relaxed. "Good to know."

"You're on, Valentine!" Daniel motioned her toward the stage and she hurried in that direction, not daring to look back at Ethan. She knew she would see the desire he worked so hard to hide.

Taking a deep breath, she took her place in front of the curtain and pasted a smile on her face. She reminded herself she was Valentine Hart and started striding down the runway.

Ethan heard the scuffle, the thud of heavy blows, and the sound of a muffled curse. He flicked a glance toward the stage, but Val was already finished. The necklace had been safely returned and she was back in her dressing room. Beau was nearby, along with a dozen other security people.

He headed toward the sound of men arguing, saw Pete Hernandez standing in front of two hard-looking biker types at the end of a dimly lit hall that opened into a room where stage sets were built.

A man with shaggy brown hair pulled into a ponytail wore jeans and a cutoff T-shirt that showed his ladder abs. The other man, taller, even harder, had tats running down both arms. Ethan wondered how the hell they'd gotten in.

The ponytail bobbed as the first guy swung, connected with Pete's lip, and blood sprayed into the hallway. Pete threw a solid punch that landed hard, knocking the guy a few paces backward into the construction room. The guy stayed on his feet, crouched low, and got ready for more as Hernandez followed him in.

The room was full of equipment: commercial saws, hammers of every shape and size, plywood tables, sawhorses. The smell of freshly cut wood rose up from the inch of sawdust covering the floor. The ponytail guy threw a straight-from-the-shoulder punch that hit Pete squarely in the jaw, knocking his head back. Pete staggered, tipped over a worktable, and went down like a stone.

Swearing softly, Ethan stepped into the fray. Catching the guy by his cutoff T-shirt, he spun the man around, grabbed his arm, and cranked it up behind his back, then slammed the guy's head into a half-built fake window. The man slid down moaning and didn't get up.

The guy with the tats stepped in front of his friend, arm cocked back. Ethan ducked the punch, tripped the guy, and he went sprawling, but he was too dumb to stay down and scrambled back to his feet. He growled as he charged, ramming into Ethan's middle, carrying him backward into the wall.

Ethan grunted, threw an underhanded punch to the guy's midsection that lifted him clear off his feet, one more for insurance, then shoved him away.

"Time to end this, buddy," Ethan warned.

"Fuck you, asshole." The colorful tats blurred as he swung a blow that would have been painful if it had connected. Ethan sidestepped, caught a tattooed wrist, and dragged the man forward, bent him over a wooden sawhorse in the corner, and dragged his arm behind his back. Sliding a plastic tie onto his wrist, Ethan dragged the other arm back and secured it as well.

It was over.

In seconds, he had the two men cuffed and sitting on the floor, their backs propped against the wall. When he looked up, he saw Val standing in the doorway in her stage robe, her eyes wide, a silent *O* on her lips.

"Everything's under control, Val. Go back to your dressing room."

Her gaze swung to Hernandez, who sat up on the floor with a groan. "What . . . what about Pete?"

He was only a little surprised she knew

Pete's name. She seemed to have a way of connecting with people, didn't matter where they were in the food chain.

Pete unfolded himself and started rubbing his temple, his lip swelling, his jaw already turning purple. "You don't need to worry, Ms. Hart. I'm okay."

"Let me take a look. You might have a concussion." She moved toward him, careful not to look at the two men on the floor. Ethan pulled out his radio and keyed it, called for backup from Dirk, told him to get the show doc, and inform the police they had intruders subdued in the set-building room off the east wing.

"Sorry, Ethan," Pete said as Val knelt next to him. She took the hem of his T-shirt and dabbed it against his bloody lip. "They got the jump on me. I didn't get a chance to use my radio. I'd just checked the room a few minutes earlier."

"Do you have a headache?" Val asked, urging him to lie back in the only clean spot on the sawdust-covered floor.

"I guess."

"How's your vision. Is it blurry?"

Ethan could see Pete didn't want to answer. He was a nice guy, but he was still a man, and Val was a beautiful woman.

"Tell her," Ethan said. "You need to get

this handled."

Pete sighed. "All right, yes. My eyes are fuzzy and my head hurts like a *pendejo.*"

Ethan's lips twitched. He glanced up to see Dirk bowling through the door, the show doctor on his heels.

"I've got this," the doctor said, nudging Val aside. She stood up, pulling her robe a little closer, but Ethan still caught a glimpse of a long, pretty leg.

"If you need anything," she said to the doctor. "If I can help with anything —"

"No. I've got everything I need in my case."

She glanced at Ethan. "What about those two?"

He looked at the two men, banged up, handcuffed, and bleeding. He wondered what she'd been thinking as she'd watched him take down the men.

"They're all right. Go on, Val. We've got this covered."

Pete seemed relieved when she started for the door.

"How'd the a-holes get in?" Dirk asked the minute she disappeared out of sight.

Pete pointed up. "Came in through the window. This place is old. I don't think the exterior alarm on the window is working." He grimaced as the doctor pressed a gauze pad against his bloody lip.

Dirk's gaze went from Pete to the men with the bound hands and surly attitudes. "Nice work," Dirk said to Ethan, grinning as he surveyed the shambles he and Pete had made of the construction room.

Ethan grunted. "I've been needing a good workout."

Dirk glanced back at the men. "So these guys decided to volunteer as a couple of punching bags."

Ethan flexed his fingers, unable to stop a smile.

"Probably locals," Dirk said, glancing back to the window. "Guys who've broken in before, so they knew how to get in."

"Probably. Listen, the cops'll be here any minute. They're gonna want a statement. Go check on Val, will you? Make sure she's okay. Then take a look around. If these two got in, there could be others." He turned a hard look on the guy with the ponytail. "You got any more buddies inside?"

"Fuck off."

"On my way," Dirk said and headed for the door. Clearly, they wouldn't be getting any help from the men.

Val still couldn't believe how easily Ethan had handled the two street thugs. He'd been standing in the wings when she'd finished her last segment. Seconds later, a David Klein rep had appeared, retrieved the diamond necklace, put it in the portable safe he carried, and walked away.

She'd turned to see Ethan striding down the hall, and something in the urgent way he'd moved put her on alert. Grabbing a robe off the garment rack, she'd followed, watched him take on the two vicious men.

In a way, she was proud of him. He had handled the situation quickly and efficiently, with minimal injuries to either man. It was certainly reassuring to know she was in such capable hands.

In another way, it bothered her.

As a kid in foster care, she'd seen more than her share of violence. She'd hung out with other misfit teenagers, getting into one jam after another. At sixteen, she met Bobby Rodriguez, two years older, a member of a local gang. Bobby carried a gun and knew how to use it. She might have followed him down that same path if he hadn't been killed.

Bobby's death had changed her. Since the night he'd died in her arms, she'd done everything in her power to stay away from any sort of trouble. She was determined there would never be any more violence in her life.

It was one of the reasons she'd decided to become a veterinarian. She'd learned to love animals on her foster parents' farm, learned that animals were a lot easier to deal with than gangbangers, drug dealers, and street thugs.

Her mind went back to the men Ethan had subdued. He'd made it look easy, just thrown a punch or two and had them in handcuffs. But security wasn't an easy job, and the incident could have turned out far differently. Pete's fat lip and possible concussion attested to that.

She reminded herself that Ethan was on the side of right, not wrong, the way Bobby had been.

Val let the thought settle in. Determined to shove images of the fight out of her head, she changed back into her street clothes, black skinny jeans with rhinestones on the pocket, an ivory satin blouse, a rhinestone belt, and killer, open-toed high black heels.

La Belle was throwing a celebration party back at the hotel. She would have to make at least a brief appearance. After an evening of interviews, the show itself, and Ethan's fight backstage, she wished she could simply go up to her room and fall asleep.

Then she remembered that Ethan would be sleeping on her sofa. Chances were she'd lie awake thinking about him, aching for him until the wee hours of the morning.

Val sighed. She was facing another sleepless night. At least she wouldn't have to worry about being murdered.

Chapter Twenty

By the time the Friday night performance was over and the cast and crew were loaded into buses for the ride back to the hotel, Ethan's mood was black.

Sitting in the back of the bus, he leaned against the plush velvet seat and scrubbed a hand over his face. He kept remembering Val in the diamonds, seeing the predatory gleam in Jason Stern's eyes as he fastened the necklace around her slender throat.

Stern was on the hunt. Val didn't seem to realize that, but Ethan did. Stern had plans for Val that included her warming his bed. She'd said she wasn't interested. Ethan believed her. Val wasn't the kind of woman to sleep with a married man.

But Stern was clearly on the prowl, which made Ethan wonder if the man was looking for a replacement for his last lover — possibly the woman who'd been murdered in Seattle.

Along with her job at La Belle, Delilah Larsen had represented David Klein Jewelers. Had Stern given her the diamonds missing from her safe?

And what if he had?

Bruce Hoover was convinced Delilah's lover wasn't involved in her death. Even if the man was Stern, the way he was eyeing Val made it clear he wasn't in mourning. If he'd murdered Delilah, jealousy likely wasn't the motive.

And the diamonds?

Ethan had checked the financials of Paul Boudreau, along with all the La Belle and David Klein top execs. A half million in diamonds — much less at cost to Stern — wouldn't mean squat to him.

Still, Ethan made a mental note to find out whether Delilah had been Jason Stern's mistress.

He glanced around the interior of the bus, saw Val sitting next to Megan O'Brien. With a killer still on the loose, he'd be spending another night on Val's sofa.

Inwardly, he groaned. Since the day he'd seen her scrubbing a wet dog at the Perfect Pup, he'd wanted her. Aside from her physical beauty, he'd come to respect her, admire the way she'd conquered her dismal youth to make something of herself.

After watching her help Heather and Pete, he was drawn to her compassion. Little by little, he was becoming completely obsessed.

It had never happened to him before, not this deep, primitive feeling that somehow she belonged to him. Not this burning need to drag her off somewhere and ravage her beautiful body until neither of them could move.

Sweet Jesus, he was in trouble.

Last night had been hell. Half the night, he'd been hard for her, aching to stride through the bedroom door and have her. The rest of the night he'd worried about the murders, wondered if the copycat would strike again, if he'd go after one of the models instead of a stripper or some other, more easily accessible prey.

Wondering if the first guy would crawl out of the woodwork and follow them, try to claim another victim.

As the bus pulled up in front of the Ritz, he glanced back at Val. He'd be protecting her again tonight, suffering more endless hours on her sofa. No way could he touch her. Rules were rules, and he had a job to do. He'd lost control and taken advantage of her the last time. It wasn't going to happen again.

Not unless Val came to him.

His jaw clenched. If she did, and she wanted him half as much as he wanted her, he wouldn't give a fat rat's ass about the frigging rules.

The La Belle after-party in celebration of the successful Dallas show was in full swing, the music from a five-piece orchestra filling the dance floor with models, TV personalities, top brass, and invited guests. Beneath a crystal chandelier suspended from the molded ceilings in the Ritz-Carlton's elegant ballroom, Val stood at one of the high round tables, each draped in a gold, floor-length cloth that matched the opulent decor.

Still wearing her black skinny jeans and killer high heels, shoes that were, ironically, now actually *killing* her feet, she took a sip of champagne from the half-empty flute that dangled from her fingers. Having managed to slip off by herself, she tried to pretend she wasn't exhausted. That the insanity of the evening hadn't set her nerves on the ragged edge.

She glanced around, searching the room for Ethan, saw him against the wall, legs splayed, arms crossed over his chest, watching her with his hawk-eyed, never-miss-a-thing, intense dark brown stare.

For an instant, his gaze locked with hers

and a tremor of heat slid through her. He was armed, she knew, beneath the black blazer he wore with his T-shirt and jeans. Tall and imposing, drawing flirty glances from a dozen beautiful women, he was the sexiest man in the ballroom. Or anywhere else, as far as she was concerned.

Sensual heat slid through her, making her skin feel tight and her body overly warm. She needed to get out of there before her flushed cheeks and the way her gaze kept searching him out gave her away.

Setting her champagne flute down on the table, she started walking toward the door. She didn't bother telling Ethan she was leaving. The way he'd been watching her, she was certain he knew.

She felt him behind her as she walked out of the ballroom, his long strides easily keeping pace with hers. Val kept walking, heading for the bank of elevators in the lobby and the safety of her suite.

Which wasn't safe in the least, because Ethan would be spending the night there.

"Running away?" he asked as he moved up beside her.

She sighed. "I suppose in a way I am."

"From me or just work?"

She stopped and turned. "I don't think I could get away from you even if I tried.

Could I?"

"No."

He didn't say more as they rode the elevator up to her floor. Ethan checked the suite, pronounced it clear, and left her. By the time he returned a few minutes later, using the passkey he carried, she had stripped out of her clothes and was just stepping into the shower.

Setting the temperature lower than normal in the hope of cooling her fevered skin, she ducked beneath the soothing spray and tried not to imagine him moving around in the living room. Beneath the water, her body felt hot and tight, her nipples stiff and achy.

By the time she turned off the water, her heart was beating too fast, her nerves more taut than when she'd come up to the suite. She pulled off the towel she'd wrapped around her hair, letting the heavy curls fall free, dried herself and reached for the white terry robe on the bathroom door.

Her hand paused inches away. Next to the thick hotel robe was the apricot satin she'd been wearing the morning Ethan had kissed her.

Every time she looked at it, she remembered that blazing kiss and thought how much she wanted him to do it again.

She heard him in the other room, making

a place for himself on the sofa. Her hands shook as she reached for the apricot satin robe and slid it on, lifted her hair out of the way, then pulled the robe back into place and tied the sash.

With a calming breath, she walked out of the bathroom and continued on through the bedroom. She knew if she stopped, her courage would falter. When she reached the door and pulled it open, she saw him, his back to her as he prepared himself for bed. He'd stripped off his T-shirt, leaving him in just his black jeans, the snap undone, his feet bare.

She'd noticed more than once the way his jeans cupped his sex, drawing her attention there. Now she saw how perfectly they outlined his muscular behind.

When he turned to face her, she could barely breathe. "Ethan . . ." she managed to force out. He didn't move, didn't say a word, but seeing her in the satin robe, his dark eyes turned nearly black.

She imagined him rejecting her, telling her to go back into the bedroom, reminding her that they couldn't break the rules. But for her there was no turning back.

She walked toward him, paused just a few feet away. "I know you want me." There was no denying it. She could see it in his eyes.

"I just . . . I need you to know that I want you, too."

His jaw knotted. He still didn't move.

"I thought that if . . . if —"

His low growl cut her off. In two long strides, he was there, hauling her into his arms, his mouth crashing down over hers. Her fingers dug into his powerful shoulders and she kissed him back, parted her lips and felt the hot sweep of his tongue.

A little sob escaped. She kissed him the way she had wanted to kiss him for days, the way she had never kissed a man before, kissed him with all the emotions roiling inside her. She felt his hands sliding into her hair, cupping the back of her head to hold her in place as he ravaged her mouth, plundered her lips again and again, kissed her until neither of them could breathe.

He bent his head and found her breasts, suckled her through the slick satin fabric, tongued her nipple, and she moaned. Heat and need tore through her, desire so hot and thick it was almost painful.

"Ethan," she whispered as he lifted her into his arms and started striding toward the bedroom. She closed her eyes, enjoying his strength, the hard muscles flexing as he moved.

He set her on her feet beside the bed,

cupped her face in his hands, tilted her head back and kissed her. A hot, wet, thorough kiss that set her mind to spinning and the blood rocketing through her veins.

"Jesus, I want you. I've never felt this kind of need before."

She understood. That same need scorched like lightning through her blood. And yet when he reached for her robe, a moment of uncertainty slipped through her. She stepped back before he could strip the robe away and expose her completely.

"What is it?" The words came out harsh. The muscles across his shoulders vibrated with tension.

"There's something. It's nothing, really, just that . . ."

"Tell me."

"I know you're kind of old-fashioned." She moistened her lips, growing more nervous. She wanted this to be perfect. Wanted to be perfect for Ethan. "La Belle has a rule . . . I mean, we model very skimpy lingerie."

"Go on," he said, impatience in his voice.

"It's just . . . well, it's company policy that all the girls . . . that we have to . . . we have to wax."

The implication hung in the air. When she took off the robe she'd be bare. Everywhere.

Ethan's eyes closed and a muscle flexed in his jaw. "Jesus, God, you're killing me."

"I just . . . I didn't know how you'd feel about —"

He gripped her shoulders and his mouth crushed down over hers. A long, thorough kiss and he reached for her robe, pulled it open, and slid it off her shoulders, leaving her completely naked. Hot brown eyes traveled slowly down her body, taking in every bare inch of her.

"I'm going to kiss you all over," he said gruffly. "I'm going to eat you alive." Then he was lifting her into his arms, striding over to the bed and settling her on the mattress.

He took a moment to shed his jeans, pull a condom out of his pocket, and toss it on the bedside table. Foil gleamed in the moonlight seeping in through the curtains as he joined her in bed and started kissing her again, ravaging her mouth as he had before, making her restless and hot.

Settling himself between her legs, he shifted his attention to her breasts, suckling and tasting until she squirmed beneath him. He moved lower, his tongue circling her navel, sliding across the flat plane below.

She whimpered at the feel of his lips against the inside of her thigh, nipping and kissing, moaned as he moved to her sex.

Keeping his word, he tasted, teased, devoured. Her hands fisted in the sheet as he drove her up to the peak. In minutes she reached an earth-shattering climax, a journey into pleasure that seemed to have no end.

It wasn't enough.

Her hands slid into his short dark hair. "I need . . . I need more, Ethan. I need to feel you inside me. Please, Ethan."

His eyes looked feral as he came up over her, his erection big and hard. His body felt solid and warm between her parted legs. Ethan kissed her, long and deep, eased himself inside with exquisite care. She loved the fullness, the way his powerful body pressed her into the mattress.

It wasn't enough.

She wanted to absorb him, mesh with him until they were just one being. She wanted to know him in the very marrow of her bones.

She arched beneath him, taking him deeper as he began to move. "I need more, Ethan," she whispered, bolder words than she had ever spoken. "Please."

He seemed to swell inside her. "I don't want to hurt you."

She realized he was holding himself back, fighting to stay in control. She didn't want him in control. She wanted him as wild for her as she was for him. "You won't hurt me. I want you, Ethan, please."

An animal growl tore from his throat. With fierce, powerful thrusts, he drove into her, moving faster, deeper, harder, giving her what she wanted. Driving her to a second shattering climax. She cried out his name, dug her nails into the muscles across his shoulders, and just hung on.

Ethan didn't stop. "Again," he demanded as she started spiraling down.

"I can't."

"You will," he vowed, driving deeper, claiming her in some way, and the words shot her over the edge.

Pleasure tore through her. She hadn't known it could be this good, this intense. For several seconds the world seemed to tilt, to spin on its axis. She clung to his neck and felt his body go rigid, every muscle vibrating as he reached his own release.

Time slowed and she began to float down, her mind in a soft, sensuous haze.

Ethan finally lifted himself away and left the bed to dispose of his condom. Seconds later, she heard him rummaging around in his bag in the living room, then he padded naked back to bed, a beautiful male animal outlined in the faint sliver of moon illuminating the darkness.

Her eyes widened when she saw the flash of foil, saw the stack of protection he set on the nightstand.

"I'm done with the sofa. Rules or no rules, from now on I'm in your bed."

She swallowed. She hadn't considered tomorrow. Just the burning need she'd had to assuage. She felt dazed and well-used. And more womanly than ever before.

Unease filtered through her. She had given him some part of herself she hadn't known existed. He'd given her pleasure unlike anything she'd experienced before. It should have been enough. It should have settled her, soothed the desperate yearning. And yet she wanted more.

The knowledge was frightening. Aside from their shared physical attraction, she didn't fit into his life. Ethan didn't fit into hers.

How much pain would she feel when it ended? Since the night Bobby had died, Val had never been more afraid.

CHAPTER TWENTY-ONE

Ethan awoke at dawn. He'd always been an early riser, looked forward to getting things done in the quiet hours of the morning. Lying beneath a comforter in the big king-size bed, he shifted, realized something was different today. It took a moment to remember last night and the soft curves of the woman whose naked bottom pressed intimately into his groin.

His morning erection stirred. He remembered he had broken the rules, remembered the hot night he and Val had shared. He heard her soft purr, felt her hips nudging, caught the flirty glance she tossed him over a pale shoulder covered by a fall of long honey-gold hair.

Reaching for the bedside table, he grabbed a condom and sheathed himself. Gripping her hips, he slid into her waiting warmth, taking what he wanted. Her moan was low and throaty, thick with pleasure as he moved. It didn't take long before both of them were sated.

Rolling onto his back, he listened to Val's deep breathing, knew she had drifted back to sleep. She'd been amazing last night, giving and taking, pleading and demanding. It occurred to him that the depth of sexual gratification they'd shared was new to her. If he were honest, the emotional attachment he felt made it new to him, too.

He refused to consider what that meant. He wanted her; she wanted him.

One thing he knew: Val had deep sexual needs and he was just the man to satisfy those needs. For now that was all that mattered. In the meantime, there were other things more important than pleasure.

There were murders to solve and people to protect. It was his job. That job wouldn't end until this was over, no matter what Matthew Carlyle said.

He kissed Val's temple and rolled from the bed, padded naked into the bathroom and turned on the shower. It was Saturday, a well-deserved day off, at least for Val. Once he was dressed, he would check his e-mail, see if he'd gotten a reply to the message he'd sent Sadie. He'd get his work done and let Val sleep.

At least for a while.

Dressed once more in jeans and a T-shirt, he sat down in front of the sofa, opened his laptop, and pulled up his mail. Sadie's reply popped up, along with an attachment.

Thursday night, as he'd worked through possible leads and tried to keep his mind off Val, he'd had an idea. During his cop days in Dallas, he'd stumbled across a group of local psychologists who conducted an interactive online forum once a month. They gathered to discuss unusual cases, get feedback between group members, though no patient names were ever disclosed.

He'd discovered the group when a female doctor named Helen Burk had helped him track down a dangerous schizophrenic who had murdered his parents. In the beginning, Helen had been reluctant to break doctor/patient confidentiality, but as the evidence mounted, along with fear the guy might kill someone else, she finally came forward.

Ethan had no suspect this time. Helen Burk wouldn't give him squat. Which was the reason he had e-mailed Sadie.

He opened her message.

Morning, hotshot. Did a little digging. (Find docs attached.) As you conned me — as usual — into doing, I went back through the chat sessions of the shrinks' monthly meetings for the past two years. I condensed them down so even a slow learner like you could get through them. They ought to keep you busy and out of trouble at least for a while.

His mouth edged up. He thought of the beautiful naked woman in the bedroom and arousal slid through him. *Too late, Sadie. I'm already in major-league trouble.*

He looked down at his e-mail. He had also given Sadie a profile of the man he believed he was looking for: a loner, someone off the grid, a guy who had probably been raised out of the city. Home-schooled. No vaccinations. Parents likely never took him to a doctor.

He read the words on the screen.

Oh, did I mention, I can probably save you the trouble of reading all that crap? I think I found your guy. Or at least where to start looking for him. When you get this, call me.

Sadie was such a smart-ass. Probably why he liked her so much.

He took out his cell. On Saturday, the fifty-year-old grandma, world's most unlikely computer genius, was usually working in the office. He punched in the number, then her extension.

She answered on the second ring. "Hey, hotshot. Figured I'd hear from you earlier. Bet I don't have to ask if you had a female keeping you company last night."

He smiled. "It's none of your business, Sadie. Now tell me what you found."

He heard her rustling around, probably putting on her reading glasses. "Okay . . . on a group chat six months ago, a doctor named Carl Weatherby mentioned a patient, a twenty-five-year-old male he'd been treating for a couple of weeks. He wasn't schizophrenic, according to Weatherby. But during the group chats, the doctor talked about the guy's violent tendencies, his wild mood swings, his fantasies about killing women — sinful, lustful women — those were the patient's words, according to Weatherby."

"I'm listening."

"The man only showed up at Weatherby's office a couple of times before he quit coming, but here's the kicker: The guy's Amish, Ethan. Or was. Left the community when he was fifteen. Weatherby figured his folks threw him out. *Shunning,* they call it."

"I've heard of it. As I recall, the Amish live mostly in Pennsylvania."

"Well, see, that's the interesting part.

You've got a couple of small Amish communities right there in Texas. One about a hundred miles southwest of Dallas, the other down near Beeville. You can Google their locations."

He felt a familiar rush. All the pieces clicking into place, the certainty he was on the right track. "Sadie, you're a gem."

"Don't forget those two tickets."

"I haven't forgotten. This lead pans out, I'm also buying your dinner."

She chuckled. "Take care, Ethan. Give the lady my best." Sadie disconnected and Ethan shoved the phone back into his jeans.

He Googled the Amish communities in Texas and found their locations. Sadie was right. The one near Beeville was over three hundred miles away, but the one out by Stephenville was a fairly easy drive. He'd head there first.

Pulling up a map on his iPhone, he bookmarked the directions, then went back to work on the Internet, digging up as much information as he could on the Amish in general and particularly those in Texas.

When he finished, he checked his watch.

He hadn't talked to Hannah in days. His daughter would be home today instead of in preschool. Seattle time was two hours earlier, but she would be up by now. He wanted to hear her voice, hear her call him Daddy. He wanted to absorb the sweet sound of her little-girl laughter.

Taking a deep breath and praying his ex would be reasonable for a change, he punched in Ally's number.

Val rolled out of bed, sleepy-eyed, hair mussed, body pleasantly battered and delightfully sore in places that hadn't been sore in years. She felt wonderful.

Smiling, she walked into the bathroom, washed her face and brushed her teeth. Since Ethan needed to work, she left the apricot satin robe on a chair in the bedroom, grabbed the white terry and shrugged it on, then headed toward the living room for a badly needed cup of coffee.

Dressed in dark blue jeans, a burgundy T-shirt, and low-topped boots, Ethan was on his cell when she opened the door. His angry scowl and the rigid muscles across his shoulders had her pausing on the threshold. She could only hear half the conversation, but it was enough for her to know what was going on.

"I just want to talk to her, Ally. I'm her father. That isn't asking too much."

His ex made some reply.

"Look, this has been going on for years.

You're dating someone. Haven't you gotten your revenge by now? I was a lousy boyfriend, okay? I would have been a lousy husband. But I'm a good father. I want the chance to be even better. What'll it take to get you to put the past aside and go forward, for Hannah's sake?"

Her reply made Ethan's eyes close in frustration. He came to his feet, gripping the phone so tight Val was afraid the plastic would shatter. "This is all just a game to you, isn't it? Well, I'm tired of playing, Ally. You'll be hearing from my lawyer — again. And this time I won't hold anything back. Unless you want your past sins spread all over the courtroom, I'd suggest you make some concessions." Ethan hung up the phone.

Val's heart went out to him. Clearly, he loved his little girl. So far she hadn't seen any reason he shouldn't be allowed to spend time with her. Val crossed the living room and slid her arms around his waist. Ethan pulled her close and pressed his face into the tangled curls at the side of her neck.

"That was Allison," he said when he looked at her.

"I know. I'm sorry, Ethan."

He pulled out of her arms and walked over to the window. The cloudless blue sky outside wouldn't do a thing to dull the heat.

"Ally was spoiled when I met her," he said. "Used to having everything her way. Her dad's loaded; the whole family's rich. I couldn't see past those gorgeous auburn curls and that sexy little body. I was a fool. Now Hannah is paying the price." When he turned, his eyes were hard. "I won't make the same mistake again."

It was a warning. He wouldn't allow himself to be sucked into another painful relationship. Did he really think she was like Allison Winfield?

The thought cut deep.

She met his dark-eyed stare. "I get it, Ethan. I get that you don't trust women. That you don't trust me. I need to know . . . last night? Was I just a conquest? A notch on your bedpost? Because the way you make love tells me you've known a lot of women. Was I just one more?"

Something wild and unsettling moved over his features. He was in front of her in a few long strides, pulling her into his arms, holding her tightly against him.

"I'm sorry. Jesus, that woman makes me crazy. You weren't a conquest. I've never thought of you that way." He tipped her chin up, returning her gaze to his. "I swear it, Valerie."

Her eyes burned. She read the truth in his face and she believed him. She almost wished she didn't. It would be easier to pretend last night had meant nothing to either one of them. That she was in no emotional danger, that her heart would be safe from Ethan.

He kissed her very softly, sinking in for a moment, letting her feel the heat, before he eased away. "Allison Winfield had nothing to do with what happened between us last night. She never will."

Relief and something deeper filled her chest. She managed to nod. "Okay."

Ethan ran a finger down her cheek. "God, I'd like to take you back to bed and show you how much you mean to me. But I can't. I've got a lead on the case. Until you and the other girls are safe, I've got to stay on it."

She shoved aside a memory of the rightness she'd felt when he was inside her and focused on what else he had said. "You got a lead? What is it?"

"There's a chance the guy who murdered Mandy Gee is Amish — or was. I need to find him. I need to locate someone who knows his name, see if I can get them to tell me where this guy is. I've got two possible locations in Texas, small Amish communities. One's only a couple of hours away from the city. I'm driving out there this morning."

"Take me with you. I'm off work today and I'd love to get away from the hotel. Let me go with you."

He hesitated a moment, clearly assessing the danger. Then he smiled; relieved, perhaps, that she had decided to forgive him, that she still wanted to be with him. But the truth was, his determination to be a real father only made her think more highly of him.

"I don't see any reason you can't come. The guy won't be there. He was ousted when he was a teen. And I might get more cooperation if I have a woman with me."

"Great. I'd better get dressed."

Ethan's mouth edged up, reminding her of last night, of his hot, wet kisses. *Everywhere.* Her stomach clenched.

"I had other ideas about how we'd be spending the morning," he said with a look that made her stomach tighten again. "Unfortunately, that isn't going to happen now."

Val just smiled. "I'll get dressed, but I need coffee first." She headed for the coffeemaker on the wet bar, poured herself a cup, and headed for the bedroom.

At least she wasn't just a conquest. She

wasn't sure if that made things better or worse.

CHAPTER TWENTY-TWO

The relentless, humid July heat bore down on the Texas landscape as Val sat in the passenger seat of Ethan's rented Buick. He was driving Highway 281 toward Stephenville, where he hoped to get the name of the man he suspected had killed Mandy Gee, a man who still posed a dangerous threat to the models.

The road stretched in front of them, a ribbon of black marked by a string of disappearing mirages, water you never reached no matter how far you drove. A thorny green landscape of elm and ash weighed down with dense, leafy branches; thickets of mulberry and fields of sharp-bladed grasses grew beside heavy stands of cottonwood at the edge of meandering creeks.

It was a foreign environment, unwelcoming to an outsider, reminding her why she loved the pine-forested hills of Seattle.

"You really think we'll find someone out

here who knows this man?" she asked, breaking the silence inside the car.

"It's a long shot," Ethan said. "But running on hunches is a lot of what my job is about. If we don't find anything here, I'll talk to the authorities in Beeville, see if I can find someone who'll do some legwork in the Amish community there."

"You worked in Dallas. Were you born in Texas?"

He nodded. "Little town east of the city called Sulpher Springs. My family had a ranch there, big one. Broke it up and sold most of it. Some of my cousins still raise cattle near there."

"Your parents still live in Texas?"

"My mom died a while back. Dad remarried, moved to North Carolina. He just adopted his second wife's kids."

"Will you have time to see your cousins while you're here?"

"I'd hoped to. Doesn't look like it's going to happen. Maybe I'll bring Hannah back for Christmas, give them a chance to meet her if —" He broke off the thought and just shook his head.

"Don't do that. You're going to get things worked out with Allison so that you can spend more time with Hannah."

He managed to smile. "I hope so."

Val smiled back. "So . . . you were more city boy than cowboy."

"I was always interested in law enforcement. My favorite cowboys were Texas Rangers. Most of the men in the family either have a military or police background."

He flicked her a sideways glance. "I know you were born in Michigan. You told me your folks died in a car accident. I read that much in your file when I first started working for La Belle."

"If you read my file, you got the cleaned-up version, what they gave to the press after I won the contest. It doesn't mention my time in juvie." She had told him the rest, about her cousins and how she had gotten to Seattle. She figured by now he knew everything there was to know about all of the models. It didn't bother her that he knew — not the way it had at first. Even if he didn't trust her, she trusted him.

"So you were chosen Miss La Belle. I'm not exactly sure what that means."

"The company picks a girl every year and awards her a six-month modeling contract. Being a La Belle model pays big. I entered on a whim, never thought I would actually win, but I needed money for school so I figured it was worth a try. I was chosen, and they gave me the number-ten spot. Until the murders, the job seemed like a god-send."

Ethan kept his eyes on the road, but his jaw tightened. "We're going to catch him."

"But you think there are two of them. Two killers."

"Yeah. And both of them are going down hard." He didn't say more, just checked the map on his iPhone, slowed the car, and turned off onto a narrow paved road.

Val smiled when she saw a yellow road sign up ahead with a picture of a horse and buggy. PASS WITH CARE was printed underneath.

"Looks like we're just about there," Ethan said, keeping the car at a respectful speed.

As they neared, she saw that it wasn't much of a community, just nine or ten small farms spread out along the road. A couple of double-wides, several cabinlike structures. All the farms had barns and gardens.

Their first stop went quickly. A man opened the door, gave a headshake meaning no, and she and Ethan walked back to the car. The second stop was the same, except the door was opened by a woman.

Unused to strangers, two kids ran out into the front yard to watch as the Buick drove away. They looked like children out of an old western movie, the boy with his flat hat, coveralls, bare feet, and rolled-up pants, the girl with her long, full-skirted dress, white apron, and bonnet.

Farther down the road, a wooden house with a porch extending off the front boasted a sign that read BAKERY. Ethan slowed and eased the car off the lane, careful not to stir up dust.

As they had before, both of them climbed out into the heat, the air damp and thick, making it difficult to breathe. She had chosen comfortable clothes: loose jeans, a short-sleeved, pale blue V-necked T-shirt, and sneakers, and she was very glad she had.

They knocked on the door, which was open, and a petite, gray-haired woman in full Amish dress — long gray skirt and blouse, white apron, white bonnet with the strings hanging down — walked up to the other side of the screen. The windows in the house were also open. Clearly, there was no air-conditioning.

The tiny woman spoke through the screen door. "May I help you?"

Ethan gave her a friendly smile. "I hope so. My name is Ethan Brodie. I'm a private investigator." He pulled out his ID badge and flipped it open. "I'm looking for a man. He might have lived here ten, maybe fifteen years ago. There's a chance he's involved in a murder."

As he had done at the other houses, he was being completely up-front, laying the facts out very clearly. Val had a feeling he was taking the right approach with people who lived such a straightforward, simple existence.

"This is a friend," he said, easing her forward. "She's helping me with the case. Her name is Valerie Hartman."

She hadn't heard her real name in so long it sounded foreign. She liked the way Ethan had said it that morning. At least he knew who she actually was.

"Please come in." The woman stepped back to invite them into the wood-frame house. "I'm Mrs. Bruckner. It's very warm today. Would you care for a glass of lemonade?"

"That sounds wonderful," Val said, fighting an urge to fan herself as she began to really feel the heat.

The woman smiled and headed into the kitchen off the living room, her long gathered skirt floating around her ankles. The smell of yeast and cinnamon filled the air, making Val's mouth water.

Through the opening, she could see a simple sink in a long wooden counter, the shelves underneath covered by a pretty yellow curtain. There was a small refrigerator off to one side. She had read somewhere that most groups used electricity, but there were certain rules they had to follow.

The woman returned with the lemonade, which was cold, homemade, and refreshing. Ethan took a long swallow, the muscles in his throat moving up and down. Why that looked so sexy Val couldn't possibly guess.

"Tastes great," Ethan said. "Thanks." He didn't try to hurry the conversation. Val had a feeling he thought the lady was about to tell him something important.

"Why don't we sit down?" Mrs. Bruckner suggested. She carried her own glass into the living room, then went back and got a tray of chocolate cookies. They sat down on a dark green overstuffed sofa and chairs situated around a newer, wood-burning cast-iron stove. A hooked rug in green and gold covered the spotlessly clean wooden floors.

Val couldn't resist sampling one of the cookies. Ethan took one, too, and munched it down. They were buttery, chocolatey, and delicious.

"It really isn't my place to talk to you about Byron," the little woman said. "Normally, my husband would do that. But as I'm recently widowed, I have no other choice."

"We're very sorry to hear about your husband, Mrs. Bruckner," Val said for both of them, meaning it, thinking how difficult losing a lifelong mate must be.

"Thank you. Now that you understand my circumstances, I feel it's my duty to tell you what I know. I pray the man you are seeking isn't Byron Mahler, but I feel no loyalty to him anymore."

Ethan made no comment. Letting Mrs. Bruckner set the pace, he took a sip of his lemonade.

"Byron Mahler was born at his parents' home in Ohio. His mother and father were good Amish farmers who moved to Texas to begin a settlement. With the weather and the harsh landscape it was very difficult, and a number of the families left the area. Jacob Mahler refused to give up. One day, Ruth Mahler, Byron's mother, just up and left. She abandoned her husband and son and never returned."

The small woman's hand shook as she took a sip of her lemonade. "Byron changed after that. He was twelve at the time, just beginning to discover girls. After his mother left, he was bitter toward women of any age. He felt they were nothing but worthless creatures put on the earth to do a man's bidding, particularly his. He began to pick on the younger girls in school. Several times he took liberties with their persons. His father tried to intervene, but disciplining Byron only made him worse."

"What happened?" Ethan asked when she didn't continue.

"When he was fifteen, there was a girl, a lovely young woman a year younger than Byron. He cornered her out in the barn and tried to rape her. Her brother stumbled onto him or he would have succeeded."

"Fifteen."

"That's right. There was a meeting after it happened. A very harsh punishment was handed out. Byron took the punishment, but he refused to apologize to the girl. He said her sinful ways were to blame for his actions. He was forced to leave. His father tried to get him help with friends in other communities, but Byron just disappeared. No one has seen him since."

"Is his father still around?"

"No. Jacob built furniture. He taught his craft to Byron, but Jacob died a few years after his son left home."

"Any other family? Anyone else here who might be able to give us information on Byron's whereabouts?"

"Not that I know of. No one's been in

contact with Byron for more than ten years."

"One last thing," Ethan said. "As I look around, I don't see any photographs. I'm guessing you don't have any pictures that might include Byron Mahler."

"Exodus 20:4, Mr. Brodie. Thou shalt not make any graven images. Though photographs are occasionally taken of us by outsiders, you will rarely see anyone face-on."

"The police need to find this man, Mrs. Bruckner. I was at the home of the woman who was murdered. What happened to her was brutal beyond description. Would you consider talking to a sketch artist, allowing someone to come here and draw a picture of Mahler as you remember him?"

She shook her head. "I don't think I can do that. At least not without speaking to the others. Perhaps they will agree. Murder is a serious crime. They will want to help if they can."

"All right. In the meantime, could you at least give me a basic description? I understand Byron was only fifteen, but was he tall? Short? Blond? Dark? Anything would be helpful."

The petite woman took a deep breath. For a moment, she closed her eyes, as if trying to dredge up memories. "At fifteen, Byron was tall for his age and quite thin, a gangly young man who rarely smiled. He was dark-haired, but his eyes were a very pale shade of blue. Aside from that, he was an average-looking teenage boy. Oh, except for the scar on his forearm."

Ethan straightened. "Tell me about the scar."

"He and his father were cutting wood with a whipsaw when something went wrong. The boy was badly injured. The accident left him with a scar about ten inches long on his forearm."

When the woman fell silent, Ethan dug out a business card and handed it over. "You've been a very big help, Mrs. Bruckner. With luck, we won't need to involve you in this any further. But if Byron Mahler is the man who murdered the young woman in Dallas, he needs to be stopped. With what you've told us, we may be able to make that happen."

"You did the right thing," Val said, reaching over to squeeze the woman's hand. "I believe it's what your husband would have wanted you to do."

The woman's eyes glistened. She brushed a drop of wetness from her cheek. "Thank you, dear, for saying that."

Mrs. Bruckner walked them to the door,

and they stepped out onto the porch. Ethan's hand settled at Val's waist as he guided her back to the rental car.

CHAPTER TWENTY-THREE

Just before they reached the highway, Ethan pulled the car to the side of the road. He didn't turn off the engine, just left it running and the air conditioner on.

"What are you doing?" Val asked, watching him work his iPhone.

"Googling Byron Mahler. Seeing if there's any chance he'll show up on the Internet. These days you never know."

"I'll check Facebook." Val pulled out her own cell and started working.

After eliminating a number of people with the same name who didn't match the description, they both came up with zip.

Next Ethan phoned Heath Ford. "I've got a name," he said when his friend answered. "Anonymous tip came in this morning. Pointed to a suspect who fits our profile."

"Anonymous? That your way of telling me not to ask how you came up with the info?"

Ethan smiled. "Yeah. Suspect's a twenty-five-year-old white male named Byron Mahler. He's Amish, Heath, or at least he was until they ousted him ten years ago for the attempted rape of a young Amish woman. He was raised in a community near Stephenville. I'm on my way back from there now."

"You get a description?"

"At fifteen, he was tall and thin. Very light blue eyes and a ten-inch scar on his forearm. A lady who lives there gave me the info."

"That'll help, if we can find him."

"I tried the Internet. No sign of him on Google or Facebook."

"We need to get a sketch artist out there to talk to the woman. Any chance of that happening?"

"Could be, but it'll take some doing. Graven images aren't popular with the Amish. You'd have to computer age it anyway."

"It's not a lot to go on, but it's way more than we had before. I'll put out a BOLO with that description, try to locate Mahler as a person of interest."

"One more thing. His father was a furniture maker. Kid learned the trade. That's how he got the scar."

"I'm on it. Thanks, Ethan." Heath ended the call, and Ethan pulled the car out onto the road.

"You're convinced it's him?" Val asked. "The copycat?"

"Yeah. Feels right. Has since I got the e-mail from Sadie this morning."

"Sadie? She's a . . . friend?"

He flicked her an amused glance. "Why? You jealous?"

Val sat a little straighter in the seat. "No, of course not."

Ethan chuckled. "Sadie Gunderson is a fifty-year-old grandmother. She works with me at the office. Believe it or not, she's a computer genius."

Val grinned so wide her dimples popped out. Ethan felt the familiar kick and his groin tightened. He clamped down on a rush of lust that wasn't going anywhere, at least not at the moment. Those damned dimples were going to be the death of him.

"You're right," she said. "It's hard to believe. It'd be more likely Sadie was a ten-year-old kid."

He smiled. "I wouldn't believe it either if it weren't for the info the woman comes up with."

Val relaxed back into her seat. "So what's our next move?"

"Our?" He shook his head. "Sorry, honey. You're a hundred miles from Dallas. That's as close as you're getting to this case. My next move is searching the Internet for stores in the Dallas area that sell handmade furniture. If that was Jacob Mahler's trade, there's a chance that's what his son is doing for a living. Heath Ford will be following that angle. If he comes up empty-handed, I'll have Sadie take a look."

"Heath was the guy on the phone? Your detective friend?"

"That's right. I'll let him have a go at it while we're driving back to the city."

She leaned forward, tilting her face into the cool air blowing out of the air-conditioning vents. "I'll be glad when we get there. I turned the A/C down when we left the suite so it would be nice and cool when we got back."

He flashed her a sideways glance. "Considering how hot I plan to make your luscious little body as soon as I get you upstairs, that was very good thinking."

Her big blue eyes widened.

"Maybe you ought to take a nap on the way. I promise you won't be getting much sleep tonight."

Val made a funny little sound in her throat, and Ethan chuckled. He wondered if she thought he was kidding. He might have to work this new lead for a while. After that, he meant to keep his word.

It was late afternoon when Meg preceded Dirk back into her suite. She'd convinced him to take her and Isabel shopping at the NorthPark Center, home to some of the most exclusive stores in Dallas. Grudgingly, he had agreed.

Unfortunately, as soon as they went into the mall, Dirk began to complain. He didn't like the limo having to park so far away. It was darker inside the mall than he liked, and more crowded. He wanted to go some-where else, someplace safer. It took Izzy's considerable charm to convince him to stay.

"No one even knows we're here," Isabel said. "And you're here to protect us."

Meg smiled at him sweetly. "We know you can keep us safe."

Dirk wasn't fooled for a minute, but clearly he was torn. He wanted to please them, but it was his job to protect them. He was cute when he was frustrated, Meg thought. Of course, he was cute when he was angry and cute when he was being sweet, which he was by taking them to the mall.

Her gaze ran over his masculine carved features, the way his mustache curved down to his hard jaw. Maybe sexy was a better word than cute.

"All right, fine, you can stay," he reluctantly agreed, as Meg was sure he would. "But you'd better stay close, and if anything happens, you do exactly what I say." He drilled her with a glare. "Understood?"

"Of course," she said breezily, because it was true. Dirk wasn't the kind of man you disobeyed.

Still, the whole time they were shopping, he was moving, constantly on alert, always on the lookout for trouble, which made it hard for Meg to relax. Fortunately, Izzy's incessant chatter helped keep up her spirits. They deserved to have some fun, whether Dirk Reynolds liked it or not.

Inside the air-conditioned corridors, they continued perusing the mall, darting from one store to the next, shopping until Dirk began to grumble again and even Isabel's energy was beginning to fade.

Dirk phoned the limo driver and the car was waiting when they reached the exit. They climbed inside, loaded down with purchases, Izzy with a fantastic Chanel designer handbag and three pairs of Manolo Blahnik shoes. Meg had found two pairs of Jimmy Choos on sale and bought a sexy, backless little black sheath at Neiman Marcus.

Mostly, she'd purchased kid's clothes, stuff for little Charlie, including a pair of miniature Burberry jeans lined with red-plaid flannel that were just darling.

As the limo drove back to the hotel, she looked over at Dirk, who lounged on the seat a few feet away. Every time she'd purchased another item for her son, his mood seemed to darken. It made her chest hurt to know how deep his dislike of children ran.

Once they reached the hotel, Dirk escorted both women through the lobby to the elevators, a bellman in their wake carrying their packages.

"*Grazie,* Dirk," Isabel said, "for putting up with us this afternoon." Izzy leaned over and kissed both his cheeks. "Now, I must have my beauty nap. *Ciao,* darlings. I will see you on the plane."

"Keep the door locked," Dirk grumbled as the heavy door slid closed. They headed for Meg's suite, the bellman following with her packages. Dirk checked the rooms. The bellman set the shopping bags down on the coffee table, walked out, and closed the door, leaving them alone.

Fatigue rolled through her. Meg felt the weight of Dirk's dark gaze and, knowing the

305

cause, her heart filled with an aching sadness.

"You don't have to stay," she said softly. "There's a guard just down the hall, and aside from Valentine, none of the other girls have full-time bodyguards."

"You have the day off and so do I. I'd rather spend my time with you."

It wasn't true. He was just overly protective, and for some reason those protective instincts had zeroed in on her.

Meg clenched her hands together. "I appreciate your concern, but really, I don't need —"

One step and he was there, gripping her shoulders, cutting off her words. "You don't need what, Meg? I saw the way you were looking at me today. Every time you bought a gift for your son, you looked at me like you wanted to cry. I know you feel something for me. More than something. And I've made no secret of the way I feel about you."

Her chin went up. "You want to have sex with me. You're a man. I'm a La Belle model. Of course that's what you want."

"Bullshit. I want you, yes. So bad I ache with it. But it's more than that, and I think it's more for you, too. Just because you have a child doesn't mean you can't have a man in your life."

"You aren't just any man, Dirk. You're wild and you're fierce. For heaven's sake, you've got tattoos! You carry a pistol and ride around on a Harley. You're not the kind of man who can settle down and raise a child!"

His jaw hardened. "That coming from a woman who's traveling around the country flashing her mostly naked body in front of a million sex-starved men."

She jerked a hand back to slap him, but Dirk didn't give her the chance, just caught her wrist and hauled her into his arms, and his mouth slanted down over hers. Heat tore through her, and a need so fierce it made her dizzy.

Her knees went weak and her pulse shot into the triple digits. Dirk just kept kissing her, first one way and then another, soft kisses, gentle and coaxing, then hot, hard, and demanding.

Meg moaned into his mouth and gripped his hard-muscled shoulders, her body on fire for him.

"You want me," Dirk whispered softly. "Admit it." He kissed her again before she could deny it. "Tell me you want me the way I want you."

She looked up at him and her throat

tightened. It could never work and both of them knew it. "I want you. You know I do."

"Yes, I do. And for both our sakes, I'm not waiting any longer." Forcing her back till she came up against the wall, he lifted her off her feet and wrapped her long legs around his waist, pushing her pencil skirt up around her middle. Dirk found her sex and stroked her through the tiny strip of satin between her legs. She was wet and ready, aching for him to take her.

"I've only just found you," he said, pressing his mouth against the side of her neck. "I'm not letting you go." She heard the buzz of his zipper. Then he was sliding inside, driving deep, giving her what she so desperately wanted.

She cried out as he took her, her body responding, climbing toward the peak, then bursting free. Her head dropped forward onto his shoulder as she rode out the wave, then came again.

She was crying when he set her on her feet, filled with emotions she didn't understand and didn't dare examine. Kissing the top of her head, Dirk left her to dispose of the condom she hadn't known he'd used.

"Don't cry," he said, easing her back into his arms, kissing the tears from her cheeks. "It's going to be all right. I promise."

But there was no way he could keep his word. He was wild and free, exactly the way he should be. She looked down at the tattoo of a dragon curling around his shoulder, climbing the side of his neck.

It wouldn't work. And yet when he carried her to bed and started kissing her again, she didn't try to stop him.

Where Dirk Reynolds was concerned, she didn't have the will to say no.

The afternoon was over and Val was back in her suite. Sitting on the sofa in front of her laptop, she went over some of the study questions for the veterinary tech online surgical prep course she was taking, but she couldn't seem to concentrate.

Watching Ethan at work on his computer, she felt as if she needed to do something to help him, something besides sitting there being protected, being a liability instead of an asset.

She fidgeted on the sofa, her gaze returning to where he sat at the dining table, head bent over his computer. She was mad for him — she couldn't deny it. The man was sex and virility personified. She kept thinking about last night, remembering what it was like to have him make love to her. She wanted more, wanted him to take her back to bed.

Which, by his occasional hot glances, she knew he would be more than willing to do if he weren't trying to catch a killer.

With a sigh, she gave up and turned off her laptop, found herself watching him again. He was searching the Internet for information on Byron Mahler, digging around for something, anything that would help the police find him.

Just the way the muscles across his shoulders tightened beneath his T-shirt made her feel hot and needy. It was embarrassing.

He sat back in his chair and blew out a frustrated breath. At the sound of his cell phone chiming, he dug it out of his jeans and pressed it against his ear. Val could only hear half the conversation, but from what she picked up, she figured it was his friend, Detective Ford.

"So you found him," Ethan said. Cell in hand, he stood and paced over to the window, looked down at the traffic moving along the street below. "Exactly. Now all we have to do is figure out where he's gone. All right, yeah. Keep me posted." He ended the call and started walking back across the room.

"Was it Ford?"

"Yeah. They located Byron Mahler's place of employment. Store just north of Dallas, sells Amish furniture."

"Just like you thought. I take it he wasn't there."

"No."

"That's not good news. Still, I'm impressed. You've been ahead of this every step of the way."

His mouth edged up. "I've been at it a while. The thing is, Mahler's in the wind. He hasn't shown up at work for the last three days."

She stood up from the sofa and walked toward him. "Are they sure Mahler's the man who killed Mandy Gee?"

"It's him. Store manager gave them his address. Mahler's packed up and gone, but the cops got fingerprints that match the ones found at the crime scene. They'll send a sketch artist out to talk to the store owner, get a decent description. Mahler's our guy, but there's no way to know where he might be headed."

Worry slipped through her. "You don't . . . you don't think he'll follow the show to Atlanta?"

"My gut says he might. Which means we can't afford to take chances."

"But you don't think this is the man who

311

killed Delilah. So we have to worry about him, too."

A muscle flexed in his jaw. "You don't have to worry about anything but doing your job, baby. I'm the one getting paid to worry."

CHAPTER TWENTY-FOUR

The Fox Theatre in Midtown Atlanta was even bigger and more problematic than the Music Hall in Dallas. Called the Fabulous Fox, it was built in 1929, one of the great movie houses of the pre-Depression era. Done in an Arabian motif, the auditorium boasted an image of the night sky filled with crystal stars and clouds that drifted across a midnight-blue ceiling.

There were ballrooms and smaller private venues, rooms as opulent as a sultan's palace, a maze of chambers and hallways that offered potential hiding places for any determined intruder.

It was a security nightmare and to make matters worse, the top floor of the theater was a thirty-six-hundred square-foot apartment. The tenant, in his late eighties, was an icon in the community who had worked at the Fox since the seventies and been granted a lease for life.

313

The apartment was hands-off to the La Belle security crew. They would have to do exterior surveillance only and hope it was enough.

"All right, you guys, listen up," Ethan said. His team surrounded him backstage on Monday morning. Matt Carlyle had pulled Beau Desmond and the La Belle crew in as well, and they fanned out behind Ethan's men. Since he'd been working with the Dallas police, Ethan had the most recent, most accurate information on the Mandy Gee slaying, information that might help keep the models safe.

Desmond and his buddy, Bick Gallagher, weren't happy Carlyle had put Ethan in charge.

"You've all been briefed on the Mandy Gee murder," Ethan began. "You also know her killer is still out there. He could be lounging on a beach in Florida. Or he could be right here in Atlanta, looking for a way to murder another woman. He couldn't get to the models in Dallas, but that doesn't mean he won't try it here. Which means we've got to have this place completely secure by this afternoon, when the women arrive to start rehearsing."

"Bick says they're letting the press in on Tuesday," one of the La Belle crew said, a fireplug of a guy with enough lumps on his face to look like he'd been cage fighting for the last ten years. "Is that right?"

Ethan nodded. "That's right. They'll be here Tuesday before the dress rehearsal instead of before the show on Wednesday. Mr. Carlyle hopes to get a little more momentum, get some additional promo."

"I don't see why he's worried," Sandy Sandowski said. "From what I hear, the show's already sold out."

"More press sells more lingerie," Ethan said. "It's as simple as that. Plus having it done a day earlier takes some of the pressure off the models the night of the performance."

"Anything new on this Mahler?" Joe Posey asked. They'd all been told the name of the primary suspect and been given a brief description, including his pale blue eyes and the scar on his forearm.

"I talked to Detective Ford in Dallas this morning." Ethan pulled out a folded piece of paper he'd made on the printer in Val's suite. "This is a copy of the composite sketch Ford e-mailed me earlier. If you see anyone who looks remotely like this guy, call for backup. Don't take chances. Don't try to take him down, but keep the guy in sight until the police get there."

"You really think he'll show?" asked one of Desmond's men, a guy with ropy muscles, long brown hair gooped back and tucked behind his ears.

"There's a chance he might," Ethan said.

"Guy's got every cop in the South looking for his sorry ass," Joe said. "I figure he'll hole up somewhere till things die down."

"Could be," Ethan said. "But a creep like this, he's crossed some invisible line in his head. He's tasted blood and he wants more. Keep your eyes open. You don't want that blood to be yours."

The men mumbled their agreement.

Ethan looked over, caught Beau Desmond's thin-lipped expression. "Anything you want to add, Beau?" He wasn't fond of Desmond, but it was always better to keep the peace whenever possible.

"Yeah, I got something to add. Mr. Carlyle expects you men to keep the women safe. Do whatever it takes to make sure that happens. That's what you get paid for. You see something, you handle it. That's why we're here. We don't need the fuckin' cops doing our job for us." He flicked Ethan a challenging glance.

Ethan kept his mouth shut. If Beau wanted to get one of his men killed, all they had to do was follow his advice.

"If there's nothing else," Ethan said, "you're dismissed. My guys, I want one more word." The other men filed away, along with Gallagher and Desmond.

"You remember what I said earlier?" Ethan said.

"Yes, sir," they agreed in unison.

"We call for backup," Joe said, clarifying Ethan's orders. "And keep the guy in sight till the cops get here."

"That's right. Keep your eyes open. Look for anything out of the ordinary. We've got a lot more to worry about than just this one guy. They still haven't found the guy who murdered Delilah Larsen in Seattle. Stay sharp and stay safe. For now, that's all."

The men dispersed. They had a lot to do to secure the building before rehearsal started at noon.

It was late, dusk setting over the landscape by the time rehearsal was over. Val sat in the bus next to Meg, Izzy, Carmen, and the first batch of models heading back to the Four Seasons Hotel, where the tour was staying in Atlanta. Ethan and Dirk accompanied them, Dirk riding in front, Ethan in the rear. Bick and Beau, the dynamic duo, as Meg had dubbed them, were on the second bus, which followed a few blocks behind.

Val was just calming down, her nerves settling after her performance onstage. It was always that way, even during rehearsal. It took a moment to realize the muffled ringing in the bottom of her purse was someone calling on her cell.

Hurriedly digging out her phone, she checked the caller ID but didn't recognize the number. "This is Val."

"Valentine, it's Jason. I gather you've all arrived safely."

The smooth male voice sent a fresh wave of nerves sliding through her. "Hello, Mr. Stern."

"Jason . . . please. Surely we're past formalities at this point, aren't we?"

Not really, Val thought. "Of course . . . Jason."

"That's better. Now that you're here in Atlanta and settled in, we need to discuss your schedule for the next two days. Will supper work for you?"

She didn't want to go. She had an uneasy feeling about Jason Stern. But she worked for La Belle, which made Stern one of her bosses. She could only put him off so long. "Yes, I suppose I can make supper work."

"Good. I'm staying at the St. Regis. I'll send a car to pick you up . . . say quarter to eight?"

She flicked a glance at Ethan, who was watching from his seat a few feet away. "All right."

Satisfaction surfaced in Jason's voice. "Then it's settled. I look forward to seeing you tonight." The call ended and Val stuck the phone back into her purse.

Meg nudged her shoulder. "That sounded a lot like a date, girlfriend. I thought you and Ethan were . . . involved."

"We're not involved. Well, not exactly. And it isn't a date. Jason Stern wants to discuss my interview schedule as spokesperson for David Klein."

Meg laughed. "That's what he's calling it? A discussion? Everyone knows what a hound dog that man is. Whatever you do, don't let him get you alone."

Val flicked a glance at Ethan, glad he couldn't hear the conversation. "He's taking me to supper tonight at the St. Regis. I should be safe enough there, don't you think?"

"My guess? It'll be supper in his suite, followed by him pressing you to join him in bed. And I mean pressing. Jason Stern is not the kind of guy who takes no for an answer."

Worry filtered through her. Apparently, Ethan was right. "Has he come onto you that way?"

Meg shook her head, shifting her silky flyaway red hair across her shoulders. "Not me. Jason prefers blondes." Meg leaned closer. "Izzy told me he was seeing Delilah before she was killed. Now that Dee's out of the picture, he's looking for someone new."

Val's interest sharpened. "Wow, Stern was the guy she was seeing? Do the police know they were having an affair?"

"They know. Izzy says they investigated any involvement Jason might have had in the murder, but he was completely cleared. Paul Boudreau leaned on his friends at the police department to keep Stern's name out of the papers."

"I knew she was seeing someone. I didn't know it was Stern."

"Izzy and Dee were friendly. According to Izzy, Dee gloried in the attention Stern paid her. He was extremely wealthy, president of the company and all that. And in fairness, Jason is a very attractive man, at least on the surface."

"He's handsome enough, I guess, but there's something a little too slick about him."

"I guess Delilah didn't see it. Add to that, he gave her very expensive jewelry. She said owning the diamonds gave her a sense of security. You know, something to hang on to when her days as a model were over."

"Well, if Stern is looking for a replacement, he's looking in the wrong direction. I don't need his brand of security."

"Then I'd advise you to get out of your date."

Val looked over at Ethan. She worked for La Belle. She'd signed a contract that wouldn't be up until the end of the tour. Aside from keeping her word, she needed the money to finish her last year of college. No way could she avoid meeting with Stern.

But maybe she could find a way to make sure he behaved.

CHAPTER TWENTY-FIVE

It was after six P.M. when Ethan stood in the living room of Val's plush hotel suite. The Four Seasons in Midtown Atlanta was first class all the way. A La Belle model definitely lived the good life.

But a lot was required of them.

By the end of the lengthy rehearsal, Ethan could read the exhaustion in Val's pretty face, in the way she rubbed the aching muscles at the back of her neck. The stage setup at the Fox was completely different from the Music Hall in Dallas, which meant there was a whole new routine for the models to learn.

In Dallas, Val had had most of her evenings free, but in Atlanta, she was required to attend several different evening functions. She had some sort of dinner scheduled for tonight, then a private event tomorrow evening, a charity benefit at the home of a wealthy Atlanta businessman. In the morning, she had to be up early for a TV interview.

As much as he wanted to follow her into the bathroom and join her while she showered, there wasn't much time, and he had his own work to do.

He wasn't getting paid to have sex with a beautiful model. His job was to protect the women and solve the murders that plagued the show.

First he phoned Bruce Hoover, where the time was three hours earlier. The killer in Seattle was the man Ethan was most worried about. He'd sent notes to ten women and managed to put La Belle's top model in her grave. He was methodical, efficient, and immaculate, leaving not a trace of himself, not a single clue. Everything about the murder shouted the guy was a pro.

Everything but the notes.

It didn't make sense. Which didn't mean the wack job couldn't be ex-military, ex-cop, ex-spook, or just a skillful serial murderer.

He dialed Hoover, who answered on the second ring. "Afternoon, Detective."

"What do you want, Brodie?"

"I was hoping to hear from you. Since I haven't, I figured I'd call. What's the latest on the Larsen murder?"

"You haven't heard from me because I got nothing to tell you. We looked for similar unsolved cases, similar MO, came up with nada. The guy's not a serial, or if he is, this is his first time out. We canvassed the area around the condo again, but nobody was up at that hour. No one saw a damn thing. For now, we've reached a dead end. How 'bout you? I hear you got a copycat down in Texas. Murdered some poor stripper."

"That's right. Guy named Byron Mahler. Lives in Dallas. Completely different MO except for leaving a similar note — which, thanks to our friends in the media, I figure he made up from the ones on TV."

"Sounds about right."

"Mahler's in the wind. Which means he may have followed us to Atlanta."

"Could well be. Plus our Seattle creeper might just be there, too. You don't think Boudreau ought to cancel the tour?"

"I'd suggest it if I thought there was a snowball's chance in hell he'd listen. Too much money at stake."

"You better do your job, then, my friend. We don't need any more bodies."

"You got that right." Ethan broke the connection.

His next call was to Heath Ford. "It's Ethan. You got anything?"

"No sign of Mahler," Ford said. "We got every cop between Texas and Georgia on the lookout for this guy. I do have something for you . . . or I should say *someone*. Friend in the Atlanta PD. Name's Rick Melon. Good guy. I gave him your cell number, asked him to keep you posted."

"Rick Melon. Thanks, Heath."

"We're gonna find this guy, Ethan. Sooner or later."

"Make it sooner," Ethan said.

Heath chuckled and hung up the phone.

Ethan had one more call to make, this one personal. He hit the contact button for his attorney, Frank Gibbs, in Seattle.

"Frank, it's Ethan. You get those papers filed?"

"I took care of it. All done nice and legal. The court isn't likely to give you full custody of Hannah — the mother has to be dangerous to herself or the child, a hopeless addict, or damn near certifiable for that to happen. But with any luck, the filing will scare the bejesus out of your ex. You've already been granted visitation, two nights a week and every other weekend. That's more than reasonable, which Allison is bound to know. The idea is to press her into abiding by the ruling."

"And if she doesn't?"

"We'll move forward in whatever way we can."

Ethan nodded, satisfied his attorney was doing the best he could. "Thanks, Frank." Ethan ended the call. Beyond the attorney/client relationship they shared, he and Frank were friends. Ethan did PI work for Frank; Frank did whatever legal work Ethan needed.

Ignoring the frustration he continued to feel about his situation with Hannah, he checked the time on his wristwatch. Almost seven thirty. He could hear Val moving around in the bedroom, then the door opened and she walked out into the living room.

For an instant he just stared. She was wearing a simple black dress that showed off her long, pretty legs, but had cap sleeves and a very modest scoop neckline. Her honey-gold hair, pulled back in a knot at the nape of her neck, gleamed in the lamplight. Only a hint of makeup touched her eyes and lips. She looked more like a schoolteacher than a model, and for reasons he couldn't explain, it really turned him on.

"You look luscious, baby. Let me grab my pistol and my blazer and we're out of here. I assume your supper is going to be somewhere downstairs."

"Actually, it's . . . umm . . . going to be at the St. Regis."

He frowned. "Been better if you'd given me some notice. I'll get a couple of my guys to go over and check things out before we leave. Is your supper in the dining room?"

She bit her lip. "I'm not really sure. I'm hoping it's in the dining room, but . . ."

Something was off. He could feel it. "But . . . ?"

"But the thing is, Ethan, I'm having dinner with Jason Stern. We're supposed to discuss my speaking schedule for David Klein."

Tension slid into his shoulders. A muscle tightened in his jaw. "You're having dinner with Stern," he repeated softly, the words requiring his complete control.

"Yes. I don't want to go, but I signed a contract. Stern is one of my bosses."

His body went solid. *She's your client,* he told himself. *Sleeping with her doesn't change the job.*

"I don't like it," he heard himself saying. "Stern doesn't want supper. He wants you in his bed."

She walked straight to him, rested her palms on his chest. "I'm afraid you might be right. I heard today that Jason and Delilah were having an affair. Now that she's dead, Meg thinks he's looking for another mistress."

"But you aren't interested." The words came out as a challenge. Stern was rich and handsome. Maybe he'd been wrong. Maybe Val was *extremely* interested.

"No, I'm not. I'm definitely not interested in Jason Stern. But I have to go anyway. Meg says Stern can be pushy. If you're there, I know I'll be okay."

He blinked. She wanted him there? She expected him to stay close while she was with Stern? The tension slid out of the back of his neck. He wished it didn't matter as much as it did.

He gently caught her shoulders. "You'll be okay, baby — I promise you that. You don't have to worry about Stern or anyone else."

As Meg had predicted, Jason was waiting in the lobby to escort Val up to his suite.

"I thought it would be quieter there, more private, easier for us to talk," he said, as if being alone with him made perfect sense. In an elegantly tailored navy-blue designer suit, his brown hair perfectly cut and styled, Jason was an attractive man. To Val, his too-smooth appearance wasn't a turn-on in the least.

Still, she gave him a smile. "Whatever you

think." Taking his arm, she started walking toward the elevators, crossing the magnificent two-story lobby with its sweeping white marble staircases, past the huge white floral bouquet on the round glass table.

Arm in arm, they walked beneath glittering crystal chandeliers into the elevator, and Stern pushed the button for an upper floor.

The doors were almost closed when a broad shoulder nudged them back open and Ethan walked in. With a nod to Stern, he chose a spot a few feet away, widened his stance, and crossed his hands in front of him.

"That's my bodyguard, Ethan Brodie." Val smiled at Jason. "Mr. Carlyle handpicked him for the job."

Stern turned a hard look on Ethan. "Ms. Hart will be under my protection this evening, Brodie. Consider this a night off."

Ethan's mouth edged up, but it wasn't a smile. "Sorry. That isn't going to happen. There are two murderers on the loose. Until they're caught, the women don't go anywhere without protection."

"That's ridiculous. She'll be safe enough in my suite."

Ethan made no reply. Clearly, he didn't agree. Neither did Val. At the moment, she was fairly certain she was in more danger from Jason Stern than anyone else.

The elevator bell dinged their arrival. Val turned and walked out into the hall. Stern followed, and Ethan fell in behind them.

They waited in front of a double-doored room marked Premier Terrace Suite while Jason used his key card to open the lock. Ethan stepped past him into the entry, walked into the all-white living room with its big glass windows and magnificent marble fireplace, then did a thorough check of the bedroom and baths.

"It's clear," he said, tossing a glance at the linen-draped table set with gold-rimmed china and sparkling crystal. A cloth-covered wheeled cart sat next to it, the food beneath the silver domes ready to be served.

"Supper smells great," Ethan said with false politeness. "The bed's all turned back. I'd say you've got everything ready."

Val's skin crawled. Dear God, Meg was right! Stern planned to seduce her. She clamped down on the urge to run out of the room. A glance at Ethan, standing rock solid next to the door, steadied her.

"You've checked things out," Stern said. "You know there's no one in here. You can go now."

Ethan ignored him, just stood beside the front door, long legs splayed, in full bodyguard mode.

Val hid a smile. "Ethan's a professional," she said to Stern. "You won't even know he's here."

Jason's face went red. He looked like his head was about to explode. From the corner of her eye, she caught a hint of amusement in Ethan's handsome face.

Fighting a grin, Val crossed the living room into the dining area. The polished mahogany table was large enough to seat eight. Through the windows, the glittering lights of Atlanta stretched for miles in the distance.

Stern moved behind her and pulled out her chair, waited for her to be seated, then pulled out a chair at the end of the table, seating himself beside instead of across from her.

An hour into the meal, Ethan's amusement had faded, replaced by a dark look that turned into a scowl when Stern reached over and took hold of her hand. By then, Jason had emptied a bottle of Dom Perignon and served her the dinner waiting beneath the silver domes.

A kale salad with roasted hazelnuts, followed by fresh Atlantic halibut and baby peas, each course paired with a glass of vintage French wine, which Jason deliberately over-poured.

Though Val was determined not to let him get her drunk, she felt a little tipsy.

Perhaps that was the reason she started asking questions she probably shouldn't. But she had been trying to think of a way to help Ethan with his murder investigation, and after what Meg had told her about Stern and Delilah, tonight presented the perfect opportunity.

Pretending to be drunker than she actually was, she leaned toward him across the table. "I want you to know how much I appreciate your giving me Delilah's job, Jason. It's a privilege to work with such a well-respected businessman."

A smile drifted over his face. "Thank you, Valentine."

She took a small sip of wine. "All the girls talk about you, you know. How handsome you are, how charming." She softened her voice. "One of the girls told me you were seeing Delilah. I guess a lot of the models knew you were having an affair."

A muscle tightened in his cheek. "Is that so?"

She ran her finger around the rim of her wineglass and looked up at him from beneath her lashes. "Apparently, Delilah raved about your prowess in bed. She said you were a fantastic lover."

Jason relaxed at that, almost preened. "All right, yes. Dee and I had an arrangement. It was pleasurable for both of us."

"She said you gave her a fabulous diamond necklace. I never saw it, but I heard it was beautiful. Was that the one that was stolen?"

He shrugged. "It must have been. The police said it was missing from her safe."

Val picked up her wineglass and took another sip. "I wonder . . . How do you suppose the thief knew where to find the necklace? I mean, how did he know about the safe? How did he know what was in it?"

Jason lifted his glass. "How would I know?"

"You must have thought about it, a brilliant man like you." She smiled, pandering to his ego, hoping he would tell her something useful. "Dee was in love with you, you know. At least that's what the girls all think. You're smart and sexy, and incredibly handsome. You knew her better than almost anyone. What do you think really happened that night?"

His gaze drifted down the front of her dress, where only a glimpse of cleavage showed above the simple scooped neckline.

He looked at her across the table. "I think

whoever killed her knew her, knew about the diamonds and where she kept them. I think she made him or someone else very angry." His lips edged into the faintest of smiles. "She wasn't sweet like you, Valentine. Dee was very self-centered. At times she could be quite unpleasant. Perhaps someone paid her back for something she did."

Her pulse took a leap. She managed to frown. "I thought it was the man who wrote those terrible notes, but maybe . . . I don't know . . . maybe she knew the man who sent them. Maybe he wasn't a stranger after all."

He sipped his wine. "Maybe not. Of course whatever happened, no one deserves to be murdered."

"No, of course not."

Still holding her hand, Jason turned it over, brought her fingers to his lips and kissed her palm. "Then again, if she were still alive, I wouldn't have had the pleasure of meeting you."

His eyes remained on her face, his intention clear. His bed hadn't been turned down for nothing. Val swallowed. She'd gone too far. She glanced at Ethan. He couldn't hear the conversation, but even from a distance, she could read the cold fury on his face.

Jason laced his fingers with hers. "Why

don't you tell your bodyguard to go back to the hotel? You're safe here. I'll personally see you back to your suite whenever you're ready to go."

Oh, dear God! Val tugged on her hand, trying to free it. Stern merely tightened his hold. Then he smiled and released her.

Val rose from her chair on shaky legs. "I appreciate the offer, Jason, but I really have to follow the rules. And as we discussed, I have an early TV appearance in the morning."

Before he could argue, she turned and started walking toward the door.

She stopped in front of Ethan, tried not to flinch at his hard glare. "I'm ready to go back, Ethan. Thank you for bringing me tonight."

His features didn't soften. "Just doing my job, Ms. Hart." Pulling open the door, he stepped out into the hall to check their surroundings, then stood back and waited for her to leave.

Val turned to the man still standing next to the table, who was every bit as angry as Ethan. "Good night, Jason. Thank you for the lovely supper."

Stern didn't say a word as she turned and walked out of the suite.

Neither did Ethan. Not a single word till

they were back at the Four Seasons in her own suite of rooms, the door firmly closed behind them. Val didn't have to wait long for the explosion she knew was certain to come.

"What the hell did you think you were doing?" His dark glare hadn't lessened since they'd left the St. Regis.

"I was getting information," Val said. "I was trying to help you."

He didn't seem to hear her. "That slimy bastard. I can still smell his cologne on you. Five more minutes and I'd have jerked him up from the table and knocked his pretty white-capped teeth down his throat."

She rested her palm on Ethan's chest, hoping to calm him, felt the too-rapid beating of his heart. "You were there. I knew I was safe."

He grabbed her hand and turned it over, stared down at the place Jason had kissed. "I hated watching him touch you. I hated seeing him put his mouth on you. If you're going to carry a man's scent, it's going to be mine."

Val gasped as he hauled her against him and his mouth crushed down over hers. It was a hard kiss, and demanding, a reminder that she was his, not Jason Stern's. She gripped his shoulders just to stay on her feet, whimpered as he buzzed her zipper down and shoved the black dress off her shoulders.

Ethan unhooked the black lace bra she wore underneath, tossed it away, and filled his hands with her breasts. He lifted and stroked them, tongued them as if he owned them, slid his palms down over her hips to cup her bottom and pull her against his rigid sex. He tipped her chin up, forcing her to look at him.

"I don't know where this thing between us is going, but as long as we're together, you're mine. I won't share you. And you won't be going to any more *meetings* with Jason Stern."

He framed her face between his hands and kissed her, holding her in place as he ravished her mouth. Heat and need poured through her, and hot, wet desire. She could feel his heavy arousal, feel his barely leashed anger, held in check only by his iron control. He was a man's man, a true alpha male. When he possessed a woman, she belonged to him.

She should have found the notion offensive. She was an independent woman who had been on her own for years. Instead, she felt desired in a way she never had been before.

When the long kiss ended, she reached down and caught his hand, kicked off her black high heels, and led him through the bedroom into the bathroom. He wanted Stern's scent gone? Well, so did she.

The bathroom was huge, black-and-white marble with a big Roman tub and a monster shower with multiple heads. Catching her intent, Ethan locked the bathroom door while Val turned on the water. Ethan shrugged out of his blazer and tossed it over the vanity stool, took off his shoulder holster and laid it on the marble counter.

Val watched as he pulled his black T-shirt off over his head and stripped off his jeans, appreciated the view of his amazing, hard-muscled body. There was a scar on his shoulder she had noticed before. She'd ask about it later.

Ethan tossed a foil packet up on the ledge in the shower, pulled her into his arms, and kissed her. And dear God, the man could kiss.

By the time he'd finished, she was mind-less and quivering, her black hip-hugger panties missing, her hairpins gone, her heavy curls loose around her shoulders.

Ethan lifted her into the shower, setting

her on her feet beneath the warm spray, then stepped in behind her and closed the thick glass door. Soaping his hands, he began to lather her all over, reaching around to coat her breasts with thick white suds, gliding his palms around the fullness.

She moaned as he reached down and soaped her sex, soaped her back and bottom. In seconds he had her panting, nearing the edge of climax.

"Put your palms on the wall," he commanded, nipping the side of her neck as he continued his relentless soapy assault.

Val trembled. Hot and achy, she leaned over and rested her hands on the smooth, slick marble. Moving behind her, Ethan nudged her legs apart, gripped her hips, and slid himself deeply inside.

"Mine," he whispered as he began to move, easy at first, giving her time to adjust to him, then driving deep, taking her hard, sending her into a climax that drenched her in pleasure and totally rocked her world.

She'd explain about Stern later, she thought vaguely as she began to drift down, tell him what Jason had said. But the thought slipped away as Ethan kept moving, as her body tightened again, and she tumbled into pleasure once more.

CHAPTER TWENTY-SIX

"Tell me again what Stern said last night while you were cock teasing him across the table."

Val flushed, soft pink rising in her cheeks. "I wasn't. . . . I told you, I was trying to help you. I was trying to get information, and maybe it even worked. He certainly sounded like he knew something about the murder."

Sitting at the dining table in the suite, Ethan took a drink of coffee. He'd almost finished his room-service breakfast of bacon, eggs, hash browns, and toast. In the chair across from him, Val sat picking at a toasted bagel and eating an occasional bite of fruit.

He tried not to think how pretty she looked with the faint blush still in her cheeks.

"Jason said he thought Delilah was killed by someone who knew her. He said she might have made someone angry, that she could be a bitch at times — well, *unpleasant* was the word he used. He said someone might have wanted payback for something she'd done."

She set her unfinished bagel back down on her plate. "So maybe he was the one who was angry. Do you think he could have killed her?"

"It wasn't Stern. The guy who killed her was a pro."

"Because he didn't leave any evidence, right?"

"Among other things."

"So Stern hired someone to do it."

Ethan had been mulling over the possibility ever since Val had repeated the conversation he'd been too far away last night to hear. "Could be. Doesn't explain the notes."

"He could have sent all ten of them as a cover for the murder."

He shoved his empty plate aside and took another drink of his coffee. "It's an interesting theory. If he wanted her dead, the notes would send the cops in a different direction."

"So it's not a crazy idea."

He'd considered it before. After Hoover had checked out Delilah's acquaintances, including her past and current lovers, Ethan had dismissed the possibility. He trusted

Hoover. Now he wondered if the detective could have been wrong.

Considering Stern's words, he was going to take another look.

Val grinned. "Admit it: I'm not just a pretty face."

Ethan laughed. "I already knew that, honey."

Her smile slowly faded. "You did?"

"Yeah, baby, I did. Not at first, but it didn't take me long to figure it out."

The smile returned, softer this time. He could really get used to that smile. The thought sobered him. He didn't need more female trouble. Allison and Hannah were all he could handle at the moment.

Ethan shoved back his chair. "We better get moving if we're going to get you down to the TV station on time."

Val just nodded. Rising from the table, she preceded him into the living room. Dressed for the show in a pale blue silk blouse, short cream skirt, and gold-heeled sandals, she walked over and picked up her purse. Val had morning TV show interviews, but they had things to do as well.

He needed to find out if there was something Delilah Larsen could have done to Jason Stern or someone else — something bad enough to get her killed.

Tuesday's dress rehearsal was over, but backstage at the theater was still chaotic. The media had finished their interviews and were packing up to leave. Set designers and costume people were putting things back in order. Most of the models were still changing into their street clothes.

Val was back in the black leggings and long silky blue top, belted at the waist, she had worn in the pre-show interviews. For the dress rehearsal, David Klein had provided her with a gorgeous diamond pendant and diamond tennis bracelet that must have been worth a small fortune. But the jewelry was now in the safe.

Feeling restless and bored, she wandered out of her dressing room in search of female companionship. She didn't see Ethan or Dirk. She figured they were working somewhere close by, making sure the theater was secure as the press cleared out.

Ethan had mentioned the stage crew could also be a security problem. A number of La Belle people traveled with the tour: experts in sound and lighting; wardrobe and makeup personnel; set designers; people who did anything and everything to make the show successful.

But a number were locals, men and women who worked at the Fox, people who knew the ins and outs of the specialized equipment in the huge old theater. They'd all been vetted, according to Ethan, but still they were strangers.

Val wandered down the corridor. Izzy and Meg were probably dressed by now. Val continued along the hall and stopped at Izzy's dressing room. Shoving the curtain aside, she froze.

There was a man inside, big and brawny, young, mid-twenties, with greasy black hair. The tattoo of a spiderweb crawled over the side of his neck. He was standing in front of Isabel, pressing the point of a knife against her throat.

Val couldn't breathe. Izzy looked over the man's shoulder and saw her, and her friend's big brown eyes filled with tears.

Val shook her head, warning Isabel to keep silent, while her stomach knotted with fear. So far the man hadn't seen her. She could slip back outside and get help, but Izzy might be dead by the time she returned. As close as he was holding the blade to Izzy's throat, a scream would be a disaster.

Trying not to tremble, her heart pounding so hard the sound filled her ears, she stood unmoving, her gaze searching frantically for a weapon. Her breath caught when she spotted a curling iron on top of the mirrored dressing table a few feet away. More than a foot long, the instrument had a thick barrel to form soft curls and an easy-to-grip handle. If she could get to it, the curling iron would make the perfect weapon.

"What . . . what do you want?" Izzy asked, trying to keep the man distracted, her voice shaking, the blade pressing into the soft flesh at the side of her neck.

The man lewdly rubbed his crotch. "What do I want? I want you to suck me, sweetheart. You do that, you get me off real good, and I'll leave."

Fear rolled down Val's spine as she inched toward the dressing table. Izzy looked as if she might faint.

"If you don't leave now . . . I'll . . . I'll scream."

He just grunted. "Make a sound and I'll cut your pretty throat." He reached for his zipper and, one-handed, buzzed it down.

Val crept closer. Izzy made a small, terrified sound as the man started to free himself.

Val grabbed the handle of the curling iron, jerked her weapon into the air, and swung it with all her strength. The barrel smashed into the side of the man's head, knocking him sideways away from Izzy, the knife flying out of his hand.

"Bitch!"

"Run!" Val screamed, rushing forward, swinging her makeshift weapon again before the man could recover, the barrel connecting hard with his jaw, sending him sprawling again. Isabel raced out of the room as the man crashed against the wall, then slid onto the floor with a groan.

Val raced toward him. Gripping the curling iron, she braced her legs apart and got ready to take another swing.

"Jesus Christ Almighty!" The roar of Ethan's voice stirred a rush of relief so strong she felt dizzy. He strode into the room, followed by Dirk and a pale-faced, trembling Izzy.

Dirk went for the guy on the floor as Ethan moved up behind Val. He wrapped his arms around her waist and tried to ease the curling iron from her hand, but Val couldn't seem to let go.

"It's all right, baby," he said softly. "We've got him. Everything's under control."

The guy didn't even struggle as Dirk jerked him to his feet, whirled him around, and slammed him face-first against the wall. Dirk kicked his legs apart, dragged his hands behind his back, and bound them with a plastic tie.

Val still gripped her weapon.

"Come on, honey, everything's okay. Let me have it."

When her fingers finally relaxed, he eased the curling iron from her hand and tossed it onto the sofa but kept his arm around her waist.

"You okay?"

She had been. Now she wasn't. She prayed she wouldn't throw up. "That man . . . he tried . . . he attacked Izzy."

"I know, baby." Ethan cast a glance at Izzy's attacker, his eyes wild, clearly high on something, now trussed up and harmless.

Val felt Ethan's muscles relax. A few feet away, Isabel stood shaking. Val wanted to go to her, but she was afraid if she moved her legs wouldn't hold her up.

"What's your name?" Ethan asked the man on the floor.

When the guy didn't answer, Dirk whacked him on the back of the head. "Answer the man's question."

"Fuck you," the guy said.

Dirk whacked him again. "Tell the man your name."

"Strickler," he said darkly.

"He doesn't fit Mahler's description,"

Ethan said, his arm still around Val's waist, holding her back against his front. "Check his forearms just to be sure."

Dirk looked him over. "No scars. Nothing there." He jerked the man's head up to get a better view. "Wait a minute. I know this guy. He was up on the catwalk working the lights." He hauled the man to his feet, jerking Strickler's bound arms up behind his back until he grunted in pain. "Now you're on your way to jail for attempted rape, you stupid fuck."

The guy spit on the floor. "I was just taking what these bitches dish out to everyone else. I read the papers, I seen those notes they got. Sluts and whores. I was just giving the bitch what she deserved."

Izzy whimpered. Val took a deep breath, broke free of Ethan's hold, walked over, and pulled Isabel into a hug. "It's okay. It's over. He can't hurt us now."

Footsteps sounded at the door. "Holy crap!" Meg walked into the room, the story apparently spreading like wildfire backstage. Her eyes went to the bound man, whose face was already turning purple on one side. "The police are on the way. Did Val do that?"

"She saved me," Isabel said with what seemed awe.

Meg's blue eyes swept over Dirk and Ethan in their snug black T-shirts, faces hard, muscles bulging.

She cocked a dark red eyebrow. "So . . . why do we need all these macho bodyguard types when we've got Valentine Hart?"

Ethan chuckled. Val felt the reluctant tilt of her lips, and even Isabel smiled.

Ethan sat next to Val, who had just eased down on the sofa in her suite. Across from them, Dirk slid in beside Meg in one of the overstuffed chairs and lifted her into his lap.

Benny Strickler, Isabel's attacker, had been hauled off to jail, and the police had taken the statements of all the parties involved. They were back at the hotel and they were exhausted.

Ethan reached out and gently lifted Val's chin, bringing her pretty blue eyes to his face. "You did good today, baby. Real good." He still couldn't believe she'd taken on a hard-edged, knife-wielding scumbag and come out the winner. The woman continued to amaze him.

Not that taking on a rapist single-handed wasn't a dangerous, insane thing to do, which he intended to have a very firm discussion about once they were alone.

"Nice work, sweetheart," Dirk said. He

slid an arm around Meg, who didn't seem entirely pleased about it. "You're a helluva lot tougher than you look."

"She doesn't need to be tough," Ethan said darkly. "She needs to be safe. Either Boudreau cancels the rest of the tour or she's quitting. Her safety has to come first."

Val pulled away. "I'm right here, you know. And I'm not quitting. I gave my word. Besides, I need the money. I'm finishing the tour."

"Listen to me, baby —"

"Forget it. You can quit if you want. I'm finishing the job I started."

Ethan swore foully. "Dammit, Val —"

She cupped his face in her hands. "I'll be safe. I trust you to take care of me. I know you'll keep all of us safe. And Carlyle needs your help to solve the murders."

Ethan sighed. A knock sounded at the door, ending the argument he was clearly losing. He walked over and looked through the peephole, saw Matt Carlyle standing in the hallway.

"It's Carlyle," he said, causing Dirk to slide out of the chair and come to his feet. Since he didn't want Carlyle to know he was with Meg, he ambled into the bedroom, out of sight. Meg sat up straighter in the

chair. Val smoothed back her hair and nodded.

Ethan turned the knob and opened the
door. "Come on in. I was just about to call
you. We need to talk."

For the first time since Ethan had met
him, Carlyle looked frazzled. His slacks were
wrinkled, his light brown hair needed combing, and the ruddy hue of his face made the
thin scar stand out along his jaw.

"If the call was about canceling the show,
you don't have to worry. Boudreau flew in
an hour ago. He says we're getting more
bad press than good. He's refunding the
money for tomorrow night's show and
canceling New York and Chicago."

"About time," Ethan said with relief.

"All we have to do now is make an appearance tonight at Peter Latham's party in
our honor and we'll head home in the morning."

Ethan's eyes narrowed. "Wait a minute.
You don't think these women have been
through enough today? Izzy was damn near
raped this afternoon. And after brawling
with the SOB — who could have killed her
— Val's still plenty shook up."

"Look, we don't have a choice. David
Klein has an agreement with La Belle. Peter
Latham's a huge investor in Klein's com-

pany. He's been planning this affair for weeks. All the models have to do is show up, drink some champagne, smile at the guests for an hour or so, and leave."

Matt turned a desperate look on Val. "Surely you can handle it if it means going back to Seattle in the morning — and of course you'll still be getting paid."

"I don't like it," Ethan grumbled.

"Beau Desmond and his men have been over the residence with a microscope. No one's getting in or out unless they've been invited. Val, what do you say? Can you do this one last thing?"

She blew out a breath. "If it means going home, I can make it."

"Megan?"

Dirk was probably in there grinding his teeth, but he was smart enough to stay out of it. These weren't the kind of women who did whatever you told them. By now, Ethan and Dirk had both figured that out.

"If Val's going," Meg said, "so am I."

He could almost hear Dirk groan.

"What about Isabel?" Ethan asked.

"She's off the hook. The guy's sitting in jail. He's hardly a threat. But one of Beau's guys will be camped outside her suite just in case. She'll be okay."

"I still don't like it," Ethan said.

"I respect that. It's your job to keep these women safe. In fact, as far as La Belle's concerned, once we get back to Seattle, you'll still be on the payroll."

He didn't argue. He wouldn't stop working the case no matter what La Belle said, but it was always nice to get paid for the job he was doing.

"I need to get going if I'm going to look presentable tonight," Meg said, rising from her chair. "It's black tie, as I recall."

"That's right. You own a tux, Brodie?"

He nodded. "Goes with the job."

"You've got the address, I presume," Carlyle said.

"I've got the damn address. I'll round up Dirk and we'll take the women over in a private limo. Like I said, they've had enough for one day."

"You've got two hours. Don't be late." Carlyle stopped at the door and tipped his head toward the bedroom. "Oh, and tell Reynolds he needs to be a little more discreet. Gallagher's seen him with Megan so many times he's starting to think they're joined at the hip. I've got enough trouble without having to fire the two of you."

With that, Matt was gone.

Dirk ambled out smiling. "Come on, honey, I'll walk you to your room."

Meg rolled her eyes. "You heard what Matt just said. He knows what we've been doing. We need to be more discreet." She jerked open the door. "Besides, we don't have time for what you're thinking."

Dirk winked at Val, then flashed an unrepentant grin at Meg. "I guess we'll just have to see." They were still arguing as the door closed behind them.

CHAPTER TWENTY-SEVEN

The white stretch limo rolled up the long curving drive and came to rest in front of Peter Latham's mansion in Tuxedo Park, one of the most expensive neighborhoods in Atlanta.

Carmen Marquez and Caralee Peterson rode in the back with Val and Meg, while Dirk sat up front with the chauffeur. Ethan lounged on the seat in the rear with the women. Val figured having her friends along was at least a nod toward discretion.

A pair of white-jacketed valets hurried to open the limo doors. Ethan and Dirk climbed out first to assess their surroundings, then Val, Meg, Carmen, and Caralee stepped out with the help of the valets.

Towering like a Renaissance castle behind a sea of colorful, perfectly tended flowers lit by spotlights and surrounded by vast manicured lawns, the mansion was unlike anything Val had ever seen.

Patterned after an Italian villa, the sprawling two-story home had turrets and chimneys and tall arched windows with balconies out front. The exterior was the soft gold of a Tuscan sunset, and dozens of lights inside glowed through the windows.

Val couldn't resist a glance at Ethan, who walked behind her as she and the other women headed up the curving path to the massive carved front doors. The man looked amazing in a T-shirt and jeans. In a perfectly tailored tuxedo with gleaming black satin lapels and a crisp white shirt with rows of tiny tucks down the front, he was magnificent.

When she caught a hint of amusement lifting the corners of his mouth, she figured he must have read her thoughts. She tossed back her hair and kept walking. So what if she liked his looks?

In her long gold-sequined, formfitting gown with its sexy slash up one side and gold spike heels, she looked pretty damn fine herself.

As they walked inside, Paul Boudreau and his wife, Marie, were standing in the entry next to the man Val assumed was their host, Peter Latham.

On Latham's arm was a woman with smooth dark skin and long jet-black hair that hinted at a Hispanic heritage. She appeared to be in her late forties, but with a little face work to hide the years, could actually be older. Though her curves were more voluptuous, her breasts a little fuller, the woman could hold her own with any of the models.

Latham was in his fifties, tall and athletic, a handsome man with silver threads in his wavy dark brown hair. Next to him stood a younger man, taller than Peter but clearly his son, handsome, with his mother's thick black hair and a leaner but no less athletic build than his father's.

Jason Stern stood beside his boss, David Klein, a man Val had met several times in Seattle. Jason's eyes came to hers and a cool smile touched his lips. Val felt a chill, offset by the heat of Ethan's gaze burning into her in subtle warning. She prayed Stern was smart enough not to challenge Ethan or make some kind of scene.

Paul Boudreau, black-haired and handsome in his sixties, stepped forward to make the introductions to their host and hostess, giving them each of the women's names.

Then, "Ladies, I'd like you to meet Peter Latham and his wife, Alessandra. They were kind enough to sponsor this marvelous affair."

"A pleasure, I'm sure," Caralee drawled.

"I am pleased to meet you," Carmen said with the sexy smile she was famous for.

"Thank you for the lovely party," Val said.

Peter Latham smiled. "Nonsense. This affair is only a small gesture of appreciation for the hard work you ladies have done to make the fashion show a success."

Meg glanced around the massive entry with its Italian mosaic floor and the gilded dome rising more than two floors above them. "Your home is quite beautiful. I've never seen anything like it."

Somewhat garish, Val thought, but undeniably impressive.

"Thank you," Peter said. "My wife came up with the concept. She's worked very hard to make it as special as it is." He turned. "And this is my son, Julian. He flew in from Miami just for the occasion."

Julian made a faint bow of his head. "It's a pleasure to have you here. Welcome to my family's home."

Peter Latham smiled. "You're the last of the models to arrive, so why don't we join the others out by the pool?"

Julian offered an arm to Meg and another to Carmen. Val and Caralee fell in behind him, followed by the rest of the group, including Ethan and a scowling Dirk.

Crossing the marble floor past rooms filled with heavy, carved Renaissance-style furniture, they moved toward the back of the house, then walked out into the warm Atlanta night.

The U-shaped home was centered around a massive swimming pool, the gorgeous blue set off by underwater lights. As Val studied the arched corridors that framed all three sides of the home, she figured it had to be thirty thousand square feet.

A white-jacketed waiter appeared with a silver tray. They all accepted glasses of champagne, and the group gradually dispersed, giving her and Caralee a quick moment to themselves, though Ethan stood not far away.

Jason Stern immediately approached Caralee, who began an amiable conversation. Val almost smiled. Caralee was madly in love with her husband and baby. No way was Stern getting anywhere with her.

As Val sipped from a tall crystal flute, enjoying the orchestra playing on the far side of the pool, she felt Ethan's presence beside her. She flicked him a sideways glance. With his dark, cop-short hair and clean-shaven jaw, combined with his broad-shouldered build, in the elegant tuxedo, he was the best-looking man at the party.

Dirk also looked amazing in his black evening clothes, though he seemed a little less comfortable in them than Ethan did. And in a different, more *GQ* way, Julian Latham was downright movie-star gorgeous.

She took a sip of her champagne. "What do you suppose Peter Latham does to make the kind of money it takes to own a place like this?"

"I don't know," Ethan said. "I haven't looked at his financials. I didn't know he was associated with Klein until Carlyle mentioned it." His lips edged up. "Latham's kid lives in Miami. He's half Hispanic. I hate to go for the usual cliché and think the family could be running drugs, but it's worth checking out."

She caught sight of Paul Boudreau walking toward her and Ethan moved back into the shadows. "I hope you're enjoying the party."

"It's lovely," Val said.

"If you wouldn't mind, there are some people I'd like you to meet. They're curious about the woman who, without the least modeling experience, managed to snag the title of Miss La Belle. A woman who has managed to do a terrific job despite difficult circumstances."

"Thank you."

She cast Ethan a quick glance over her shoulder but let Boudreau guide her into the throng of guests around the pool. Pasting a smile on her face, she settled into doing the job she was getting paid for.

Ethan moved off through the crowd, giving Val the chance to work the crowd with Boudreau. His crew was on-site. He made a round to check security, talked to Joe Posey, then Sandy Sandowski, checked in with Walt Wizzy, and Pete Hernandez.

"Latham has things running like clockwork," Pete said. The bruise on his jaw had faded to a dull yellow. He'd recovered from his concussion and the doc had pronounced him fit. "I haven't seen anything out of the ordinary."

"Good, let's hope it stays that way."

He caught sight of Beau Desmond and walked in that direction. "Any problems?"

Desmond shook his head, his silver earrings glinting in the soft light illuminating the patio. "The place is secured like Fort Knox. Nobody's getting in here tonight."

"What about the catering staff? The valets? The servers? They all been vetted?"

"Latham's own people handled that. Latham insisted and Carlyle agreed. I haven't seen any problems."

Unease filtered through him. Much as he disliked Desmond, he trusted him to do his job, part of which was doing background checks on the staff.

Ethan glanced around, saw the blond Russian model, Katerina Stoyanov, talking to Julian Latham, saw Carmen speaking to Mrs. Boudreau. The two women put their heads together and Mrs. Latham laughed. Carmen left her there and started toward the house. She paused next to Val, said something, and the pair continued on together.

He'd been given a layout of the mansion. There were fourteen bathrooms, the biggest in the private spa in the wing closest to the pool, clearly the women's destination. What was it about females that they couldn't go to the head by themselves?

He spotted Meg, now talking to Julian and Caralee, looked for Dirk, but didn't see him. Just to be safe, he fell in a distance behind Val and Carmen, then positioned himself in the outside corridor next to the bathroom door to wait for them to come out.

After what felt like ten long minutes, he checked his watch, found it had only been five. *Women,* he thought. In the last few weeks, he'd been around enough females to last him a lifetime.

A pretty, dimpled face appeared in his imagination, but he forced it aside. He'd deal with his feelings for Val when the time came.

He looked back at his watch. What the hell were they doing in there?

He started to knock on the door, which he knew would cause female hysterics, looked up to see Dirk striding toward him down the hall with a hard look on his face.

"What is it?"

"It's not good, Ethan. Looks like we've got a hostage situation."

Ethan looked at the bathroom door and his body turned to ice.

Chapter Twenty-Eight

"You two women. Get over there and sit in front of the door. If they try to shoot their way in, you'll be the ones who get killed. Do it now!"

Val watched in horror as Carmen and Ursula scurried forward and sat down on the white marble floor, their backs against the eight-foot bathroom door. The room was huge, all white marble with gold nozzles and gilded molded ceilings. There were three separate toilet stalls and a mirrored dressing table that seemed half a block long.

The bathroom was part of a private spa with a steam room, a Jacuzzi, a nail and hair parlor, even a massage table.

A noise started in the distance. The rumble of a helicopter descending over the house kicked Val's wildly speeding pulse up another notch.

"You! Get over here by the phone." He was in his mid-twenties, tall and thin to the point of gaunt, with longish brown hair and very pale blue eyes. If Val could see his forearm beneath the sleeve of his coat, she could be certain it was Byron Mahler, but deep down she already knew.

He was pointing at Amarika, who stood in front of the mirror, shaking all over. Beneath her ebony skin, her features actually looked pale.

"The police are going to call," the man said. "When they do, you're going to answer. You understand?" He'd been waiting when she and Carmen walked in, had shoved them into a corner with Amarika and Ursula, who were already inside the spa.

"Yes . . ." Amarika's voice shook, but she moved over to the phone, stood stock-still as the man's pale eyes slid over her. His short white jacket and the black pants he wore matched those worn by the valets and serving people, exactly how Mahler had managed to gain access to Latham's private party.

Val thought of Ethan and fought not to tremble. Ethan would be frantic by now. She amended that: Ethan would be calmly, fiercely in control. And he would do whatever it took to save them.

She held on to the thought as she looked at the man pointing a big black semiautomatic pistol directly at her heart. She wondered if the knife he had used to kill Mandy Gee was the one stuffed into the top of his pants, and a tremor ran down her spine.

She figured he had come in through the rear entrance leading to the spa from inside the house. The heavy massage table now barricaded that door.

Mahler started pacing. Sweat gleamed on his forehead and trickled down the side of his neck. Val moistened her lips and clamped down on her fear.

"You're Byron, right?" She couldn't stand there a moment longer. She had to do something, find some way to reach him, try to talk him down, or at least keep him occupied till Ethan and the police could figure out a way to get them out of there.

He stopped pacing, his pale gaze sharpening on her face. "How do you know my name?"

"My bodyguard figured it out. We talked to Mrs. Bruckner. She said you had a very difficult childhood." Not exactly the truth, but she needed to make some kind of connection. She had seen that done on TV.

He sneered. "That old woman talked to you? She never did know her place. Just like the rest of you women. You all need to be taught a lesson." His gaze skimmed up and down her body, and a shiver of fear moved through her.

She tried not to think of what he'd done to Mandy Gee, but she'd read the gruesome details in the paper. Now she wished she didn't know.

He walked over to where she stood, reached out and wrapped a hand around her throat. "My mother was a whore, just like all of you. Did old lady Bruckner tell you that?"

She didn't move. If he squeezed, she wouldn't be able to breathe.

He let go of her and reached into the pocket of his short white jacket, pulled out a folded sheet of paper. He flipped it a couple of times till the sheet opened up.

"Read it out loud," he demanded.

Val swallowed. Her mouth felt dry. "Sinners, sluts, and whores — repent or burn in hell." The words on the printed page were all in different fonts, many in bold letters. It was modeled after the original notes, just like the one he had left at Mandy Gee's.

He tossed the note on top of the dresser. "I'm going to teach all of you a lesson. Just like I did that stripper. And I'm going to start with you."

A shot of dizziness struck her. She imagined Mandy's beaten and bloody body and thought she might faint.

"Byron Mahler!" A shout came from the other side of the door. "This is Lieutenant Alvarez with the Atlanta Police Department. Come out with your hands in the air!"

Mahler walked to the door. "I'm not coming out!" he shouted back. "I've got a .45 caliber pistol and an eight-inch knife. And I've got four of your women! Make a move and I'll kill them, one by one. You hear me?"

The phone rang just then, startling Val out of her petrified trance. Mahler turned and motioned for Amarika to answer it. Her hand shook as she picked up the receiver and pressed it against her ear.

"Hello, this . . . this is Amarika." Her eyes looked huge as she stared back at Mahler. "It's . . . it's Lieutenant Alvarez. He says to put the phone on speaker. Is that okay?"

Mahler nodded. "Go ahead."

"Are you listening, Byron?" the lieutenant asked, his voice calm but firm.

"I hear you."

"There's a SWAT team out here. You're not getting out of there alive unless you cooperate."

The police had arrived in the chopper. They would be doing their best to get the women out safely. Val just hoped whatever they were planning didn't get them all killed.

"We've got every exit covered," the lieutenant continued. "There's only one good way for this to end, Mahler, and that's for you to toss out your weapons and surrender to the police."

Mahler just laughed. "You thought I couldn't get in, didn't you? I guess I showed you. Now I'm gonna show these little whores. I'll tell you what. I'll let two of them go, but the other two stay. You can have them after I've had my fill."

Nausea rolled through her. Val's legs felt weak. She knew what he was thinking, that he couldn't control all four of them but two he could handle. She gripped the marble counter to stay on her feet.

"That isn't going to happen, Byron," the lieutenant said. "I'll tell you what. You let two of the women leave right now, then we'll make some kind of trade for the other two. Does that sound fair?"

A grating chuckle pushed up from his throat. "How would I know what's fair? I'm insane. That's what the doctors are all going to say. I won't have to go to prison. They'll just put me in some cushy institution."

The lieutenant made no reply because it was probably true.

Val looked at the other women. They were

all thinking the same thing. He couldn't kill all four of them at once. But if they went after his gun, at least one of them was going to die.

"I'll tell you what," Mahler said. "I'll let three of the women go, but one stays here. I mean to take her, use her real good, then you can have her."

"Just take it easy, okay? We've got plenty of time. Let's try to work this out."

"You've got ten minutes to make the deal. You give me the one, and I let the others go. If not, I kill them all, one at a time. I'm going to cut their throats and let them bleed out on the floor." Mahler pushed the button on the phone, ending the call.

Val just stood there, feeling light-headed, trying to force air into her lungs.

"Look, Lieutenant, Valentine Hart is my assignment. I need to get in there." Ethan tried not to let his desperation show, drew on everything he had ever learned to stay in control. "I'm an ex-cop, all right? I know the drill. Let me go in with you." Val was way more than a job, but if the cops knew that, he didn't have a prayer of going in.

"Sorry, you're a civilian. I can't allow you to get involved."

A big black plainclothes detective stepped

up beside him. "This is Ethan Brodie, Lieutenant. He's the guy who fingered Mahler. He's ex-Dallas homicide. How about letting him go in as backup?"

The black cop turned to Ethan, stuck out a meaty hand. "Detective Ricky Melon. Heath Ford says he owes you, asked me to look out for you."

He gripped Melon's hand, nodded a quick thanks. "Appreciate the help." Time was of the essence. He turned back to the man in charge. "I'm armed. I just need a vest, Lieutenant."

Five ten and completely bald, Alvarez released a slow breath. "Damn, I know better than to do this." He tipped his head toward one of his men. "Get Brodie a vest and let's get this show on the road."

Relief and resolve filtered through him. Ethan shrugged into the black body armor the cop handed him, settled it in place over his tux, then pulled out his Glock and checked the load.

"Call him," the lieutenant ordered the officer working the portable phone. "After what this guy did to the stripper, we don't have time to get eyes and ears in there. See if we can get him back on an open line."

"You got it."

Moments later, Byron Mahler was talking

again, making more threats that Ethan believed he absolutely meant to carry out. He moved in behind SWAT as they headed for the rear entrance to the spa, silently praying they would get to Val and the others before it was too late.

The lieutenant's voice sounded scratchy as it came over the speakerphone line. "I need you to listen to me, Byron. You don't want to hurt those women. They haven't done anything to you. You need to let them go."

"Time's running out, Lieutenant. What's your answer? We got a deal? One for three?"

There was only a moment's hesitation in the police officer's voice. "All right, we've got a deal." There was really no choice. Three women would be safe. Only one left to save, only one life at risk instead of all four of them. Val shivered.

"Send three out," the lieutenant agreed. "Then we wait, give you time with the other one. Soon as you're finished, you give yourself up. Okay?"

Mahler's satisfied smile made the bile rise at the back of Val's throat.

"Three for one. Here they come."

Striding to the door, he dragged Carmen and Ursula to their feet. "You on the phone," he said to Amarika. "Get over here."

With a terrified glance at Val, Amarika raced across the room to join the other two women.

Val stood frozen. She shouldn't have said anything to Mahler. She shouldn't have done anything to get herself singled out.

Mahler shot her a malevolent glare. "You stay where you are, you hear me?"

Val nodded, but she was ready to bolt the minute Mahler opened the door.

"You still there, Lieutenant?" Mahler asked through the open phone line.

"I'm right here. Don't do anything you'll regret, Byron."

"I'm sending three of them out to you. You better not shoot or you'll kill them." Mahler jerked open the door and shoved all three women out into the corridor. At the same time, an explosion rocked the room, blowing the back door off its hinges, and the vent in the ceiling crashed open.

Val screamed as six men in full body armor carrying assault rifles stormed the gigantic bathroom. Another SWAT officer dropped down through the opening in the ceiling. The last man to enter, a pistol gripped in both hands, wore a tactical vest over a black tuxedo.

Val saw Mahler's hand come up, then she was jerked out of the way as Ethan stepped in front of her, shielding her with his big, hard body. Shots rang out. She couldn't count how many, but they didn't come from Mahler's weapon. She didn't see him die, but she heard his body hit the floor.

She grabbed hold of Ethan and buried her face in his chest.

"I've got you," he said, holding her so tight she couldn't have moved if she'd wanted to, which she didn't.

Ethan smoothed back her hair. "You women and your goddamn bathroom breaks. Sweet Jesus, lady, you scared the piss out of me." He took a deep, steadying breath and kissed the top of her head. "What am I going to do with you, Valentine?"

Val stared up at him, her ears still ringing with the echo of gunshots and the chaos around her. A single sob escaped. It turned into a moan that seemed to tear loose inside her. The moan dragged on, then turned into a giggle. She started laughing, laughed harder, laughed so hard she was shaking all over.

Ethan's arms tightened around her. "It's okay," he said gently, moving her toward the door. "It's just the adrenaline. It'll pass in a minute."

The laughter shifted, changed back into

sobs that turned into uncontrollable weeping. Ethan lifted her into his arms and started striding past the SWAT guys, outside into the fresh night air. He didn't stop until they were well away from the chaos overrunning the mansion.

"You're all right." He sat down in a chair at the table farthest from the pool and settled Val in his lap. "You're safe, honey. We're going home tomorrow. Everything's going to be okay."

Hysterical laughter threatened again. She finally managed to stop crying. Dragging in a shaky breath, she sniffed and wiped the tears from her eyes.

"That's right. How could I forget? We're going home tomorrow. Back to Seattle — where another maniac is lying in wait to murder us. Everything is going to be just great."

CHAPTER TWENTY-NINE

By the time the chartered jet landed at Sea-Tac Airport, Ethan had given up any pretense that he and Val weren't in some sort of a relationship, Carlyle and the rest be damned. He was staying with Valerie Hartman until the riddle of Delilah's murder was solved and the models were completely out of danger.

All he had to do was convince Val.

They were riding in the back of the limo, one in a line of private cars that were waiting when the models arrived at the airport.

"There's something we need to talk about," Val said before he could broach the subject. "We might as well talk about it now."

"All right, go ahead."

She released a slow breath. "I know you're still worried about my safety, but this . . . this bodyguard thing can't go on forever. You said yourself we were going home and everything would be okay. Byron Mahler is no longer a threat. The tour is canceled. The models are no longer in the media spotlight. I can't live under house arrest for the balance of my life."

"You aren't under house arrest. You have personal protection. So does Bill Gates. So does Lady Gaga. A lot of people do."

"Well, I'm not one of them. I need to get my life back in order, and that doesn't include spending every minute with an armed guard."

His jaw tightened. "That's the way you think of me? As your jailer?"

Surprise flickered in her eyes. "No, of course not. I didn't mean it that way." She reached for his hand, held it between both of hers. "I've never met a man like you. I've never felt the things you make me feel, but . . ."

"But what, Val?"

"But that's just it — I don't know! A man in your line of work . . . I don't know how I feel about that. I still have a contract to fulfill with La Belle and now David Klein. I have online classes to finish. I've got a part-time job waiting at the animal clinic, then school in a few more weeks. I don't know where this relationship could possibly go, and I don't think you do either."

He clamped down on an urge to show her exactly where it could go — straight back to bed. But maybe she was right. Maybe he didn't have everything completely worked out. And clearly he had his hands full with Hannah and Ally.

It didn't mean he was anywhere near ready to end things between them.

And it didn't change the fact that he needed to keep her safe.

"Look, Val, Mahler didn't kill Delilah — we know that. Nothing about the two cases matches up. Someone else killed her, and that means your life could still be at risk."

"You said her killer was a pro. That's some kind of hit man, right? That means it was personal. Someone wanted her, specifically, dead."

"That's only a theory. Just because the guy was thorough doesn't mean he couldn't be as crazy as Byron Mahler. It doesn't mean he couldn't be lying in wait, getting ready to take you out or kill one of the other girls."

She fell silent. Her big blue eyes searched his face. "You really think the killer might come after me or one of the other models?"

He reached toward her, cupped a hand beneath her jaw. "That's the thing, baby. I don't know. Until I do, I need to be close enough to protect you." He didn't tell her he'd nearly gone out of his mind when he'd realized she was locked in a room with the crazy son of a bitch who had raped and brutally murdered Mandy Gee.

That it still haunted him that he hadn't been there when she'd needed him most.

He tipped her head back and settled his lips very softly over hers, began a gentle persuasion. He wasn't beyond using sex to get what he wanted. One thing he knew: Val liked sex and she liked it with him.

Ethan deepened the kiss, kissed her until she moaned into his mouth. If the car hadn't been so close to the duplex, he might have had the driver raise the privacy partition and taken her right there on the seat.

Instead, he eased a little away, kissed the side of her neck, dropped slow kisses along her jaw. "I'll give you as much space as I possibly can, all right?"

She slid her hand behind his neck and pulled his mouth back down for another steamy kiss. Her lips were soft and moist and he was rock hard. Ethan bit back a groan.

The limo pulled up in front of her house. Steeling himself, he ended the kiss and shifted his erection into a more comfortable position.

The driver opened the door. "We're here, Ms. Hart."

Ethan climbed out of the car and made a quick check of their surroundings. His Jeep was parked in front of Val's garage, where his brother had moved it for him.

Seeing nothing but a woman out walking her dog and a man riding his bicycle beneath the trees overhanging the street, Ethan helped Val out of the limo while the driver took their suitcases out of the trunk.

The door to the other duplex swung open and an elderly lady dressed in turquoise Capri pants and a loose white cotton blouse shuffled out. She waved, setting her thin gray curls in motion.

"Welcome home," she called out. "Kinda surprised to see you. I didn't think you'd be comin' back so soon."

Val hurried up her neighbor's walkway, then climbed the steps to the porch and gave the old woman a hug. "We weren't supposed to be back, but the tour got canceled. Long story. Thanks so much, Mrs. Oakley, for taking care of Snoozie. I hope he wasn't too much trouble."

"Not a bit. But I think he's been missing you. He wanders out in his yard and prowls around like he's looking for you. He'll be glad you're back."

The women chatted while the limo driver carried the luggage up to Val's front door. Ethan tipped the man, then walked over to join the women.

Val turned to her neighbor. "Mrs. Oakley, this is Ethan Brodie. He's my . . . he's a friend."

The older woman's eyes took him in from top to bottom. "Well, aren't you a big strappin' fella. 'Bout time Valerie found herself a man."

Val flushed and he felt a trickle of amusement. "Nice to meet you, Mrs. Oakley."

"You too, Ethan. You be good to our girl now, you hear?"

"I will, I promise."

Val tugged him down the steps and over to her side of the duplex. She waved at her neighbor, who went back inside and closed her door. "She's a sweet lady, but Mrs. O. will talk your ears off if you aren't careful."

But the lady thought Val needed a man and he was currently that man, so he kind of liked the old woman.

Ethan took Val's keys and went inside to clear the house. Her big gray tom sauntered up to him and meowed. Ethan scooped him up and stroked his short gray fur, making him purr as he carried the cat back to the living room.

"Snoozie!" Val hurried over and took the big cat from his arms. "Mama's sweet baby. I missed you so much."

Ethan grinned. Damn, she was cute.

While Val carried the cat into the bedroom and started to unpack, Ethan got on the phone to his office. He spoke to Ian, bringing him up to speed on Byron Mahler's recent demise, as well as the idea of revisiting the people in Delilah Larsen's past. He talked to Luke, who was back in town after picking up his latest bail skip.

Once his calls were made, he set up his laptop. Basically, he was moving in with Val, a notion that should have made him run as far and as fast as he could. Instead, knowing Val was in the house, that they would be sharing a bed, he felt completely at ease.

He walked over to his suitcase. He didn't have much to unpack. His tux would have to go to the cleaners. His underwear and socks, T-shirts, and jeans needed to be laundered. He had a feeling Val wouldn't be thrilled if he asked to use her washing machine. She might feel he was getting too close, penning her in — exactly the way *he* should have been feeling.

Hell, there *was* something kind of intimate about it.

Ethan grinned and started walking toward

her bedroom. Almost sex had gotten him this far. Maybe he needed to finish what he'd started in the limo. His groin tightened as he imagined her lying on her big king-size bed, imagined himself driving hard inside her.

With any luck, what he had in mind would convince her she was glad he was there.

Maybe even after they caught themselves a killer.

Meg had been putting it off. Now that she was home, she couldn't wait any longer. "We need to talk, Dirk." He'd checked the house, then made himself at home as only Dirk could do, rummaging around in her fridge, grabbing himself a beer and cranking off the cap, drinking half the bottle in a few long swallows.

She'd only recently purchased the newer home in Madison Park, but it was perfect for her and Charlie. With four bedrooms, a family room, and three and a half baths, there was plenty of room for a family. The best part was the large fenced backyard, a great place for Charlie to play.

Dirk ambled toward her. "You want to talk, then talk." He upended the bottle and took another long swallow of beer.

Meg pulled in a slow breath. Just watching him made her wish he would carry her off to bed. He was the hottest guy she'd ever met. More than that, he was sweet and smart, and she was crazy about him.

Meg ignored the soft lump rising in her throat, her gaze still on Dirk. With his colorful tattoos, sexy mustache, and cocky grin, he looked completely out of place in her practical single-family house, where a little boy would soon be playing on the floor with his toys.

It was a tract house, roomy, more expensive than most because of its Madison Park location, fairly ordinary in design. But there was nothing the least bit ordinary about Dirk Reynolds.

"So . . . my mom and dad are coming over later tonight," she said, forcing out the words. "They're bringing Charlie home."

He plopped down on the sofa. "Good. I'll finally get a chance to meet him." He looked up. "And your folks."

Meg shook her head. Just the way he sat there, one of his muscled arms resting on the back of the sofa, made her yearn for him. Made her heart hurt at the thought of losing him.

"As much as I appreciate everything you've done to protect and keep me safe, I can't introduce you. My parents would never approve of me dating a man like you, not when I have a child to think of."

His lean-muscled body went rigid. He sat forward on the sofa. "A man like me? What the hell's wrong with me?"

"Nothing! There's nothing the least bit wrong with you. You just . . . you aren't the kind of man I need."

He set his beer bottle down on the coffee table and got up off the couch. "Bullshit. I'm exactly the kind of man you need. I have a job. I work hard. I have money in the bank. I'm not some loser you picked up on the street. I can take care of you as well as any other man." His gaze slowly raked her, fastened on the swell of cleavage above her pink tank. "Better."

She ignored the tingling that shot through her body. He had certainly taken care of her in bed.

"I know that. Physically, we're very . . . compatible. But it has to be more than that. Please don't make this any harder than it is already."

He grabbed her hand, pressed it against the fly of his jeans. "I can't get much harder, Meg. That's the way I walk around half the time when I'm with you. I can't get enough of you, honey. I wanted you the first time I saw you. I still do."

Her throat felt tight. "Don't you see? Wanting isn't enough. I'm only going to be modeling for another year, two at the most. By then I'll have enough money put away so I can stay home and take care of my son full-time, work at something I really want to do. I've always wanted to own my own business. I might give that a try."

"So you'll own a business. Whatever you do, you'll do it well. That's just the way you are. Doesn't mean we can't be together."

Her heart squeezed. She hadn't realized he would think they could continue. "Maybe not, but once I'm ready to settle down, I'll be looking for more than just a fling, more than just sex with a man I'm wildly attracted to."

His hazel eyes sparked with interest. "Wildly attracted? That's how you feel?" He caught her hand. "Come on, let's go to bed. You always see things more clearly after you're relaxed."

Meg jerked free. "That's the problem, Dirk Reynolds! You think sex is the answer to everything. Maybe if I didn't have Charlie, it would be. At least until you got tired of me or . . . or I got tired of you."

His masculine features tightened. "Is that it? You just wanted a fling and now you've had enough?"

"No! You know . . . it . . . it wasn't that way. But now we're home and things . . . things are different."

A muscle clenched in his jaw. "You're really serious about this. You want us to be over."

She didn't want that. She didn't want it so badly she ached. "It has to be. I have a son. He's got to be my first priority."

She saw the moment the barb struck, when he realized she meant every word. He paced away, turned back to face her. "See, that's the thing you don't get, Meg. You wouldn't have to choose between us. You could have both of us in your life. You didn't have to choose, but you just did."

Meg's heart seemed to stop beating.

"Until we're sure you and the other models are safe, you're going to need some kind of protection. I'll put a man out front. You'll be covered twenty-four seven."

She started trembling. "I wish . . . I wish it could be different."

"It could have been, Meg. If it was what you really wanted." Dirk crossed the room and yanked open the door. "Have a good life, baby." And then he was gone.

The sound of his footsteps descending the front stairs made her feel dizzy. Meg heard him fire up his Harley and rev the engine.

Dirk popped the clutch, gunned the motor, and roared away, the sound of his muffler slowly fading.

Her heart throbbed dully. He wouldn't be back. She knew it deep in her soul. Dirk Reynolds wasn't the kind of man who came back once a woman turned him away.

Meg dropped down on the sofa. Her eyes burned and hot tears scalded her cheeks. She'd done the right thing. She'd given up Dirk for little Charlie. But dear God, she hadn't realized it was going to hurt so much.

CHAPTER THIRTY

"You up for a ride? I've got something I need to do and it'd be better if you went with me."

Which was Ethan's way of saying he wasn't about to leave her there alone. With Byron Mahler dead, the immediate danger was over. But the man who'd killed Delilah was still out there, waiting, perhaps, to make good on his threat to murder another model.

Seated behind the computer in her bedroom late the next morning, Val glanced over to where Ethan stood in the doorway in his usual T-shirt and jeans. The man was eye candy no matter what he wore, but her favorite would always be Ethan Brodie in a tuxedo — accessorized with a black tactical vest and a big black semiautomatic pistol.

For a moment, she smiled. Then she remembered how terrified she had been, remembered the sound of bullets smashing into flesh, and her smile slid away.

"A break sounds good," she said. "I've got more studying to do, but I could use a chance to get out of the house for a while. Where are we going?"

"Down to my office. Sadie's expecting me. I've got some ideas I want to run past her. Since you're not just a pretty face, maybe you can help."

Her smile returned. "Okay." Besides, she was interested in seeing where he worked. She didn't know if she could handle the dangerous sorts of jobs he did, but — Val broke off the thought.

What Ethan did for a living was none of her concern. They would only be together a little while longer. Sleeping with him was just a matter of sexual gratification, something that worked for both of them.

Or was it?

How much of a lie was she willing to tell herself?

"Grab your purse and let's go." He set a hand at her waist as she walked past him out into the hallway. Just that light touch sent shock waves the length of her body. They were definitely compatible physically. Still, she wasn't ready for a complicated relationship. She had too much on her plate already.

It didn't take long to reach Ethan's Bellevue office. The sign etched into the door read Brodie Operations Security Services, Inc.

Ethan led her inside, into a black-and-chrome interior that was very tasteful and masculine. Nothing like the scarred wooden desks and linoleum floors she had imagined from old detective movies she'd seen.

She spotted Dirk the minute they walked in, sitting at his desk, his feet kicked up on top, staring off into space. There was none of the restless energy she always associated with him, only a darkness she knew instantly had been caused by his breakup with Meg.

"Hey, Dirk," she called out.

"Hey, Valentine."

"It's Valerie now. Or just plain Val."

"I know. Somehow Valentine always seemed to fit you."

She smiled, wishing there was something she could say to make the darkness go away. She knew he and Meg were over. Her friend had called in tears. Meg was crazy about Dirk, maybe even in love with him, but she was sure it would never work, and she had Charlie to think of.

Meg was probably right. Neither one of them should have gotten involved with the men assigned to protect them. But when she glanced over her shoulder at Ethan, when she felt his solid, reliable presence behind her, she couldn't regret a single moment they had shared.

Her chest tightened. She didn't regret a thing, but looking at Dirk and thinking of Meg, she began to realize how much losing Ethan was going to hurt.

"Sadie's office is on the second floor." Ethan led her in that direction. Before they reached the stairs, the front door opened and Nick Brodie walked in, looking as handsome as he had the last time Val had seen him. The family seemed to have amazing genes.

"Hey, Val," Nick said, then nodded to his cousin. "Ethan. I heard you two were back."

"We ran into a little problem in Atlanta and the tour was cut short."

"I heard. You still working the Larsen case?"

Ethan nodded. "That's why I'm here. I need to talk to Sadie."

"Good idea."

"Tell Samantha hello for me," Val said.

"Will do," said Nick.

They passed by the conference room with its long mahogany table and black leather chairs. Beneath the staircase, Val noticed a big black gun safe, probably de rigueur for a successful security firm.

They climbed the stairs to the second floor, then headed down a corridor with doors off each side, stopped in front of an open doorway where a handsome blond man sat behind his desk.

The office was large, with a nice window looking out over the street. The room was furnished in the same black-and-chrome motif as downstairs, with a butter-soft black leather sofa against one wall. A little girl's pink plush rabbit sat at one end, carefully positioned as if the animal were there for a visit.

"Ian, this is Valerie Hartman. Val, this is my cousin, Ian. He's also my boss."

Ian stood up from behind his desk, tall, athletic, nicely dressed in tan slacks and a yellow Oxford shirt. He walked around to greet her. "A pleasure to meet you, Val."

"You too, Ian." They briefly shook hands. She glanced over at the rabbit. "Ethan mentioned you were married. Do you have children?"

His friendly smile widened. "I have a beautiful little four-year-old girl."

"She and Hannah must be great friends."

Ian's smile slipped. "I'm sure they will be, once Ethan gets things worked out."

A noise sounded in the doorway before she had a chance to respond. Because she had no idea what to say, she was grateful for the interruption.

"Hey, bro. Good to see you." A tall, lanky, amazingly good-looking man with sun-streaked brown hair and incredible blue eyes sauntered into the office. "This your lady?"

Ethan's lady? Was she? And why didn't she correct the impression before it was too late?

"Luke, this is Valerie Hartman. Val, my brother, Luke."

Those brilliant blue eyes assessed her. "Nice meeting you, Val." He gave her a lopsided smile. "My brother's always had good taste in women. He's definitely out-classed himself this time."

"Thank you . . . I think. I understand you work here, too."

"More or less." At first glance, Luke seemed far more laid-back than his brother. But there was something about him . . . Perhaps it was the same core of steel she recognized in Ethan.

"It's a family business," Ian said. "Though Luke tends to be a bit of a wanderer."

Luke grinned and a sexy dimple dug into his left cheek. In a different way, he was every bit as hot as his older brother. "Wandering's kind of a job requirement. I'm a bounty hunter."

"Wow." The word slipped out before she could stop it. "That sounds . . ." *Dangerous as all bloody hell.* "Umm . . . exciting."

Built more like Dirk than Ethan, he shrugged a pair of lean, hard-muscled shoulders. "Money's good, if you know what you're doing."

"I can imagine."

She felt Ethan's hand at her waist. She wondered if it was meant as a subtle message. "Come on. Sadie's waiting."

They left the office and headed farther down the hall, into a room with an oversized desk and triple computer screens. The fifty-year-old computer wiz Ethan had talked about, Sadie Gunderson, had very curly platinum-blond hair with dark roots that matched her dark eyebrows. She was a big woman with more than her share of wrinkles and a serious look on her face.

She glanced away from the monitor and looked up at Ethan. "So . . . more dead bodies, I hear. You seem to be collecting them lately."

"Two since we left. One in Dallas, one in Atlanta. Unfortunately, the one in Atlanta didn't die soon enough." He tipped his head toward Val. "Sadie, this is Valerie Hartman."

"Valentine," the woman said. "You're one of the models. I'm sorry about your friend."

"We weren't close, but thank you."

Sadie's gaze ran over her, taking her measure in some way. Val fought not to squirm under the woman's stern, all-seeing regard.

Sadie turned her attention to Ethan. "So where are we now on the case?"

He motioned for Val to sit down, then took a seat himself. "Pretty much back to square one. I'd like you to take another look at Jason Stern. Turns out, he and Delilah Larsen were lovers."

"Ahh . . . that's news."

"Along with that, I need everything you can find on Peter Latham, his wife, Alessandra, and his son Julian. Latham's the second-largest shareholder in David Klein. They're loaded, and I mean megabucks. He and his wife live in Atlanta. Julian's in Miami."

"Miami. You're thinking there might be a connection to drugs? Kind of a stretch, isn't it? Just because the family's got money."

"I know. At this point it could be anything. Still, it might be interesting to know how the family made their fortune and what Julian does for a living. Whether or not he's in and out of the country, how often, and where he goes."

"All right. Anything else?"

Val shifted in her chair. "Maybe you could . . . umm . . . check out Jason's wife," Val said, drawing Sadie's shrewd green eyes back to her. "I think someone told me her name is Myra, but I don't know for sure."

"Myra Stern," Sadie said with a nod. "I remember the name from my preliminary search."

"Could be Myra found out her husband was being unfaithful," Ethan added. "Maybe it pissed her off enough to have his mistress killed."

"What about the notes?" Sadie asked.

"Yeah, well, that's the problem. The notes don't work with that theory, but they could have been sent as a cover."

"Seems like you're reaching to me. You know, if you go down that road and you're wrong, if the guy who killed her is as crazy as he seems, it could get another model dead."

Ethan rubbed a hand over his face. "I know."

Sadie nodded. "Okay, then. Anything else?"

Ethan looked over at Val, who shook her head.

"Not at the moment." He rose from his chair and so did Val.

"It was nice meeting you, Sadie," Val said.

"You too." Sadie looked from Val to Ethan, noticed the way his hand rested possessively at her waist. A frown pinched a line between her eyes. "Looks like you two are getting pretty friendly."

Val felt heat sweeping into her cheeks.

"We're together," Ethan said. "If that's what you want to know."

Sadie's dark eyebrows shot up in surprise. Clearly, she hadn't expected that answer. Val was a little surprised herself.

"Hey, none of my business," Sadie said.

"You're right, it isn't." But he was smiling as he urged Val toward the door. "I appreciate your help with this, Sadie. I haven't forgotten those tickets."

The older woman's features softened. "I'll let you know what I find out."

They left the office and headed back to the Jeep.

"I think your Sadie is afraid I'll try to take advantage of you."

Ethan chuckled. "She's kind of protective. She considers us all part of her family."

"That's nice."

"Yeah, I guess it is. Right now she's not too happy with Megan. Sadie has a way of finding out what's going on. She figures Meg hurt Dirk and she doesn't like it."

"Meg had to think of Charlie."

"I think she's underestimating Dirk, but that's just my opinion."

Val didn't agree. Dirk was wild and, as far as she could tell, not the least bit ready to settle down. "So where do we go from here?"

"I'm at a dead end till I hear from Sadie. What's on your schedule?"

"I checked this morning. Tomorrow's the tenth anniversary of David Klein. I've got an early morning TV interview on CBS Seattle. I'm supposed to show off some of the more affordable pieces of jewelry Klein sells."

Ethan shook his head. "I don't like you back in the media spotlight. It might draw the killer's attention to you."

"It's part of my job, Ethan."

"I know." He released a slow breath. "So nothing till morning. Let's go home. We'll get on the computer and do a little more digging ourselves."

Val just nodded. Ethan helped her into the Jeep, then went around and slid in behind the wheel.

"If we stop at the grocery store," Val said, "I could fix us supper at home tonight."

"You cook?" The look on his face was priceless.

Val grinned. "What, you think because I'm

a lingerie model I can't fry an egg? Cooking's one of my hobbies. I started learning a couple of years ago. Samantha and I take classes together whenever we can. I'm not as good as she is, but I'm not half bad."

Ethan smiled. It was a relaxed, really handsome smile, the kind she had rarely seen.

"You look like an angel," he said, "and now I know you really are one. We'll stock up, fill the fridge with everything you need."

"Do you like veal parmigiana?"

Ethan rolled his eyes. "Oh, man." Reaching down, he started the engine, eager to get back home.

CHAPTER THIRTY-ONE

In celebration of David Klein's tenth anniversary, Val was asked to wear a floor-length sapphire gown with a low-cut sequined bodice and a slash up one side. The necklace Klein provided was a gorgeous diamond pendant on a thin platinum chain and an elegant-but-simple diamond bracelet. A slender three-inch string of diamonds dripped from each ear.

"You look lovely this morning, Valentine. We're glad you could find the time to be on our show." The morning host, Don Murray, was a heavyset, balding man with a jovial personality and a knack for making people comfortable in front of the camera. Val had been on his show before when she won Miss La Belle, but never for David Klein.

"Thank you, Don. It's nice to see you again."

"You too, Val. I see you're dressed for an anniversary party. Tell us about the David

Klein pieces you're wearing."

She lifted the pendant, and the camera zoomed in. "It's a single pear-shaped diamond set in platinum, designed by David Klein himself. It's eight-point-four total carat weight, valued at just under two million dollars." She went on to describe the rest of the jewelry she was wearing, the diamond bracelet and earrings.

"It's all really lovely," Don said. "But for most people this stuff is way out of their price range. I understand you've brought a few things that are a little more affordable."

"That's right. We have some very special items over here." She walked to where the display was set up and Don followed. With her high spike heels, she was five inches taller than he was.

Val tipped back the lid of a polished walnut box, one of three positioned on the table in front of the cameras. On a bed of dark blue velvet, an array of much smaller diamond pendants flashed beneath the bright overhead lights.

"As you know, all the diamonds used by David Klein are very high quality. These are smaller, more affordable stones, but they're no less precious." She went on to a second box that held diamond tennis bracelets, quarter-to-half-carat stones, then a box filled with pavé diamond earrings, jewelry that ranged from two thousand dollars to twenty.

"As you can see, Don, almost anyone can afford to own good-quality diamonds."

Don chuckled. "I just hope my wife isn't watching the show."

Val grinned. They talked a moment more, then the interview was over. As she crossed the stage to where the David Klein security people waited to take charge of the diamonds, Ethan stood in the wings.

He strode toward her, waited close by as the several-million-dollar necklace, bracelet, and earrings were removed and returned to the portable safe they had arrived in.

"I need to change out of my gown," Val said. "Then I'll be ready to go."

Ethan followed her to the dressing room, waited outside while she stripped out of the sapphire gown. She changed back into her street clothes — black skinny jeans and a loose-fitting, belted, soft pink top — then they headed back to her apartment.

She hadn't gotten five feet inside the living room before he tossed off his leather jacket, shrugged out of his shoulder holster, and set the weapon on the table.

"Come here," he said softly.

Drawn by the dark, restless hunger in his

eyes, Val walked toward him, her heart jumping into a faster gear. Ethan caught her shoulders and drew her against him, bent his head and very thoroughly kissed her. She loved the feel of his lips over hers, the way they sank in, urged her to open for him, took complete control. She loved the feel of his big hands sliding down over her hips, cupping her bottom, pulling her into the hard ridge between his legs.

Desire curled into her stomach, spread out through her limbs. Warm male lips pressed against the side of her neck just below her ear, and goose bumps feathered across her skin.

"Damn, you looked so gorgeous in that dress it was all I could do not to walk into that dressing room and have you right there."

Val draped her arms around his neck. "In that case, now would be good."

Ethan growled low in his throat and kissed her again, a long, deep, thorough exploration that had her melting against him, pressing her body even closer. He was backing her up to the wall, his erection making all kinds of promises she knew he could keep, when his cell phone started to signal.

Ethan cursed, and Val felt a sharp stab of disappointment.

He took a deep breath and set her away, dragged the phone out of his pocket and checked the screen. "It's Sadie." He pressed the phone against his ear. "You got something?" He listened, flicked Val a glance. "Hold on while I put you on speaker."

Surprise filtered through her. He was including her, understanding that she was part of this, respecting what she might be able to contribute. She had come to respect him, too.

The notion unsettled her. She was getting sucked in, her feelings for Ethan growing deeper every day. She couldn't afford to fall in love with him. Ethan couldn't afford to fall for her. Not with the problems he was already facing with his ex and his little girl. They'd wind up like Megan and Dirk, both of them getting hurt.

Val took a deep breath. Forcing aside the unwelcome thought, she moved closer to the phone.

"Go ahead," Ethan said. "What have you got for us?"

"Oh, just all kinds of juicy little tidbits. Starting with Myra Stern. Turns out Jason's wife is Peter Latham's twin sister."

Ethan whistled.

Sadie chuckled. "So you probably see

that's the reason Jason got the job at David Klein. He was hired as president four years ago, after Latham took a major shareholder position in the company."

"You're right, that is juicy."

"At the time Stern took over, the company was close to bankruptcy. David Klein himself was getting older, mostly interested in doing design work. It was Jason who turned the business around. He now owns a sizable number of shares, and the president's job pays a bundle."

"Interesting. I did some digging this morning myself. Klein is well past seventy. A pillar of the community. From what I could tell, he and Stern don't seem to have much of a personal relationship."

"They don't socialize, leastwise I didn't see them linked in the papers or in social media."

Val spoke into the phone. "Do you know how Jason turned the company around, Sadie? What changes he made that pulled Klein out of the red and put them back in the black?"

"I surely do. Stern introduced a line of less-expensive jewelry." Ethan remembered the stuff Val had been modeling that morning.

"He was also the guy who came up with

the idea of partnering with La Belle," Sadie said, "using glamorous lingerie models to show off Klein's million-dollar necklaces. Same way other designers use actresses to advertise their jewelry on the red carpet at the Academy Awards."

"Sounds like a smart guy," Ethan said.

Val made a disgusted sound in her throat. "More likely Peter Latham is the guy with the brains."

Ethan eyed her closely. Val knew Stern better than he did. He didn't want to think of the dinner she'd had in Stern's suite, but she very well could be right.

"I can't tell you who thought of it," Sadie said, "but you get the idea. Having hot babes like Valentine wearing David Klein jewelry gets women flocking to the stores."

"Val's taken Delilah's place as Klein's spokesperson," Ethan said carefully, interested in what Sadie might have to say about that.

When the phone went silent, he cast a worried glance in Val's direction, his gut telling him this wasn't good.

"What is it?" he pressed.

"Nothing I can put my finger on. Just that Julian Latham is also a Klein shareholder. One who makes some very interesting trips out of the country."

"Mexico?" he guessed.

"South America."

"Colombia," Ethan said. "Latham's gotta be involved in the drug trade."

"Could be drugs, but Julian isn't going to Colombia. Every three months, he takes a first-class American Airlines flight direct to Caracas, Venezuela. Simón Bolivar International Airport. He makes a return trip home three, sometimes four days later."

"Sounds like drugs to me."

"According to his tax records, Julian runs Latham Property Management, a company his father owns. They manage apartments and strip malls owned by Latham Enterprises."

"If it's legit, why's the son going to Caracas?"

"Good question. Whatever he's doing, he isn't doing it in the city. He takes a suite at the Gran Melia the night he arrives, checks out the next morning, then checks back in a few days later, the night before he heads back to Miami. No idea where he goes in between."

Ethan's glance returned to Val. He didn't like her working for people who might be involved in an illegal drug operation.

He turned back to the open phone line. "The question becomes, is Julian's little

408

enterprise personal? Or does it have something to do with his interest in David
Klein?"

"And if it's connected to Klein, does it
have something to do with Delilah Larsen's
murder? That's the real question, hotshot.
Guess you'd better figure it out."

He sure as hell better. "One more thing:
Any idea how Latham made his money?"

"He was a hedge fund manager. They all
seem to walk away rich, don't they?"

"Seems like. Thanks, Sadie."

"I'll keep digging. Go to work," Sadie said
and ended the call.

Val walked up beside him. "Maybe Peter
Latham didn't really make his money in the
stock market. Maybe he made it running
drugs, then used the drug money to buy
shares in David Klein. Maybe he and Jason
partnered up, infused some of the drug
money into the company to turn it around."

"Maybe. I've got a friend, a guy who
works for the DEA in Miami. I'll give him a
call, see if Latham or his son are on any of
their watch lists."

"That's a good idea."

His cell phone chimed again. He glanced
at Val, had a bad feeling his plans for getting her naked were going to have to wait.
"Brodie."

"Ethan, this is Ross Mosher, Seattle PD."

He knew the guy, a detective in the vice squad, tried to think why Mosher would be calling instead of Hoover. "Hey, Ross, what's up?"

"Sorry to be the bearer of bad news, buddy, but your ex-girlfriend got busted for drunk driving a couple of hours ago. She had her kid in the car with her. She says you're Hannah's father. You need to come down here, Ethan. Your little girl's asking for you."

His stomach knotted. Sweet Jesus, Ally was drunk before noon, his little Hannah sitting alone at the police department. "Tell her not to worry, Ross, I'm on my way."

"I'll make sure she's okay."

"Thanks, buddy." Ethan ended the call.

"What is it?" Val asked.

"It's Allison. Cops busted her for DUI."

"Last night?"

"Sometime this morning. Apparently she's got a serious drinking problem. I've got to go get Hannah. She's at the police station. I know this trouble isn't yours, and I really hate to ask, but —"

"Don't be ridiculous. Of course I'll come with you."

Ethan released a deep breath. "Thanks." Allison had royally screwed up this time, but Hannah was safe. He just needed to get to her, bring her home.

Unfortunately, it wouldn't be that easy. With the info Sadie had dug up on Julian Latham and the family's possible connection to drug smuggling, he needed to keep an even closer eye on Val.

He grabbed his shoulder holster and dragged it back on, pulled out his Glock, checked the clip, and shoved the gun back in. "You ready?"

She nodded. "Let's go get your daughter."

Ethan shrugged into his leather jacket, covering up the Glock in his shoulder holster, then escorted Val out to the Jeep. In record time, they reached Seattle Police Department Headquarters, downtown in the six-hundred block of Fifth Avenue.

As Val walked next to Ethan through the front door, a plainclothes detective, midthirties, sandy hair, and a nice smile, walked up to greet them.

"Hey, Ethan." He reached out and the men shook hands. "Don't worry, Hannah's okay. She's in the back entertaining some of the guys in the break room."

Val didn't miss the relief on Ethan's face.

"Thanks for watching out for her, Ross." He tipped his head toward Val. "This is

Valerie Hartman. She's a friend."

"Detective Mosher," the man said. "Nice to meet you, Valerie."

She started to say it was just Val, but the men started walking, Ethan anxious to get to his daughter. The break room down the hall was full of male and female uniformed police, some sitting at tables drinking coffee from Styrofoam cups, a good-looking young officer in the corner reading a *Sports Illustrated* magazine. A constant stream of men and women moved in and out of the room.

Following Detective Mosher, Val spotted Hannah sitting on a gray vinyl chair, swinging her legs back and forth, talking to a female police officer whose name badge read Mills. The woman laughed at something Hannah said and the little girl laughed, too.

Hannah looked up and saw Ethan and her laughter faded. Big tears filled her eyes. "Daddy!" Her bottom lip trembled as she reached out to him, and Ethan caught her up in his arms.

"It's okay, sweetheart. Daddy's here now. He's going to take you home. Everything's going to be fine."

Val felt a tug at her heart. Hannah was so darling. And clearly she adored her father.

What would it be like to have a child with Ethan?

He was an amazingly handsome man. The baby would be beautiful, boy or girl. And strong-willed, like both its parents.

Shock hit her. What in the world was she thinking? She had vet school to finish, a career ahead of her that was her life's dream. Add to that, she had vowed to stay away from trouble, and Ethan's whole world revolved around violence and crime.

"They took Mama away," Hannah said, hugging Ethan's neck and sniffing back tears, dragging Val's attention back where it belonged. "Mama was crying."

"I know, sweetheart. We'll check on her and make sure she's okay. But you'll have to stay with me for a while, until things get straightened out." He kissed her temple, turned to Detective Mosher.

"Thanks again, Ross. I really appreciate this."

"No problem. You just need to fill out some paperwork before you leave. You and her mother are both legal guardians so it shouldn't be any big deal. There's a release form, just to confirm you're the one who picked her up. But with her mother in custod . . . with her mom away, things are going to get complicated. I suggest you call your attorney."

"I'll do that right away."

Mosher led them into an office to wait, then returned a few minutes later carrying a clipboard. Ethan signed the paperwork, took the copy Mosher handed him, and they headed for the door.

"We need to get her car seat," Ethan said. "I keep one at my apartment. It's not that far away."

"I'll sit in back with Hannah," Val said as they climbed into the Jeep.

"You're daddy's friend," Hannah said, looking at Val.

"That's right. My name is Val."

"That's for Valentine. I remember you from the hospital. I wish my name was Valentine."

Val laughed. "Hannah is a beautiful name, sweetie. My real name is Valerie. That's not nearly as pretty as your name. And it fits you because you're pretty, too."

Hannah's eyes shot to Val's face. Her hair was pulled into a messy ponytail on top of her head. "You think I'm pretty?"

Val smiled. "Yes, I do. Very pretty."

"I hope I grow up to be beautiful like you."

As the Jeep rolled along, Val reached over and hugged her. "You're beautiful right now, sweetheart."

CHAPTER THIRTY-TWO

While Hannah sat in the living room of Ethan's modestly furnished Belltown apartment, playing with some of the toys he kept there for her, Ethan pulled Val aside.

"We've got a problem."

"Ya think?" she teased, mentally going over the long list of problems they faced. His mouth edged up in that sexy way it did when he was amused.

"The thing is, you're working for Klein, and the job might be involving you in something illegal — even deadly. Stern is a big philanthropist here in town, which means that isn't something the cops want to hear so they won't be much help."

"What are you saying?"

"That's the situation behind door number one. Behind door number two, there could be a psycho out there, a crazy still lying in wait to kill you or one of the other models. Either way, until we figure things out, you could be in trouble."

"I know that."

"Now Hannah's in the picture. I've got to figure a way out of the quagmire Allison has dropped us all into and still make sure you're safe. I'll have Ian put a man on your apartment. That's what Dirk did for Meg. In the meantime, I'll stay here till I can find someone to take Hannah. She can't stay with me — not yet. I've still got a murder to solve. I can't quit until this is over." He touched her cheek. "Will that work for you?"

He was moving out. It had to happen sometime. Every day he stayed just made it harder. She still had a job, Internet classes to study for, and the first of the month she'd be starting her part-time job at the animal clinic.

She looked into Ethan's dark eyes and emotion tightened her chest. *Tell him that's a good idea,* her smart self said.

"I won't feel safe with anyone but you," her heart said. "Let's take Hannah back to my place. Surely with you there she'll be safe. She can stay until you can find someone you trust to take care of her."

"You aren't used to kids."

She smiled. "I'm used to animals. Some of them can be pretty hard to handle. I can manage a three-year-old girl."

His mouth faintly curved. "Whatever happens, she can't go back to her mother until Allison gets herself straightened out. Even then, there's no way Ally can keep me away from her after her DUI. I just need a day or two, time to figure things out."

Val rested a hand on his arm, felt the hard muscles tighten. "I want you to stay. I want both of you to stay." Her heart squeezed just saying the words. Dear God, was it already too late? Was she already in love with him? Already falling in love with his sweet little girl?

"You sure?"

No. I've completely lost my mind. "I'm sure."

She could still read the worry in his face. "We could stay here," he said. "I can make my calls, get things rolling."

"Have you got anything in the house to eat?"

"No, but —"

"We've stocked the fridge at my place. My clothes are there. I've got a yard Hannah can play in. Snoozie's there. And I have to say it's a little cozier than this place."

He glanced around his basic, furnished-apartment living room with its plain brown sofa and chair and almost no decorations.

"All right, your place. Like I said, it's just

for a day or two." Bending his head, he very softly kissed her. "Thanks, baby."

Her insides melted the way they always did when he said the word. "It's no big deal." She turned away before he could see the mist that sprang into her eyes. "I'm sure Hannah won't be any trouble at all."

He nodded. "I'll call Frank Gibbs right now. He's my lawyer. He can make sure we do everything nice and legal."

While Ethan made the call, Val filled a box with some of the toys and clothes he kept in his apartment for Hannah. The clothes were probably a size too small — Allison hadn't let the child visit her father in weeks.

By the time they got back to the duplex, the little girl was asleep in her car seat.

"Wait for me. I'll be right back."

Val watched the gentle way Ethan carried the child into the house, her head snuggled against his shoulder, and emotions rose Val usually kept locked away.

For years after Bobby, she had closed herself off, kept herself apart from all but the most superficial relationships. Not even the men she'd dated over the years had ever gotten close. Only Mom and Pops had been able to break through the barrier she had created.

In the past few years, that had begun to

change. She'd made friends with a couple of girls in college. She'd met Samantha and they had become close friends. Through La Belle, she'd met Meg. Isabel and Carmen were friends, too.

After what had happened in that bathroom in Atlanta, Val and Amarika had been e-mailing back and forth.

Now there was Ethan and his little girl, touching her even more deeply.

It was the wrong time. The wrong man.

Then why did it feel so right?

Ethan checked the duplex, settled Hannah on the sofa, still fast asleep, then returned to the Jeep for Val.

"Come on, let's get you inside."

She slid out of the vehicle, all long legs and grace, and he felt the same tightening in his groin he'd felt when he'd seen her in the sapphire dress that morning. He wanted her with the same deep hunger, but again he would have to wait.

A faint smile touched his lips. Being a father had its drawbacks. He thought of the sleeping child who had nestled against his chest. There were drawbacks, but there were far more perks.

The sky remained overcast, but a few holes appeared in the dense layer of clouds.

Sun was predicted for that afternoon. Ethan urged Val along beside him as they climbed the front porch steps. He'd go back and get Hannah's toys and clothes, but he wanted to get everyone safely inside the house first.

They had almost reached the porch when something in the distance moved at the corner of his vision, glinted for an instant when the clouds opened up.

"Get down!" Ethan shouted as the sound of a muffled rifle shot split the air and a wood chip flew off the column holding up the overhanging roof. Val screamed as he shoved her down behind the three-foot partition enclosing the porch, pinning her beneath him, jerked his weapon, came up, and fired off two quick rounds. A second whizzing shot ricocheted off the top of the railing.

His jaw hardened. *Sniper rifle with a sound suppressor.* This guy wasn't playing games.

Val crouched behind the half wall around the porch while Ethan changed position and popped off two more shots in the direction the bullets had come from.

"We need to get inside." Grabbing Val around the waist, he positioned her in front of him and they raced, bent double, through the open front door.

Hannah was sitting up on the sofa, her

eyes wide, her lips parted in a silent scream of terror. Ethan grabbed her and dragged her down on the floor.

"Stay down. Both of you." His gaze shot to Val. "Call nine-one-one. Tell them we've got a shooter. Tell them I'm a private detective and I'm armed." Moving at a crouch, he made his way back to the window.

Glass shattered above his head and Hannah started crying. "Daddy!"

"She's okay," Val said to him. "I've got her."

Ethan fired off two rounds, then ducked as a bullet shattered another pane in the window. Glock in both hands, he popped up and fired again.

Quiet fell. His blood pumped, adrenaline roared through his veins. He itched to go after the shooter, make this end once and for all. "I want this guy," he said through clenched teeth. "But I can't leave you and Hannah."

Turning away from the window, he saw Val huddled over Hannah, protecting her with her body. The little girl was shaking and crying, curled up beneath Val on the floor. His heart jerked hard at the splashes of crimson on Val's blouse.

"You're hit!"

"I'm . . . I'm okay. It's . . . my arm. I

don't . . . don't think it's too bad."

His heart was hammering, blood rushing as he clamped down on his fear. The wail of sirens in the distance was the sweetest sound he'd ever heard.

He took another look out the window but saw no sign of the shooter. Belly crawling across the carpet, he settled himself next to Val.

"It's all right, honey. I'm right here. We need to stop the bleeding." He smoothed back her long, blond hair. "I'll buy you a new blouse, I promise." Grabbing a handful of fabric, he ripped the blouse away, then tore the material into a strip long enough to tie around her arm.

He took the cell phone she still gripped in her hand, the line still open, told the dispatcher to send an ambulance along with the patrol cars already on the way.

Hannah was still curled into Val, still shaking. He kissed the top of his daughter's head. "It's all right, sweetheart. The police are coming. They'll take care of Val, and we'll all be okay."

"I'm scared, Daddy."

"I know, honey. Just stay down on the floor with Val. She needs you to take care of her, okay?"

She nodded. "I will, Daddy."

"Good girl." He kissed her forehead, then headed to the back of the house to be sure it was still secure.

He heard the screech of tires as he moved back into the living room, raised his head enough to see two black-and-white police cars slamming to a stop at the curb. Two more pulled up in the street. Doors flew open. Officers poured out, guns drawn, and relief surged through him.

They were safe.

At least for the moment.

He opened the front door with his hands in the air, holding the pistol loosely between his fingers, showing them his weapon. He bent and set the Glock on the ground, then went back to Val to wait for the ambulance. Ethan prayed she'd be okay.

"We've got a problem," the man said into the phone.

"I don't like problems. What is it?"

"The hit didn't go down as planned. Our man got away, but it puts Brodie on alert. He won't give us another opening."

"Brodie will think the shot was meant for the girl. He'll be worried about her, not himself. Brodie's been sniffing around the Internet, setting off all kinds of alarms. I want him stopped before he stumbles onto something."

"Killing him might just stir things up, make things worse than they are already."

"The police have moved the Larsen case to a back burner. Brodie's an ex-cop and a PI. He's got all sorts of enemies. If he gets killed, it could be anyone. Once we get rid of him, this will be over."

"What about the girl? He's been staying with her. She might know something."

A long pause ensued. "She's a model. All they think about is their hair and makeup. She won't be a problem."

"And if she gets in the way?"

"Then get rid of her, too. Call in some help if you need it, but this time get it done."

The call ended and he made another, this one to the man who'd been hired to take Brodie out. "You've got another chance. Get some men and take care of it. You know who to call."

"You know I prefer to work alone."

"Yeah, well, you tried it your way; now you'll do it mine. And you'd better not blow it. You do, you'll be the one dodging bullets." He hung up the phone and sat back in his chair.

He didn't like this business of murder. But with the money involved, sometimes unpleasant things had to be done. He'd make sure Brodie was taken care of; then things could get back to normal.

Rising from his chair, he walked outside into the humid summer air. The sexy little redhead he'd been seeing for the past couple weeks waved in his direction. She was sunbathing topless. Wouldn't take much to get her out of her bikini bottoms. He watched as she dove into the pool, started unbuttoning his flowered shirt and stripped it away, leaving him in just his swim trunks.

He liked the good life. He wasn't about to give it up. He smiled and dove into the water.

Ethan sat in Val's living room with Val and Detective Bruce Hoover. Two police cars still sat out front. Hannah was next door with Mrs. Oakley, helping the old woman make chocolate chip cookies.

Val's neighbor had come over as soon as the ambulance arrived. As the EMTs worked over Val, Ethan explained to her about the shooting and the statements they would need to give the police. Mrs. Oakley volunteered to take care of Hannah, bribed her with cookies and kindness, and so far it was working.

Next to him, Ethan's arm around her waist, Val looked pale and brave, her arm bandaged where the bullet had gouged an inch-long groove into her flesh just above the elbow. He didn't want to think what would have happened if the shot had gone sideways, hit her in the chest or even the heart.

The EMTs said the injury wasn't that serious but insisted she go to the hospital to be checked out. Ethan had done his best to convince her. Val had refused, though her arm probably hurt like hell.

"I'm studying to be a doctor," she'd said. "Well, an animal doctor, but still . . . I know how to take care of a wound like this."

Then Hoover had arrived and started asking questions, pacing back and forth between the sofa and the shattered front window. As usual, he was in a grumpy mood.

"So you think the shooting is related to the Larsen murder. You think our killer is back."

It made sense. Though at the moment, he wasn't sure of anything.

"The killer left a note at the Larsen murder scene threatening to take out another model. The job he did was neat and clean, in and out, and not a clue left behind. The MO here is different, but a sniper's bullet is just as neat and clean, the shooter's identity equally hard to track down."

Hoover held up a chunk of lead Ethan had dug out of the leg of the sofa. "Caliber could be a .308, but until forensics gets a chance to weigh it, we won't know for sure."

"You'll find a couple more embedded in the porch."

Hoover studied the misshapen piece of lead. ".308s aren't that uncommon. Marine snipers shoot an M-40 rifle that fires a .308."

"That's right."

"Maybe it was someone from your past." Hoover turned, the top of his fringed head gleaming as if it had been polished. "You think of that, Brodie? Could be someone you investigated or arrested, someone you pissed off real good."

Ethan blew out a breath. His gut said this had nothing to do with the past and everything to do with the present. "It's possible, but I don't think so."

"But you don't know for sure."

"I know one thing for sure — I need to get my little girl somewhere safe, and being with me isn't it."

"What are you going to do?"

"I've got a call in to my cousin. He didn't pick up. I'm waiting for him to call —" His phone started chiming. He checked the caller ID, pressed the phone to his ear. "Hey, Nick, thanks for calling. Listen, I've got a problem. I'm hoping you can help."

"This a new problem or just more of the old?" Nick asked.

"Both. Allison got arrested for DUI. Hannah was with her, so now she's with me. The thing is, when we got back to Val's apartment, a sniper was waiting. Val got creased protecting Hannah."

"Jesus. She okay?"

He swallowed, tried not to think of the blood. His own he could handle. Seeing hers . . . not so much. "She's okay. Wouldn't even let them take her to the hospital." He wondered if his cousin could hear the pride in his voice, though she probably should have gone. "The cops are here. I don't know what the hell is going on, but I need Hannah somewhere safe."

"Yeah. Sounds like you're in the middle of a real cluster-fuck, cuz." Nick was ex-military. He didn't mince words.

"You can say that again."

"Take it easy, okay? You look out for Val and we'll take care of Hannah. Samantha loves kids and she especially loves your little girl. On top of that, I'll watch out for her myself, make sure no one comes near her, yes? You don't have to worry, okay?"

His chest felt tight. "Okay . . . all right. Thanks, Nick."

"The cops are still there, right?"

"Yeah. They're combing the area. Guy's long gone."

"Okay, I'll bring Samantha. We'll come get Hannah."

"I really appreciate this, Nick. I can't tell you how much."

"Don't be an ass. She's family. So are you. We'll be there as fast as we can."

His chest clamped down as the call ended. Worrying about Val, nearly getting her killed, had him strung right to the edge. Worrying about his kid, putting Hannah in danger . . . it was a gut punch he never wanted to feel again.

The worry was muddling his brain, making it hard to think. He had to get his head on straight and he had to do it now.

"So you believe this guy could be our killer," Hoover said, picking up the conversation where they had left off.

"I think it could be, yeah." *Or it could have something to do with drug smuggling.* But he couldn't say that, since he hadn't had time to develop the lead, and Hoover wouldn't appreciate Ethan looking at Stern without a damned good reason.

Add to that, he couldn't think of a motive

for Stern or anyone involved with David Klein to take a shot at Val.

"I've talked to Matthew Carlyle. He's put his team back on alert. He's got a man with each of the models who live in Seattle, and all of the ones who received a note, even if they live out of town."

Ethan nodded. "Good. That's good."

Hoover stood up from the sofa. "You need to go through your old case files, see if there might be someone who wants you dead. I want a list of anyone who might have a motive."

"I'm an ex-cop. I do P.I. work. I've got plenty of enemies. But I don't think —"

"Don't think, just do it."

"Fine." He'd do it. There was always a chance he was wrong.

"And I want that list ASAP, so don't dally."

"Okay, I'll start on it today."

"All right, that's it for now." Hoover got up from his chair. "Anything comes up, you know where to find me. In the meantime, keep your head down."

Ethan felt the pull of a smile. It felt out of place considering the circumstances. "Good advice." Reluctantly, he released his hold on Val and walked the detective to the door. "Thanks, Bruce."

Hoover waved as he crossed the porch, heading back to his car.

CHAPTER THIRTY-THREE

Two patrol cars remained at the curb and yellow police tape fluttered across the porch. The CSI people had finished their work, had taken photos and dug out bullets. They had studied the angles from which the shots had been fired and managed to discern the shooter's location.

Officers still scoured the area where they believed the man had been positioned: the rooftop of an empty two-story residence for sale at the end of the block. No shell casings had been left behind.

Aside from the officers in the patrol cars, the rest of the police were gone. Hannah was home from Mrs. Oakley's, back in the apartment with Ethan and Val. Nick and Samantha were there, getting the child settled enough to take her home with them.

The blouse Val had been wearing was in tatters and covered with blood, so she'd changed into baggy jeans and a soft, loose, short-sleeved gray sweatshirt that was easy to get off and on and allowed plenty of room for her bandaged arm. NO PLACE LIKE HOME in red plaid letters decorated the front. She closed her eyes and tried not to feel as if her safest place had been invaded.

She glanced around the living room. The curtains throughout the apartment were closed just as a precaution. Ethan had found a thin sheet of plywood out in the garage and nailed it over the broken front window. Samantha had vacuumed up the shards of glass scattered all over the carpet.

Val looked over at Hannah. The little girl sat on the sofa, gripping a plastic bag full of homemade chocolate chip cookies as if they were the last food left on planet Earth. Sensing the child's distress, Snoozie had curled up beside her.

A memory returned of the child shivering with fear on the floor beneath her, and Val fought not to tremble. She glanced up to see Samantha crossing the living room toward the sofa.

Sam crouched in front of the little girl. "This won't be for long, sweetie. I know you want to stay with your daddy, but he needs to find the man who shot at you."

"At me and Valentine," Hannah said solemnly.

"That's right, sweetie. He shot at you and Val, but Val's okay."

Hannah looked at Val with big blue worried eyes. "Does your arm hurt bad?"

Val's heart squeezed at the child's concern. She managed to smile. "It hurts a little. Not too bad." It had hurt like bloody blazes until the meds the EMTs had given her kicked in. She'd only taken one, though, instead of two. She needed to stay as alert as possible in case someone else tried to kill her.

Or Ethan. Neither of them could be sure exactly what had happened.

Beneath the bandage, her left arm continued to throb. She still couldn't believe she had actually been shot.

"I'll call every day, sweet cakes," Ethan said as he approached. "I promise."

Hannah stared up at him, tiny lines cutting into her forehead. "What about Mommy?"

Ethan's jaw tightened. He wasn't happy with Allison's DUI. Val couldn't believe the woman had been drunk with her daughter in the car. Clearly, Ethan figured Allison deserved some time in jail.

"You're mama's gonna be fine." Ethan

crouched next to Samantha. "You won't see her for a while." Or so Ethan's lawyer had assured him. "But you get to spend time with your Aunt Samantha and Uncle Nick."

They were actually her cousins, but Ethan and Nick were nearly the same age and very close, and aunt and uncle seemed easier for a child to grasp.

Samantha took hold of the little girl's hand and urged her up from the sofa. "We're going to have a great time, Hannah."

"What about the Busy Bee? And Chrissy?"

Samantha turned to Ethan for help.

"The Busy Bee's her day care," he explained. "Chrissy's her babysitter. Ally's gone a lot."

Sam cast Val a disgusted look they both understood. Allison wouldn't leave the little girl with the dad who yearned to spend time with her, but she thought nothing of handing the child over to day care or a babysitter so she could party with her friends.

"We'll make sure they know you're visiting your aunt and uncle," Ethan said. "Okay?"

For the first time the child seemed to relax. Apparently, order had been restored to her young world. "Okay."

Nick scooped her up and propped her on his hip. "I need kid practice, anyway," he said with a grin. He was going to be a dad soon himself, and clearly he was excited about it.

"Thanks again," Ethan said as he walked his family to the door. Val could almost feel the emotions rolling through him. She wished she knew what to say to make him feel better.

He watched through the curtains as Nick's SUV drove away. The engine noise slowly faded. Though the police were still outside, with everyone gone the house seemed strangely silent.

"I know how you must be feeling," Val said, walking up behind him. She rested her head on his broad back and slid her arms around his waist, hoping the contact would soothe him.

Ethan turned to face her. "I don't think you could possibly understand. Until today, I had no idea what it would feel like to see two of the most important people in my life looking death square in the face."

Val's throat tightened. "Oh, Ethan, I'm so sorry. If I'd let you stay at your place instead of insisting you and Hannah come back here —"

His warning glance cut her off. He eased her into his arms. "This isn't your fault, honey. None of it. We don't even know if you were the target. Hoover's right. It could have been me."

She nestled her head against his shoulder and Ethan just held her. She could feel the tension coiling through his big hard body, the worry, the weariness. "What are we going to do?"

"The cops are still outside, so we're okay for the moment, but we need to get away from here. Trouble is my apartment might not be safe either. I called Dirk while you were giving your statement. He's got a place we can use. You'll need to pack a few things."

"Okay. I'll do it right now."

He reached out and touched her cheek. "I'll never forget the way you protected my daughter, Val. Never. You were amazing."

"Ethan." She rose a little, pressed a soft kiss on his lips. His arms tightened around her, pulling her fully against him.

"I was so damned scared," he said. "I don't scare easy, Val, but I was so afraid for you and Hannah."

"Oh, baby." Her eyes burned. She leaned into him, very gently kissed the side of his neck, trailed soft kisses along his throat, the bottom of his hard jaw. She pressed another kiss on his lips.

Ethan cupped her face between his hands.

"Valerie, honey. I don't want to hurt you, but Jesus, I want you."

Her chin wobbled. She wanted him, too. Needed him in a way she never had before. "You won't hurt me." Wrapping her good arm around his neck, she kissed him the way she'd been wanting to since she had sensed his pain.

Ethan took the hot kiss deeper, made it wetter, then he was pressing her back against the wall, reaching for the buttons on her jeans. She shoved his hands away and unbuttoned them for him. Toed off her sneakers, pushed her jeans and panties down to the floor and kicked them away.

Careful not to hurt her arm, Ethan lifted her, and she wrapped her legs around his waist. His lips were hot as they moved over hers, plundering her mouth, making her burn. She heard the buzz of his zipper sliding down, knew he was freeing himself, and a fresh wave of heat pulsed through her. He was big and hard, and she knew how good it would feel to have him inside her.

"I could have lost you," he said, stroking her with a big talented hand, sending soft heat into her core. "I don't ever want to lose you."

"You won't lose me." She prayed it was a promise she could somehow keep.

"I need you, honey." Filling her slowly, he took her, joining them in a different, special way. For an instant, he held himself back. "I won't let anyone hurt you, baby, I swear it." Then he kissed her and started to move.

Deep, driving thrusts sent heat burning through her. Slow, erotic strokes pushed her toward the edge. Pleasure rose, fierce and wild. Ethan gripped her hips, holding her in place as he took her, lost himself inside her. She wanted to give him this, wanted to lighten his burden, to let him know how much he meant to her.

With a soft moan, she picked up the rhythm, moving with each of his thrusts, bringing him closer, absorbing some of his pain. Giving him the comfort he so desperately needed.

The pounding increased, along with her own sweet pleasure. Her sex tightened around him as he drove her higher, nearer the peak. Reaching the crest, she tipped over into climax and cried out his name, slid into deep, saturating pleasure.

Moments later, Ethan followed, his muscles tightening, his head going back, the cords flexing in his powerful neck and shoulders.

For seconds they clung to each other. Ethan pressed a last soft kiss on her mouth, but he didn't pull away. She'd needed this as much as he, she realized as they continued to spiral down. Needed proof they were both okay. Needed to believe they would find a way out.

Maybe even find a way to each other.

Ethan stood at Val's front door, surveying the area around the house as they prepared to leave. He waved at the officers sitting in their patrol cars.

"All clear," he said to her. "Time to go." The Jeep was in the driveway, the key in the ignition. Their suitcases were packed and loaded into the back. Mrs. O. had volunteered to take care of Snoozie again.

Val joined him in the doorway. Ethan took a last look around, spotted four cars coming in their direction, eased her back inside and stepped in out of sight. Since they were four of the least threatening vehicles he had possibly ever seen, his heart rate returned to normal. He came out of protection mode and watched as the cars approached.

Joe Posey, in an older-model Ford, rolled his window down and waved. Ethan waved back, giving the cops in the patrol cars the all-clear signal. Behind Joe, a white Ford Fusion pulled up and Sandy Sandowski climbed out. Walt Wizzy unwound his long, bony frame from a little silver Prius he could barely fit into.

Last but not least, the red-and-white, lowered '56 Chevy Pete Hernandez drove pulled up to the house, the muffler overly loud in the quiet street.

"I guess we aren't leaving just yet," Val said with a grin as the men walked toward them.

Ethan flashed her an amused glance touched with a remnant of heat. "Good thing they didn't show up a few minutes sooner."

Val's cheeks flushed a pretty shade of pink.

"Joe's got a police scanner," Pete explained as he climbed the porch steps, half a foot shorter than Walt, who ascended the steps right behind him. "Joe heard the call come in and remembered Val's address from when the media was here after the Larsen murder."

"Joe phoned and filled us in," Walt added. "We thought you might need some help."

Ethan nodded. "Appreciate it. Come on in."

Now that the fashion show tour was over, La Belle had let its temporary security team go but kept Beau Desmond and its full-time crew in place. Ethan was still working the murder investigation, but after today's shooting, he was off the grid till this was over. So was Valentine Hart.

They all settled in the living room. "We don't have much time," Ethan said. "We need to get somewhere safe." He debated telling the men where he planned to hole-up, but he had been working with them for weeks. He trusted them completely.

"I'll be taking Val to Dirk's place. If you're serious about helping, I could use some backup."

"Serious as a heart attack," Joe said. "Just tell us what you need us to do."

After a little back and forth, Ethan laid it out. He figured six-hour rotating shifts. They would need to be careful not to be followed to and from the location, but if the shooter found a way to track him and Val to the safe house, with a lookout in place outside, they'd have a chance of spotting him, arresting him, or taking him out.

Maybe they could make this end.

"We'll try it for a couple of days and hope a lead will break."

"Sounds good," Joe said. Once the plan was set, Ethan went out to the Jeep to retrieve the burner phone he kept in his glove box. He programmed in their numbers, then the men programmed the throwaway's number into their own phones.

"All right. Pete's volunteered to go first." Ethan turned toward him. "I'll see you there two hours from now. That'll give me time to go by my office and pick up my old case files. You got a car you can borrow? Something that won't stand out?"

"I should have thought of that," Pete said. "I'll trade with my girlfriend. She loves to drive the Chevy."

Joe chuckled. "If she drives like my wife, you'll be lucky to get it back in one piece."

Pete groaned. "You had to say that."

"You need to bring your weapons," Ethan said, sobering everyone up. "You're all licensed to carry. You never know what you might run into."

They ran over a couple more points, wound up the discussion, and headed out the door. The sky had turned a dull pewter gray and a light rain had started to fall. The wind kicked up as the storm drifted in.

The men returned to their cars, and Ethan guided Val out to his Jeep. Things were moving forward. He damned well hoped they were moving in the right direction.

CHAPTER THIRTY-FOUR

His first stop was the office. Hoover wanted Ethan to revisit his old case files. He'd be going stir-crazy without something to do anyway, so he figured it was a good idea.

And there was always a chance the detective was right. Maybe the sniper had nothing to do with the threatening notes or Delilah Larsen's murder or Val or any of the other models. Maybe someone wanted revenge for something Ethan had done and that person had just been waiting for him to get back to Seattle.

Maybe the shooting and the murder were nothing but coincidence.

It was possible. Too bad Ethan didn't believe in coincidence.

Turning another corner, he checked his rearview mirror for the dozenth time. The sky had grown even darker and the light rain had turned into a steady downpour that sloshed against the windshield wipers and puddled on the street.

Though it wasn't likely the shooter had stayed in the area once the police had arrived, he took a long, circuitous route to his office to be sure he wasn't being followed. He had no idea how the sniper had found them, but after Delilah's murder, photos of Val's home, surrounded by a boatload of media, had been all over the news. It wasn't much of a secret that he had been staying with her.

Before they'd left her apartment, he had checked to be sure there was no GPS attached to the Jeep, nothing in Val's purse or in their luggage. He had also removed the batteries from both their cell phones.

"I'll be using the disposable," Ethan told her. "Dirk'll have a few at his place." *Along with a small arsenal of weapons, should they be needed.* He didn't say that to her. "He'll have one there you can use."

"But no one will be able to reach me," Val grumbled. "What about my mom and dad? What about Meg?"

"You can call them when we get there, give them the throwaway number."

She leaned back in her seat, released a slow breath. "I never realized how hard it was to hide from someone."

"You got that right. Cameras everywhere.

GPS tracking. It's tough to stay off the grid."

"I hate this."

"I know, baby." He didn't say more. He didn't like it either, but until he got another lead, there wasn't much he could do.

Once they reached the office, he shoved through the door, guiding Val in front of him. Seated behind a desk across the open room, Luke shot to his feet.

"Jesus Christ, where the hell have you been? Valentine, are you okay? E, why didn't you call me?"

"So I guess you heard about the shooting," Ethan said mildly.

"Nick called. I've been phoning your cell every few minutes, but the calls go straight to voice mail."

"Your brother's been worried," Ian said diplomatically as he and Sadie came down the stairs. "He figured he should be helping you fend off the bad guys."

"I took the battery out of my phone so the bad guys couldn't track us."

Luke raked his fingers through his sun-streaked brown hair. "That's what Ian said. I just . . . man, a sniper. That is so not good."

"No, it isn't. Even worse news is we don't know for sure if the guy's target was me or if it was Val."

Luke's blue eyes widened. "The hell you say."

"I'm here for my old case files. Lieutenant Hoover thinks the shooter might be someone from my past, someone I pissed off enough to want me dead."

"What do you think?" Ian asked.

"Too soon to say. Once we get settled, I've got some phone calls to make. The most important goes to Jack Morrell. He's DEA in Miami. I'm hoping he'll be able to help me figure a few things out. But my gut says this has nothing to do with an old case and everything to do with what's going on in South America."

Luke whistled. "South America. So now you're pissing off some drug cartel?"

"Could be."

Sadie ambled up to Val, lifted the sleeve of her sweatshirt, and looked at the wide white bandage on her arm. "Never say Ethan doesn't know how to show a lady a good time."

"Very funny," Ethan said.

"How are you feeling?" Sadie asked Val. "You okay?"

"I took a pain pill, so at the moment I'm fine."

"She's okay for now, but I need to get her settled in somewhere."

"You got that covered?" Ian asked.

"Yeah."

Ian tipped his head toward the back of the office. "Let's go into the conference room and you can fill us in."

Setting a hand at Val's waist, Ethan guided her toward the door to the conference room.

Val sat quietly as Ethan talked to Luke, Ian, and Sadie, going over the events of the day. As the story unfolded, with Ethan dramatizing Val's bravery in protecting his daughter and embarrassing her, Sadie kept tossing her glances.

Their gazes met, and the look in the older woman's eyes softened. Apparently, Val's rating had moved up on her women-suitable-for-her-favorite-men's list.

"So you're staying at Dirk's," Luke said with a nod of approval. "It's private. Good access in and out in both directions. He's got Wi-Fi, and he keeps plenty of hardware there."

"Hardware?" Val asked, wondering why they might need maintenance tools.

The question seemed to amuse the men. Ethan gave her an indulgent smile. "He means weapons, honey. Dirk's got a gun safe. He could outfit a small army with what he keeps inside."

"Oh. Right." Dirk and his toys. But then, guns and ammunition were hardly toys. A shiver ran through her.

Sadie leaned over and squeezed her hand. "You need anything, you call me. Women have different needs from men. You call, I'll make sure you get whatever it is."

Val smiled. "Thank you, Sadie." She yawned. The pain pill was making her groggy and it was hard to concentrate.

"So that's it," Luke said. "You need to leave the house, you call and I'll come stay with Val. You or your boys need backup, you call. Yeah?"

"All right." Ethan smiled. "Thanks for the worry, little brother."

"You're welcome, pain-in-my-ass big brother."

Ethan chuckled. "I've got to get those files." He rose and the conversation came to an end. In minutes, Val was back in the Jeep and Ethan was heading for the safety of Dirk's house.

Val just prayed the place would actually *be* safe.

Dirk's ranch-style home sat on a road in an area south of Bellevue off Lakehurst Lane. Ethan glanced at Val, who sat next to him in the passenger seat as they drove through the heavily treed area toward their destination. The rain continued, pounding against the hood as the Jeep rolled along.

"So will Dirk be home while we're there?"

Val hadn't said much since they'd left his office. The pain pill was making her sleepy. Ethan figured the ache in her injured arm was probably coming back — if it had ever actually gone away — and a trickle of guilt slid through him. He was supposed to protect her. But damn, this whole thing made absolutely no sense.

Or, more likely, it made complete sense and he just hadn't figured it out yet.

"Dirk left town for a couple of days. I think he needed a break." He turned down a narrow lane, into a neighborhood of homes on large, tree-covered lots, the properties so overgrown he could barely see the houses through the dense, leafy foliage.

"Doesn't look like Dirk's kind of neighborhood," Val said, surveying the nondescript family homes in the area.

"For years in his spare time, Dirk's been buying foreclosures and turning them for a profit. He got this house in an estate sale about a year ago; an old woman who died without any kids. It came with all her furniture and it's only a few blocks from the lake. Dirk's got a boat, so he decided to keep it, at least for a while. He's got a one-bedroom apartment in Bellevue. He stays there most of the time. It's closer to the action."

"Dirk seems like a restless kind of guy, someone who'd get bored fairly quickly. I think that's one of the things Meg was worried about."

Ethan's gaze swung to hers. "Meg thought Dirk would get bored with her?"

She shrugged. "She says he's a chick magnet — that's what she called him. She doesn't think a guy like Dirk could be faithful to one woman. I have to say, he seems like kind of a tumbleweed."

He scoffed. "My brother, Luke, now he's a tumbleweed. Dirk, not so much. Like I said, besides doing his job, he buys and sells property. It takes hard work and brains to make money at that, and it doesn't happen overnight."

She looked up, clearly reconsidering her original impression. "He never said anything."

"It isn't his way."

Val fell silent as Ethan turned into the gravel driveway, pulled up, and got out to retrieve the spare garage door opener Dirk kept in the mailbox along one wall. He climbed back in, opened the double car garage, and drove the Jeep inside. A dirt bike sat in the second car parking space.

"I thought he rode a Harley."

"He does. His Viper's in the shop, and he's off on the Harley." Ethan grinned. "The dirt bike's mine."

She studied the knobby tires and racy design. "I guess Dirk's not the only one who likes his toys."

Ethan chuckled. "It's an off-road machine. It isn't meant to be ridden on the freeway. It's more about getting out of the city and into the woods."

Val smiled. "I used to like camping. I used to go on the weekends with Mom and Pops. We'd pitch a tent and Pops would fish. Mom and I would hike or sunbathe or just loaf around in the forest all day."

"You like to fish?" Ethan asked, trying to imagine her in rubber waders instead of a skimpy bikini. Good luck with that.

"I used to fish with Pops. I haven't done it since I got out of high school."

"Maybe we could go out on Dirk's boat sometime." At the same instant, both of them realized how unlikely that sounded.

"Maybe" was all she said.

Dirk's batten-board house was built in the seventies, a single-story structure that faced backward, out toward the lake. With an eye to making a profit, he had slowly been improving the place. New roof. The exterior dark wood recently stained. He'd pruned the overgrown landscape, though he liked his privacy, so he hadn't trimmed too much.

When Ethan opened the door leading in from the garage and they stepped into the kitchen, the interior smelled of lemon oil. The appliances were old, but everything was neat and clean. Dirk was ex-military. The lessons had stayed with him.

Ethan cracked the window over the sink to let in some air while Val went to open a window in the living room. When she pulled the drapes, there was a partial view of the lake down through the trees and rooftops of houses on the lanes below. A newly stained wooden deck opened off sliding glass doors.

Val ran a hand over the old-fashioned burgundy velvet sofa next to a matching chair. "I can feel her in here — the lady who owned the house. I bet she loved this place. It's not exactly Dirk's style, but it's quaint and very charming."

"Dirk said it reminded him of his grandmother."

"Maybe that's why he kept it."

Ethan set down his bag and the one Val had packed. "Nothing so romantic. The boat dock's close by. He's got a Scarab 215 with twin two fifty engines. That's five hundred horses. Dirk loves to water ski."

"Anything that involves speed, I guess."

He shrugged. "And fishing. Boat's not exactly built for slow going, but we make it work." He grabbed the bags and headed down the hall. He could hear Val's footsteps right behind him. "The house isn't big, but Dirk keeps one of the bedrooms for guests."

Ethan walked in and set the bags on the floor. "Queen-size bed." He looked at Val, thought of her there beside him, and arousal sifted through him. "I guess we'll have to snuggle."

Val smiled up at him. "I don't mind."

He didn't either. Though he'd just had her, looking at the bed beneath the old-fashioned handmade quilt made him want her all over again. "How's your arm?" he asked, afraid he might have hurt her when he'd taken her before. "When will you need to change the bandage?"

"I'm okay. I don't have to change the dressing till tonight. I brought everything I need."

Worry filtered through him. "Maybe you should take another pain pill."

"I might. If it starts hurting again. But later, once we're settled."

He knew she was afraid something else might happen. Hell, he was worried about it, too.

"There's a bath at the end of the hall. Why don't you get settled while I set up my laptop?"

"I need to do that, too. Oh, darn, that reminds me. With everything that's happened, I forgot to tell you what I found out."

"Yeah, what's that?"

"Since I'm not just a pretty face, I decided to see what else I could find out about Myra Stern. I Googled her and started digging, and guess what?"

"What?" he asked with a hint of amusement, glad she was smiling after all she'd been through that day.

"Myra wasn't jealous of Jason. Certainly not enough to hire someone to kill his mistress. In fact, she has a thing for younger men."

His eyebrows went up. "I remember reading in her file that she's a few years older than her husband."

"Eight years older. Jason's forty-six. Myra's fifty-four, but she stays in shape, and she's had enough face work to look years younger. Jason's actually getting too old for her." She grinned and her dimples appeared. "It seems the lady is quite the cougar."

"Is that so?"

"That's right. In the tabloids, she's been linked with several young, wannabe movie stars. Even a young pro golfer. Jason has his ladies, but Myra has her much younger men."

His lips twitched. "Another perfectly good theory shot to hell."

Val laughed. "So where do we go from here?"

His amusement instantly faded. "I need to make that phone call. This is the first chance I've had to talk to Jack Morrell."

"He's the DEA guy in Miami, right?"

He nodded. "I worked a case that led down there a couple of years ago, got a tip on a big shipment of drugs coming into the country. Jack handled the bust. He's a good man."

"So he owes you for the tip?"

"Let's hope he thinks so."

The phone call to Jack Morrell went better than Ethan expected.

"I've got trouble here, Jack. Big trouble. I'm hoping you can help." Ethan told him about the murder, the investigation that had led to a copycat killer in Dallas and a hostage situation in Atlanta. He mentioned the sniper who'd been waiting for him this morning, here in Seattle.

"Sounds like you're up to your ass in alligators, good buddy."

Ethan grunted. "I'm not sure what the hell is going on, Jack, but I really need to find out."

"So how can I help?"

"One of the leads I'm following involves a guy named Julian Latham. Thirty years old, lives in Miami. Peter and Alessandra Latham, Julian's parents, are big money, Jack. The kind that might just come a little too easy."

"And you're saying that because . . . ?"

"Julian works for one of his father's companies, Latham Property Management. Interestingly, he travels three or four times a year to Caracas, disappears for a couple of days, then comes home. I've got a feeling he's doing more down there than managing company property."

Ethan filled Jack in on as many details as he knew, including the hotel, the Gran Melia, where Julian stayed when he was in the city.

"Your tip was good the last time," Jack said. "I'll check this out. We've got a man on the ground down there. He may recognize the name. If not, I'll have him do some digging, see what he can come up with."

"Thanks, Jack."

"I'll call you when I've got something. Meantime, stay out of range."

Ethan smiled. He was getting plenty of free advice lately.

Most of it was pretty good. "I'll do my best."

He hung up the phone and turned back to Val. "Morrell's got a man in Caracas, an agent or informant, I'm not sure which. He's going to see what Julian's up to."

"I hope he does it fast."

"Yeah, so do I."

CHAPTER THIRTY-FIVE

Val walked with Ethan down the hall to the third bedroom to retrieve a disposable cell phone. This room was all Dirk Reynolds, a man cave that included a closet holding several pairs of camouflage pants and a pair of black tactical vests, a basketball and football in the bookshelves along the wall, a weight rack and bench, tennis racquets, a snowboard and winter outdoor wear, a racy-looking single ski, and a ton of other miscellaneous sporting equipment.

Most noticeable was the heavy steel gun safe nearly as tall as Ethan that dominated one wall. Val figured the fishing rods were out in the garage, along with motorcycle helmets and God only knew what else.

She couldn't help wondering what Meg would say if she saw all this — which reminded her that she needed to talk to her friend.

Ethan pulled a throwaway phone out of a

459

drawer and handed it over. "It's untraceable. Dirk keeps a couple of them charged just in case. Program in my number, nine-one-one, and anyone you might want to call."

"Okay."

"I'll be in the living room on my computer. No e-mails, by the way. And no Facebook, okay?"

She nodded. Ethan walked back out the door, giving her some privacy to use the phone.

She called Mom and Pops first. She had phoned them every day since she'd gotten back to Seattle, but after being shot and nearly killed, she needed to talk to them again.

"Hi, Mom, it's me."

"Hi, honey." She could almost see her mother's smiling face, framed by the cloud of silver hair she usually clipped back at the nape of her neck.

"It's good to hear your voice," Val said.

Her mother must have caught the tremor in her words. Val could almost feel the mother radar kicking into gear on the other end of the phone.

"What's going on, sweetheart? Are you okay?"

She wasn't okay. Today had been a nightmare. So far, she'd been able to control her emotions. Now she was fighting not to burst into tears.

"I'm . . . I'm okay." *Except for being shot.* "I just . . . I miss you."

"Oh, honey. We miss you so much."

"When are you coming up to see us?" her father asked, picking up the bedroom extension. For once, he was in the house instead of outside working on the farm.

"Well, see, that's the thing. The police . . . umm . . . may have some more questions for me. They're still trying to catch the man who killed Delilah Larsen." *And may have shot at Ethan and me this morning.*

"Delilah . . . she was that model who was murdered," Pops said. Tall and thin, with blond hair turning silver, he actually looked like her, though they were not blood relatives.

"Lord, it seems like that happened ages ago," her mother said.

"I can't believe they haven't caught the bastard yet," Pops grumbled.

"The police are still looking. They're doing their best, but they might need my help. Or Ethan's." She said the name just to hear how her parents would react.

"He's your bodyguard, right?" her mother asked.

"Yes, but . . . our relationship has gotten a little more complicated lately."

Silence fell. "Well, it's about damned time," her father said. "Beautiful young woman like you. Could have men beatin' down your door if you wanted. Though I can't say I'm sorry you been so choosy."

"I know if he means something to you, he has to be a very special man," her mother said. "We can't wait to meet him."

Some of the tightness loosened in her chest. She thought of Ethan and how much he loved his little girl. She thought of the way he had risked his life for her, thought of the fierce way he protected her.

"He is special, Mom. I'm not sure what's going to happen between us, but I'd love for you to meet him."

"Glory hallelujah," her father said. "And he damned well better be good enough for my little girl."

Val laughed. It felt unbelievably good. "We aren't close to getting serious, Pops, so you don't have to worry. Look, I have to go. We'll talk again soon, okay? Love you both."

"Love you, too, honey," they said in unison, and Val pressed the End button on the phone.

Blinking back tears, she took a minute just to absorb the love they'd sent her with every

462

word they'd spoken. She had been on her own for years. Been away at college, had her own car, her own home, her own life. But when things got tough, her parents were the ones she turned to, and they were always there for her.

She sat down on the weight bench to make another call. "It's me, Meg. Can you talk?"

"I've been trying to call you. Your phone keeps going straight to voice mail. Is everything okay?"

"Not exactly. I'm surprised Matt Carlyle hasn't called."

"He probably has. Charlie wandered off with my cell phone and I haven't had time to track it down. What's going on?"

"You remember I had that anniversary interview for David Klein this morning on the local CBS station?"

"I remember. What about it?"

"Well, when I got back to my house, someone tried to shoot me."

"What!"

"Or they might have been shooting at Ethan. We don't know for sure. We're staying somewhere safe until we can figure things out."

"Oh my God!"

"I know. I . . . umm . . . got shot in the

arm, but I'm okay."

"You got shot, but you're okay? Oh my God!"

"Really, it's all right. Ethan's guys, his team from La Belle, they're helping us stay safe. They're probably outside right now. You have someone there with you, right?"

"Dirk took care of it. There's a man from Brodie Operations in front of the house twenty-four seven."

"That's good. I'm sure your security guard knows about the shooting by now."

"They're very efficient."

"That's right, and that's a good thing. If the guy who shot at us is The Preacher, he could be after any of us."

"Oh, God, I hate this."

"Me too."

"At least you have Ethan. Is Dirk there, too?"

"Dirk took his Harley and went out of town for a couple of days. He was hurting, Meg. He didn't want to lose you."

"I didn't want to lose him, either, but . . . I just . . . I did what I had to." There was no way to miss the tears that sprang into Meg's voice.

"I know you did. I'm not ready to give up Ethan. I probably should. I don't know if it can work. I don't know if I can handle his job. All the violence . . . I'm getting to see it firsthand." She sighed. "Maybe I don't need to worry about it. I really have no idea what Ethan feels for me. He cares about me, yes. But maybe that's just his protective instincts kicking in."

"Maybe. Or maybe he's in love with you."

Her stomach clenched. Was it possible? Because it was becoming very clear that she was in love with him. But even if they loved each other, that didn't mean it would work.

"Does Dirk know about the shooting?" Meg asked.

"Ethan called and told him. As I said, he's out of town. Ethan's brother, Luke, says he'll back Ethan up. I have a feeling Luke's a very capable man."

"If he's anything like Ethan and Dirk, I'm sure he is."

"As I said, the guy out front probably knows about the shooting, but you might want to make certain."

"I can see him out the window. I'll call him."

"Listen, I've got to go. Take this number down. We aren't using our own phones. We don't want the people after us using GPS to track us."

"You don't want the people after you . . . oh my God! This is all so scary. I can't help

465

wishing Dirk were here."

"If you called him —"

"No way. I'm not doing that."

"All right, I get it."

"Let me find a pen." Meg returned and wrote down the number of the throwaway phone. "Call if you need anything — and I mean anything. Okay?"

"Same here."

"In the meantime, you both stay safe."

"Thanks, Meg. You, too." Val disconnected the call and headed back to the living room.

Two days passed. Early morning rain pounded on the roof and a gust of wind rattled the window, rousing Ethan from a deep, erotic dream. In the dream, Val had awakened him with soft kisses that traveled from his chest to his navel, then went lower. He could almost feel the silk of her hair brushing his skin as she worked over him.

His morning erection stirred. Something hot and wet licked over his hardened length. Ethan groaned and his eyes cracked open. Not a dream. Better than any dream he'd ever had. His hand slid into Val's heavy blond hair as she took him into her mouth, laved and teased, and pleasure tore through him.

Jesus God, she was amazing. He clamped

down on his control and let her play for a while, enjoying the hot sensations spearing through his body. Then, careful of her arm, he lifted her up and settled her astride him.

"You want to take charge. Go ahead."

She grinned devilishly, displaying her dimples, then rose up and took him deep, began moving sweetly and driving him insane. Ethan cupped her breasts as she tilted forward, her soft blond curls swinging down, cocooning them both as she rocked back and forth and started to come.

He ground his jaw, caught her hips, and drove into her until she came again, then allowed his own release.

Afterward, she snuggled next to him in the queen-size bed, her back to his front, his arm draped over her waist.

Damn, he was crazy about her. He couldn't lie to himself any longer. Hadn't since the moment he had seen her huddled over his daughter, protecting the child with her life. He'd figured out early she was nothing like Allison Winfield. But as bullets flew around them and blood soaked her shirt, he realized that unlike the disdain he felt for Allison, he felt only admiration for Val.

And before Ally had turned his life upside down, Val would have been everything he wanted in a woman.

He wondered what she would say if she knew.

But Val had suffered enough violence in her life and she didn't want more. She didn't want a man whose job required him to own a Glock and a tactical vest.

And he wasn't the kind of man who'd be happy doing anything else.

Ethan sighed into the quiet. He needed to get dressed and get going. It was almost time for Pete to spell Joe. Careful to park his vehicle down the lane out of sight, the outside man positioned himself in the location they had chosen, which provided the best vantage point to watch the house. Every hour, he walked the perimeter, then returned to his place out of sight among the trees.

Ethan had instructed the men to phone if they spotted anything the least bit out of the ordinary. They were not to engage except in self-defense. They were the eyes and ears of the security operation.

Ethan was the primary line of defense.

But two full days had passed since he and Val had taken refuge in the house. Ethan had gone through each of his old case files and managed to come up with a couple of names, but he didn't believe the men he'd helped put in jail posed any actual threat. He had talked to Hoover and given him the names. Hoover would follow up, but so far the police had come up with squat on the shooter.

Time was ticking away, and though the men on his team hadn't complained, Ethan couldn't allow their vigil to go on much longer. The immediate danger was past. He couldn't stay locked away forever. And he wasn't sure how much longer he could convince Val to stay cooped up either.

In the meantime, he planned to call Luke, ask him to stand in while he did some badly needed legwork. He intended to go back and knock on doors in Val's neighborhood, see if someone might have remembered something after the police were there.

At least getting out of the house might get his brain working, spur his mind to come up with some fresh ideas. Something that would give them a break in the case.

He showered and pulled on jeans and a long-sleeved thermal in concession to the rainy weather, passed Val as he came out of the bathroom. She went up on her toes and kissed his mouth, then yawned and went in to take her shower.

Her arm was feeling better, she'd said, but every time he thought of how the shot could have been a few inches lower, could have hit some vital part of her body, how the injury could have been fatal, he felt sick to his stomach.

The familiar two-and-one rap at the door told him Luke was outside. He hadn't phoned his brother yet, but Luke had uncanny intuition.

He figured it was Luke, but when he looked through the peephole, Dirk stood on the porch. Dirk turned and waved to Pete, who was heading up the hill in a dark gray rain slicker to take his shift.

Ethan pulled open the door. "You look like hell," he said, assessing the three-day growth of beard on Dirk's face, the water plastering his too-long hair against the dragon tattoo crawling up the side of his neck. His black leather jacket and denim shirt were soaked, his black leather pants running water all over the floor.

"Yeah, well, I was all the way to hell and gone out in the San Juans when you called two days ago. It was sunny when I left Seattle, rained all the way back. My timing sucks." He scrubbed a hand over his face, sliding away a palm full of water. "I shouldn't have left in the first place, not with everything going on."

"There's nothing you could have done.

The shooter came out of the blue."

"How's Val? She okay?"

"I'm good," Val said, walking toward them down the hall in a pair of jeans and a sweatshirt, her blond hair pulled up in a bouncy ponytail on top of her head. Just looking at her made his chest feel tight. "My arm doesn't hurt much anymore."

Dirk eyed her gravely. "Jesus, Val."

"Really, I'm okay."

"What about Meg?" Dirk asked, clearly worried. "Have you talked to her? Is she all right?"

"She's fine. She said you put a man on her house."

Dirk sighed. "I'd rather it was me, but that isn't what she wants."

When Val made no reply, he looked at Ethan. "You think it's him, The Preacher?"

"Hoover doesn't think so. He thinks the shooter was aiming at me, not Val. Old case, somebody I pissed off."

"Yeah? What do you think?"

"Not convinced. Hoping to hear something from Jack Morrell. He's checking Latham's connection to South America."

"South America? You're still gnawing that bone? You really think this has something to do with drugs?"

"Call it a gut feeling, but yeah, I do. A

couple of things turned up while you were gone. Why don't you get out of those wet clothes and we'll talk?"

"I'll make some coffee," Val offered. "And see what there is to eat."

"Sounds good." Dirk headed down the hall, his leathers squeaking, black boots muddying up the floor as his long legs carried him into his bedroom.

Chapter Thirty-Six

"You always thought Delilah was murdered by a pro," Dirk said while Val worked in the kitchen and Ethan finished summing things up. A lot had happened since Dirk had left the city.

"For a while, I thought maybe I was wrong and it was just a crazy," Ethan said. "After Stern came on to Val and started talking about the murder, hinting that the victim was killed because she'd made someone mad, I decided to take another look. When Sadie found the info on Julian Latham and his travels to South America, it all seemed to fall into place."

"So you think the whole note thing was a setup. Just a way to throw the cops off the trail."

"Yeah, but I could be wrong."

"You could be. I guess we won't know till you hear from Morrell, and that could take some time."

"I hope not."

"What can I do to help?" Dirk asked.

"I was just about to call Luke. I need to get out of here for a while, clear my head. I thought I'd go back to Val's, take another look around, knock on some doors, see if someone remembers something they didn't think of before. We've got to come up with a lead."

"I'll stay with Val." Dirk yawned. "I could use a little downtime after all that riding. My muscles haven't stopped vibrating yet. They think I'm still on the road."

Ethan chuckled. He was still smiling when his disposable started to ring. He picked it up off the dining table. "Brodie."

"You been on your computer?" Sadie's voice sounded sharp over the line.

"Last night, not this morning. Why?"

"They planted some kind of Trojan horse, Ethan. I was afraid of that, so I set up an alert. It's real smart software. They know it was you looking at them. That's probably how they found you at Valerie's place. They're tracking you through your computer. They know where you are."

"Christ. You said *they.* You talking about Latham?"

"Julian Latham and everyone he knows. Not sure where you picked it up. Now get

474

the heck on the road."

"Thanks, Sadie. I'll call when we get somewhere safe."

Val walked out of the kitchen. "I've got biscuits in the oven. Breakfast is almost ready, but . . . umm . . . I might have seen something outside."

"What?" Ethan asked.

"Two men on the lower road. I only caught a glimpse, but it kind of looked like they were trying not to be seen. It's probably nothing, but —"

Dirk moved toward the window above the kitchen sink. "We got visitors. I can see two from here. Where the hell is Pete?"

Ethan grabbed his shoulder holster and slid it on as he moved to a spot in the dining area where he could see Pete's location through the trees. "Pete's down. I can see a little of his rain slicker in the mud behind some bushes."

"We're gonna need some firepower." Dirk started running down the hall.

"What's going on?" Val asked.

"You need to get down, honey." Dragging the heavy antique oak dining room table away from the window, he turned it onto its side. "Over here." He ignored the knot in his stomach and the sudden pallor of her face. "Stay as low as you can and don't get up. You got your phone?"

She swallowed, nodded.

"Call nine-one-one. You know how to shoot?"

"Bobby taught me." Her voice shook. "It's been a long time."

"Good to know, but it probably won't come to that."

Val's hands trembled as she tugged the disposable out of her pocket and punched 9-1-1.

Dirk raced back into the living room, an AR-15 assault rifle slung across his chest, a tactical vest in his hand. His Browning 9 mil rode in the clip holster at his side. An extra clip protruded from his pocket.

He tossed Val a vest and Ethan a semiauto S&W .45. Ethan checked the clip, racked the slide, and put the safety on, then shoved the second gun into his waistband behind his back. Catching the extra clip Dirk tossed him, he jammed it into his pocket.

While Dirk headed for the rear of the house, Ethan covered the front. As he moved into position next to the dining room window, the first shots rang out, a burst of automatic rifle fire that shattered the glass next to where he pressed against the wall just out of sight.

Ethan stepped out and returned fire, sending one of the attackers running. "Put the vest on, Val."

She made a sound in her throat.

"Do it, honey."

From the corner of his eye, he watched her struggle into the vest while trying not to hurt her arm and keep her head down.

"It's going to be okay," he said. "We've got enough firepower to defend our position till the cops get here."

More rounds went off, plowing into the windowsill. A couple of shots shattered the glass over the kitchen sink. The men in front moved forward. Ethan fired, taking one of them down. The other fired wildly and ducked into the foliage. Ethan heard Dirk blasting away out back.

"Where're the police?" Val asked from her place on the floor. "Why don't the cops come?"

Dirk hurried out of the back wearing a vest and loaded down with more weapons. He grinned. "When seconds count, the cops are only minutes away."

Ethan just grunted. "What's going on?"

"They're on the move. The hill's too steep at the back of the house. They'll be coming in the side windows or through the front door." He tipped his head toward the garage. "You need to get her out of here."

"We can defend till the cops come."

"We could — if the bastards hadn't set the house on fire."

Ethan's gaze sliced to Dirk. "You're fucking kidding me."

"I wish. My bike's out front, but you'd be too much of a target. Take the dirt bike. You can get out through the side door in the garage. I'll throw down enough lead to give you time to get away."

"What, and you stay here and turn into a crispy critter?"

The corner of Dirk's mouth lifted a little, then thinned to a grim, hard line. "I was thinking I'd make a move before it came to that." He turned, fired off a round through the kitchen window. Ethan fired a couple of shots out the dining room window. On the other side of the living room, he could see the deck burning. No one was coming in that way.

"I can get out," Dirk continued. "Long as I don't have to worry about you or Val. Besides, one of you is the target. They'll be after you as soon as they figure out you're gone."

It was a point and a good one. Ethan knew Dirk well enough to believe he could escape.

Ethan could smell the smoke now. The back of the house was burning. The roof was on fire.

Where were the fire trucks, dammit? Where were the effing police? "We gotta go, baby." She came to her feet, her eyes big and blue and full of trust. Ethan's jaw hardened. No way was he breaking that trust.

Moving her back from the window, he cinched the black Kevlar vest a little tighter around her, but it was still way too big. *Better than nothing,* he thought.

"The key to the boat is on the wall by the door," Dirk said. "If they've got the lower road covered, head for the lake, take her out that way."

A barrage of shots tore through the front door. These guys weren't waiting. Dirk positioned himself off to one side and blasted back in their direction, cutting the door nearly in half. "Go!" The fire chewed through the ceiling and a chunk of it fell into the hallway.

"Time to move." Glock drawn, Ethan grabbed the boat key off the wall, opened the door into the garage, dodged a shot that splintered the jamb, and fired, taking down a man near the side door. He spotted another guy and fired. The man grabbed his bloody leg and jerked back into the cover of the bushes.

Ethan shoved his pistol back into his shoulder holster and ran for the bike, Val close behind him. Grabbing the helmet sitting on the seat, he turned and shoved it on Val's head, climbed on and turned the key in the ignition, felt her swing on behind him, felt her arms lock around his waist.

"Hang on!" As they shot through the open side door and headed downhill along the narrow dirt path toward the lake, he caught a glimpse of the barrel of Dirk's AR-15 above them as he fired a short burst out the window, then fired again. The engine roared as Ethan raced toward the lower road, praying Dirk would escape the house without getting killed.

Or burned up in the fire that was fast collapsing the roof.

A black SUV with dark-tinted windows, a drug dealer's cliché, sat on the lower road, its engine running.

"It's them!" Val shouted. Ethan couldn't believe it when she pulled the .45 out of his waistband behind his back, flipped off the safety, and fired two shots through the windshield. Glass exploded. The car swerved right, then jerked left, then swung right again.

"Hold on!" Ethan gunned the engine and the bike lunged across the road, got a little air and landed on the path on the opposite side. He could feel Val's arms lock back around him, the gun still in her hand, the barrel pointed at the ground between his legs. He hoped like hell she didn't accidentally pull the trigger.

He almost smiled. Stupid damn time to realize he wanted more kids.

The SUV tore off down the road, tires squealing. They'd be turning at the end of the lane where the road curved down to the lake.

Ethan planned to get there first.

From the bottom of the trail, he could see the dock stretching into the water. Dirk must have been planning to use the boat because the cover was off. The bike hit a patch of mud and spun sideways. Ethan righted it and kept going. He shot onto the wooden dock and slid to a halt. Shoved the kickstand down with his boot, and the two of them leaped off and ran toward the bright orange twin-engine Scarab.

The jet boat roared to life. Ethan shoved the accelerator forward and the boat jumped out of its berth as if it had been caged too long. The Scarab could really haul ass.

By the time the big SUV pulled up and men began pouring out, taking up firing positions along the dock, the boat was way out in the lake, out of range.

Ethan kept the Scarab headed north. There was a roadhouse on the water a few miles away, where he and Dirk always stopped for a beer after a day of fishing. There was a dock there where he could tie up. Mulkey's Tavern was a locals' joint, hidden away in a cove, not easy to spot; it was a long way around to get there by car.

Tucker Mulkey, the owner, was a Vietnam vet, a tough old bastard, and a friend. Ethan could count on Tuck to keep Val safe while he went back to help Dirk and Pete.

Mulkey's drew near, an old wooden building up on the bank, picnic tables outside and a view of the lake from inside the rustic interior. With the weather so chilly and wet, no one was sitting outside.

Ethan pulled up at the dock, took the pistol Val still clutched in her hand, and stuffed it back into his waistband behind his back. "We need to hurry." With his hand at her waist, both of them started jogging along the walkway.

Ethan prayed Dirk had gotten out safely. Prayed the cops and the EMTs were there by now, taking care of Pete, prayed he had gotten medical attention in time. Whatever had happened, he had to go back and find out.

He clenched his jaw as he hurried toward the roadhouse, hoping like hell Mulkey was there, as he usually was.

The best sight he could have seen was Luke striding toward them down the hill.

Standing on the shore at the end of the dock, Val trembled in the misty cold, her arms wrapped around her.

"How'd you know where to find us?" Ethan asked his brother.

"I was in the office when Val called Sadie, said you were taking fire. I knew you'd bail. I figured you'd wind up here. I thought you might have bogies on your tail."

Ethan's gaze swung to Val.

"After I called nine-one-one, I phoned Sadie. She always seems to get things done."

His mouth edged up; then he thought of Dirk and Pete and his mood darkened. "I've got to get back. Dirk's still there and Pete's been shot. You stay with Val."

She looked up to see an older, silver-haired man striding purposefully down the hill, a big black pistol holstered at his waist.

"Tuck's going to look after Val," Luke said. "We need to get back there before it's too late."

Ethan looked torn. Val knew he trusted his brother, but if Luke wasn't there and the shooters came after her —

"You have to go," she said. "Dirk and Pete need your help. I'll be okay with your friend."

Ethan's jaw tightened, but he nodded. "Tuck knows what he's doing. Not much chance they'll find this place, but if they do, he can protect you till we get back."

Ethan's disposable started ringing. He dragged it out of his pocket and pressed it against his ear, listened, and started nodding. Val couldn't miss the relief that swept over his face.

"We're at Mulkey's," he said. "We'll wait for you here." He ended the call and turned toward them. "Dirk's out safe. Pete's on the way to the hospital. Took a bullet to the shoulder. Hit his head when he went down. He's probably got a concussion. He'll have to have surgery, but they think he's going to be okay."

Relief hit her hard and her knees went weak. She started shaking, felt Ethan's arm go around her waist.

"Let's get her inside," he said. Removing the tactical vest she still wore, he guided her up the hill.

Luke strode along beside them. He was wearing camo pants, heavy leather boots, and a long-sleeved, olive-drab T-shirt. A band of bullets draped across his chest, a holster rode at his waist, and there was a knife strapped to his thigh. His hair was wet, making it look darker, though the rain had lessened to a drizzle. Luke's jaw was set, his features iron hard.

There was nothing of the handsome, casually friendly man she had met at Ethan's office. This man was hard through and through, a battle-trained soldier.

Val thought of the men who had attacked them at the house, remembered her insane ride behind Ethan down the hill, remembered pulling the pistol, how it had felt in her hand. She thought of Bobby Rodriguez, could almost hear the gunshots that had killed him, feel his blood sliding hotly through her hands. Her stomach rolled. For a moment, she thought she would be sick.

"You okay?" Ethan asked.

She swallowed the bile rising in her throat. She remembered something else, something important, or at least thought she did. "I just . . . I need a minute."

Ethan didn't hesitate, just swept her up in his arms and carried her inside the tavern. By the time he set her down at a corner table, she was feeling a little steadier.

"I'll get her a glass of water," Tucker Mulkey said.

"Yeah, and a brandy," Ethan added.

"You got it."

"And bring us a couple of beers," Luke said as he sat down at the battered wooden table across from them. The place was old, with a long wooden bar, exposed rafters overhead. All kinds of posters covered the ceiling, beer ads, pinup girls, photos of guys kneeling next to their hunting trophies. Mounted deer heads hung on the walls.

Val forced herself to concentrate. "Did they catch them?"

Ethan shook his head. "No."

Val gripped his hand. "While you were busy trying to keep the bike on the trail, I recognized one of the men. Not at first. He was out of place, you know? I didn't put it together until a few minutes ago."

His eyebrows went up. "You recognized one of the bastards who was shooting at us?"

She nodded. "Bick Gallagher. You shot him in the leg. At the time, all I could think of was getting out of there alive."

"Yeah, me too."

Tucker arrived carrying a tray with two mugs of beer, a glass of water, and a shot of brandy. Val watched as Ethan pulled out his phone.

"Sadie, beautiful, it's Ethan. Thanks for

saving my ass today. Mine and Val's. Dirk's, too." He chuckled at something the woman said. "Yeah, yeah, I hear ya. Listen, I need you to go in, take another look at a guy named Bick Gallagher. He's second in command at La Belle security. Val says he was one of the men shooting at us. While you're at it, you might as well run Beau Desmond again."

He nodded. "I know. You'll have to go deep. Nothing shows up on the surface." Sadie said something, and Ethan hung up the phone.

"She's taking a second look. If there's another Trojan horse, she'll know how to get around it."

Val looked at the men sitting at the table. "What are we going to do? We don't have any clothes, nowhere to stay."

Luke grinned. "Leave it to a woman to worry about the luxuries. Doesn't matter if a horde of cutthroats are trying to gun her down — she wants to look good while she's running for her life."

Val laughed, reached over and punched him in the arm. At least he'd made her laugh when she felt more like crying.

Luke kept grinning. "Don't worry about it, sweetheart. We'll go to my place. It doesn't have all the comforts Dirk's place has, but —"

"Make that had," Ethan interrupted darkly. "Bastards burned the place down."

"What? Jesus, I liked that house."

"Yeah, so did Dirk. Add to that, my Jeep was in the garage."

"Fuck. Like I said, my place might not have all the comforts, but it's secure."

"Luke's got a cabin up in the hills above Gold Bar. It's on the side of a mountain, looks down over the town. Perimeter alarms, security cameras, chain-link fence. Damn thing's a fortress. Probably should have gone there in the first place."

"We didn't think they'd find us," Val said.

Ethan shook his head. "These guys have been one step ahead of us from the start. I'm tired of it. It's time we stepped up our game."

Luke set his beer mug down on the table. "You're thinking instead of waiting for them to come at us again, we go after them." Luke grinned, more relaxed, blue eyes sparkling, looking more like the Luke she had met in the office. "Good idea" was all he said.

CHAPTER THIRTY-SEVEN

"Loser stays with Val."

"Wait a minute," Val said, pinning Dirk with a glare.

Ethan chuckled. They were in the living room of Luke's rustic one-bedroom log cabin. The place had a galley kitchen with an old freestanding white stove, a propane fridge, and a counter with a sink. There was a small bedroom with a queen-size bed, a tiny bathroom with a shower, and a living room with a cast-iron woodstove, the only heat in the house. A windmill and propane ran the generator that provided electricity, which ran the lights and the well pump.

When Luke wanted to, he could stay way off the grid.

The good news was, Dirk had gotten out of his house without being hurt. He had crashed Ethan's Jeep through the garage door to make his escape, so the vehicle hadn't burned up. It ran, but the bad news was, it was going to take a lot of bodywork to repair the damned thing. Still, Ethan was grateful.

He held up the matchsticks he'd broken into lengths. Both Dirk and Luke pulled one and held it up.

"Looks like you stay, Dirk," Ethan said.

Dirk said the f word beneath his breath.

"Hey, you already had your fun," Luke said. "Now it's my turn."

But the truth was, Luke always did his best to avoid a firefight. He'd been Special Forces, a Delta operator. He'd still be there if he hadn't taken a bullet in some foreign country on a mission he still couldn't talk about. By the time he'd gotten back into fighting form, he'd moved on with his life. He'd given his all for God and country, would again if he was needed, but he'd discovered he wanted more.

Unfortunately, he hadn't yet figured out exactly what that more was.

"You know, maybe you should take Val instead of me," Luke teased. "I hear she shot the hell out of those bastards from the back of your dirt bike."

"You should have seen her in Atlanta," Dirk said proudly. "Knocked some perv loop-legged with a curling iron."

Luke grinned. "My kind of woman."

Ethan glanced over at Val, but she was no longer smiling. Fat tears rolled down her cheeks. Ethan threw a hard look at his friends. "All right, you two, now look what you've done."

Pulling her up from the sofa into his arms, he led her into the bedroom and closed the door. Val clung to him, held on tight while she cried against his shoulder. She'd been so damned brave. Sometimes he forgot that normal for him was far from normal for her.

Hell, who was he kidding? This wasn't even normal for him.

He kissed the top of her head and just held her. Dammit, she deserved a good cry.

She snuggled closer and her crying eased to soft little sobs. She was wearing a pair of Luke's sweatpants and one of his faded army T-shirts instead of her wet clothes. He could feel her soft breasts pressing into his chest and, bastard that he was, he started getting hard.

Val sniffed and eased a little away. Ethan lifted the bottom of his T-shirt, found a Kleenex among the change of clothes he kept at the cabin, and used it to dry her tears. "You okay?"

She nodded. "I'm sorry. I didn't mean to do that. It's all just . . . so overwhelming."

"Hey. You were really great back there.

You were tough when you needed to be. You've got nothing to apologize for."

She looked up at him, gave him a tremulous smile. Ethan felt the power of that smile all the way to the bottom of his boots. Jesus God, he was in love with her. Crazy in love. What a crappy time to figure it out.

His phone rang just then. He was still using the disposable. The fact that Luke could get cell service up here was one of the reasons he'd bought the property.

"It's Sadie," said the familiar voice on the other end of the line.

Ethan opened the bedroom door and walked back into the living room, the phone against his ear. Both men's heads came up. Both looked guilty for making Val cry. Ethan just smiled.

"Hey, Sadie, what have you got?"

"Not a darn thing on Beau Desmond. He was a cop before he went private, just like it says in his file."

"And Gallagher?"

"Valentine was right on the money. Bick Gallagher, aka Ray Bickford. Paramilitary. Worked in South America for a while. Showed up in Seattle three years ago."

Ethan's instincts started screaming. "South America. He connected to Julian Latham?"

"Not that I could find. Beau Desmond was the one who hired him at La Belle. I don't know who recommended him. I have a hunch Desmond doesn't know anything about Gallagher's past. It was buried deep, Ethan. By someone who really knew what he was doing."

"Desmond might not know who he is, but someone does. My guess — that someone paid him to kill Delilah Larsen. I want to talk to him. You got an address?"

Sadie rattled it off. "By the way, the shooting's all over the news. Dirk and Pete were both mentioned. Said Dirk's house was destroyed but Pete's condition is good. Nothing about you or Val."

"Glad Pete's okay. Thanks, Sadie." Ethan hung up and turned to the men. "It's beginning to come together. I think it's time we had that little chat with some of our closest friends. First on our list, Bick Gallagher, aka Ray Bickford. He's paramilitary, worked in South America."

"I never liked that prick," Dirk said. "Gotta be connected to Latham."

"Sadie couldn't find it."

"Doesn't mean it's not there," Luke said.

"We talk to Gallagher, then talk to Stern."

"Maybe you ought to call Hoover," Dirk suggested. "Tell the cops Val recognized

Gallagher as one of the shooters. If he's carrying a bullet, they'll at least be able to hold him."

"Yeah, and if I do that, we won't get a chance to have that chat. I want to know who he's working for. We still don't know who Gallagher had in his crosshairs. Could be me for digging into Latham, or it could be Val. Maybe whoever hired Gallagher thinks Val knows something — the same something Delilah found out. Hell, it could be anything."

"Ethan's right," Luke said. "We need to get to Gallagher first."

"If the guy took a bullet," Dirk said, "there's a good chance he's already on the run."

"Could be. If he is, we go to Stern. One of them's going to tell us something — one way or another."

Luke reached for the holstered weapon lying on the coffee table, pulled his customized M9 Beretta out and checked the load, then checked his ankle gun, a subcompact Glock 27.

Dirk's Browning rode in his side holster. Ethan rechecked his Glock, slid it back into his shoulder holster. All three men were reloaded and ready. The phones had been recharged.

Ethan strode over to Val, pulled her into his arms, and very thoroughly kissed her. She was clinging to his shoulders by the time he was done. "Just a little longer, baby. Then this is over. Can you make it?"

"Do I have a choice?"

Ethan kissed her again, looked into her gorgeous blue eyes. "You'll have one later." He wondered if she understood the message, wondered if she would be willing to consider making a life with him.

Her eyes filled for the second time. She went up on her toes and kissed him. "Be careful."

Ethan just nodded. He and Luke headed for the door.

Val sat in an overstuffed chair near the iron stove, where a small fire burned against the chill. Dirk stretched out on the brown plaid sofa, sound asleep, long legs hanging over the arm.

His weapon lay on the floor within easy reach, though he had told her the security alarms had all been set and there was no way anyone could reach the cabin without setting them off. He looked tired. He'd ridden hard to get back to Seattle to help Ethan. He was a good man.

Val couldn't help wondering if Meg had

made the right decision.

She looked over at Dirk, and an image arose of him striding out of the back bedroom of his burning house, an assault rifle strapped across his chest. She tried to imagine Dirk with Charlie, a father to Meg's little boy, but the image wouldn't come.

She thought of Ethan and the shoot-out, and the echo of gunfire filled her head. For a minute she was back on the street, cradling Bobby's head in her lap, her heart breaking as she watched the crimson flow of his blood sliding through her hands.

She had vowed never to enter that world again and yet here she was. Surrounded by gunmen, bullets flying, running for her life. One of them could have died today. Did she want to live that way? Live with the fear and the worry?

After her wild motorcycle ride, her arm had started throbbing again, a reminder of what it would be like to live in Ethan's world.

He had said she would have a choice. Was he hinting at a future for them? She was in love with him. Of course she wanted to be with him. But could she handle the uncertainty? Never being completely sure that he would be coming home?

She glanced over at Dirk. Maybe Meg had

done the right thing. But Val wasn't Meg. She didn't have a child to consider. Was giving up Ethan the right choice for her?

She leaned back in the overstuffed chair and closed her eyes, praying the answer would come.

Praying the men would stay safe.

Ethan swore as he strode through Bick Gallagher's empty apartment. As Dirk had rightly guessed, Gallagher was in the wind. His closet door stood open. The hangers were bare, his clothes missing. Dresser drawers were left open. A locked desk drawer had been opened, then hadn't been pushed completely shut. Ethan figured Gallagher probably kept another passport, another identity in that drawer.

He phoned Bruce Hoover, told the lieutenant Bick Gallagher, aka Ray Bickford, was one of the shooters at Dirk's house. Val had recognized the guy and Ethan had shot him in the leg. He told Hoover about his hunch that Gallagher was the guy who had killed Delilah Larsen.

Ethan wouldn't get the chance to interrogate the bastard, as he had planned, but with any luck, Gallagher wouldn't escape.

Hoover spoke into the phone. "I need you, Valentine Hart, and Dirk Reynolds to come

497

into the station," the detective said. "You know how it works. I've got irate neighbors and cops swarming the area around Reynolds' house. I've talked to Hernandez, but I need a statement from everyone involved."

Hoover needed a statement, but Ethan couldn't mention the evidence Sadie had come up with, because it wasn't exactly obtained by legal means. Besides, at the moment he had more important things to do.

"Later," he said. "I'll tell Reynolds you're looking for him. I'll bring Val with me and we'll both give you statements. At the moment, there's something I need to do."

Hoover was still talking when Ethan ended the call. He flicked a glance at his brother, who prowled up beside him. "Time to talk to Stern," Ethan said.

"Oh, yeah," Luke agreed.

They headed back to Luke's vehicle, a beat-up black-and-tan Ford Bronco at least ten years old. Being a bounty hunter required stealth. The old SUV could pass without notice. Unless you looked under the hood.

The Bronco sported a brand-new Ford Racing Aluminator XS 5.0 liter Coyote 500 horse engine. The SUV had been fully rebuilt. It had top-of-the-line four-wheel drive for off-road terrain and the speed of a gazelle.

Luke slid in behind the wheel and fired up the big V8 engine. "You got the address?"

Ethan rattled off a number on Olympic Drive in the Highlands, one of the most expensive neighborhoods in Seattle. Luke drove his battered Ford up to the tall iron gates at the entrance to the exclusive community. Ethan smiled at the look on the gate guard's round darkly suntanned face.

Just to be obnoxious, Luke gunned the powerful engine.

The man's black eyebrows went up. His dark red uniform jacket suited him perfectly. He looked like he'd just gone AWOL from the Bengal army.

"May I help you?"

"We're here to see Jason Stern," Luke said.

"Your name, please."

Ethan leaned over to speak through the driver-side window. "You won't find our name in your visitor log. Call Stern, tell him Ethan Brodie needs to talk to him."

The guard's mouth lifted in a smirk. He didn't think for a second Stern would give them permission to drive through the gate.

The Bronco idled, growling like an impatient tiger.

The guard spoke into the phone, listened, and started nodding. "Yes, sir. Of course, Mr. Stern. I'll send them right up." He turned, cast them an imperious glance. "You may proceed."

The gate swung slowly open. Luke stepped on the gas and the beast rolled forward. They wound their way along the road through the lush green foliage, then up the circular drive, around the fountain in the middle of the circle.

The dented old Bronco looked completely out of place when Luke stopped directly in front of the house. Tudor style, constructed of brick, more than two stories high, the mansion had to be ten thousand square feet.

Ethan's phone began to chime as Luke turned off the engine. "Brodie."

"Jack Morrell. I've got news."

Fortunately, the disposable had a speaker feature. Ethan pushed the button, then set the phone so his brother could hear.

"Good news or bad?" Ethan asked.

"Depends on how you look at it. Julian Latham isn't involved in drug smuggling. From Caracas, he's flying private into a little town called Santa Elena. It sits on the borders of Venezuela, Guyana, and Brazil."

"What the hell is Latham doing down there?"

"So here's the good news. Like I said, he isn't smuggling drugs. The bad news is he's smuggling diamonds. Venezuela is one of the world's biggest diamond producers. Santa Elena is the hub of the black market trade in the country. It's big business."

"That so?"

"That's right. Worldwide about seven billion in rough stones are stolen each year. They call it *leakage*. It's a big problem."

"How are they getting them out?"

"They're smuggled through Guyana into other countries. Some of them go to Holland. The Dutch cut the stones for half the regular price, then ship them to Antwerp. From there, they make their way into the good ol' U S of A."

"Diamonds. Makes perfect sense. Julian's father is one of the major investors in David Klein Jewelers. That's where the company's getting their stones. A few years back, the company was in the red. They started using stolen diamonds, and that's how they got into the black."

"The FBI's stepped in. The Venezuelan authorities are holding Julian in Miami while the feds go after Peter Latham and whoever else is involved."

Ethan felt a rush of satisfaction. They were going to make this end. He'd have a chance to talk to Val, convince her not to run the way Meg had.

"With the son in custody," Ethan said, "it shouldn't take them all that long to figure things out. I really appreciate this, Jack."

"Are you kidding? I'm looking like a hero, thanks to you. Let me know if you ever need anything else." Morrell hung up the phone.

Luke stared up at Stern's impressive Tudor mansion. "Stolen diamonds. The profit's got to be huge."

"I'm betting that's what got Delilah Larsen killed," Ethan said.

Luke's jaw tightened. "Why don't we go find out?"

CHAPTER THIRTY-EIGHT

Side by side they climbed the wide front porch steps, Ethan's shoulder holster hidden by a black Windbreaker, Luke still wearing his camo pants, his gun clipped out of sight behind his back beneath his olive-drab T-shirt, along with the seven-inch KA-BAR knife strapped to his waist.

Ethan rang the doorbell. Seconds later, the ornate wooden door swung open and a small, gray-haired man in a black suit and neatly pressed white shirt stood in front of them. The edge of Luke's mouth tipped up when he realized Stern had a butler.

"Which of you is Mr. Brodie?" the little man asked.

"That'd be me," Ethan said.

"Mr. Stern will see you in the library. Your friend may wait in the drawing room."

Luke grinned. "I don't think so."

The butler's bushy gray eyebrows shot up. He took another long look at Luke, must have decided he wasn't a guy to argue with, turned, and started off down the hall.

Ethan followed, Luke behind him, into an impressive wood-paneled chamber lined with shelves filled with leather-bound books. Paned windows looked out over a manicured garden behind the house. Flames curled over the grate in a mantel-topped fireplace at the end of the room.

The butler backed out and closed the door, giving them privacy. Stern rose from his chair behind a wide cherrywood desk and walked around to greet them.

"This is my day off, Brodie. Whatever you and your friend here want, I'd appreciate if you'd make it fast."

Ethan tipped his head toward the man beside him. "My brother, Luke."

"Another Brodie, fine. What do you want?"

"We came to ask you some questions. In particular, we're interested in your diamond-smuggling operation."

Stern's face went pale.

"We'd like to know if Latham is giving the orders or if you're handling the business yourself," Luke said.

"I don't know what you're talking about."

Ethan moved closer. "What we really want to know is whether you're the one who ordered the hit on Delilah Larsen."

"I want you out of my house."

"I don't think so." Ethan caught him by the front of his starched yellow button-down shirt and shoved him backward till he slammed into his desk. "First we're going to talk, then I'm calling the police."

"I don't know anything about any smuggling. Go ahead and call the police. I've got nothing to hide."

"As I said, first we're going to talk. I want to know why you had your mistress murdered. Did she figure out what you were doing? Did you have her killed to shut her up?"

"I'm not saying anything. You have no right to be here. You're trespassing. Get out."

Ethan's fingers tightened on the front of Stern's shirt. He dragged Stern up, then slammed him down on the top of the desk, sending papers into the air and an antique inkwell flying. He let go of the shirt and wrapped a hand around Stern's throat. "It was Gallagher, right? Did you hire him or was it Peter Latham?"

When Stern didn't answer, Ethan squeezed until Jason started wheezing, gasping for breath. "Was it Gallagher?"

"Let . . . go of . . . me!" He clawed at the

hand choking off his air, and Ethan eased his hold. "You don't scare me, Brodie. You're a cop. You aren't going to hurt me."

Ethan let him go but didn't back out of his space. "You're right. I'm an ex-cop. I don't torture suspects. My brother, Luke — now that's a different story. You see, Luke was Special Forces. He doesn't see things quite the same way I do."

Luke nudged him aside, got right in Stern's face. "All right, now we're going to do this my way. My brother is going to ask again. This time I expect you to answer." The KA-BAR appeared in his hand. He laid the blade across Stern's throat, and there was no doubt of the threat he posed.

"Was it Gallagher who killed Delilah Larsen?" Ethan asked.

Stern swallowed. Luke nicked his Adam's apple and a thin trickle of blood ran down his neck. "Answer my brother's question."

"It was . . . it was Gallagher."

"What about Valentine? He the one who shot at her?"

A noise in the room drew Ethan's attention. He turned at the sound of a husky female voice.

"Bick wasn't shooting at Valentine, Mr. Brodie. He was shooting at you."

Ethan had never met Myra Stern, but he'd

seen her picture. Brunette, nice figure, fifties, looked to be in her late thirties. She was still a beautiful woman. He didn't know Myra, but he knew the blond man standing next to her pointing a big black semiauto at the middle of his chest.

Bick Gallagher, aka Ray Bickford.

"Step away from Jason," Gallagher said to Luke. "Do it now before I shoot your brother."

Instead, Luke hauled Stern up off the desk and locked an arm around his neck. The big knife rested at the base of his throat. "Looks like we're at a standoff," Luke drawled. "You shoot Ethan, I slice Stern's throat."

The woman's dark eyebrows went up. "Are you certain I care?"

Stern trembled. "What are you doing, Myra? I realize we have an unusual relationship, but I always thought you loved me."

"I do, darling. Of course I do." She ran a hand tenderly down Bick Gallagher's arm. Bick was years younger. Clearly they were involved, or at least had been.

"You're a good husband," Myra said. "I wouldn't want to lose you." She turned to Ethan. "Perhaps we could make a deal. How much would it take for the two of you to forget whatever it is you think you know about our diamonds?"

"So it was you, not your twin brother," Ethan said. "You're the one calling the shots."

"That's right. Peter's a good boy. He's always done what I told him and look how well it's paid off for him."

"He lives like a king," Ethan said. "No doubt about it. Too bad it's all about to end."

"Is that so?"

"That's right. The cops know everything. It's only a matter of time. The best you can do is use whatever connections you've got to get out of the country."

"Let me kill them," Gallagher said, his hand steady on the trigger of the pistol. "We'll be gone before the police figure out what happened."

"You fool. You can probably kill Ethan. But I know people." She pointed at Luke. "You kill his brother, that one won't let you live."

"I'll take my chances," Gallagher said.

"You'll do what I tell you."

"Why'd you have Delilah killed?" Ethan asked her, stalling for time. And frankly, curious after all the trouble he'd had because of Myra Stern.

"Little bitch found out about the smuggling — thanks to Jason's carelessness. She tried to blackmail us. No one blackmails Myra Stern."

Ethan flicked a glance at Luke. Both of them were ready to make a move. "You send the notes?"

She smiled coldly. "Brilliant, wasn't it? Bick came up with the design, but the idea belonged to me."

"It was fairly ingenious, I'll admit. Even had me fooled for a while."

Myra turned from Ethan back to Gallagher. "You really think you can kill both of them, darling?"

"I know what I'm doing."

"Myra, wait!" Jason pleaded, struggling against Luke's hold. It was the moment they needed. Luke shoved Stern between Gallagher and Ethan. Gallagher fired, Ethan sidestepped, and the shot slammed into Stern. Jason moaned as he hit the floor. Ethan ignored the burning pain in his side that told him the bullet had gone through Stern into him and launched himself at Gallagher.

The men crashed onto the Persian carpet, Ethan on top, Gallagher on the bottom. He was a tough man, a professional soldier, his blond hair and good looks disguising the hard man underneath. Ethan thought of Val

509

and how close Gallagher had come to killing her, and slammed a fist into his pretty-boy face. Ethan thought of Pete and Dirk and the fire, and punched him hard again.

Gallagher threw a right that cut into Ethan's eyebrow. He grunted as the man rolled on top. Ethan slid his hands around Gallagher's throat, rolled on top, and squeezed until Bick's face turned beet red. He struggled, kicked, fought for air. Ethan thought of Val and squeezed harder.

"Don't kill him, big brother," Luke called out to him. "We don't have time to dick with the cops over this."

Ethan held on a little longer, till Gallagher's eyeballs were bulging and his body went limp, but his brother was right. And the wound in his side was beginning to make him dizzy. He rolled to his feet, caught the plastic tie Luke tossed him, flipped Gallagher onto his back, and bound his wrists.

He looked over to where his brother had Myra Stern in plastic cuffs. Jason was bleeding out on the floor. Looked like the bullet had nicked his heart. Myra didn't seem all that concerned.

"You call it in?" Ethan asked, wiping blood from his eyebrow, wiping his bloody knuckles on his jeans.

"Yeah. Cops and an ambulance on the way."

The room spun. He was losing blood. He pressed a hand to his side and it came up red.

"What the hell?" Luke strode toward him. "Jesus, you're hit!"

"Gallagher's bullet went through Stern into me."

Luke eased him back into a chair, yanked his T-shirt off over his head, and pressed it against Ethan's side. "Keep the pressure on."

He nodded, leaned back in the chair, and closed his eyes. The good news was, it was over.

The bad news was, once Val found out he'd been shot, he'd never get her to marry him.

CHAPTER THIRTY-NINE

The antiseptic hospital smells overwhelmed her, reminding Val of the night Bobby had died. After the shooting that night, she'd been taken to the hospital, though the blood on her clothes and hands had belonged to Bobby, not her.

She paced the floor of the waiting room. Ethan was still in surgery. The bullet had damaged his spleen. He could die in there. A little sob locked in her throat. Dear God, she couldn't take anymore.

Her mind returned to the events of the evening. As soon as Luke had called and she and Dirk were on their way to the hospital, she had phoned Mom and Pops and told them what had happened. They were coming to Seattle, but they couldn't leave the farm until they'd made arrangements for someone to take care of the animals.

She had phoned Meg, but Meg was in

Chicago, on a modeling job for La Belle. Meg had wanted to fly back, but Val had said she'd be all right as soon as she knew Ethan was okay.

Both of them had cried.

The door swung open and Luke strode in, Dirk following in his wake. "You need anything?" Dirk asked.

She just shook her head.

"Why don't we go get some coffee?" Luke asked softly. He was an interesting man, hard in some ways, gentle in others.

"Not right now. I don't want to leave." Val sat down on the gray vinyl sofa, her gaze going to the other two people in the room, an older, heavyset woman and her short, stout husband, there for their son, she'd heard the woman say. The couple looked as worried as Val.

"He's gonna be all right, you know." Dirk sat down beside her. "Vardon's supposed to be a brilliant surgeon. Sadie checked him out."

"That's what she told me." Sadie and Ian were both in the hospital somewhere. They'd been pacing, trying to make time speed up, finally headed outside to get some fresh air.

"He'll be okay," Dirk repeated, returning to his feet. Rightly figuring she couldn't be persuaded to leave, he and Luke sat down in chairs across from her and each picked up a magazine.

The door opened again and Samantha walked in, her fine brown curls subdued with a clip at the nape of her neck, her baby bump getting bigger every day. Val rose to her feet and went into Sam's arms for a badly needed hug. Both of them started crying, then finally pulled themselves together.

Through the waiting room window, she caught a glimpse of Nick, out in the hall with Hannah. Uncomfortable with two crying women, Dirk and Luke left to join him.

"I'm so glad you came," Val said.

Samantha nodded and leaned in to give her another hug. Through the window, Val watched Dirk take hold of Hannah's small hand, and the group headed down the hall to the cafeteria.

"We decided to bring Hannah with us," Samantha explained. "She heard Nick talking to Ian on the phone. When she realized her daddy was in the hospital, she was so upset we figured it would be better to bring her down, let her wait for news with the rest of us."

"She was in the hospital before. Ethan was there when she needed him, so she wants to be there for him. You did the right thing."

Tears welled. Val dragged a Kleenex out of the pocket of her borrowed sweatpants and dabbed at the wetness.

Both of them sat down on the sofa. "He's going to be okay, Val. No one's in better physical condition than Ethan. Ian told us the doctor said he should come through the surgery very well."

"I know. I wish I could convince myself. Even if he gets well, I can't make myself believe everything will be all right between us. It isn't going to be all right. Not now or ever."

"Don't say that. I know you're worried. I know what you've been through. But Jason Stern is dead. The police have arrested Myra Stern and Bick Gallagher and everyone involved in Delilah Larsen's murder. Julian Latham's been arrested. Even Peter Latham and his wife are in custody."

She nodded. Luke had told her all that. "What about the men who shot at us at Dirk's?"

"Nick says they were Gallagher's hired guns. It wasn't personal to them. Gallagher will probably make a deal, give them up to the authorities in exchange for a lesser sentence. Even with that, he'll be in prison for a very long time."

Fresh tears welled. "How do you do it? I

don't understand. Nick's a private investigator. How do you handle the worry? Never knowing exactly where he is or what he's doing? Whether he's been shot or even killed?" Her heart squeezed painfully. "Even if Ethan wants a future with me, I don't think I can do it."

"Listen to me, Val. Ethan and Nick are good men. So are Dirk and Luke and Ian. These guys are the best. The kind of men the world needs. It's a better place because they're in it, helping protect the rest of us."

"I know, but . . ." Val shook her head. "I'm not tough enough to handle the kind of lives they lead."

Samantha reached over and caught her hand. "You may not be tough, but you're strong. You've proved that again and again. Men like Nick and Ethan need strong women to come home to. That's what makes *them* strong. Do you love him?"

Val glanced away, wiped another tear from her cheek. "I love him so much. I can't stand to think of him lying in there in pain."

She swallowed past the ache in her throat. After the phone call from Luke and her wild ride with Dirk down the mountain to the hospital, she'd been frantic. Ethan had been shot. She didn't know how badly he'd been injured, didn't know if he might be dying.

Dirk had tried to keep her calm, but too much had happened. By the time they'd reached the hospital, she'd been nearly hysterical. No way could she handle anything like that again.

"Ethan loves you," Sam said. "I could see it in his eyes every time he looked at you."

Val glanced away. Sometimes loving someone wasn't enough.

"Our men are tough," Samantha continued. "And you know how capable they are. But they have a heart and soul just like everyone else. They need someone to love them, someone they can lean on, someone to help them stay strong. Ethan needs you, Val. He needs you to be strong for him."

Val looked at Sam and an odd feeling moved through her. She had survived the loss of her parents, survived Bobby's death, and had pulled herself up by her bootstraps. She had survived the terror she had endured on the fashion show tour, and that took guts. She *was* strong. She knew that deep down.

But she had never thought she might have something to give to Ethan. She had always thought he would be the protector, the one to take care of her, even though she was a self-sufficient, independent woman.

But Samantha's words stirred something

517

deep inside her, some sense of rightness that seemed to put everything in its proper place. For the first time, she realized Ethan needed someone to take care of him, too. Maybe needed her even more than she needed him.

"What you've been through," Samantha said. "I know what it's like. I told you what happened to Nick and me in Alaska, how close we both came to being killed. But their job isn't usually so dangerous. Now that Nick's married, he's more selective about the cases he chooses. Nick wants to be a husband and father. He wants to be around to raise his kids. I think Ethan wants that, too."

Val swallowed, the pressure in her chest beginning to ease. Maybe there was hope for them. If she was truly the woman Ethan wanted.

The doctor walked in just then. At the serious look on his face, fear poured through her. Her heart jerked and started pounding.

Then he smiled. "Ethan's out of surgery. He did great. We only had to take a small portion of the spleen, not all of it. He'll be in the recovery room for a while. The nurse will let you know when you can see him."

Val turned to Samantha and the two of them hugged. "He's okay," Val said, repeating the doctor's words. "He did great."

Samantha grinned. "Yes, he did."

The news spread throughout their worried little group. People went in and out of the waiting room, went for coffee, then returned. Hannah sat on Val's lap for a while. One of the nurses handed the little girl a coloring book, and once she knew her daddy was going to be okay, she sat on the floor and colored.

Then the door opened and a nurse in green scrubs walked into the waiting room. "You're Valerie, right? His girlfriend?"

She nodded. "I'm Val."

"He's asking for you. You can see him, but only for a few minutes."

Val came up off the sofa. "Thank you."

Samantha caught her hand as she started for the door. "Remember what I said."

But all Val could think of was Ethan.

She followed the nurse out the door, down the hall into the recovery room, up to his bedside. His skin was pale, his eyes closed. Black lashes fanned his cheeks. He was hooked up to a heart monitor. Bags of saline hung from a rolling IV stand, dripping fluid into his veins.

Her heart hurt and fresh tears blurred her vision. She reached out and took hold of his hand. The warm, strong feel of it steadied her.

Ethan's eyes cracked open. He saw her and an uncertain look came over his face. "I'm . . . okay, honey. Or I . . . will be."

She tried to smile, couldn't quite make it happen. "I know, the doctor said."

"You don't need to worry. I'm a very fast . . . healer."

She almost smiled, swallowed back tears and nodded, couldn't manage another word.

"Promise we'll talk . . . before you say no."

A tear rolled down her cheek. "You think I'm going to say no?"

"I'm afraid . . . you will." He lifted her hand to his lips, pressed a kiss into her palm. "I love you. Stupid time to tell you."

It wasn't stupid. She managed to force her lips into a teary smile. "You sure it's not just the meds talking?"

His mouth edged up. "I've loved you . . . for a while. I just hadn't . . . figured it out."

Tears rolled down her cheeks. She bent over him, brushed the faintest kiss over his lips. "I love you, too. Didn't take me long to figure it out."

His eyes slid closed. "Who needs a whole spleen, anyway?"

She was caught between laughter and tears. "I just need you," she whispered softly.

But Ethan didn't hear her. He had drifted back to sleep.

"I'm sorry to interrupt," the nurse said, "but Ethan has another visitor. His little girl is here. She really needs to see him."

"Of course." Val eased back as the nurse led Hannah up to her father's bedside. She saw the tubes and needles poking out of him, saw the pale color of his skin, and her face scrunched up with tears.

"He's going to be okay, sweetheart." Val reached down and took hold of the little girl's hand. "I promise."

Ethan slowly opened his eyes. "Hey . . . sweet cheeks . . ."

"Daddy . . ." Hannah leaned against the bed and started crying.

"I'm okay, sweetheart. Daddy just had a little . . . accident. Like when you fell off your trike. But I'm already . . . getting better."

Val smoothed a hand over Hannah's hair. "I know how you're feeling. I was really scared, too. I know you love your daddy. I love him, too."

Hannah turned to look up at her, eyes wet and glistening. "Is he really gonna be okay?"

"Yes, he is." Val smiled down at Ethan. "He's a very fast healer."

Ethan's lips twitched. "My two best girls." His eyes slid slowly closed, then opened. "Listen to Valentine . . . sweetheart. Everything's going to be okay."

Hannah's serious gaze swung from Ethan to Val. "I think Daddy loves you, too."

For the first time since Luke had phoned Dirk, the smile that curved Val's lips felt real.

EPILOGUE

It was Saturday, a sunny September morning with only a slight breeze blowing in off the Puget Sound. Ethan sat on the comfortable overstuffed sofa in Val's cozy living room. He'd been staying there since he'd been released from the hospital. Val had insisted he needed her help to mend. He wasn't about to argue.

Even after he'd gone back to work, neither of them had wanted to end the arrangement. Two weeks ago, he'd given up the lease on his apartment, making their living together official.

Ethan still hadn't asked Val to marry him. Not yet. It had taken all his willpower to keep his mouth shut, but he wanted to be absolutely certain she'd say yes. He understood her misgivings about the kind of work he did, knew she wasn't crazy about marrying a guy who carried a gun. Being shot hadn't exactly helped matters.

They had talked about it, though, which was a major step. She knew how important his job was to him, knew she had to accept what he did for a living if they were going to make it work.

He'd promised her from now on he would try to take cases that wouldn't get him shot or killed, couldn't believe she actually seemed satisfied with that.

Val was working part-time at the animal clinic and had started back to school. She was busy and so was he, but they still managed to have plenty of time for each other.

Ethan looked over to where she sat on the floor playing dolls with Hannah. Snoozie curled in the sunshine a few feet away. Val didn't have much family, just Mom and Pops. He'd met them at the hospital, then again at their small family farm. He thought they were great. Fortunately, they seemed to like him, too.

Val laughed at something, and Hannah giggled. Val didn't have much experience with kids, but during his stay in the hospital, she and Hannah seemed to have bonded.

Val helped the little girl dress her Barbie doll in some kind of long sequined gown that reminded him of the dress she had worn on the local morning news and the hot sex they'd had later.

Ethan felt a jolt of heat and found himself smiling.

It had been seven weeks since the shooting. The case was wrapped up good and tight, everyone rounded up and sitting in jail for a list of crimes a foot long. Everyone but Stern, who had died in his house that day.

Bick Gallagher, aka Ray Bickford, had turned state's evidence and rolled on his former lover, Myra Latham Stern; her twin brother, Peter Latham; and his wife, Alessandra, also neck deep in the diamond smuggling operation. Julian Latham was a major player, now locked away.

Because the case involved international crime, they were all considered flight risks, so none had been granted bail.

Ethan hoped they all rotted in prison.

On the home front, Pete was healing, doing occasional work for BOSS, Inc. Allison had fought the DUI charge, which turned out to be her second. With the help of an expensive lawyer her daddy paid for, she'd managed to get off with three months' probation, rehab classes, and two hundred hours of community service.

Not wanting more trouble, Ally had agreed to full joint custody of Hannah, which included a visitation schedule that gave

Ethan plenty of time with his daughter. No way would Allison be giving him any more hassles.

Leaving Hannah to play with her doll, Val wandered over and sat down beside him on the sofa. Ethan gently brushed a lock of golden hair off her cheek. "You two having fun?"

She gazed down at Hannah. "I had a great childhood, but all the bad stuff later kind of blocked it out. It's fun playing with Hannah."

He chuckled.

She lifted his T-shirt to check out the scar on his side. "It's looking better all the time. I think your doctor wanted to keep you looking pretty."

"Looking sexy, you mean."

She laughed. "You know . . . I never asked you how you got that other sexy scar on your shoulder."

Ethan managed to smile. "I never told you?"

"No."

"It's kind of embarrassing."

"Really?"

"Yeah. I fell off my trike when I was a kid." No way was he telling her it was another bullet hole. He was still on shaky ground as it was.

"I see . . ." But she didn't look convinced. "So when are you going to ask me to marry you?"

He grinned. God, he loved her. "You sure you're ready to say yes?"

She smiled. "More than ready."

"Will you marry me?"

Val grinned so big her dimples popped out. "I'll think about it," she said.

AUTHOR'S NOTE

I hope you enjoyed *Into the Fury,* Ethan Brodie and Valentine Hart in the first of my BOSS, Inc., novels. If you haven't met Ethan's cousins, I hope you'll look for Dylan, Nick, and Rafe in *Against the Wild, Against the Sky,* and *Against the Tide.*

Up next for me is *Into the Whirlwind.* Catch up with Dirk Reynolds, Ethan's best friend, and Val's friend, Megan O'Brien.

It's been five long months since Meg ended her brief but passionate affair with Dirk. She's a single mother, while Dirk loves hot cars and Harleys. He's not the kind of man to settle down and be a father to her son.

But when little Charlie is abducted and held for ransom, Meg must set aside her pride and her broken heart and go to Dirk, the only man she trusts to save the life of her precious little boy.

I hope you'll join Meg and Dirk on their

emotional journey, *Into the Whirlwind*, a high-stakes adventure filled with passion and intrigue.

Till then, very best wishes and happy reading.

Kat

The employees of Thorndike Press hope you have enjoyed this Large Print book. All our Thorndike, Wheeler, and Kennebec Large Print titles are designed for easy reading, and all our books are made to last. Other Thorndike Press Large Print books are available at your library, through selected bookstores, or directly from us.

For information about titles, please call:
   (800) 223-1244

or visit our Web site at:
   http://gale.cengage.com/thorndike

To share your comments, please write:
   Publisher
   Thorndike Press
   10 Water St., Suite 310
   Waterville, ME 04901